the gatemaker

the
gatemaker

CHRISTINE DWYER HICKEY

NEW
ISLAND

the gatemaker
published 2006
by New Island
2 Brookside
Dundrum Road
Dublin 14
www.newisland.ie

Copyright © 2000 Christine Dwyer Hickey

Original edition published 2000 by Marino Books

The author has asserted her moral rights.

ISBN 1 905494 15 7

British Library Cataloguing in Publication Data. A CIP catalogue record for this book is available from the British Library.

Printed in the UK by Cox and Wyman

New Island receives financial assistance from
The Arts Council (An Chomhairle Ealaíon), Dublin, Ireland.

10 9 8 7 6 5 4 3 2 1

In memory of Liam

CONTENTS

PROLOGUE

Crumlin, 1953

Now it is winter. Through the frame of his window there is darkness; through a lace curtain, silence. Across the road a squint of yellow street light outlines a house, exactly like his house, in a row, just like his row; facing each other like trains in an overnight depot.

His wife has gone out somewhere. She indicated the hour of her return, along with instructions of a domestic nature, which he can't remember now. He steps into the kitchen.

Where the light hangs down on the shapes of his life. Four chairs and a table; too large for the kitchen, which is more of a pantry, with a one-eyed sink and a cooker that lights at the top. There is the pot of potatoes waiting to be boiled. Peeved from the wait, they are beginning to snot their starch into the water.

Was that one of his instructions? Turn gas on at some time? He clicks at the pilot and turns the knob gently. The flame bounces up to him and he lights a pleat of newspaper. Then a cigarette. The paper dwindles down to the pinch of his fingertips. He tosses the remains into the sink, where the last bit of light withers away, whispering into a spear of crisp black flake.

His finger pokes into the potato water and wiggles like a cancan leg. Then he brings his hand back down to the gas knob and turns it off again. Leaving the kitchen door open behind him, so that he can only see what he needs to see, he comes back to the parlour.

It's cold in the house. He has let the fire go out. His wife plans its construction like a master confectioner: a newspaper base first, now the sticks and cinders the street Arabs have sold her at the door, this much coal at this exact time, now a wad of turf. If things turn out a little dull, then there is always one of his worn right shoes packed with yesterday's coal dust, dampened down. He thinks about relighting it, but he is reluctant to interfere with the theatre of her firegrate.

Yet he feels he might like to do something. He stoops to the hearth and begins to roll up knots of newspaper, the way he has so often seen her do, watching the words crawl into each other, world events and in-house palaver; a woman's face and camera-clever smile. When he has wrapped them all away he ties the paper in a bow and perches it carefully on the hearth. He continues until he has a bundle made and piled together in a neat arrangement of knots and frills. Then he stands up. 'And now what else?' he asks himself. 'What else now?'

Behind him is his wife's work corner, where she makes dresses for Communion children. He has stumbled across them, from time to time, when they come for a fitting. In from his walk or down the narrow staircase in search of something: a book, a pen, a cup of tea – some such prop to while away his day. He has seen their startled eyes look down at him from the pedestal his wife has placed them on – a kitchen chair or that paint-stained stool, the only piece of furniture he can seem to recognise from the old house in New Street. Necks scrubbed from behind, ears rooted into by a hungry flannel corner. Vests tucked into knickers; freshly laundered. They have been prepared for her, as carefully as if she were their doctor. He has watched with amusement the effect of his presence; that flash from sanctity to fear, he finds quite charming. And oh, those Catholic children; frightened of him, they are. Frightened in his den. Outside, of course, where they run with the pack, it will be a different story. Singing behind him, little cheerful songs: 'Proddy, Proddy, on the wall . . . ' or other ditties concerning his game leg. They like his game leg and the way it leans heavily on his right shoe, wearing it down, so that he must do with two left shoes and walk with that funny little gait that two left shoes insist on. It gives them endless pleasure. But he can understand that. In a way it gives him pleasure too. And comfort. Much more comfort. Sometimes they call him Charlie, after Chaplin. And then, if he's feeling up to form, he might waddle just a bit, give his cane a bit of a twirl and then *hup* – raise his heels together to the side – and *click*. And they like that too; that always makes them laugh.

It's the other things about him they dislike: his silence, for example. And the way he ignores, through the railings, the small fist from next door, tightening and spreading to him each time he makes for his front door. Tightening and spreading. A small, dirty fist. Crying, 'Baba, Mister Baba, Mister Ba . . . '

He flicks the cigarette into the firegrate, then turns to his wife's work table. Ruffles of white and a sewing machine. Tinned pins and flimsy pattern cut-outs. A tape and cotton reels. A scissors and wreathed rosebuds skulking among the tulle and best lawn. Nun's muslin too, for the poorer kids. But all cloth looks the same in this muted light: vaguely white, vaguely grey.

He moves to the dressmaker's dummy in the corner. It is fully attired with veil and pinned frock; a wealthier communicant. They come from as far as Rathgar for the benefit of his wife's fingers. How they like her tricky fingers. He stops for a moment and his hand almost touches – almost – a small headless bride, a ghost of a child. But a girl-child. Not like the face through the railings: 'Mister Baba, Mister Ba . . . '

He puts his hand away. Into his trouser pocket for a rummage at the bits inside. A few loose matches; a coin or two; the familiar feel of a bookie's docket. He claws his fingers through them for a while, listening to his breath singing in his chest. Rising slow and high, shorter on the the way back down. Climbing up again, then down; shorter. Shorter today. Shorter than yesterday. Shorter than the yesterday before that.

He wonders what he should do now. Now that his cigarette is finished. And the rhythm of his chest has been recorded. And the contents of his pocket. He wonders what he should do to put in a winter's evening. How should he fill all this time? All this black, buttery silence.

He recalls a summer's evening – any summer's evening. And how it brings its own scraps, its own sounds. Rope-swings whipping around a lamp-post, a child's arse cutting down on it, a child's mouth opened wide and screeching. Loose-bosomed women at garden gates; laughter or complaint or the hushed, uneasy rumble of confidences being bartered; the occasional throwaway chide to a youngster in the background. That is the sound of the women.

Saint Agnes's Church cracks open the angelus and the evening changes. The women become distracted. They glance out of their conversations to the top of the road, where the first city bus falters and hesitates, gobbing men from its platform one by one. The black frames of bicycles rattle into a sharper focus as they turn from the Armagh Road. Some skirt the periphery of the green, others are dismounted and carried across the grass, through the disgruntled flaps of outraged seagulls still searching for the city dump that has long been filled in and puffed up with grass. Why don't they know? Somebody should tip them off.

But the men are coming home. There are meals to be served. Even the idle ones will be given a plateful, a reward of sorts for obeying the unspoken rule of staying out of doors; keeping out from under Her feet during the daylight hours. In from a day spent hiking in the mountains or lounging about on the old quarry green playing cards and drinking milk from bottles, like schoolboys. The craftier of them will have stretched the few hours into the artificial darkness of an afternoon pub. These are always the last to make an appearance, straggling behind. Pausing at corners to pass Silvermints and excuses: 'Now what you say, is this . . . and what I'll say, is that . . . '

As each one recognises her own particular man, the group of women will divide and cut. And, making for the gate of her house, she will pass through the front door that leads, in a step, to her hallway; in another few, to her kitchen and the cooker that lights at the top.

He might like to read for a bit. Finish off that book he stole from Kevin Street Library. And then sneak it back in under his coat, the way he sneaked it out, twenty-odd years ago. When he had started with just one empty box and filled it; then another box and yet another. Filled them all full of books: Kevin Street, Rathmines Library, Thomas Street as well. And then working backwards had emptied them all again, squeezing them back into shelves where they had long been forgotten. Did anyone notice? Only a few left now. In the very last box. What then? Start again?

He slides his hand along the parlour wall until it comes across a diddy-bump: the light switch. But the electric light annoys him, picking out distractions in every corner of the room. Photographs mostly: his son George leaning on a willy jeep in Belfast, the dangle of a cigarette at the side of his mouth, one eye caught winking to the camera, American soldiers lounging by his side.

Another one: George again, sprawled on a lawn at Belfast City Hall, long legs stretched out in front of him, young people all about: bare-headed men, bare-armed girls leaning back on the heels of their hands. All along the mantleshelf there's George and George and George again. Belfast George and New Street George. And Dublin George, who lives now in a city-centre hotel.

On each side of the chimney breast, the other photographs make do. Bits of other children; bits of other occasions. And into the recesses, where his wife has made a gallery of his past and better days – days before he knew her; days she regrets, as if they were her own – commemorations of events he can't quite place, playing parts he can only half-remember playing. A boy in a sailor suit, standing at a women's knee. A young man with a straw boater, a tall sister at either side. A brother; a son; a page-boy. Bridegroom. Uncle. Father. Could all those people really be the one person? Could all those people be him?

The light bulb, like a woman, makes much of photographs. Bringing things to life; snatching at moments that are long since dead. Like the ghost-child in the corner behind him. The girl-child in her veil and pinned frock.

The man across the way has one of those lamps on a stem. He

wouldn't mind one of those lamps himself; one of those lamps on a stem. Standing over him, protecting him with its muted privacy, shading him with the fringe of its Reserved Enclosure hat; just enough for one man and his book. He tries, in these winter evenings, to do his reading during the day. Up in the back room, in those vacant hours between the going and the coming of scheme dwellers. Between the creaks of gates; first outward, and then later back in. Or if the day is fine, to take his book away altogether from Crumlin. Off on a bus or two, to a bench somewhere: the Phoenix Park or St Patrick's Park or the park where the fat ducks live. Once he preferred a bench facing the side of the Zoological Gardens. A green bench, it was, with wrought-iron side-burns. And, standing reverent and unobtrusive behind him, was the old Officers' Club. Called something else now. Some other Free State name. And he was happy on that bench; well, at least, almost contented. Until one day, glancing up from the page, he caught the eye of a giraffe looking over the wall at him. Tall as the trees – taller than some – its long, benign face watched him un-flinchingly. And it first frightened and then enchanted him. And they looked at each other for a considerable time. He quite enjoyed it. Yet he never sat on that bench again. It was better to sit with the ducks; the fat, predictable ducks, who wouldn't dream of doing a thing to disturb or surprise you.

He might like to go down to Mooney's. But the drink now burns his stomach up and the men keep talking at him. Expecting him to discuss things he cares nothing about. Expecting him to reply. Waiting for something of himself to emerge. How easily they could be pleased, if only he had a mind to.

He might like to do a lot of things. But the practicalities are all against him.

Once, when he was younger, he would take a walk at this hour. Catching the Liffey from behind. And the lights spearing down through the water, punting him gently along. Down quayside until he reached the pub, where half-ones took him through the rest of the evening, and somehow he would find himself at home. But that was when he was younger, and now he is old. That was when he lived in New Street, in the city. Where they used to call him the Dancer.

And he misses the city at times. Misses its lack of inquisitiveness. Though he still keeps its scape inside his head for taking him to and from sleep. And he still sees himself then cross over its streets, as he used to do, with neat steps; neat space between them. Up narrow laneways to the back of the theatre houses. Onto a stage with the shuffle of his feet just discernible; the tap of his cane; the spotlight that he made his moon, full of itself, in its final quarter. And houses with the coffee smell coming through the walls. And houses with sweet balls of gaslight and endless marbled counters; and kind, brown boxes snugged along the walls. With the glitter of liquor moaning out from behind curved glass: amber and red and indisputable black. And the house, too, where the Turkish bath took him into a room and smoked him like a cigarette. And at last the houses where he danced for strangers, his feet alive with whiskey that they fed him.

Now he lives out here in the sticks, where he knows only one house. Out here where they don't call him anything at all. Not that he knows of, anyway. And besides, there is no river to direct him. To tell him which way to go.

He slides himself into his overcoat and, settling himself into a chair, wraps it kneewards about him. He can hear the boy next door crying to himself. 'A disgrace,' his wife says every time they hear him, every time they see his sad, neglected face.

How old would he be? About what age? Would he be as old, say, as the other boy was when he died? Although *his* face at least was often clean. If you rubbed away the dirt, whose face would you see?

And how old would he be today, that other boy, if he was still here? A man now, anyway. Gone, like the rest of them. A man. Like one of those people who is careful to leave before his welcome has worn, he just left a little earlier, that's all. He just took a shorter route.

He reaches over to his side and his hand pushes a button on the wireless set. A light comes up. He twists the knob, following the vertical search line with his eye, and with his ear the whirr and twitter of the search pip. He finds a spot. A sensible voice speaks from behind the woven screen, strolling into the room with its impudent tones. There is nothing entertaining on the wireless set now. Nothing worth a damn. Churchill was always good for a laugh, chawing out his words like a dog on a bone. Or Lord Haw-Haw . . . he was good too. The voice; the cheek; the menacing tone. Used to get a great kick out of him; the things he came out with. But now he too has gone. The haw-haw knocked to the other side of his face.

He listens for a moment, then he turns the knob again. He prefers the whirr and ooh of the search pip.

He lays his head onto the back of the armchair and closes his eyes; tired, he's feeling, just a little. He should pull himself up before he gets too comfortable, back into the kitchen for a sup of water and a glob of bread soda to ease the indigestion he appears to have acquired from eating nothing since ... That piece of bread and butter his wife shoved into his hand a long time ago now, at the opposite end of the day. A little snooze first. A little snooze might be just the ticket, to take him up to bedtime. He searches for a street in his mind. Golden Lane should do nicely, with its four corners of hell: a pub on every one. Yes, Golden Lane.

He moves along it gently, recalling rooftops and huckster shops and the familiar quirks of pavement under his feet. But after another few steps he notices that the pavement is beginning to give and he can hear the sound of concrete gently shattering. When he looks down he is walking on gravel. A wide stretch of gravel, with a smooth green lawn to each side. And in the distance – where the entrance to Stephen Street should be – there's a stone-faced house. He can see along its granite steps a group of people. Watching him. These people; those steps: he recognises them, without knowing who or what they are. There is a woman, a man, a small boy. And two young girls with hair to the waist, bouncing up and down on button-backed boots. Waving and waiting. He stops for a moment and looks behind him. But there is nobody else on the street only him. Waving at *him?* Why him?

Well let them, he thinks, spinning on his heel and making a brisk return up the lane, where he takes the corner smartly for Bride Street. And gladdened for a moment by the sight of it: the great bulges of oxidised copper, sunbasking on the rooftops of the Iveagh Buildings; ripened green. Always liked them, the Iveagh Buildings, always pleased by them; he smiles. But then he sees the stone-faced house has skipped over him somehow and the warm red bricks of the buildings have melted away. And there they are again, those people; still waving, waiting. Laughing silently, out through the holes in their faces.

Perhaps he has just picked the wrong street. Perhaps Winetavern Street would have been better. He opens his eyes and looks around the room and, pulling his coat closer to him, shuts them again. Once more. Try once more: Winetavern Street. Where once he was publican to a pub on the corner, that spread itself out between the street and the quay; and once he was the watcher from the window up above. Down onto the river; the grey, indolent river. Dyspeptic at high tide; over-indulgence. And at low tide, when its belly was empty, you could see all the way down, under the bridges, right down to its tonsils, gullet and all. And passing the balustrade, a pedestrian flicker that darkened its tiara of fat, white pearls.

The Irish House; the name of the pub. Where it was his key that opened the door and his hand that unbolted the bolt. And where once they called him master.

But he finds himself moving across the gravel again and he feels it squirm as his foot presses down on it. And he finds the big stone house getting larger. Or is he just getting nearer? He can see, quite clearly now, the two Lombardy lions perched on each side of the steps. There's a charabanc parked to the side of the house; men in holiday hats, ladies with holiday hampers sitting up on their laps. Waiting for something? Waiting for him? And his mind refuses all interest now in Winetavern Street, in the Irish House; Wood Quay. And only seems concerned with the names of the faces waving from the steps, descending them now, down as far as the lions, and coming forward in an orderly fashion, each one taking a bow. Into his memory . . .

Kate and Maude. Mama and Papa. The faces from the photo-graphs. So *that's* who they are. Of course. Of course. That's them. But who is the boy? He is afraid to look. Who will it be?

But the boy in the sailor suit has covered his face. His two hands slapped over it: peep-o. Mama wags a playful finger at him and reaches out for his hands. But the boy is too quick for her: peep-o.

Each time the boy pulls his hands away, he is wearing a different face. He has seen the dead boy in there, in amongst the changes; he waits and watches for its turn to come round again. Preparing himself, knowing that if it does come again, he will go to it. If it does comes again, he will go.

Mama says, 'Oh, you naughty boy,' and then she laughs. This time when she grabs his hands, she manages to keep a hold of them. Then he hears himself call the name. The name he never mentions.

'Danny, is it? Danny, is that you son?'

Mama smiles and turns towards the charabanc, one hand stretching out to him, the other lifting the skirt of her dress, ready to move off, in her busy-mama way. There is no one left on the steps now: all are running towards the charabanc; all urging him; all calling back. 'Take mama's hand, Benjamin, *take* it.'

When the pain comes, he is expecting it; he opens his eyes and waits for it to come to him. He can hear the child next door increase his volume. He can hear the wireless woo and pop. He can feel the orchestra in his chest tune tighter. Tighter. Drawing the strings to snapping point. He looks over to the side of the room, where he knows his hat and walking cane are placed behind the door. He wonders will the pain subside long enough for him to get up and fetch them. He will be needing them both now, his hat and his cane.

He is going on a journey.

PART ONE

GEORGE

I

Belfast, Summer 1939

Up the steps of Amiens Street Station, the Dancer followed his
son; one foot lifting, the other joining; climbing like a toddler
climbs, one step at a time. He noticed his son pause at intervals,
to give him a chance to catch up. 'You go on ahead,' he said to
him after a while. 'You go on and get your ticket.'

He watched the young man spring up and over, heeling the
risers away in pairs, so that they seemed to tumble back down the
incline like a deck of cards collapsing. When he had skimmed
over the final step, they pulled themselves together again; steep
and insurmountable. The Dancer let out a sigh through his teeth.
'How do you eat an elephant?' he asked himself then. 'One bit,
one little bit at a time.'

A spree of activity came up behind him and he decided to wait for an
easier moment. A flutter of priest hem; a gaggle of baggage boys
touting and shouting for cases and bags; a woman struggling with a
baby carriage. He reached his hand out instinctively to help her, but
the woman's instinct was stronger and she declined his offer with a
'not at all' nod of her head. He could see his own frailty written all
over her face. So he stayed where he was, leaning on the banister and
watching her gradual ascent. Then he filled up his lungs and, looking
back down, persuaded his foot to move off again.

Naggedy-nag; now, sitting on the bench, his foot was making him pay; niggling away at him; naggedy-nag. It didn't mind the flat so much, it was the climb it hated. It would crab all day. The only thing to shut it up would be a sup of whiskey.

Whiskey? What he had in his pocket would hardly do the trick: a couple of bob – enough to tease but not to cure. So where did that leave him? Samuel would be along in a minute after he'd parked the car, perhaps he could ask . . . No, he couldn't do that. But then again, perhaps it might be offered.

He eyed the crowd until his son was found. There he was – there. Edging up along the queue to the ticket office. It gave him a shock for a second to note how much he looked like a man from behind. But he *was* a man; a tall man; impatient. Shuffling into the line, craning his neck; counting the heads in front, no doubt. (How many left now? How many more to go?) No patience at all. In a few minutes, he would be back with the ticket; in another few he would be on the train for Belfast. God knows when they would see each other again. He would have to say something – but what? What do you say to your son when he's already a man; a tall man; impatient? What can you tell him that he's likely to believe? Or that he doesn't think he already knows? If he said nothing at all, he would have his wife to face when he got home; her questions charging at him the second he crossed the door. (Well . . . ? How did you get on? What did he say? What did you say? Did you . . . ? Did he . . . ? Did you not . . . ?)

Then there would be two nags to contend with: his foot and his wife. And it would take more than a sup of whiskey to lay Greta off.

He looked at the queue again; only five from the top. Which would he buy? Second-class? Or third, maybe? Although he could afford first, if he wanted. He had enough. Isn't that what he said when I asked him? 'How much did you say you got out of Tully, George?' 'Enough.'

Enough could mean anything. And you could be sure Samuel would have slipped him something too, last evening. The pair of them in the yard for ages, squeezed side by side on the window ledge outside, like the Sugar Loaf Mountain, blocking the light to the room. Chatting sometimes, or sometimes not bothering. Close as toes, the two of them.

Like I once was with Sam myself, when I was the same age as George is now. What was I like then? A married man; a businessman. (Look at me now.) Younger-looking than him too, much younger; shorter as well. And once George was a boy, what was he like?

Between his fingertips, the Dancer rolled the neck of his cane and tried to remember his son. What *was* he like? But nothing came into his head.

He could remember the other boy all right: every feature, every word. Every turn of his little body. But he was easy because he was dead; his memory frozen. He could remember Herbert too. Watched him more; the interest you take in a child that's supposed to be yours but isn't: spotting the little differences, almost like a hobby. Charlie was still young enough, no need to remember him yet. But what about George?

Samuel's form slid through the crowd and the Dancer raised the crook of his cane to guide him over.

'Well?' Samuel asked.

'He's gone to get his ticket.'

Samuel nodded, sitting down beside him; and about to settle

down with his Sunday paper when the Dancer began to speak.

'Did I ever tell you about the incident with the laced-up boots?'

'No, I don't think so.' Samuel put down the paper.

'Oh, let me see . . . How old would he have been then? Not yet three. Herbert was older, but it was the other fella always led the way, even at that age. Wintertime down in the pub; on the way home from town, they stopped in. Christmastime, it was. I was up to my eyes with the turkey draw. And their mother had insisted they wore the new boots, even though I had warned her: the cobblestones; they'll break their necks; icy weather; all that. She'd still insisted – you know what women are like.'

'Indeed.'

'And then she'd sneaked off upstairs to hide their Christmas presents. I left them in the back kitchen while I sorted the raffle prizes; thought them out of harm's way there; a biscuit each; the Red Cross box to rattle between them. "Huh-mon, Berbie, huh-mon," I heard the other fella saying. He couldn't even say Herbert yet – that'll tell you how young he was. Of course I didn't pay it much heed. The next thing I knew there was an almighty clatter outside in the yard, and when I ran to look there was the two of them, flat on their faces out on the stones. The top latch opened, sweeping broom on the floor, kitchen chair pulled up beside the door, it swinging on its hinges. He'd climbed up onto the edge of the sink with the sweeping broom in his hand and opened the latch. The roars out of the pair of them; little noses dappled with blood. Opened the latch. Who would believe it? With the sweeping broom? Not three years of age. How did he manage at all?'

Samuel laughed.

'And who do you think got the blame? "Oh *you!* Oh *you!* I thought you were supposed to be watching them!"'

'The boots, of course, were never mentioned?' Samuel smiled.

'Oh, don't you know?' The Dancer nodded and then, looking away, fell silent again.

'Do you know what I remember?' Samuel asked, in an effort to bring him back.

'What?'

'The incident with the cartridges.'

'The cartridges from the foundry?'

'That's right. He was about what, then? Nine, maybe ten? We'd just come back from New York.'

'I remember; he found one of the cartridges still loaded. "I wonder, now, what would happen if you hit it with a sledge-hammer?" *Bang* – he found out soon enough. Like a shot from a gun, *bang*. The whole neighbourhood out. A splinter of it in that young one Enright's leg, from across the way, her mother screaming for the police. Another bit in his own leg. He ran away. I found him that night, with the blood gushing out into a filthy rag, crouched in a corner of Hennessey's barn, in the dark. Not afraid, either, of the dark or the rats. He'd only gone there at all because he thought he was going to be arrested. Up to the Meath then, kept in overnight, nurses fussing over him, combing his hair. Wild out, he was. Impetuous.'

'He leaves his mark, no doubt about that,' Samuel said.

'He left it in that young one, anyway: the mother still won't look at me.'

'He's afraid of nothing.'

'No. No fear. Thinks that'll keep him safe, but if you ask me, there lies his danger.'

'Ah, he'll be all right.'

'Well, we'll see. We'll see.'

Samuel studied the Dancer's face.

'What?' the Dancer asked.

'I was just thinking.'

'What?'

'Ah, nothing really. Just that it's a long time since I heard you talk so much.'

The Dancer shrugged. 'And it'll probably be as long again.'

Samuel waited for a minute. But the Dancer had already drifted away.

He was watching his son make his way back from the ticket booth; handsome but clumsy; the way he was carrying his new suitcase, anyway. Maude bought it for him. Leather and brown; too big for the sweet f.a. that was inside it. Difficult to balance; too light. The case took a swing to the right and hit the shoulder of a small girl. Owww. The mother, not pleased. Or was it the grandmother? Widow, anyway; all in black. He saw his son stop and give a half-arsed apology. The woman not satisfied, glaring after him; the little girl rubbing her shoulder; rubbing it in. Familiar face on the woman. Did he know her? Not pleased at all. But it didn't mean he wasn't sorry, just clumsy in his apology; clumsy with the case. Keen to get away too; thinks he never will. The Dancer pushed his weight down on his cane and, pulling himself up, walked slowly to meet him.

'You got it all right?'

George nodded, lifting his hand to show.

He nodded back. 'Good.'

George looked up at the clock then, anxious. Thinks he'll never . . .

'How are we for time?' he asked George.

'Ten minutes . . . I better . . ' and he gestured towards the platform with the side of his head.

'Yes.'

Samuel came over and stood beside them. He took George's

hand and shook it, then patted him on the arm. 'Good luck to you, Georgie, and be sure to keep in touch, let us know how you're getting on, won't you?'

'I will of course.'

'And you have my telephone number, if you need anything? Anything at all.'

'I have of course.'

'Good.'

Samuel started to walk away. 'I'll bring the car around,' he called back to the Dancer. 'You take your time.'

Now they were alone.

George looked down at his father. 'I suppose you'll have moved to Crumlin by the time I get back.'

'I suppose . . . '

'You will go this time?'

'I might . . . I'll have to see if they make us another offer first.'

'Why wouldn't they?'

'Because I've refused twice already. And if there's a war . . . '

'They'll stop building.'

'Exactly.'

The Dancer grinned and looked down at the ground.

Ten minutes, did he say? Eight by now; maybe seven. Now, I suppose, I better. Now or never. He began to speak. 'I've only this to say to you, son . . . ' Then he stopped for a moment and scratched the back of his neck. He said a few more words then, and stopped again. George was looking away. He looked away himself. Shifting his eyes along the smoked rubbed walls to the happy faces of billboard ads: Paddy's whiskey; Beatty's curtains; Thompson's shirts; one by one. Everything belonged to someone; everything had somebody's name.

Back to Paddy's whiskey again. Then back over to George, whose face was all flushed; itchy-looking. What was *he* looking at? The circular steps from the buffet restaurant; speckled and gaining width, the nearer they got to the ground. Feet, flittering up and down them. Women's tippy-clicks, men's flat slaps. What now? Where? The ceiling, ah yes. The light pressing down on the slashes of iron crossing each other from all sort of angles. Triangles and squares; neat little hatches of sky. The smoke from the trains, like black muscular arms stretching up, up, up; groping around the harlequinade screen; looking for an escape. Looking to get out.

The advice carried on of its own accord while the two pairs of eyes continued to wander, bumping into each other now and then before jumping away somewhere else. He could no longer hear himself. Had he stopped? Or was it that the sounds around him had suddenly increased? A ragbag of shouts – rhythmless shouts – and a sharp whistle toot that took a short cut through his head. Now a rumble of trolley wheels down at his feet; now a bump at his elbow, then a shove at this back. The voice from the public-address system spoke down through its nose: 'All aboard, all aboard the Belfast train, departing in . . . ' How many minutes did it say? How many more?

He glanced down at the ticket. First-class or . . . ? But the hand was too big, he couldn't make it out. First-class or . . . ? Hand like a shovel, and it used to be so small. Used to hold it, pulling it along, endlessly questioning everything, never stopped asking. Ask him one now. Will I? Ask him? Just a couple of bob . . . a few swift, small ones. Just a few.

Now his son was saying something . . .

'What's that? What's that you said?'

George sucked in a breath and shoved out a bigger voice. 'I said of course I will.'

Cheerful response. But the face was tight.

And it could have been a response to any one of his questions: a suggestion that he might think about writing to his mother now and then. Or a request to mind himself; avoid all talk political, all women blousey. An instruction to get the hell out at the first call of war. Any question that had been included in the list of hints his wife had given him; her mother-script. But then he saw his son reach into his inside pocket and pull out a note. And he knew then it was a reply to his own request: 'I suppose you couldn't spare me the loan of . . . '

It looked like a fiver. Five quid; far too much. He could always refuse. He lifted his hand up to block the money; to say, No, no . . . far too much. You'll need it yourself; a quid will do fine. Two quid even; more than enough. Three would be plenty. Maybe four, just in case . . .

But then he watched his hand turn and slowly lift the five-pound note and then pull back quickly to shove it down into his pocket, where it finally ceased to tremble.

He brought the hand back out again, stretching it this time, out in front of him; a handshake.

George accepted it and that was that. It was over now. The two of them free. And a smile at last began to form. They exchanged the smile. And that awful ache of mutual embarrassment that had been there all morning, like a queer smell around them, suddenly drifted away.

He stood at the barrier and watched his son walk down along the platform, his head tilted, scanning the length of the train for a suitable spot. He found it. Turning sideways now, shoving the case in before him. Second-class. A second-class carriage. A shadow at a window next. Was it him? He would stay and wave at him. If he caught his eye. If he *let* his eye be caught. Five quid. It was a lot to give; but even more to take.

But he hadn't asked for that much. He'd only asked for . . . what? A couple of quid, not any more than that. 'I'm badly stuck, son, otherwise I wouldn't . . . A couple of quid . . . ' Wasn't that what he'd said? Not *five* of them.

He could see at the corner of his eye the shape of the woman and the little girl emerge. The woman looking over at him; recognition. She knew him. Then a screech from the little girl as she broke away from the woman's hand. Running to greet someone just off the train on the far side of the platform. Full wave; full, bouncy wave; pitching her little-girl screech; high and clear. 'Eddie, Eddieee.'

Eddie, a young man, stooping to lift her, swinging her around; the heels of her shoes spinning a white, dizzy circle. The little girl landed now, swaying on her legs. 'Who's your best brother?'

'You're my best brother.' And a hand patted the top of her head. 'Where's mother?'

The little girl pointed and pulled her big brother by the hand.

'Hello, son,' he heard the woman say.

The Dancer looked over at her; happy now; smiling. She nodded at him. He doffed his hat. He knew her all right. She used to go racing. Helped him out one day with the other boy. In Baldoyle, long time ago. Hadn't seen her since. She told him her name once; what was it? Mrs Abbey, or something. He hoped she wouldn't speak to him. Ask, 'And how is your little boy . . . ? How is he coming along?' Widow's weeds. Wouldn't hold back on the sympathy so; butter him all over with it; roast him with her spuds.

He doffed his hat again and turned away, stepping through the barrier, a few steps nearer to the train.

Which window? Which window? they all looked the same now, pushing away from the grip of the platform. In the few seconds he had taken to turn away, he had lost the window he wanted.

And incidents, he thought. Only incidents. I won't remember what he looked like today, what was said; by him, by me. Or even this ache in my foot. Soon that'll be gone too; this particular ache. I'll only remember that he bumped his case into a small girl. A small girl who said 'Owww'. And a woman who once held my dead child in her arms glared out at him from under her hat. Glared out at him with her vaguely familiar face. Leaving his mark again; by an incident.

*

The train roused itself and squeezed slowly away, and through a gap in his fingers George took a last peep at his father, standing out there on the platform. Alone amongst the flags and the Sunday trippers and the fuss of other people's farewells. Five quid he'd wormed out of him, and he'd been determined not to part with as much as a shilling. Five big ones.

He set his eyes on a boy in a school uniform sitting opposite and unravelling a parcel: of white, spongy bread and tight brown cake and a tin of cream crackers. The little bollix had cream crackers. Packed, no doubt, by his mother. That woman out there, crying into the corner of a handkerchief, a man's arm around her shoulder. His own mother had done plenty of crying too, last night out in the scullery, when he had insisted she take the fiver Samuel had earlier stuffed in his pocket. But there the similarity stopped; no cream crackers, no spongy bread; only plenty of tears that cost nothing. But he didn't want to think of his mother now. And he didn't want to think of her scullery. And he certainly didn't want to think of how she had stopped the others from coming to the station with him; Herbert and Charlie and even his cousin Mo; they had all begged to go. But his mother had seen to it, thought it best, that he should have had those last few moments with his father. Just the two of them alone. Unbearably alone.

He lifted onto his lap his new leather case and, after a bit of a struggle with the unfamiliar straps, the lid was up. He took out a newspaper and a packet of cigarettes. He was away now, anyway – what did it matter? He'd make another five soon enough and plenty more after that too. He was away now and free. Five quid, and cheap at the price.

He stood up and slid the case up onto the luggage rack and on the way back down stooped to take a look out the window.

But he couldn't see his father, just faces on the platform, shrinking into the distance. He was about to sit down again when he spotted the familiar hat, bobbing up and down in tune with his limp. Making his way to the stairs and the exit and moving much quicker, now that he was on the way back out, than he had on the way in. Couldn't wait to throw the money over the counter. Just couldn't wait to get started. Couldn't even have been bothered to wait and give a wave.

George sat back down and watched the shadow of the station slip back from the train and the sky of the city open out to it. He gave himself a minute and then lit up a cigarette. And, with the first slow puff of it, passed across the compartment his message of disdain: cream crackers and currant cake were for kids, cigarettes and newspapers for men.

II

Belfast: by tall buildings and shaded streets, he carried his case, turning sometimes right and sometimes left until he passed the three Castles: Street, Junction and Place. He was hungry now; the money burning a hole in his pocket. A feast, that's what he felt like, a big shove-it-into-you, soup and spuds and a clatter of meat. Dessert too, maybe a slice of apple pie looking out from under a quiff of yellow custard. Looking out at him like Veronica Lake. But the streets were deserted, the cafés all closed. Every time he stretched his neck to look over another half-curtain, it was empty tables and empty coat-stands. And every time he put his hand to a doorknob, the door refused to be pushed. Not even a shop open. So this is what they meant by the Christian Sunday. He'd heard they took their Sundays seriously up here, but he hadn't realised they took it to the death.

He stopped and looked back the way he had come; just a few watery shadows now at the end of the street, the humpback of a taxicab turning off to the right and the box-back of a country bus waddling off into the distance. He picked up his case and continued on in search of a brighter corner.

Up High Street towards a clock in a tower, then back down High Street again, his reflection skimming the broad, curved windows of paltry shop displays. The butcher's bare enamel trays and a row of empty meat-hooks hanging like music notes from a stave. The grocer's baskets lined with empty nests of flimsy fruit paper, and a scales in the background with a hood over its head. The last one then: the bakery, where he stopped to watch his reflection smoke a cigarette, into a shadowy interior of silver stands and empty glass cases and a large cut-out board of two odd hands threatening a knife down onto a three-tiered, cardboard cake. And still more shuttered doors and awnings rolled tight to the wall.

Now he was out at City Hall. All roads seemed to lead to City Hall. A buxom declaration of Portland stone; nooks and crannies; humps and bumps. And the Union flag farting softly to itself way up there, like a cat on its own chimney pot. With its grass topped off and shaved to the bone and its row of monumental representatives here and there: victim and victor. And Victoria too. The *Titanic* and the Boer War; the two Eds – Carson and Harland; there they all were.

But where were the real people?

He took a couple of turns around Donegall Square, where nothing moved except himself and a random tram or the wheels of an occasional car that always seemed to be going in the opposite direction. He was unable to shake off the notion that he was being watched, and found himself glancing backways and sideways. But the only eyes he saw were the eyes of masonry heads puckered out from the frieze of a building, or a statue perched on a parapet somewhere, or the triplet of long-necked mannequins staring out of a big department store, or this lot here at the front of City Hall. All ash-grey eyes; ash-grey irises; all dead.

Now, at Great Victoria Street, he spotted a street map on the corner and carefully plotted his route. He had wanted to put off going to his digs for as long as possible; but he wanted to get it over with now. Having no one around to notice him was making him feel more aware of himself instead of less so. But worst of all, it was making him think of home; past Sundays; hanging around, waiting for them to be over. The oul'fella in one of his hangdog moods, in and out of the kitchen, up and down the yard, until you gave him whatever you had in your pocket, just to get shut of him. His mother busying herself with the dinner dishes and hints for someone to go with her up to Danny's grave. And then pretending he had somewhere else to be other than out on the empty streets. Where the afternoon bells from the two black cathedrals were always waiting for him. Following him around like a litter of sick pups. Yelping after him, no matter how many turns he took. He hated them. He had always hated them. Last Sunday in Patrick's Park, he'd hoisted Charlie up onto his shoulders and danced good riddance to them. He never dreamt he'd ever think of their lonely sound again. But he was now. Sort of. At least on Sunday, once you got into the centre of Dublin, you could buy yourself a bit of company. A few minutes' stroll would see you in the hub of it: people out walking, queuing for the pubs to open; queuing to go to the pictures. Or in for a cup of tea. A bar of chocolate even, in the pokiest corner shop. All you needed was the money. Here he was at last with his pocket stuffed, and what good was it to him now?

He was having difficulty keeping a careless swagger to his walk; he was having difficulty keeping up form. And this feeling of being an intruder; a burglar casing the rooms of an empty house, wondering what time its owners would come back in and catch him: he'd had more than enough of that.

The streets were beginning to lose their looks. Sharp-faced factories or plain-faced warehouses or gable ends of meeting houses posted with black, biblical warnings. And family enterprises with a strip of faded cobblestones leading to an archway and a thick wooden door that was invariably locked. He knew what would be inside: cars, maybe, or parts of cars. A handcart sitting back on its hunkers. Drums of paint stacked against the walls. Sacks mumpish with coal or spuds. A squiggled mess of scrap iron. That was the sort of thing you'd see when you passed under the arch and through the shortened tunnel that opened out to a yard inside. Outhouses on one side, living house on the other. And a family in a kitchen, crouched over plates of Sunday dinner. That's what you'd find in there.

He stopped often. Uphill was a struggle, and his cap was transferred to his pocket. Then his jacket was transferred to his shoulder and finally prised through the handles of his suitcase. Through congeries of alleyways and damp-brown houses on gardenless streets, with the occasional cutaway between the terraces; a sly, dark slit you wouldn't want to chance. And down at his feet, the unfamiliar – kerbstones painted red, white and blue. And over his head, the unfamiliar – a jut of iron flagholders on every single house. And all about him, the all too familiar – the smell of poverty clenched behind shut Sunday doors.

A few kids were out; bare-footed boys pulling at each other's jerseys or heavy-booted girls playing piggy beds, who looked up from the pickeycan to watch him walk by. In a side entry a group of men were playing marbles, huddled together like a conference of tinkers. He stopped to look, but their eyes turned white on him from the darkness inside and he moved quickly away.

His heart was too tired to really sink but it managed a scowl. At the thought of his Aunt Maude and how she had arranged his digs with some Charity contact she had up here. He remembered her promise to his mother then: 'Don't worry, Greta dear, I'll find something suitable, never you fear . . . '

He could picture them both now, his aunt and her contact, matching him up; a poor chap, not used to much. Best to keep him with his own kind. She should have given him a spotty handkerchief on the end of a stick instead of this swanky case. He didn't want it now; the good had gone out of it. He wondered how much he would get for it in the pawn or anywhere they took goods that were both new and second-hand. Or, either way, unwanted.

When he found the house, there was nobody in. So he sat on the windowsill, watching the pigeons fall down from the rooftops to totter over cobblestones or pick at the dents in between. He waited for ages; maybe an hour, shyness dragging him up and making him walk away any time he saw someone coming. Then two men on bicycles rolled up beside him; one an older version of the other – a father, a son. The older man spoke to him, asking him questions he answered himself.

'Who is it you're looking for, sonny? The Cleavers, is it? Number twenty-four? You'd be the boy from the South?'

George nodded.

'Aye, well, they wouldn't be in. Sure, go on you round the back.'

'Naah, it's all right, I'll wait.'

'Go on, go round the back. The door's allas open.'

'Naah, I'm all right, thanks. I'm grand.'

'Go on, don't be shy nay. Don't be daft. Percy here'll go with you.'

'No . . . really, I mean it. I'd prefer to wait.'

In the Cleavers' back door then, straight into the kitchen: a bucket of nappies, a jug of milk. Percy poked his finger into the bucket.

'Shite,' he explained. Then he picked up the milk jug and helped himself to a slug. 'Have you any money?' he asked, and George pretended not to understand.

He followed Percy into the parlour and watched him root about the room, opening drawers and pulling up cushions from a settee shiny-skinned with stains and age. Like an old man's suit, it looked. A knockabout's suit.

'Because if you do have any money, and you find yourself wantin', then I'm the boy to sort ye out.'

'Thanks, I'll keep that in mind.'

Percy walked over to the sideboard and picked up a Coronation tankard, stirring his finger around the bits inside. 'You'll be up in the front room. They all have to sleep together in the back room, on *your* account,' he said accusingly and then upended the tankard onto his palm. 'How much you paying them?'

'We haven't discussed that yet.'

'Aye, nor you won't. Cleaver's not a man to discuss. We have a spare room in our house. Me ma is dead. There's only me an' him.'

'Is that so?'

'Aye. We're having bacon and cabbage for dinner. And spuds.'

'And spuds? Imagine.'

George turned away and looked at the first wall. Pictures and a tapestry. Royalty mostly: stutterin' George and dumpy Mary. The Duchess and Duke of Kent next. The queen again; the princesses. The king again. The king's oul'one; the . . .

'Do you know who they are?' Percy asked him slyly, returning his handful to the tankard and putting it back in place.

'The royal family.'

'Correct. We have a wireless set. A good-toned wireless set.'

'You don't say?'

Percy pulled the lid off a cardboard box. He rummaged over a stack of paper, then pulled out something that looked like a rent book. He flicked the pages over, pausing now and then.

'Should you be doin' that?' George asked him.

'How do you mean?'

'I mean, it's not your house.'

Percy lifted his eyebrows. 'Fuck away off,' he said, 'it's not yours neither.'

George walked over to the next wall. Family photographs this time.

'That's him there.' Percy's finger came over his shoulder and landed on a face in a crowd. Of bowler-hatted men: tall ones at the back, short ones sitting in the front. All set out like a surly football team. A banner stretched between the two wingers on each end of the back row, a Lambeg drum squeezed between the knees of the centre-forward. Face after crabby face bulged out between the black of hats and the black of suits; some older, some younger, but the one shared expression made them all look the same.

'You want to watch him. He's a hard man to nick. Look, there he is again.'

This time he pointed to a man on a motorbike. Goggles pushed back against a ledge of straight hair and eyes like a boy's, tucked up in a smile.

'He looks all right to me.'

'A hard man to nick,' he repeated warily.

George walked back to the tapestry. Elaborate with Orange threads and Orange symbols: an open Bible; a ladder; a heart and star. And in the centre, wouldn't you know – William of Orange. He had seen him already outside the Belfast Orange Hall waving his bronze sword from the broad, bronze back of a butty-arsed horse.

And then again at the end of this street, in flatter form, painted on the gable end of a house. Astride a rearing horse; a white one this time.

'Tell me something,' he asked, 'is that a man or a woman?'

'How do you mean?'

'With the fancy hairdo and that. I just wondered.'

'That's King Billy you're talkin' about,' Percy snapped, and then stepped away.

George turned to the last wall. The dockyard. The ships. The *size* of them. They were magnificent; only magnificent. The men like midgets against the scale of them; the men like bits of fluff. He identified the parts in his head: the stern, the hull, the aft, the bow. That thing projecting into the air: now that would be the bow.

'You're gonna work in the yard.'

'I know.'

'Doin' what?'

'I don't know yet.'

'I do. Making tea. Or nabbin' rats.'

'You're in charge, are you?'

'Maybe I am.'

Percy sat down on the arm of the settee and waited for a moment.

'Do you think there'll be a war on?'

George shrugged.

'My da says there won't be. Cleaver says there will. Cleaver knows nawthin'. Sure what would Hitler want with us?'

'What would he want with anyone?'

'Aye well, it'll not make much difference to you cute boys down south.'

'I'm here now, amn't I?'

'You'll not stay. You'll away the first sign of trouble. And even there's no war on you'll still get plenty of trouble.'

'How do you make that out?'

'They don't like Free Staters working in the yard, so they don't. Think they might be spies. But don't you worry your head, I'll speak up for you.'

'I can speak up for meself, thanks very much. I don't need you to do it for me.'

'Oh, you will, boy. You surely will.'

Percy took a packet of cigarettes from his pocket. 'Ye want one?'

'No.'

'They're Gallagher's Blue.'

'I said no.'

'Suit yourself.'

Percy poked the cigarette into the side of his mouth. 'What do you know about the yard?' he asked.

'I know a bit.'

'You know nawthin' about the yard. See me? I've been working there these five years. I'm a welder now, this past twelvemonth. I know all about it. All about the yard. And I'm tellin' you, they don't like Free Staters. Especially ones who think they know it all.'

'I never said I knew it all.'

'You don't *have* to say it.'

'Ah, fuck off.'

'Did you ever hear tell of Hersel and Pounder?'

'No. What are they?'

'Who. You mean who.'

'All right, who?'

'Oh, they only invented the Harland and Wolfe Burmeister & Wain airless-injection diesel engine.' Percy stood up and took a step towards him. 'Now you know something. Somethin' about the yard.'

George took a step forward himself. 'Is that right?' he asked. 'Tell me, do you know what a suppository is?'

'A what?'

'A suppository. Do you know what it is?'

'No, what is it?'

'It's somethin' you stick up your arse.'

They were both laughing when the Cleavers came in.

*

Mrs Cleaver said they had no wireless set because it killed the art of conversation. Mr Cleaver poked at the bonnet of his pipe and said he would have to agree with his wife. Then they both fell silent, with the odd exception, for the remainder of the evening. There were four small Cleavers – the eldest about eight or nine, the youngest a toddler with an old man's face, who later turned out to be a girl. George discovered this when Mrs Cleaver changed her nappy right in front of him. Even though he had no sisters, he knew that girl babies were never changed in front of men; they were always whisked into another room. He nearly died at the sight of her little peach, instead of the widdler he had been expecting.

The evening squeezed itself out dribble by dribble. Hardly a word was spared, until prayer time just before bed. Mr Cleaver then opened the Bible and read aloud. The children lowered their heads to their chests and stayed perfectly still. Even the baby was so quiet that at one time it looked like it might be dead. George wanted to go home.

He stared at the wall. And the photograph of the ships again. Two big bruisers, they were; dangerous-looking animals: locked in a cage, waiting to be launched. They must launch them stern-first. To be part of building that. Have some little section in its vast body that you could point to and say, that was me, that was my workmanship. That bit there . . .

He saw Mrs Cleaver whisper something to her husband then and the Bible was closed. 'And Lord,' Mr Cleaver began, 'we want to welcome among us young George, on his first steps to manhood, and ask you, Lord, to watch over him and guide him in the right pathway. We ask you to consider his family, his mother and father, his brothers, and especially his dear, departed brother Daniel, who is this day looking down with you from heaven. Thank you Lord.' And Mrs Cleaver twitching over at him, as if she had done him a favour. As if she expected him to be pleased.

George looked down at his feet and found himself wondering what sort of a wireless set Percy had, and if, when he had said bacon, he meant real bacon or just a few oul' scabby cut-offs.

III

In the morning Mr Cleaver became another man as soon as they left the house, reviving the art of conversation – or at least talking a lot, and not like a man that was too fond of the Bible. He spoke all the way to High Street. About the shipyard, mostly, and how he came to be the man he was. His mother was a tracer; his father, like himself, a riveter. 'The only trade worth its salt,' he said, clearing his throat and spitting on the road. 'Welding, my arse. My brown hairy arse.'

George looked down at the cobblestone with the goo of Mr Cleaver's spit perched on top and something about it was almost appetising. He was starving. He thought of the silent supper the night before. A large tin plate with one sausage, one egg and one piece of bread huddled in the centre. A big spoon then coming towards it loaded up with what looked like bread sauce that had been plucked up off the floor – with a 'Would you like a wee squib of plum duff, son, or are you too full?'

More plum duff for breakfast and a mug of tea with a scum of sour milk beaded on top.

He held under his arm what Mrs Cleaver had referred to as his 'piece', squeezing it in between elbow and rib to prevent it from falling. He knew by the feel of it that it couldn't amount to much. He looked over at Cleaver's piece – it was by far the healthier specimen – his elbow winged to make room for it. George thought his face would fall off with hunger and exhaustion. The baby whinging all night. The family in the room next door scuffling and whispering together, trying to accustom themselves to their new, cramped conditions. The sounds of them pissing in turns into a tin pot. Little trickles and mightier efforts that made him cringe inside.

'Would you know, nay, who was the first shipwright, son?'

'No.'

'Well I'll tell you nay. It was Noah, so it was. He was the first shipwright.'

'Oh, Noah.'

'Aye, Noah. You'll be taken on anywhere in the world if you done your time at Harland and Wolfe. Anywhere. Do you mind me nay? We'll leave you as a helper for a few weeks until we see where your knack lies. But keep you away from that welding. Sure it's no trade at all. That Percy can manage it; any fool can do. It's dilutee's work, that what it is.'

'Dilutee's?'

'Aye. And you'll get the blinks.'

'The blinks?'

'Aye, the fuckin' blinks.'

George wanted to ask him what a dilutee was, or what he meant by the blinks, but he had already turned to the story of his grandfather.

'He came down from thon Holywood hills, my gran'far. He painted them big cranes, way up there. He could see them goin' to work on the Isle of Man. He could see them picking their noses. He swang from the cradle at the top, with the wind pushin' at him and shovin' at him. With the wind cuttin' through his head. And not a stroke was missed. Do you know why?'

'No . . .'

'Because he was a craftsman. That's why. Now they're talking about opening a school for welders. Dear sake, but you'd want to be a wee bit lackin' not to pick it up in a week. See that Percy? He'd cry himself sore if he had to take on a task like painting the cranes. See his elbow and scalded? He'll burn another hole in his arse one of these days if he's not careful. So you can forget about welding. Are we agreed upon that?'

George nodded but George would have agreed to anything by now. By the time they turned into High Street, he had a pain in his head listening to Cleaver and his tales from the shipyard.

But then he felt as though he'd been kick-started. Or as though someone had thrown a bucket of cold water over him. The street was black with men. Gangs of them. He had never seen so many men in his life. Where had they all sprung out of? Where had they all been hiding yesterday? Wasn't this the street he had wandered up and down; the empty street? And look at it now . . . the shops all open, long-aproned shopkeepers carrying crates under and out of awnings; all tilted down now. Slim-hipped chickens and split-bellied pigs swaying at the end of hooks outside the butcher's; barrows stuffed full with green frilly cabbages and cranky brown spuds outside the grocer's. Shop boys sweeping the paths out front. Delivery boys piling up their baskets with mounds of new bread. Newspaper boys scurrying and shouting in and out of men, trotting along the street towards the trams or travelling on shoals of bicycles or in clumps together on top of carts. You wouldn't see it on Derby day in the Curragh. You wouldn't see it on a dozen Derby days all rolled into one.

Mr Cleaver broke into a run and George picked up pace beside him. He felt Mr Cleaver grab a hold of his coatsleeve, then he felt himself being lifted up and on.

He looked around at bodies, all about him, blocking out any bit of light inside the tram; thick as hops, they were. Packed in tight over the platform, corkscrewed together all up the stairwell and even scutching like street urchins on the outside. Jaysus, what if one of them was to lose his grip? He held his breath. The smells, the smells; there were too many smells, punching each other out of the way. Linseed oil and engine oil, wood shavings and rust, red lead and oakum, not to mention the inevitable, thick, sweaty hum of a heap of workmen piled in together. He felt his lunch slip out from under his arm and the last he saw of it was a flattened scrap collapsing onto the platform and then sliding off down onto the road as the tram made a slow struggle for the Queen's Bridge. He was shoved forward then and a large hairy arm swung around his neck, where it remained without apology for the rest of the journey.

By the time ten o'clock came he thought he would go off his head. His nose and throat were thick with dust and fumes, as if he'd eaten them out of a bowl for breakfast. His ears were stinging. He wanted to put his hands over them and then stick his head between his legs, then stick himself into a hole somewhere. He was numbed by the noise of the hammers; banging on, rapping on, hour after hour. And the roar of the foundry and the whoosh of pneumatic machines, all joining in. He felt like joining in himself after a while, throwing his head forward and screaming back at them, 'Shut up! Shut up! Will you shut the fuck up?"

There were men everywhere, in dungarees and caps, passing him by in all directions; sometimes in squads or sometimes perched alone high up on stagings. Up there on catwalks, shouting down to those on the ground. There were scrawny-looking scuts carting big steel plates up onto gangways. There were fat slobs up on planks that kept swaying with each movement – he couldn't bear to look up at them. Down in the workshops there were slow-hands shaving at pieces of wood or swift-fists bashing away at sheets of steel. And all over the place, appearing out of nowhere, others, back-bent, pushed buggies of angle irons and other bits of heavy metal he couldn't begin to put a name on.

They gave him messages to run. Up to the boiler-room, down to the blacksmith's shop. Back to the coppershop. Up to the shipwright's shop, then over to the slips. Up on a shipdeck, twenty-foot ladder to a bockety landing, then up again, all the way; maybe a hundred and twenty feet. And then that ordeal just over and behind him and another one waiting. This time below: down to the welders, down to the hold. Down in the black, black bowels of it; red sparks spitting all around and the arc of the weld scorching his eyes. Staying with him then, for the rest of the morning, little crimson flecks decorating everything he looked at.

And he had always been used to working alone, under the belly of a silent car, nothing but his own thoughts to amuse him and his own hands to concern him. Between the yard and the digs, he began to see the foolishness of himself. All that trouble for this? For this bloody bang, bang. For this bloody bang. His head was lifting away from his body. His legs were travelling the opposite way.

The messages were passed and returned: sometimes verbal, sometimes no more than a bag of nails, bolts or washers. Or a lump of black putty he was that hungry he felt like taking a bite out of. Nobody seemed to notice he was new. Nobody asked him his name or his business. Nobody spoke to him, unless to give him orders. Until it came towards the meal hour and he set himself about making the tea. A big man called Crawford was not impressed.

'Och, what do you call that? Horse's piss? You have to let the tea leaves at it till they turn over on their backs. Where did you get this dunce, Cecil?'

Mr Cleaver frowned and, laying his lunch on the ground between his legs, began pulling at its wrapper. 'He'll larne,' he said.

'Aye well, he better.'

'Where's your piece, sonny?'

'I ate it already,' George lied, although he almost told the truth on the off-chance that it might tempt their better nature. But then he stopped himself; being called dunce once in a day was enough.

George sipped at Triple-X tea and looked over the cup rim at Mr Cleaver's sandwiches. Loads of them, there were, in a big pile, and the first of them stuck now in his dirty big gob. Fat lumps of bread with rashers peering out at him through the buttery slits. And him with nothing to swallow but his own spits. He wondered what time the next train was leaving for Dublin.

When the horn sounded he was busy finishing a task Crawford had set him, and so he paid it no heed. Then he glanced up and saw he was surrounded by spattered legs and battered boots: Cleaver and Crawford and a few other squad members, all looking down on him as if he had been caught with his trousers around his knees.

'Are you stoppin' the night?' one of them snarled, and Cleaver gave him an impatient nod. George stood up and ran after the men, seized with the terror that, if he lost sight of them, he would never find his way out of this place and might end up having to do just that.

He packed himself on with the rest of the herd. His head was a yo-yo, his neck was the string. It spun away from him and then reeled back up again. Dropping and rising; dropping again. The sounds from the shipyard were still beating in his head. The shapes, diluted to shadow, but still there, just the same. His eyes lured him down. Deeper and down. Into the hold; the black, silent hold where there was nothing, only darkness and sharp red rain moving across it at a slant. The tram gave a petrified screech and he jerked his eyes open, just in time to catch his head snoozing on Mr Cleaver's shoulder. Cleaver graced him with a tolerant grin and a pat on the arm. That was when he decided on the bicycle.

Percy got it for him. 'That'll cost you two quid,' he said.

'Two quid? For that crock?'

'A bicycle's a valuable piece of property in this town, I'll have you know.'

George handed him the two quid. 'Where did you get it?' he asked.

'It's me da's.'

'Does he not mind?'

'Not for two quid, he don't.' Percy smiled and pucked him on the arm. It was then that he noticed Percy's weeping eye and the small red circle, like a rubber band, that held it in place. And he grinned to himself, returning the puck: the blinks.

IV

He almost got used to the noise; he almost got used to the accent. And that sleight of tongue, with its upward curve that made every remark sound like a question he would eventually stop feeling obliged to answer. It amused him anyhow, the observations of the men; their opinions about women, their rows about the war. And the notions they had about the South, their disapproval of what they referred to as its 'Continental Sunday'. He thought that was gas. And the way they gave their senses to matters such as 'Popery' or 'DeValerism'. The amount of time they wasted on it too. When did anyone at home ever bother their arse discussing Belfast, or who would even know the name of its prime minster? And to hear them then, big gruff men, in the middle of bawling and cursing, suddenly coming out with granny expressions like 'For dear sake' – that always made him want to laugh.

It was a bit like being a baby all over again. Another language; a whole new vocabulary to learn. Dunchers were caps, mutton duffers were canvas shoes. And a foot adze was an ancient implement that Noah used to carve the Ark. An implement that would slice the mickey off you if you took your mind off it for a split second. Granpa Cleaver's two big cranes were known as Samson and Delilah. A ceiling wasn't called a ceiling; it was a deckhead. The walls were bulkheads and every ship had a double skin at the bottom.

He learnt the names of dockyard jobs and the pecking order

involved. The dilutee was way down the line: an unskilled man. A welder was a dilutee that had been hastily trained in a skill that didn't merit much respect, especially since it was a skill that would eventually shove the riveter onto the scrapheap. Dilutees tended to skulk together. Tradesman of the higher order stuck together too; these were the ones who wore collars and ties under their overalls. They washed their faces as well as their hands before eating and took their pieces out of a hand-carved box instead of a paper wrap; such were the traits that set them apart.

He became familiar with the politics of the yard too. Unless you were prepared to carry your crucifix up twenty-foot ladders all day long, you'd better accept that the craneman's palm was there to be greased; his arse was there to be licked. He learnt how to recognise and keep dick for the relevant foreman. And that when he asked you for a light on Friday, it wasn't your matchbox he was interested in, but the small fold of money that was stuffed inside; money that would buy you another week's work.

Every day that passed he became a bit more familiar with the geography of the yard; every day he discovered another section of it around a different corner. His sense of direction had been developed when he was a boy, running for his schoolmaster to bookie shops all over Dublin city, and he was glad of it now as he negotiated his way through the vast continent of Harland & Wolfe. Like a cartographer on an expedition, he recorded names and exact locations: the yards and the channels – Musgrave and Victoria. The basins and docks – Abercorn and Hamilton. And later in the evening, he sketched them down in his notebook so he would know their positions off by heart. He didn't intend staying too long, but as long as he was here, he wanted to cut down on the occasions when he might get lost and then have to make a fool of himself by asking directions back to his squad. And besides which, he wanted to know the yard. He wanted to take that much away with him, at least.

He even got to be fond of parts of it, like the engine room. He had only ever seen the engine of a car or a motorbike before, but this was something else. He felt like a fly that had wandered in under a car's bonnet. The enormity of it all. And he couldn't make his mind grasp the notion that this structure, with men crawling over and about it, would one day have a ship built around it that would tear a strip through the ocean.

He learnt how to get through the day, how to make tea you could trot a mouse on, how to pick up his board in the mornings and finish what he was at the second the horn blew south in the evening. He learnt that Percy didn't just have bacon and cabbage on Sunday, but every evening when he got home. Or cold in a parcel for lunch. And how to accept part of his greasy offering during the meal hour and then to return the compliment in the chip shop later on. He stuffed his head full of all these things: things that he didn't already know, and things he only thought he knew. Like how to play cards.

He was coming to the end of his second week and his plans to escape were almost finalised, his excuses, when he got there, in need of just another little polish. He planned them all as if they were homecoming gifts; for his mother, the skimpy food and the nappy-changing should do the trick. He might add in a bit of public breastfeeding, for extra effect. (She could share that with Aunt Maude – for all her bother.) For the oul'fella, the Bible-reading, the Cleavers' disapproval of gambling and the fact that the yardmen gave him no credit for being a Prod and insisted on calling him 'Free Stater' instead of George. For Herbert and his other pals, he'd have to spice things up a bit: the dullness of the place; the lack of prospects; the lack of women. Maybe he could throw in a rucky-up with one of the foremen: a split lip, a burst nose – something on that line. For Samuel? Well, he wouldn't need anything for Sam: he could tell him the truth, more or less, when the time was right.

He had it all organised, all in the bag: the Sunday train timetable off by heart in his head; all he needed was the opportunity to fit in with it. They went out on Sundays, the Cleavers. As soon as they were off the street, he'd be out that back door like a hare out of a trap. Let them think what they liked. The important thing was to get the hell out.

No more waking up to the sound of the manic rapper-up running up and down the street banging on doors to call the men for work. No more nights of falling asleep to the tell-tale clang of Cleaver's big brass bed and the grunts that always went with it. Never again would he have to look at their ugly mugs or listen to them pissing in their pot. And the days, too, of grinning at the jokes of the squad were almost behind him. Jokes that were invariably at his expense. Them always the big men and him always the boy. He would leave this kip behind him and never come back. Never again.

His mind was turned homewards, the wind at its back. His mind was an athlete, down on its mark and ready to go. But then, when he least expected it, the wind changed direction. And his mind stood up and walked slowly away.

'Here, Free Stater, can you collect a bet in itself?' Crawford asked him, Friday dinner time. 'Can you be trusted to do that much?'

And him frowning down at the tea leaves, which still hadn't

quite managed to master the backstroke. 'Now, do you mean?'

'Aye, now I *do* mean.'

'But . . where like?'

'Like down the toilets at Deep Water.'

'The toilets?'

'Aye, the toilets.'

'Right.'

George stood up and brushed the few crumbs from his overalls. 'Where's this Deep Water is again?' he asked.

'Where's this . . . ? You don't fuckin' know, do you?'

George shook his head.

'Horace here'll show you. Get you down there. The second cubicle. Big Sam. You'll not miss him – he's only the one eye. Although he's not the only one with one eye, mind you. But he's the only one with one eye in that cubicle. Am I right, Horace?'

'Oh aye.'

And George complimented their little routine by obliging with a grin; the same stupid grin he'd been using all week.

'Here's the docket. Now be sure you and count it. If you come back short, I'll hit you a looter. Do you know what that means?'

George nodded and skittered away.

Restful now in the meal hour, with the machinery lulled and the walkways all cleared, George and Horace walked through the yard. Past scattered groups of tired men mumbling together, eating bread and smoking cigarettes, boiling cans for second tea or pressing slow folds into greaseproof paper to take home for tomorrow's piece. Some of them sat on upturned crates reading bits out of the newspapers to each other. Some more snoozed with their backs to the wall; others had made little beds for themselves out of coats spread on the ground or rolled into pillows over their toolboxes.

In between were several vacant spaces strewn with traces that had been left behind, like cowboy camps that had suddenly been abandoned. Tin cups and tin cans; half-eaten crusts; the shell of an egg. A coat here, a duncher cap there. The stub of a cigarette that wasn't quite dead.

'Where have they all gone?' he asked Horace.

'Who?'

'The rest of the men.'

'Oh, they'll be up the casino.'

'Casino? What casino?'

Horace laughed but he didn't answer.

When they got near Deep Water, Horace nodded him in the right direction and left him to it. George turned a corner, making his way down to the row of cubicles at the end of the walkway, where he took his place in the queue. All the doors of the toilets had racing papers pinned up and yardmen, acting as bookies, were perched on downturned toilet seats, checking out dockets and totting up sums. He handed his docket to Big Sam and counted the money. A bald man with a hooked scar on the back of his head was having a barney. With himself, it would seem, as Big Sam was paying not the slightest attention.

'See you . . . ? You're nothing' but a robbin' bawstard, you. You'd rob your own mother, you. You probably robbed your own eye out of your own head. Well, you'll not fuckin' rob me. I'm going thon ship, where the price maight be better. Aye, that's where I'll be taking my business.'

Ship? What ship?

George thought about asking him, but the man had already moved away. So he pushed the money into his pocket and followed him down to the jetty. Where he had to pause for a moment, to catch himself on, then he had to light a cigarette to give himself a moment before he looked back down to the ground. There were men in circles everywhere, all over the ground as far as the eye could see. There were coins hopping and cards flicking and little hills of money in the centre of each group. He'd never seen anything like it in his life. He had to force himself to move away after the bald man, keeping his eye on the scarred head and the two black boots that were picking their way through the players and over to the ship.

He could hear the sound of the man's boots clunk urgently ahead of him up the ladder. He pulled himself on, stopping every few rungs to look down on the long stretch of bent heads and genuflected knees; caught between the shadow of the ship's huge stern and the high, grey wall of the works. A long corridor of toss schools and card schools made up from all corners of the yard; from tradesmen to can-boys, there they all were. All humped in together; everyone the same. He hoisted himself aboard ship, where the commotion was even greater. On the far end of the deck, he could see the smooth head of the man stopping to consider the first of several pitches. George flicked his cigarette overboard and walked slowly along the deck.

There were rubby-dub men with rubby-dub boards and the day's racing hung up on sheets behind them. There were shouts and roars and odds being bartered with harsh Northern accents turned suddenly sweet. Another few steps and his feet started to move faster; he could hear his steps echo into the iron. He could feel his heartbeat thicken into his blood. He put his shoulder to the crowd and shoved. One more push and then he would be in. One more push. But first he had to stuff his fist into his mouth to stop himself from laughing out loud.

He thought he might stay another few days, then another few weeks. And then he thought he might see the summer in and go south, like a bird for the winter. By the end of the month, he no longer collected bets: now he put them on. And he sat with the men discussing form; they were impressed by his knowledge. All except Cleaver.

'Christ on a bicycle,' Cleaver spat, 'you're like Jesus in the temple, surrounded by the rabbis. Or should I say "rabbits"? Have youse none of youse a mind youse can call your own?'

But nobody seemed to listen to Cleaver these days, because everyone was listening to George. And nobody could place a bet either without George's opinion; George's advice. The day Crawford went against him and lost nearly half his wage packet, trying to prove a point, George dipped into his own winnings and gave him the loan of a couple of quid, without being asked. After that, George never had to make the tea again. Crawford organised his own tea and sometimes even passed George a share of his piece: two slabs of bakery bread, buttered to the corner and damp with the sweat of ringed raw onion.

V

In the evenings he went out with Percy and they exchanged the tricks of young men. Percy showed him how to talk to girls. Even out on the street, Percy thought nothing of barging into their company with no more to offer than the front wheel of his bicycle and a great deal of guff. This amused as much as embarrassed George. He knew he had little or no experience in that field; not yet. But he knew that when he was ready, his approach wouldn't be Percy's. Nor would his choice of women. In the meantime he was glad enough of the bit of practice and so he let Percy lead a field; he sometimes chose to follow.

Then it was George's turn to take the lead. Up to the dogs in Celtic Park two evenings a week, where he showed Percy how to place a bet and, more importantly, how to handle a result: not to get hysterical if you won or into a huff if you lost. If they came out ahead, they went for a feed: the bigger the winnings, the bigger the plate. And then later downtown to the International Bar, up three brown flights to the billiard rooms, where there was no alcohol served and the men were steady-handed.

By a long window that gave out over Royal Avenue, they waited for a table, Percy keeping a jealous eye on their spot in the queue while George considered the contrast. Between the agitation of dockyard and dogtrack, and this smooth, hushed atmosphere:

panelled wood and low-slung lights and swishes of hard colour gliding across a dark baize table. And easy sounds: the dry toc of billiard balls as they clipped each other in passing, or the occasional rustle of subdued applause from the spectator seats behind. Agitation or tranquillity; opposite ends of the line: one stopped you from thinking, the other allowed you to think too much. The difficulty was in deciding which disturbed him the more.

On other evenings Percy showed him the inside of Belfast. The two of them rolling down from the snuggery of clumped-up terraces, through streets that would gradually widen, until they were out into the city and part of its traffic. If the time was right they might stop across the road from the row of theatre houses on Great Victoria Street where Malone Road toffs poured out of cars, passed under canopies and finally disappeared through tall glass doors. And they would tell each other then, from their safe distance, that next pay day they might chance it themselves. The Grand Opera House, the Hippodrome and then the Ritz; to dance and dine; to see a show. Next pay day, or maybe the one after that.

Percy always seemed to believe it. But George wasn't so easily fooled. He knew that this was something that could only happen at a later time, and that when it did, it wouldn't be with Percy. The only picture houses he had known up to now had been fleapits. But this was no fleapit with the kids pissing on the floor and flinging things at each other across the aisles. This was somewhere he wanted to belong – or to feel he belonged, at any rate. The only way he could ever allow himself to pass through those glass doors was when he was as good as any other punter: a date on his arm and a suit on his back; spanking and new, and none of your cut-off jobs either. And maybe a wristwatch too, showing a half-moon of itself from under a shirtsleeve cuff; straight and sharp and without the trace of a fray.

Sometimes they cycled down as far as the Queen's University. Percy liked to stop and heckle. But George liked to stop and look. He liked the colours; the way the northern sun transmuted them at evening; it made him feel as if he was at the pictures, looking up at the big screen; that's how far removed it was from his reality. Mellow brickwork and mullioned windows; the flap of a scarlet-robed don. Young men striding on thick, green lawns, coming back in from the cricket field; jerseys slung over shoulders and loose, flannel legs folding down to join one of several circles of loafing cronies. He felt neither envy nor concern for their lives; it was their confidence that interested him: their sense of belonging.

He saw a different sense of belonging then one night; a different sort of confidence. But that didn't interest him at all. Near Carlisle Circus, where they came across a practice parade of Junior Orangemen. All done up in cocked hats and cross-belted tunics; slow-marching to the sounds of pipe and wind and a three-pace roll of drums. This time it was George who wanted to stop and heckle. But he took one look at Percy and the pride welling up in his watery eye and kept his mouth shut. He lit a cigarette and leaned back on the bar of his bike, watching the turn of kilt hems and sporrans and the rise and fall of shortbread-box spats. Percy took him through the tunes: 'That's "The Seventy-Ninth's Farewell to Gibraltar",' he whispered. 'That's "From Kantara to El Arish".' By the time they got to 'The Burning Sands of Egypt', he thought Percy was going to cry. So he stubbed out his cigarette and cycled away.

When they had seen all there was to see of the city, George suggested they go further afield. And Percy, who had been unused to travelling – other than the occasional Sunday-school trip to the Fresh Air Colony in Bangor or the odd tram ride up to Bellevue Zoo – was a willing companion. They cycled together up to the rise of the Springfield Road, looking westwards to the Black Mountain and the first screeds of darkness blotting the light from the lough.

George felt himself moved in a way that was almost threatening. He wanted to say that he thought it was beautiful, but the words got stuck in his throat.

And when Percy said, 'Did you ever see anthin' as nice? Would you ever see anthin' as nice in this world? I bet you now, youse have nothin' as nice in the South,' he heard his own voice lash out and say, 'Oh for fuck sake, Percy, it's only Belfast, not the hanging gardens of bleedin' Babylon.'

George looked over at his friend's face and knew he had humiliated him. He wanted to tell him he was sorry, but he couldn't say that either.

When Percy shrugged it off and said, 'Aye, I suppose. Will we go on down for the chips so?' it made George feel even worse. After that, whenever he went to the hills, he went alone.

On Saturday afternoon, by the time he got off work it wasn't worth the cycle to the races, so he stayed in Belfast and made do with the bookies. On Sandy Row, where he placed the first of his bets, he watched the women take on the street traders and the street traders take on each other. And in the bookie's shop, the men slipping in and out from the pub next door, while neglected wives hung around outside like beggars, hoping to catch their husbands midstream. And he hated them sometimes, these people he lived with. He hated their acceptance; a whole week's slavery for just one afternoon. An afternoon of drink and half-considered bets, of items redeemed from the pawn until the weekend was over. Of matinée picture queues; eager Saturday faces, with honeycomb to suck, boiled pigs' feet to guzzle. He hated them, but mostly because they reminded him of home.

After he had cycled back to his digs to hand up his keep, collect his clean clothes and decline Mrs Cleaver's weekly offer of a tin bath and a hot kettle, he took his roll up to the public baths, where he steeped himself in salts and steam and watched the water bruise black and blue with dockyard dirt. Lying back in his private cubicle, the racing page held at arm's length, he studied form to the background sound of boys beating each other outside in the pool. The whack of dry Corporation towels, the slap of wet Corporation togs. The name-calling under the half-doors of dressing rooms that lined the poolside; in a high, muffled cacophony of utter, joyful nonsense. It made him remember when he was a boy. And that made him feel like a man.

He came back into town then and met up with Percy. In Donegall Square they sat in cafés and snackeries eating and smoking, watching the women turn in and out of doors. Women in hats, off the brow or brim-dipped over one eye. Their fingertips strung through parcels that lurched when they moved their hips. When they took off their hats, when they peeled off their gloves, their mouths were red gashes, their nails red claws. These were the women George liked the look of. Sometimes they went to Woolworth's Emporium, where Percy liked to look at the younger girls. They didn't do much for George, but he had to agree with Percy at least that these were ones you felt you could talk to.

Perched up on high stools, licking at pokes of ice cream and swinging their ankle-socked legs, grinning at nothing; charmingly shocked by the antics of Percy. He would leave Percy at it, to check on the progress at the bookies, returning from time to time to check on the progress of his friend. Like a doctor doing his rounds, he divided his time between patients.

On Saturday night, Percy did his dancing in the Painters' Hall on Dee Street. George went there with him once. He stood at the back wall, watching Percy move aross the floor with one or another from the shelf of girls under his arms, sending puzzled winks of encouragement over her head to him. Percy couldn't dance if his life depended on it, but George didn't dance at all. Later, when Percy pressed him, he confessed that that was because he didn't know how. Percy offered to show him, but he said he'd rather learn from someone who didn't dance as though he was trying to knee himself in the bollix.

So he enrolled himself in a dance class, where on Friday nights he learnt to dance: one-steps and two-steps and how to trot like a fox. Sometimes with a sweet-smelling dandy named Sylvester; sometimes with a pissy-smelling oul'one named Doris; sometimes with a chair.

In the meantime he took to cycling out to the country towns, where he watched the country people stretch out their day. He would buy a slab of roasting beef or a brace of chickens and later, in the market place, a bag of vegetables. These were given to Mrs Cleaver, who took them as tokens of apprecation (although in fact they were just a guarantee that he would have a decent Sunday dinner). In the market square, an open-air prayer meeting: cornets and drums playing gospel hymns and a soapbox preacher spitting on the crowd. And the farmers' wives and daughters wandering through, with baskets of vegetables pressed against crossed-over dresses of thin, shabby cotton. When the sun took a slant you could see through the dresses, and that took the shabbiness away.

Once he saw a dying bull. In the open countryside, a stupid dying bull who had got his head stuck between the bars of a gate. There was no one around, so George tried to free the bull himself. But the thick, damp head just wouldn't turn. The more he tried to help it, the heavier the head became; it was as if his horns had been welded onto the bars of the gate. Only the eyes turned; the big, soft, crying eyes. He couldn't figure the bull out at all: if he had the brains to get himself in, why couldn't he get himself back out again?

In the end he decided there had to be a knack to freeing the bull and so he cycled away to look for help, monitoring the series of long, deep moans that skimmed across the fields behind him. They stopped and then started again, a little weaker each time, the intervals of silence growing longer. By the time he had found a farmhouse, the silence had taken over. And he knew the bull must be dead. So he didn't bother knocking on the farmhouse door. He just cycled straight on past. And, moving like the clappers, he thought he'd never get away, as if somehow he was responsible. Or somehow he would be blamed.

Then back into town to hang around, like he always did, until the dance was over, and if Percy hadn't clicked, they'd go home together. If Percy had a girl, she would sometimes have a friend, and they'd all go in together then to sad-eyed Enzo for a fish supper. If the friend was a dog, he'd talk to Enzo; if she was all right, he'd do a bit of showing off. If Percy's girl had no pal, he'd leave the two of them go ahead down the street, Percy with his arm like a plank around her shoulder. He'd go home alone then, by a different route, stopping off occasionally to join in on a game of banker on the street.

Until the night Big Sam cuffed him.

He was in a side entry dealing the cards when he heard his name being called out from the street. He recognised the voice without having to take his eye off the cards.

'I'm dealing, Sam, hold on a minute.'

But Big Sam didn't want to hold on. 'Get you out here nay,' he shouted.

When he got out he hardly recognised Big Sam, all done out in mufti. His huge frame shouldered the street light; he wore a long, pale-coloured mackintosh coat with a belt snapped onto the middle. Only his one eye popping out from under his hat was entirely familiar. George gave a whistle to let Big Sam know how well he looked, but Big Sam wasn't flattered.

'Come here to me, you.'

'What's your problem, Sam?'

'Here's my problem,' he said. And then he cuffed him.

He nearly knocked the ear off his head.

'If you want to play cards, play like a man, not like some fuckin' rat in an alleyway.'

George would have liked to hit him back. But he knew that was stupid. Big Sam would have flattened him, and besides, you couldn't hit a man for telling the truth.

After that he stopped playing cards in the street. After that he played with Big Sam and his crowd, in different houses all over the city. And sometimes outside as well: Bangor, Omagh. And once they even travelled as far as Carrickfergus. Although Big Sam made him wait long enough before inviting him along for the first time. George reckoned that was because he was testing him to make sure he'd really given up playing in alleyways. But George didn't mind that. A man like Big Sam would always have to be sure. A man like Big Sam couldn't afford to court messers.

Sometimes he found time to write letters to Herbert and poems to himself. In the poems he wrote lavish words about sweet-smelling gorse and the blaze of trapped sunlight in the country hedgerows of the Holywood Hills. Or the white fingertips of a dark-eyed girl, turning softly in her hand a big, blond onion picked from the basket perched on her hip. In the letters he wrote:

> Dear Herbert,
>
> I went on a cycle today. It was all right. A bull got his head stuck in between the bars of a gate. I tried to save him but the stupid bastard couldn't turn his head and choked itself to death. You should come up some time, it's not too bad at all. In any case, it could be worse. Work is all right, the weather is good. I'm learning how to dance. How is the pen-pushing coming along? Are you still going with whatever girl you're going with now? Tell Charlie I asked after him. Am enclosing a few quid. See that it doesn't fall into the wrong hands.
>
> Your brother G.

This was his first summer in Belfast; the summer before the war.

HERBERT

I

Herbert moved through a narrower world: dingy hallways, swollen walls and rooms at the top that daylight skipped over. Where slow-handed chief clerks made him wait while they eased documents into envelopes and then dismissed him with them, as if he was a boy. And this was how he carried his day: traipsing the interior alleyways of these decrepit buildings, negotiating brittle stairwells turn by turn, past doors of half-forgotten offices or disused corridors that may once have intended something. This is how he wandered, like a thought lost in an old man's head, and the stairs that wavered under his feet loosened teeth that had long since shrunk from the gum. His was the life of a solicitor's clerk; the obeisant life of a solicitor's clerk; the all-brown life of the legal lackey.

It was a wish that had been granted, in a half-arsed sort of a way. A wish he had nursed since his last term at school, when Walter Caper had taken him to the Four Courts to see his oul'fella perform. Wally's oul'fella had a face like nothing on earth; a face that was plush with the colours of affluence. Mauve on the outskirts, coming in purple, a tip of lilac here and there, and a nose in the middle you could light a cigarette off. Besides all this, he still managed to carry a couple of chins as soft as chamois cloth and drag along behind him an arse very close to the ground. He was the ugliest man Herbert had ever set eyes on. But he spoke like an actor in the theatre and behaved like an actor up on the screen, and when he moved, he went like a clockwork toy on feet that seemed too small and too fast for the load they had to carry. Herbert had never met anyone so utterly pleased with himself. But after a few minutes in his company, it was an opinion he found himself sharing.

Under the portico of the Four Courts building, Wally's oul'fella looked him over. 'So this is your chum? He's tall enough, anyway.'

'The tallest in the class,' Walter confirmed.

'I don't doubt it. What height are you, son?'

'I'm not sure, sir.'

'You're not sure, sir? Would you say now, you were six foot one? Two, maybe?'

He took a step back and with the flat of his hand drew a line from the top of his wig to the hub of Herbert's shoulder.

'I'd say, in all probability, you're six foot three, from top to toe.'

'Three and a half, actually.'

'Aha, so you *are* sure? I knew it. Fella's as tall as you, always knows it to the fraction. What do they call you, tall man?'

'Herbert.'

'Herbert? Not much of a name for a giant, is it? Still, it will have to do until we come up with something better. You two wait inside, I've someone to meet – we're due in court in twenty minutes. You'll have to forgive me, I couldn't come up with anything very exciting today – neither debauchery nor mutilation, I'm afraid. Not even a common-or-garden murder.'

'What have you come up with then?' Walter asked.

'A drunk in charge of a motor vehicle.'

'Is he guilty?'

'Of *course* he's guilty. Do you know what disappoints me most about the human race, tall man?' Herbert shook his head. 'How little we murder each other – considering the nature of the beast, that is. You'd think there'd be at a lot more, wouldn't you? Still, we must have our dull days, I suppose, and today, much to my shame, is one such. You will forgive me?'

'Of course,' Herbert said.

Wally's oul'fella gave a little bow. 'I am eternally grateful.'

'Tell you what,' he continued, 'by way of compensation for the dullness of the case, I'll treat you to a spot of lunch. I suppose you generally eat a horse. I warn you, you won't get a horse in the Clarence, but I dare say we'll get you a slice of something. That suit you all right?'

'Oh yes, sir, thank you very much.'

'Excellent. I'll see you inside. Enjoy the circus.'

Sitting on a ringside bench in the Great Hall of the Four Courts, Herbert watched the crowd pass over a circular floor, ascending or descending short flights of granite steps that curved at intervals off the arena. Behind the fluted columns, the mouths of courtroom doors creaked open and a dribble of silence rolled out for a second before being snapped up by the din. He couldn't follow the voices; the voices were too many and kept barging into each other and then smashing into senseless fragments. But the footsteps managed to stay clear. Chattering footsteps rising up with the walls and narrowing into the bowl of the dome above. From time to time he felt Walter's elbow take a proprietorial poke at his ribs, directing his attention to this or that, and he nodded, half-listening, with the stilted politeness of a guest who doesn't altogether respect his host. Then he returned to his own thoughts about men and their footsteps.

Not all feet made noise, he noted, nor did all feet want to. An occasional man took to the floor as if he had come in late for a funeral service. His step was hesitant and soft; this was the man in trouble. The brisk, resonant step belonged to the man who would get him out of it. You could identify each man's purpose by the way he walked or by the way he wore his clothes. Barristers were bulked out with wig and gown, but that didn't cut their canter. Solicitors, pared down in their suits, looked in comparison a bit like plucked chickens, but they carried their bags if they knew what they were at and kept a steady eye in their head. The man in trouble wore his suit as if he was afraid of it. Policemen, tugging at their uniforms, seemed afraid of something too, which he found surprising. And even the plucked chickens seemed, if not exactly afraid, then at least a little wary. Only the barristers were completely brave – the barristers and the porters, who conducted themselves and everyone else with a graceful balance of deference and disdain.

He could have sat there all day, just looking at the faces and pinning them down to crimes and misdemeanours, defenders and defendants. But then in the distance a low, long voice pressed down on the noise, and within seconds everything had stopped. He felt Walter's hand pull on his sleeve, instructing him to stand up. An entourage came out of one door, a comic-book judge at its centre, and then nobody seemed that brave any more. All heads bowed until the procession had passed, then all heads bobbed back up again. And in a moment the chattering footsteps resumed.

Up the steps and into a corridor then, they took up position beside Wally's oul'fella, one at each elbow, struggling to keep up. The oncoming traffic forced them to step aside and they lost him a few times. But Wally's oul'fella never gave way; he left it to others to take to the wall. They caught up with him again outside the library, where he came to a sudden halt.

'You're my devil,' he said to Herbert out through one side of his mouth. 'You're devilled to me, if anyone asks.'

From the other side of his mouth he then dismissed Walter. 'You stay outside.'

'But . . . ?'

'You don't look old enough. You stay out here.'

Into the law library, he followed behind. Into the panels of dusty light where black wings fluttered and straw scrolls on heads were pushed informally to the crown. Leather-bound books muddled up to the ceiling and then tumbled over each other back down to the ground. Long, narrow benches stretched out between walls, leaving a small gap where barristers squeezed by, brushing flimsy pages off their trays and toppling files that seemed purposely to be stacked out of alignment. And everywhere paper in scraps or thick wads, and hands playing with paper: shuffling them together, thinning them apart or even discarding them in a heap to the floor. He'd never seen such a mess in his life; in school, you'd get a kick up the arse for even a fraction of it. And yet there was an air of organisation about it all, as if someone had taken an immense amount of trouble to mastermind this perfect disarray. He heard them call out wittily to each other or gesture across the room like schoolboys taking advantage of an absent master. Or slip outside sometimes and slide away into a corner to bend an ear and nod a head to a client he felt sure they were only pretending to believe.

And later in the courtroom then, he followed a case and the course of a point, batted from left to right and back again. Until finally it settled down, between an incredulous chuckle on one side of the room and an exasperated hand slapped against a forehead on the other. While in the dock a downcast face lied through its teeth. And got away with it too because Wally Caper's oul'fella was such a clever Dick. Herbert the schoolboy had lapped all this up. Herbert the schoolboy heard a voice in his head that had always been there but up to now had only been muttering. 'This could be you,' he heard the voice say. 'This could be your way of making a name, not begrudged to you. This could be how the black sheep rises.'

For almost a year it had overpowered his thoughts, squeezing out what, up to then, had been his principal preoccupation: all shapes female. Women, girls; objects, too, that borrowed the female form. That cello in the window of Walton's, the genitalia that had somehow melted into the bark of a tree in Stephen's Green. Such things he put behind him now, with marble swaps and Hotspur comics; these were mere extensions of boyhood. From then on his mind had houseroom for only one notion. The vision of his future self, strutting across the courtroom floor, bending the will of the jury in his hands. Ordering lunch in the Clarence Hotel the way Mr Caper had done, as if he was ordering for everyone in the room, or as if the waitress was deaf. And all the time with his voice still running, despite a mouth stuffed with roast beef or a glass that rattled with ice and shone with large measures of American whiskey. To be such a man . . . No sacrifice would be too great. He would even be willing to risk such a face. A man of position; a master of the chicane. A man with 'SC' after his name. A name not begrudged to him.

But all that was before.

Before that Monday four years ago when his mother had gone to see Aunt Maude. He hadn't wanted her to go at all in the end. He had begged her not to. 'Write,' he had said. 'Can't you write instead?'

But she wouldn't listen. She just wouldn't listen. Her mind

was on Charlie. Pulling him to her by the lapels of his outgrown coat, dragging at its hem, as if that would make it long enough. Now whipping his cap off and lightly slapping her fingers across his hair.

'Mother, please . . . ' he tried again.

'Don't be so silly, Herbert. I have to show her your exam results. If she doesn't know you've passed, how will she know she's supposed to pay for the university?'

'But are you sure that she said? She actually said?'

'It's always been understood.'

'But she mightn't.'

'Of course she will. She's paid for your schooling so far. She's hardly going to stop now. And I told her the last time I met her. I said it to her, Herbert is going to go for the bar. He has his heart set on it. I told her out straight, so you see she's no excuses now. None at all.'

Herbert watched his mother take Charlie's face in her hand and then he watched Charlie's face squirm under the point of her spit-damp hankie as she scoured it across dirt nobody else could see. Leaving red marks like swabs of warpaint.

'I've changed my mind,' he muttered. 'I don't want to be a barrister. I want to go to Belfast, like George.'

'Belfast? Don't make me laugh. If you were to heed everything that fella says . . . '

'I'm telling you, he's going.'

'And miss his racing? And his motor cars? That'll be the day.'

'There's racing in Belfast. And motor cars too. Ask Samuel, then, if you don't believe me. Samuel is going to get him a job as soon as things pick up in the dockyard. I could ask him to get one for me.'

That got her attention all right.

'Now listen here to me,' she began, and Charlie's face was suddenly dropped. 'George can go where he likes. But you're not going to any Belfast nor to any dockyard either. I'm not having you throwing your brains away.'

'George is brainier than me.'

'George is different.'

'You mean I am.'

She turned away and dragged Charlie with her to the door. Herbert stepped up behind her, softening his tone. 'Ah, what do I want with studying, mother? It'd be years before I'd make a bob. If I went up to Belfast, I could get a proper job, send money home every week. So there's no need to go near Aunt Maude, no need at all.'

But then she gave a little laugh and slapped him on the arm as if he had made a joke that was only slightly funny.

'Stop your nonsense, Herbert. Stop causing confusion. We're going to see her and that's that. You wait here – we won't be long.'

But she was long. She was never longer.

He could remember sitting on the floor beside the door for hours; he could remember the scullery sink. Pulling himself up, walking to it, taking a scoop of water into his hand and sucking it up. Going back to his place, getting up again, standing at the tap, turning it in his hand, playing with the water; now a little splash, now a bit more, now a full-throttled blast, now a splash again; watching the water twitch and fall. Watching the water twitch. Going back to the floor. One more time, then back to the sink and just looking down into the plughole. Doing nothing, just looking down through the iron web into the deep black hole beneath it. The walls of the room creaked up behind him. The clock on the mantle ticked into his face. The beetles in the wainscoting scratched another quarter of an hour away. And still no sign of them. Still not here.

Charlie's mouth was stained with jam. His cap was rolled into his pocket. He held a ten-shilling note out in front of him. He spoke to Herbert but his eye looked elsewhere, as though he was ashamed of something. 'Here,' he said, 'she gave you that. She gave you that for passing your exam.'

Herbert looked up and saw his mother cross over the yard. He didn't have to see the face bent under the brim of her Sunday hat to know that Aunt Maude's promise had been just another notion inside her hopelessly hopeful head. The ten-shilling note had already told him.

He glanced back down at Charlie.

'Let her stick it up her arse,' he said.

He walked past his mother out to the barn, raising his hand slightly, bringing it up like a drawbridge. Saying with the gesture: Not a word. Don't even begin to explain.

That was the first time he could remembering crying since he was about nine or ten. Crying made him angry. Anger dried the tears up. And that was a lesson well-learnt.

Aunt Maude must have felt guilt just the same, because there came a night, after weeks of many, when he didn't have to study the *Evening Mail* and write stiff letters proclaiming his suitability for jobs he felt were beneath him. While his mother went on and on giving out shite about her sister-in-law. Smearing it into his face.

'When I think of that one, the cheek of that one. Making a fool of you, that's what kills me. And her with money to burn. You should have seen the house; stuffed to the seams, it was. Two pianos. *Two*. What would anyone want with two pianos? She doesn't mind keeping strangers, of course. Doesn't mind how much she spends on that Lucia Carabini one – oh no – grinning in the corner like a black-eyed moon-calf. And well she might, living off others.'

'Maybe that's why she has two pianos,' Charlie suddenly put forward.

'What? What are you talking about?'

'So she can play one and Lucia can play the other one.'

'Who asked you? Who asked for your opinion? You eat your dinner and keep your mouth shut.'

'I was only saying.'

'Well *don't* only say. Leading you on like that. Raising your hopes. Making a fool of you. Making a fool . . . '

But as far as Herbert was concerned, they had all made a fool of him, one way or the other. His mother marrying a man who wasn't really his father, trying to pass him off, building a litter around him then, as if he wouldn't be noticed. His Aunt Maude sending him to a school that was way above his station. Where boys had fathers with motor cars who went to work in offices, and mothers who had maids, like his own mother had once been. And always having to fret about that. ('You're mother was a *what*? Did you hear that, chaps? Did you hear it? His mother was a skivvy.') And always having to avoid the crowd he would really have liked to have been part of, sticking instead to the likes of Wally Caper, who was too selfish to be interested in anyone's personal life and who nobody else could be bothered with anyway. Although the one advantage in having a mother who was once a skivvy was, at least you could manage a few bits of cutlery if you were ever asked to the likes of the Clarence. If you were ever more than once in your whole poxy life asked to the likes of the Clarence Hotel.

And mothers called 'mummy' instead of 'ma' and fathers who were often called 'sir'. And accents that didn't sound the same as the ones on the street where he lived. So he never knew for sure which way he should speak. And a brother he had thought would last forever, suddenly dying while he was still just a child. And now even George . . . George who he thought would always be here, and whose oil-smudged face he would always expect to see sliding out from under any stationary car that happened to be parked on New Street and whose broad back he would always expect to turn every time he looked and saw a broad back in the window of a bookie's shop. He was going to swan off to Belfast to live his own life. Leaving him behind with one small, silent brother, a silent oul'fella and a mother who never knew when to shut up. They had all made a fool of him all right. They had all had their turn.

His mother wasn't too long about changing her tune, all the same. The minute Aunt Maude's message arrived telling him to present himself in Findlater & Co on College Green. His mother read it out to him, breathless with joy; one hand holding the letter up, the other wagging away. 'Now listen to this, Herbert. Are you listening to this? She says:

> Of course, for the first year or so he'll be expected to act as a messenger boy in the mornings, but in the afternoon he'll be trained to be a clerk. Then after seven years he can apply to be a solicitor, and if he has been satisfactory, Mr Findlater tells me there's every chance they'll offer him an apprentice-ship, after serving which he'll be an assistant solicitor and eventually fully qualified . . .

'Oh isn't she very good to have gone to all that trouble? I knew she wouldn't let you down. Didn't I tell you she wouldn't let you down? Oh isn't that just marvellous news? Herbert? Herbert?'

'How much are they paying?'

'She doesn't say. What does that matter? Think of the prospects, son. A solicitor. Only seven years as a clerk and then . . . '

Herbert turned his face to the wall.

'You're talking about ten years in all,' he said. 'Ten years stuck in the same oul' office.'

'But ten years is nothing, Herbert. Ten years? Don't make me laugh. Here, read the letter. Read it for yourself.'

'Why should I? It isn't even addressed to me.'

Ten years to turn himself into a plucked chicken. This was his aunt's consolation prize.

It worked for his mother; her bursting with pride. Braggadocio. Off she went like a blue-arsed fly, through the house and over the neighbourhood. It kept her going for nearly four years.

'A solicitor. Imagine that now. A professional man.'

And every time he walked out on the street some other oul'one took over. 'Ah, there you are, Herbert, I believe you're goin' for the law. A sol-icitor. I know who to come to if I get into trouble. Ha ha ha.'

And every night when he came home from Findlater's, he had to listen to his mother's countdown again. 'Only another six years, Herb, before you can apply.' 'Only another five. Where does the time go? Oh, where does it fly?'

And he wanted to slap his hand over her mouth when she started; to make her shut up. Because when he looked out the window of Findlater & Co, down over College Green, he saw the railings point their iron fingers up at him and the brisk heads of students stoop away from him, in through the thick, iron gate of Trinity Entrance. And the building itself snigger behind its long smears of soot; and that voice always in his head that shouted: That should have been you. He didn't feel consoled, he felt passed over. He felt sickened inside.

To some small extent he had got what he wanted, but it was worse than not getting it at all. Because he was the skivvy now. The eavesdropper at the half-opened door; the man at the back wall with the tray in his hands. Herbert the schoolboy had grown up to be a clerk. And a barrister's coat was something other people wore.

He wore his disappointment like a smell around him. Keeping his distance from people he didn't want to offend. Sometimes ashamed, other times defiant, like any other tramp you'd see on the street. He could see it in his face when he looked in the mirror. He could see it in the faces of others. Clerks leaning on counters who suddenly straightened up and made a bit too much room whenever he came over. Charlie leaving the room whenever he came in. Even George, saying goodbye the night before he finally left for Belfast, could hardly look him in the eye. His mother too, laying his plate down in front of him in the evening, had recently taken to scarcely saying a word, keeping her mouth shut, the way people do when they come across an unbearable stink. Only the Dancer, sitting in his corner, seemed unaffected. Only he seemed unaware.

Sometimes the smell became too much for even him to bear. He tried to shrug it off, but with little success. It lifted once for a short time only, the day Samuel took him to the bespoke tailor to collect his new suit. It lifted then and Herbert was glad. The tailor pulled out a full-length mirror and invited him to step inside. 'Admire,' he said. 'Admire your fine self.'

He drew his eyes upwards along the lines of expensive cloth, from the upturned cuffs on the trouser legs to the sleeves of the jacket that tipped over his wrist. And then up to the sharp-nosed lapels and finally across to the very square shoulders. All the way up, the smell had lifted. He glanced through the mirror at Samuel clapping his wallet open. He glanced at the tailor playing with the ends of his measure tape. He heard him say, 'A fine suit; a perfect suit. A suit like this is well worth the money. A suit like this will last him ten years.'

Ten years. He looked up at his face and the smell had come back again. He tried to be rid of it. He wanted to be rid of it. But he couldn't think of anything to make it go away.

*

When he needed to see light, he looked out of windows; that way the backgrounds remained the same. Morning windows were grimy, masked yellow to the sash and, in a crescent over the top, the name of a firm, where glimpses of light rubbed around black-rimmed letters – or in shreds, where the chipped gilt had fallen away. Behind him, a wood-partitioned room; a brass bell on a long counter that he could vaguely recall having shoved a ding out of some moments before. The snap of a typewriter key against taut judicial paper; the scream of a startled telephone. The voice of a big shot behind the walls of an inner office, speaking down into a Dictaphone machine or across the desk at a mumbling client. From Chancery Place to Merrion Square, it made no diffence where he was; like traffic heard in the distance, it always sounded the same. Only the view from the window could hint at the location.

Afternoon windows were longer and gave a clearer view. The sounds behind him were softer too: a porter's grunt behind a stack

of books, the thud when they hit the counter. The mouse-scratch of a clerical pen or the scrape of a nib as it sniffed around the bottom of an inkwell. The coughs; the snuffles; the groans of old wood. The occasional childlike sigh.

In the Registry of Deeds, where he could never seem to settle, he would slide down from his high stool at intervals to go to the window. Abandoning another half-constructed sentence that, like all sentences before it, had shadowed his pen along double pages. Letter to letter; word after word; confined by his hand between narrow, endless lines. And as the afternoon progressed, the words had become, to his eyes, like small animals caged in the zoo.

From the side of the building the city stretched out its left arm: church dome and spire; cupola and campanile; diagonally arranged, patient as chess pieces on a board. From the front of the building, the bars of the railings protecting the lawn of Kings Inn from Constitution Hill. Where the light came through in vertical stripes, interrupted on occasion by the face of an urchin or a gleam of streamlined black dragged over by a hearse on the way to the cemetery.

And a tree he watched throughout the summer. Bald in springtime; bud-fluffed for a while; and as the weeks moved on, a fleeting blossom that turned to rust before its time. Turned to rust before July. When the rain came down, the leaves ran fluid, like the wattles of innumerable cockerels: soft, red and constantly wagging.

In the mornings, when he played runner-boy from office to office throughout the city, and in the afternoon, when he learnt his trade – in every room he happened on, he found himself by the window. Until eventually, he began to feel like the man he used to call father, who had always looked at the world through a frame. And then he knew he would have to stop. He would have to look elsewhere if he felt the need for light.

II

Dublin became a city of clocks. Tin clocks in the armpits of bus shelters; triangular clocks frowning on public-house brows; rendezvous clocks where anxious heads gathered below; Clery's or the Ballast Office, or in D'Olier Street – the darkest street – the *Irish Times* clock, stark on its wrought-iron spandrels. He measured his footsteps from one to the other: from the Four Courts to the King's Inn and all the little clocks in between. These were the only faces he wished to consider. The only voices were chimes, Westminster or Whittington, letting him know how many more minutes his journey would take. And all day long then, as he trudged to and from the repositories of his trade, he chased the fingers of time from dial to dial. Through Arabic numerals or Roman numerals, or sometimes just little dashes, that took longer to decide. Until the West Clock at Trinity College told him: Almost over now; almost done. You've broken the back of another useless day.

Sometimes a human face came unexpectedly through, but he usually managed to duck it. He saw Aunt Maude glide out of Thomas Cook's Travel one day, fiddling with a pair of gloves. Before she had settled her fingers down into the first one, he had slipped himself inside the doorway of Fox's Tobacconists, where he weighed the bowl of a pipe in his hand and told some yarn about his grandfather's birthday.

He spotted his old master in Grafton Street another day. His old master Mister McDaid, who that last day of school had invited him into his study to share a farewell cup of tea. He shook Herbert's hand when he was leaving; his eyes were damp; his voice was dry. 'I know you will do well,' he said. 'I know you have what it takes. And that someday I'll come across your name again and will turn proudly to whomsoever happens to be beside me and say, "I taught that boy. I always knew he'd make a name for himself." You are going out into the world today and in a sense I am too – as you know, I retire this year. I hope you'll keep in touch and let me know how you're getting along.'

Then he lifted his hand to stop Herbert from speaking. 'No,' he continued, 'please make no promises. I expect no more than an occasional card – at Christmas time or any time – I don't wish to interfere with your studies. It may be a long time ago now, but I still remember how demanding college life can be. Exciting days but busy days. And I do so want you to make the most of it. The very, very most of it.'

He ducked into Lipton's when he saw his old master and, over a stack of cheddar-cheese wheels and a pyramid of Chinese tea caddies, he watched the top of McDaid's black hat pull his kind old head slowly by.

Walter Caper wasn't so easily dodged, nabbing him one day on Dame Street. Wally had nearly three Trinity years behind him and was well settled into the role. His accent swerved at the bend; his voice skimmed over the crowd. 'I thought you were supposed to be . . . ' he began, nodding back towards the college.

'Changed me mind.'

'You changed your mind?' (Herbert recognised the incredulous little chuckle.) 'And why, may I ask, would you want to do *that?*'

Herbert looked down at fat little Walt, studying for a moment his childish face and the small, white hands that held the lapels of his jacket while he rocked himself on the heels of his size-six shiny shoes. Herbert looked at the Trinity colours scarved around his neck and remembered the long conversations they had had about what it would be like to be a student and what it would be like to be called to the bar. And that day in Trinity College, when they had ventured into its cloisters just to see what it was like inside. Through the dark entrance, they had avoided the porter's eye by engaging each other in deep conversation that probably hadn't made much sense. Out into the light then, they took a shy stroll and tried to look as if they knew where they were going. He could remember feeling ashamed of Walter, and how, as they made their way around the quadrangle, he had been slightly ashamed of himself too. At the sudden resolution that had slithered into his head: that he would drop his friend like a hot potato as soon as he had his foot in the door. Or as soon as he met anyone better.

He thought of all those wasted winter mornings when he had left the house, sometimes without any breakfast, so he could meet Walter at the bandstand in Stephen's Green to check his homework for him. Or those last days of term and the walks they had taken together up and down Harcourt Street during the weeks of their final exams. While step by step Herbert had coached him through the relevant points, over and over and over again, nailing it into his thick, fat head.

And look at them now. Look how it had all turned out. Walter's face smug with his own future, while Herbert could see no further than the stack of envelopes under his arm. Envelopes that could be delivered by any penny-boy in town.

'Look, Walt, the way I see it, it's no life for a man. I had enough of schooling and being talked down to. Just decided it wasn't my bag, that's all. I'm thinking of going to Belfast, as a matter of fact. I've a brother up there, he's cleaning up.'

'*Belfast?* With a war around the corner? Are you mad?'

'Of course I'm also considering America.'

'*America?* First Belfast, now *America?* it seems to me you don't know what you're at, if you don't mind my saying so. Besides, there's no money in America, not any more. America is gone to the dogs. No, I'd rather give that idea a knock on the head, if I were you.'

'I've a cousin in New York; he's doing all right for himself. He'll set me up till I get on my feet.'

'But you can't stand him.'

'I never said . . . '

'Yes, yes. Correct me if I'm wrong – Bennie, isn't that what he's called?'

'That's right.'

'Now you always led me to believe you couldn't stand the fellow. You said he was an absolute . . . '

Herbert brought his face down to Walter's.

'Well, I'll learn to fuckin' well stand him,' he snarled.

When Walter heard Herbert curse, a jittery laugh popped out of his mouth. He looked down for a moment from left to right and then brought himself back up with a frown.

'Well now, I heard you were working for Findlater, as a clerk, but aiming to become a solicitor in time.'

'Come on, Caper, who the fuck wants to be a solicitor?' This time he didn't laugh.

'Yes. Yes, I see your point, of course I do. But there's nothing to be ashamed of, you know, if family circumstances . . . I mean, you can always apply for the bar later on, you know.'

'What do you mean, "family circumstances"?'

'Oh come on, Herbert, I know. I've always known. Everybody at school . . . Well, we all always knew. It's not your fault. You can still be a barrister. There's more than one way to skin a cat, don't forget.'

'Barrister, solicitor, what difference does it make? I've had plenty of time to study their carry-on and, let me tell you something, they're no better than a pack of old women, cutting the back of each other and counting their pennies. I wouldn't be part of that set-up, not if you paid me.'

'A pack of old women? Oh now, come on, really . . . ' Walter snorted. 'Look, I'll speak to my father, if you like. He was very much taken by you, you know.'

'You'll speak to your father?'

'Yes. I would be quite willing to do so. Now he may not be able to help you, of course, but if you want some sound advice, there's no better man to give it.'

'Listen, Wally, if I wanted advice, the last person I would go to would be that fat little puce-faced toad. No, thanks all the same. I'd rather make me own way, if you don't mind.'

That shut him up all right.

He took one last look at Walter's face, pink to the gills with wounded pride. He looked like a boy dressed up for the school play. A boy that had lost his lines.

Herbert walked away and felt suddenly better. Now he had found a reason to be consoled.

Who the fuck *did* want to be a barrister? Or a solicitor, for that matter? A life amongst men with old faces; and even the younger ones, with their girl-soft hands – who would want to be like them? He wanted to lead a real life. A life like his brother's. Not this . . . this life among clerks: cheap-suited clerks gathered together every Friday evening in the Land Registry jacks. Hands slicking hair back with Brylcreem; thumbs looping ties forward from under the knot. Going off then together to huddle in the corner of a pub or in the back booth of an ice cream parlour. To spend their few shillings and go over the week: what they should have said; what they could have said. Who the fuck wanted to be like that?

Gammy-armed Gibson was a solicitor. Although they kept him out of court. Kept him away from clients too. As soon as there was the sniff of one, Findlater's head came around the door and gave him the nod. Then Gammy would slink off to the filing room to shove his one arm down into dusty boxes until the coast was clear again. Herbert was his charge. The sleeve of his jacket pinned into his pocket, he took Herbert under his wing, literally. Teaching him things he didn't want to know, showing him ropes he never wanted to pull. Making up a stupid little sample book for him to take home: Notices of Appearance; Notices of Motion; Common Process; sworn affidavits and folio file plans. Every law clerk's desire.

And every afternoon before he was sent off to the Registry of Deeds he got the same oul' guff from Gammy: 'Now . . . a memorial of a document is a synopsis of the important and relevant details of a property transaction. Which is why we must abstract with the utmost caution; the utmost care. Are you with me now?'

'Oh, I am all right.'

Gibson wore a Homburg hat with a stiff-lipped brim and a black town coat that ran bald around the edges. His one hand did the work of twenty, poking and prodding his points into the air; flying blind all around him, like a bird let out of a cage. He was there when you arrived in the morning, and there when you left at night. Except for the times when he wasn't there at all; then his desk would lie empty for weeks at a time. For reasons Herbert couldn't quite work out, he was tolerated by all and even seemed to be respected by some. Although Herbert had no doubt in his own mind that Gibson kept a few rats in his upper storey.

Fell at Ypres, he said, that's why he sometimes had to go down to the country for a little rest.

'Fell off a bar stool, more like,' the chief clerk mumbled, when Herbert happened to mention it.

Whatever he fell off, he landed on his head. The way he stared at you with his green eyes glowing. The speeches that he gave, through a constant mouthful of Cough-No-Mores: 'The Great Jewish Plot to overtake the world', 'The Great Catholic Plot to brainwash the people', 'The Great Homosexual Plot to build air-raid shelters so they would all have somewhere to bugger each other to death.' The Corporation workers pissing in the reservoirs; the waiters in Jammets spitting in the soup. There was a plot around every street corner, and in every situation another one in the making. And the way he took your arm when you met him in the street, walking beside you, talking all the way. Raising his voice whenever a Jewish establishment was passed.

'Bloody Jews. Don't talk to me about the Jews, smirking up to your face and doing you behind your back. I could tell you a thing or two about the chosen people. Chosen to do what? Well might you ask. Chosen to wipe the rest of us off the face of the earth, that's what. If you ask me, that Hitler fella should be canonised. Canonised, that's what Herr Hitler should be.'

The day after he met Walter Caper, Gibson asked him to stay after work. Herbert asked him why.

'"Why?" he says. Why do I ever ask you to stay late? Because I can't teach you with all the distractions going on in this place, and if I can't teach you, you can't learn. And if you can't learn, you'll never be articled. And if you aren't articled, you'll never be a solicitor. Does that answer your question in a full and satisfactory manner?'

'Well, I can only stay a while.'

'A while is all it'll take.'

Gibson crossed over the empty office with a roll of paper under his arm and then went back to a press in the corner to fill his pocket with bits of stationery. He cleared a space on his own desk then, chopping his hand gently along the paper roll until it was flat, and when he had found a marble weight to keep it that way, he began to empty his jacket pocket. A pencil-rubber, a bottle of ink and a small silver box all came out and were laid side by side in a row. Finally, he reached down into his trouser pocket and edged an oblong box upwards into his hand. Herbert thought there was something religious about the way he had laid the table – but that he was less like a priest than a magician about to astound.

'Now,' he said at last, 'this here is . . . parchment paper.'

'I know.'

'I know you know. But do you know how to handle it?'

'What do you mean?'

'"What do you mean?" he says. This isn't any old paper, I'll have you know. This paper is like a woman: you have to treat it in a certain manner before it'll take the pen. Are you with me now?'

Herbert nodded.

Gibson lifted the pencil-rubber and held it up for Herbert to view. When he was satisfied that its importance had registered, he took it down onto the paper.

'First you rub her over like this. You must take great care – you don't want to rent a hole in her. Now we're ready to move on to the next step.'

He lifted the silver box in his hand, holding it out for Herbert to open. Then he started again.

'You give her a good sprinkle for herself. Oh, she loves this stuff, she loves it – this is powdered French chalk, by the way. This stops the pen from slipping. Now, she should be gameball. I want you to take the pen. There in that box there, show it here. Careful now . . . careful. It's a special pen; only to be used on the parchment. It doesn't care for clumsy handling. Now sit yourself down here and see if you can copy out this memorial for me.'

Herbert sat down and tried to ignore Gibson's breath coming in over his shoulder: a three-tiered gust of menthol and sour cheese and the sly, gingery whiff of a recent whiskey mac.

'Good,' Gibson whispered into his ear. 'Oh, very good indeed. That's a fine hand you have there. A fine, delicate hand. How old are you, Herbert?'

'Nearly twenty-one.'

'"Nearly twenty-one," he says. When I was twenty-one I had a fine hand too. Yes I did, I certainly did. But by the time I was thirty-one, I didn't.'

He turned away and walked over to the door. 'Keep at it now. Keep at it. Be firm but be careful. I'll be back to you in a couple of shakes.'

He came back just as Herbert was thinking about leaving. The door opened with a snap and there he was with a face like thunder. 'Come up here a minute, would you? Come up here and have a look at what I've just found.'

Herbert followed him up the stairs and into the gents' lavatory, where Gibson lifted his foot and kicked the door of the cubicle open.

'Have a look at that, what? Did you ever see the like of that?'

'Of what?'

'There. Look, in the toilet. Isn't that a disgrace? Now doesn't that just take the biscuit? Go on, take a look.'

Herbert stepped in and looked down at a very large turd, like a big brown trout peering up at him from the throat of the bowl.

'What do you make of that, now? Will you kindly tell me?'

'The chain must be broken.'

'"The chain must be broken," he says. Don't be daft. I'll tell you what the story is there. That's the work of a homosexual. Oh yes. Only a homosexual could pass the like of that.'

Herbert stepped out again and edged himself back to the sink.

'A homosexual?' he asked.

'Oh yes. I'm telling you there's a homosexual in this office. And I have a fair idea just who it is.'

'So have I, as a matter of fact. Flush the chain.'

'What?'

'Flush the fuckin' chain, would you?'

'Now hold on a minute. I know you're upset, naturally you're upset – we're both upset. Naturally we are. Of course. Of course. But there's no need for foul language, just the same.'

'I'm going home,' Herbert said.

'I'm not finished with you yet.'

Herbert took a step towards the door. 'Look, I don't know and I don't care how you get your thrills . . . '

'My what? My what? I hope you're not suggesting . . . Come back here, I said.'

'Look, I just want to *go.*'

Gibson's voice howling down the staircase; the crashing flush of the toilet. The snap of the pen in his hand, the crackle of parchment paper. These were the sounds he took home with him. These were the sounds that would stay in his head.

'I'll be making a new start,' he explained to the chief clerk a couple of days later.

The chief clerk folded a will in four and patted it into a drawer. 'You don't say? Your aunt . . . ? Does she know?'

'Why should she?'

'And Mr Gibson? Have you told him?'

'He's away on one of his little holidays.'

'He'll have to be told, just the same.'

'Why don't you tell him then?'

'I see . . . You've been getting along all right with Mr Gibson, have you? No problems or anything?'

'No. Why do you ask?'

'No reason. And might I venture to ask to whom you are giving the honour.'

'To the Misses Rooney, the law searchers.'

'The law searchers?'

'That's right.'

The chief clerk picked up a bone-folder and rubbed the snout of it against his knuckles. 'How long are you with us now?'

'Two and a half years.'

'Almost three years? In another four you'll be eligible to sit the solicitor's entrance exam. Think how quickly the last three years have gone.'

'Not for me, they haven't.'

The chief clerk lifted the bone-folder higher, this time to tap on his chin. 'Well, there's nothing more to be said then. Except . . . '

'Yes?'

'Well, if you had told me you had decided to take another direction in your career . . . If you had told me that you wanted to go into the bank, or the insurance – a trade, even – I would have understood. But to leave a position as a law clerk to become a law *searcher;* a mere scrivener. Well, frankly I don't see the sense in it. You do know it's a step down?'

'The money's a hell of a lot better and I feel I'm a bit long in the tooth to be delivering messages – which, by the way, was only supposed to be for the first year.'

'A step down is a step down, my boy.'

'Do I look as if I give a shite?'

*

The Misses Rooney twitched and twittered at him. The Misses Rooney made him tea. A chocolate Mary from Bewley's on Friday; an extra quid in his pocket at the end of the week. On the rare occasion that he had to visit a solicitor's office, it was to collect money due on the Rooneys' behalf. He got attention then all right; sometimes he even got a chair.

The crowds came against him in the morning. The crowds came against him in the evening. Pushing to or from the factory horns; select little bunches of women or men. Men with lunch packs under their arms or bicycles between their legs. Women with scarves knotted on top of their heads or flat white bonnets that made them look bald; Jacobs' mice going off to cut biscuits; Dennys' dames to cut rashers. New buses nuzzled like hogs into street channels, snortling out fag-ends with their new-bus breath. 'Stop Press' boys called out as he passed. The war was on. The war was off again. And the city filled up with knapsacked foreigners who seemed to stop him in every street to ask for directions. Otherwise, little had changed.

The Registry of Deeds was his permanent pitch now. The streets around it his beaten track: a narrowing circle of poverty and destitution from the stinking debris of the fish and fruit markets, to the cow-shite islands with their bluebottle clouds stretching across the cobbles of Smithfield Square. There were no crowds on this far side of the river and so he no longer worried about bumping into a familiar face. He stopped looking for clocks on the street too, because clocks weren't a feature of Arran Quay Ward. But he began to notice other things instead.

Through the doors of the tenement buildings in King Street, cow-hair struck out from the walls. Pink, distempered walls, where little brown bugs came out to play and take a sniff of the air: damp and piss and paraffin oil or the permanent hum of yesterday's cabbage. In the mornings the drunken farmers fell in and out of the market bars; in the afternoons the old people dragged kitchen chairs out to their doors. On sunny days khaki-eyed kids pushed each other on kitty carts made from crates they had nicked from the markets. On stormy days blobs of fish-and-chip paper skipped on the wind up the street.

And a prostitute he saw in Yarnhill Street one day, a German sailor poking her up against the door of a shed. The sailor wore a red bobbin on top of his hat. The bobbin wagged when he did. The door rattled in time. The prostitute's eyes were closed; her lips made coaxing noises. He was about to walk away again when her eyes suddenly opened. And then, looking over the sailor's shoulder, she winked and held his eye until the little red bobbin had fallen down on her arm and the shed door had fallen silent. Held his eye with a brazen gleam. As if she expected that to turn him away.

III

The prostitute's wink brought him back to himself, and at night thoughts of women started again to slip into his head. He thought of the sailor too, on occasion; the muscles of his tightened arse like a cannon ball in his trousers and the hem of her skirt balled up in his paw. And how tidy his dark figure had looked – almost formal, in fact (considering what he'd been up to) – how alone he had looked too, as if the girl wasn't there at all. Like one of those crack-shot sailors you'd see at the shooting gallery, who always appeared to be on their own.

But it was the prostitute in particular that loitered in his mind: not her face, though – he couldn't remember her face – only her knee. And the thigh sloping up from it and the calf sloping down from it, and the ruffle of a dropped stocking at the ankle. The way they all curled together around the sailor's low-slung hip. And the wink, of course – the wink meant everything – even though he could scarcely recall what class of an eye it had flipped out of.

He might have had a go at himself only for Charlie asleep at the end of the bed and the memory of a promise he'd made after Danny's death. It was a childish promise he had made to God, to give up pulling his plum. Why he had made it he wasn't quite sure. Maybe as a kind of a deal that Danny would be looked after – maybe as a kind of deal he'd be looked after himself. Whatever the reason, he had felt at the time that a sacrifice would be appropriate. As this was the only pleasure he had that didn't cost any money and didn't rely on anyone else, this was what he had offered. And even though it had been a long time since he'd had any truck with the idea of God, he didn't want to go back to that rampant phase he had wanked himself through in his earlier years. He didn't want to go back under its power. And the fear that went with it; fear that any moment someone might burst in the door and catch him at it; fear of how he might end up too. Maybe like one of those manky oul'fellas you sometimes saw cycling along the banks of the canal: flies undone, baggy tackle flopped out on the saddle. They had all started somewhere before they had come to that. They had all once had their dark corner.

For a while he believed his father must have known what he was up to, which would explain why he didn't seem to like him that much. He also believed he was the only one to have this secret little world. There was no one to confirm or deny this suspicion. It wasn't a subject discussed in his school, although in Catholic schools, he gathered, it may very well have been. In any case, his cousin Bennie used to try the odd joke on him before he went back to America, but he wouldn't give him the satisfaction of pretending to know what he was on about, and anyhow he didn't think it was a subject that was particularly funny. There had been no point talking to George either. George had his own way of dealing with things. He had his own dark corner: his gambling. Although at least when he won he felt better. But Herbert never felt better after the event.

What would start as a tingle would end up in the jacks bowl: a few seconds of joy that couldn't wait to get away from you. Then a short-lived ticker-tape reception lashing out in all directions as the ship pulled away. Another few seconds of relief. And what would be left at the end of it all? What did you feel as you got down on your knees to blot up the squirts of phlegm? Or as you scanned the walls and the rim of the jacks to see where else it had landed? What did you feel as you washed the slime of yourself from your hands? Shame. Only shame. Because only the shame ever lasted. And a vow that that would be the last time, the very last time. Until the tingle started again.

Like that day in Heather's shoe shop when he was fourteen years of age and his mother had taken him to buy his school shoes. A plump assistant had stooped down beside him, lifting his foot up onto her lap. The sole of his foot melted into her thigh. His toe pointed due north. His mouth refused to speak. Couldn't get it to utter a word; not even if he had wanted it to.

She spoke to him and she spoke to his mother all in one go. But when she addressed him, her voice slowed down and pitched itself higher, in a way that made it obvious she thought him a bit simple.

'Does it feel comfortable, love?' she asked him. 'No? Too tight, is it? I think it's too tight, madam,' she said then, turning to his mother.

'Will we get you a bigger size, pet – something with a bit more width?' Then, to his mother, 'I think he might take a bigger size, madam.'

And she climbed up the stepladder one more time for him and stretched her arm to pull another box from the wall. Her arm was dark in the pit, but not with the expected sprigs. It was more like a lining of black suede; a sort of five o'clock shadow. She must have shaved it. How did she shave it? Naked from the waist up?

Naked all the way? And what did her diddies do when she stretched her arm up and took the razor to the hollow? Did they go their separate ways? Or did they cower down together like frightened rabbits in one corner? And what sort of diddies did she have in there anyway: ones with pink buttons, or brown? Billy Cartwright said some women had no buttons at all and some others had two on each knocker. Was she one of them? These were the thoughts that made his head light. But the sight of her arse made it weightless. Arse on the descent; full arse on the descent, step after step, with a nice hefty sway as it moved.

His mother gave him a knuckle in the back. 'Will you ever pay attention and stop your daydreaming. He's always dreaming, this fella; lives in his own little world.'

The assistant's mouth smiled, understanding. And then she was back down on the floor again. Back down beside him.

'Now,' her mouth said, with her fingers tipping the tissue paper away from the fifth pair of shoes. 'Now,' it said again, with her voice growing distant, so he could hardly hear her at all. 'I'll just get you to slip into this.'

Then he fainted. The pleasure had became too much to bear and he had simply fainted with desire. All that plum-pulling must have made him sloppy. But he got some mileage out of the shoe-shop woman just the same. For weeks to come he conjured her up in the outside jacks that he had converted into his own private barber's shop specialising in women's hairy armpits. Naked women's armpits. Dent after dent, all waiting for the swipe of his razor.

The shoe-shop woman was definitely his best customer (which was only fair, seeing as how she had put the idea in his head in the first place), and by the time he had tired of her, she had as many diddies as a farrow sow. Other customers dropped in from time to time, smiling out between upstretched arms: Myrna Loy; Maureen O'Sullivan; the woman in the Pond's powder advertisement; the woman with the Sunbeam stocking leg. Between the lot of them, he was run off his feet.

Beatty Bumbury made the odd appearance too, but he always made sure to give her rough handling. And once he drove the razor down so hard on her that he made her cry. Which served her right for being so full of herself. And went some way towards making up for the raw egg yolks his mother had made him gulp down every day since his fainting fit had had her convinced that he was anaemic. But he was a kid then. A kid with no control. Someone who had always believed you had to be married to go the whole way. Now he was a man and could act with a man's composure. Now he was ready for the real thing.

Once the prostitute's wink had brought him back to himself, he started to look at girls again and found after a time they were looking back; sometimes even getting there before him.

Up to now he'd had his few moments, starting off early with Billy Cartwright's sister in a back lane off Brabazon Square. Where he had pressed his lips onto her tight little pucker, gnawing on it round and around – because that's the way they did it in the pictures – until he thought it would fall like a snail off her face.

Her voice buttered into his ear, 'You can have a feel if you like . . . Go on, you can. I don't mind . . . '

And his heart nearly burst for those few seconds it took to get his hand into position. Relying on instinct this time – because the feel was something they didn't do in the pictures – he slowly edged it up and over, inch by inch, and tried not to appear too keen. But when he got there, the cupboard was bare.

Billy Cartwright's sister might have been a bit more willing than most, but Billy Cartwright's sister was as flat as the wall. He didn't want to hurt her feelings, so he left his hand there for a minute. And he didn't know what to do then, so he edged it away again.

As he got older there were other occasions: clammy hands in the back of picture houses; bony knees under the table of Cafolla's café. There had been a series of walks with a girl from the Iveagh Buildings, when they had dragged the conversation like a dead dog between them until it was time for the goodnight fumble in Hanover Lane.

There was a tall girl he thought he might love, who made him feel nervous because she seemed so refined. He waited at the corner of Clanbrassil Street for nearly an hour, but she didn't show up.

Her bunty sister came instead, barrelling up the road. She said, 'She's not coming.'

'Why?'

'She's not coming because you're a president.'

He pretended not to know what she meant. 'A president? What are you on about?'

'No. A prosident. You know – a prod.'

'Oh, you mean a *Protestant.*'

'That's right. She says she hopes you don't mind and that will you please excuse her. And if you ever look at her again, me big brother, who's in the animal gang, says he'll knock the fuckin' shite out of you.'

These were the years for local girls.

When he started working in Findlater's, office girls stepped into the picture and local girls stepped out. But office girls were a trickier proposition: office girls had their notions. He asked one

113

of them out one time – a clerical typist named Ivy. He asked her out because she reminded him, in a very slight way, of Beatty Bumbury. At least she had the same sort of figure and the same sort of pout to her gob. She didn't even bother to pretend to be flattered. 'My mammy doesn't allow me go out on dates with strangers,' she said.

But then he saw her playing up to an apprentice solicitor – an ugly-looking bastard at that – and knew then what she really meant to say was, 'My mammy doesn't allow me go out with strangers unless they have their pockets stuffed with prospects.'

'Fuck you and your mammy,' he said to himself, and never spoke to her again. She had made him feel stupid. But worse, she had made him feel unworthy. And then she had *really* reminded him of Beatty.

After that he mostly forgot about office girls and, if the exceptional one should start him tingling, he made himself forget about her as well.

Now that he was back on form, he no longer cared if he was worthy or not, nor did he mind the risk of rejection. It began to occur to him then that the one drawback in leaving Findlater's was that you didn't get to see many girls. At least when you delivered envelopes you occasionally got to visit insurance offices that had girls running around instead of a couple of old bags peering down their specs at you. And although he hadn't allowed himself to think too much about them at the time, he thought of them now all right; he thought of them often. Girls in navy office coats, bottom button gaping when they stretched one leg over the corner of the desk. Girls gossiping together, pressed against bookcases. Or walking to Dictaphone machines, wax cylinders held tenderly between two fingers of each hand. Elasticated hands working on switchboards. Affectionate hand stroking the slated belly of a roll-top desk. Girls eating almond buns, licking their lips.

In hindsight now, he missed such treats and cursed such lost opportunities.

Working for the Misses Rooney, the opportunities would hardly trip you up. Except for the woman in the Credit & Loan company downstairs; the woman with the bun in her hair. She kept the door of her office open, so he saw her every time he passed by. Looking up at him from a gale-day book; looking down at him from an upper shelf. Or backways from a pigeon-hole, looking at him.

Her 'good day' was always a prissy affair, but her head, he noticed, was always cocked in a 'chase-me-Charlie' kind of a way. But she was a bit on the old side, anyway. She must have been tipping thirty.

Apart from her, there were only the girls on the street. Sitting up on bicycles, the saddle holding them firmly in place and the hems of their skirts bubbling up when they came flying around the corner. Standing beside him at bus stops or curling before him up the stairs of the tram. An eye caught in a compact mirror, or in passing through the window of a shop. A step that stayed with his until a busy street was crossed. Pleasures that passed on too swiftly for any move to be considered, let alone made.

The only one he really came into contact with was the only one he didn't want. The girl in McKinney's shop on the corner beside his house. The one his mother had been promoting since she had got it into her head that he would love his job if only he found himself a nice girl to go out with. A girl to 'make him take an interest in himself'; 'a girl to give him ambition.' Every other day sending him into the shop on whatever pretext she could manage to come up with: 'Oh, I forgot to get your father's buttermilk. You know what he's like if he hasn't got his buttermilk' or 'Would you ever pay a few bob off my account when you're passing?'

And afterwards then sniffing around for his reaction. 'Wouldn't you feel sorry for her all the same stuck in that poky hole all day, with that pair?'

'What pair?'

'That pair that own it, the McKinneys.'

'I never see them.'

'No, nor you won't. Planked on their backsides in that kitchen all day, drinking tea and poking around at jigsaw puzzles. And if they hear her get into any sort of conversation, the watery eyes on them peering out behind the lace curtain to make sure she's not wasting her time. Lovely girl like her. Do you not think she's a lovely girl?'

'She's all right.'

'Do you know her, Mo?' she asked his cousin one day, dropped in for one of her visits. 'Do you know her at all? The girl who works in McKinney's?'

'I've seen her, yes.'

'What do you think of her? Now is she or is she not a lovely girl?'

'Oh now, I'm sure, Aunt Greta, Herbert would prefer to pick his own friends.'

And Herbert had to laugh to himself because you could nearly read what his mother was thinking about cousin Mo, who was supposed to have a crush on him since she was a child – 'Well, you would say that, wouldn't you?' – although she managed to confine herself to, 'Oh of course, I know that. I was only saying she's a lovely girl. Lovely brown eyes. Do you know what her name is, Herbert? Her name is Amy.'

'Oh is it really?'

And doe-eyed Amy would go scarlet in the face whenever he stooped in through the door. Her little hand would shake when she turned the pages of the accounts book looking for his mother's name. He looked around the shop at the touches she had set to it – pyramids of withered turnips and doily-wrapped potatoes. A bucket hand-painted with a smile: 'Lucky bags, 1d a dip.'

And sometimes he did feel sorry for her, surrounded by dreariness and Mrs McKinney's well-mauled home-made apple tarts that only the flies seemed to appreciate. But she was one of those girls who was looking for love. And that wasn't what he was after.

He had an idea of what she should be like. Nobody real, just a vague representation; someone to get him on his way, that's all that concerned him for now. She'd have to be givish, even if she started off coy. He'd have to know she'd come across in the end. Somebody young, but not too young – maybe with a face like Deanna Durban. Or she could look like Movita too, if she liked. A sweet-smelling thing, whatever her age, whoever she was – with layers of underwear he would have to rummage through. And a dress he could hold in the paw of his hand.

Yet he was willing to consider almost any girl at all. Even the fat one in the butcher's shop in Queen Street. He'd always preferred girls that were a bit on the roundy side, but this one exceeded all specifications. Cramming the window, first with herself and then with hunks of raw meat, her large hands seemed almost to bring to life rings of pudding bursting out of their skins, slabs of curly-faced tripe, bunches of plump grey sausages and big-arsed sides of home-cured ham. She made him look at the meat like he'd never looked at it before. And besides all that, he felt sure she would be game.

He stopped to watch her one day through the window, just to follow the loose way she handled her wares. First placing a ball of mince on a cut of damp paper, then lifting it gently on the palm of her hand. Now letting it slide off onto the scales. He thought about going in and standing at the counter and what he should say if he did.

But then he noticed the doorway was active with the movement of women. Women going in and then coming out with newspaper cones of meat parings under their arms and the glint of experience in their eyes. All looking at him, all knowing. Nudging each other with those experienced eyes. They knew what he was at; what he was after. They knew every move of the game. And that was the difference between women and girls.

Which took him back to the woman with the bun.

Dropping in one day on his way up the stairs, he stood in the doorway, watching her pretend not to know he was there, while she clawed through files in the cabinet drawers.

'I brought you the afternoon post,' he said at last, taking a step inside.

'Why did you do that?'

'Thought I'd save your legs.'

'Do they look as if they need saving?'

'No, they look fine to me, miss . . . '

She whacked the middle drawer shut with a twist of her hip.

'Call me Daphne,' she cooed. 'But don't call me daft.'

He took her to the Capitol restaurant and bought her creamed mushrooms on toast. She took him back to her flat for a drink and apologised for her old-fashioned gramophone player. She said she was getting a black box player next month and Herbert nodded and said, 'Oh, right', as if that was a point that needed clearing up before they could move on to anything else.

She cleared up a few more points while she was at: she had a new settee on order, the one in the window of Pimm's – had he noticed it? – and that tallboy in the corner, she'd been meaning to get rid of that old thing too. And as for her coffee-percolating machine, she'd lent it to a friend and, wouldn't you know, she hadn't even bothered to return it. By the time she was finished apologising and explaining, he was beginning to think he'd lived his whole life in this room – or that he might be expected to in future. Then she left him for a few minutes.

When she came back, her feet were bare and her bun had exploded down onto her shoulders.

She held a record up between the sides of her hands and blew her breath in a circle around it. 'Do you like Chopang?' she asked him.

'Sorry?'

'Chopang? Do you like him?'

'Well enough.'

She closed her eyes when the first notes slipped out. 'Oh God,' she sighed, 'I just love him.'

She thought he was a solicitor and nearly died when he put her right. He almost felt sorry for her as she tried discreetly to remove his hand from her leg.

'But don't they have solicitors working up there?'

'No, we're law searchers. I told you, we work for solicitors.

'Oh, but you're so well spoken,' she said, 'I just assumed. And with your suit and your attaché case and everything . . . I mean, I can't be blamed for assuming.'

'Nobody's blaming you, love,' he said. 'No need to feel bad. You're a bit too old for me anyway, and to be honest I only really came up because I thought you'd be on for it.'

After that remark she had no trouble removing his hand.

He made as much noise as he could as he came back down her stairway because she had told him to 'shh' on the way up. He left the front door open too, because a sign on the wall told him not to. He walked all the way home because the creamed mushrooms and the taxicab had left him skint. Office girls – he should have known better. It was time to go back to the drawing board.

Now he was getting desperate. He even considered one of those shady establishments in the basement of a house in Bolton Street just to get the first time over.

It was said that the girls there were fairly clean and you'd be less likely to end up like one of the Great War pox-veterans that went about with their tongues hanging out. He knew he'd never have the nerve to knock on the door and make his intentions known, but if what he had heard was true, he mightn't have to go as far as that. The Bolton Street girls were supposed to be recognisable by their smart sense of style: two-piece costumes with spots all over them. One colour for Sunday, the other for the workaday week. And every time he saw a spotty two-piece, he thought about running after the girl and asking, 'How much?' But once he started looking, it seemed that every second woman in Dublin seemed to have a spotty number on her back. So the two-piece theory was gradually dropped, and so was the search for the shady lady. Because if he was to be honest with himself, he had to admit that he couldn't recognise with any certainty a prostitute in the street. Unless of course she happened to have a German sailor pinned to her front.

Now the summer was nearly over and he was almost ready to throw in the towel. Then Martha Enright came into the barn.

He was writing a letter to George.

'What are you doing, Herbie?' she asked.

'Don't call me Herbie.'

'Why not?'

'Because I said so. I'm writing to George, now scram.'

'Will you tell him a message for me?'

'Scram, I said.'

'All right, I'm going. I can take a hint.'

She stopped at the barn door and started again. 'Your brother George . . . '

'What about him?'

'He left a hole in me leg.'

'Did he now?'

'Yes, that time when he shot me.'

'He didn't shoot you.'

'He might as well have. Me ma says he could have kilt me.'

'Pity he didn't.'

Herbert returned to his letter.

'Do you want to see it?'

'What?

'The hole in me leg.'

'Go away.'

But Martha was beside him now, raising her skirt to show.

'There,' she said. 'There, see?'

Herbert looked up. At a stick-white leg speckled pale brown and a dent on the calf looking out like an eye from a circle of little gold lashes. And up-country then, everything bare and unsheltered. Everything there.

'See?'

'I see.'

'It *is* a hole. You can put your finger in it, see?'

Herbert put down the letter.

Martha Enright was hardly a sweet-smelling thing; she didn't look anything like Deanne Durbin. Nor had she any layers to negotiate. And if the fat girl in the butcher's shop exceeded his specifications, skimpy Martha was way below the mark. But Martha Enright was there in the barn. And that was good enough for him.

'PS,' he wrote at the end of the letter to George, 'Martha Enright says hello.'

CHARLIE

The albino horse was half-in, half-out of the water. His front legs, scooped to the air, were ready to pounce on the river bank that wedged unevenly out of the water and then ran in a smoother line into a hill. On the top of the hill were other horses mounted by a row of cowboys. You couldn't see the cowboys' faces because their hats had shelved them over, but you could tell by the lazy way they were leaning their forearms down on the horses' withers that they believed themselves to be safe. The hilltop horses weren't a patch on the albino – a couple of mustangs, a nice fat pinto, a sorrel mare and a pair of Morgan cattle-cutters. Each one could have been a beauty in its own way, but the albino had made them seem like nothing special. They stood side by side like a row of back-lane shops, bits of things hanging off them: tin pots and leather bags, hairy-skinned water bottles and other cowboy bric-a-brac.

Back down on the river bank a man was watching the albino, a coil of rope in one hand, the tail of the rope in the other. You could see this man's face because his hat had fallen onto the ground. It was an alert face; a face at the start of a boxing match, ready to dodge but more likely to throw a punch. It was a face that was expecting to win.

Everything framed the albino; he was the only one who had made things happen. He had battered the water, slicing it up into smithereens, some of them still dangling from his front hooves, or bouncing off the barrel of his thick white chest. He had mastered the river, forcing it to veer around him as if he was an island. He had made the other steady-legged horses seem weak and stupid, and the men harmless and without judgement. Charlie had no worries about the albino horse. He knew he would get away all right. He would die rather than allow himself to be dragged off somewhere to be reshaped – re-formed until he became something else. Something you hung things off. Something that obeyed. He would flay his hooves until they found a grip on the breast of the river bank. He would push the front half of himself up and then pull the back half behind. Next there would be one final struggle until both halves came together. And then the horse would be free. None of these movements would be random; each one would be part of a careful pattern. Only his mane might shiver in an unnecessary way, but that wouldn't be his fault; that would be the wind. The man with the rope would fall on his snot, then turn his face, dripping with muck, to watch the albino pound up the hill. Like an avalanche rolling backwards. The hilltop cowboys would wrestle with the necks of their horses, struggling to collect the reins; struggling to keep control. But there would be no control. The albino would scatter the horses apart. The albino would make them forget they had ever been tamed.

Charlie could see all this happening when he closed his eyes. He would have liked to have heard the splash and suction of the water as the albino pulled himself out. He would have liked to have heard the squelch when the man who thought he was the champ hit the ground. He leaned his head closer. But no sound came from the poster.

Charlie didn't take his eyes off the albino until the doors of the Tivoli sprang open and gangs of kids came gushing out. He watched them take Francis Street, all the way up to Dean Street and back down past him to Thomas Street, pouring through all the gaps and cracks in between. They were moving their legs in a funny way, up in a sharp little jump before landing them again, a fraction of a second between each footfall. Sometimes they slapped themselves on the arse and shouted 'Yaaa!' They were pretending to be horses, but they were pretending to be riders too. They thought they were great. But Charlie thought they looked stupid – you could only be one or the other.

He'd never seen a horse in full flight before. Only the lazy street horses pulling carts, or the muzzle of a thoroughbred over the high door of a horsebox that was passing through town. But he was familiar with their isolated movements just the same; he knew all their breeds too and could name all the parts of their bodies from a book Herbert had won in school. He knew for example that the little dark wart on the inside fetlock above the pastern was called a chestnut. That was three things he could name in just one small sentence about one small area. He knew something else too – that all horses had elbows. Teddy Daw said he never heard such nonsense: how could they have elbows, when they didn't even have arms? But Charlie knew they had. Although he didn't tell Teddy how. Some day Teddy might find out for himself. And then he might feel like a right sap.

Charlie also knew the only place to really see a horse was at the pictures. The pictures would be the very best place, because you could follow the horse and see where he was going. The camera would make you go as fast as the horse. He noticed that about the pictures: if someone went on a train, you could go with them and travel as far down the line as they did. If someone got into an Otis elevator, you got on too and went whizzing up as many floors as they did and saw the same view; then they always brought you back down with them again. You were never left behind at the pictures. He'd only been a couple of times with Herbert – once on their own, another time with their cousin Mo. But neither of those pictures had horses in them. Only girls. The time they went with Mo, it was to one of those stupid singing pictures. Herbert didn't like horses, but Herbert liked girls. Hundreds of them in long rows across the screen grinning like crackpots with their legs going up and down, up and down as if they were saluting Hitler. Herbert looked at the girls. And Mo just looked at Herbert.

Before George went away he sometimes said he'd bring him to the races. But he always seemed to forget. Charlie knew this was because he might get lost. He never meant to get lost; it just always seemed to happen. First he would fidget on the spot and then the spot would grow too small for him; then he would have to step out of it, gradually edging himself away until he was out of sight. Then he would be lost. They called him 'the explorer' because he was always wandering off and then someone would always have to go and find him. George wouldn't be able to concentrate on the races if he had to go looking for his kid brother. So he just forgot. But Charlie didn't mind. He understood George's predicament. It was 1939; it was the summer; he had just turned eleven. He understood a lot of things. A lot of predicaments.

First the wireless set was on very loud. An endless programme, kept on all day. Then Uncle Sam went away, taking Mo and Bennie, and the volume was turned down. Then George went away and the volume was turned off altogether. Herbert didn't go away. But he might as well have, because he stopped being part of the family. Leaving the house early in the morning and coming home late at night. Sometimes he didn't bother coming home at all. Even when he was home, you could tell he'd prefer to be someplace else. Everyone had somewhere to be: George had Belfast; Herbert had his job; even Danny had heaven. Uncle Sam had his spanking new garage in Rathmines; his cousins had their new house with a grass garden and a toilet at the top of the stairs. Charlie had a silent house, and a wireless set that made no sound. When everyone was there you couldn't hear the secrets. But when the wireless was switched off, you could hear them again. He couldn't make out what the secrets were. But he could hear them just the same.

Ma said, 'I knew he'd start again as soon as the boys went their own way.'

He asked her what she meant. She said, 'Nothing. I mean nothing.'

But he knew she meant his da would start again, and he knew when she said 'the boys' she meant George and Herbert. And he felt like saying, 'I'm a boy too, ma. Why can't you ever mean me?'

Once Herbert stopped being part of the family, Charlie put his eye on the barn. Charlie liked the old barn. But it had always been somebody's else's territory. The last person to have it was Herbert, but first it was ma's, when she used it for a henhouse, but Charlie couldn't remember that. He could remember when it was a garage, though, where Uncle Sam and George and sometimes even Herbert used to work on cars. And da used to sit in a corner on a bench with one of the neighbours, filling out forms or writing letters for them. He used to refer to the corner as his 'Chambers' and the neighbours as 'the Illiterati' – but only behind their backs. They gave him cigarettes and baby bottles of whiskey. He would ask them questions then, rearranging the answers until they were fit for the dotted lines. Or, looking up from the letter to suggest another way of phrasing a sentence, he would play around with their versions until it became his own. At the end of the session he would take out a notebook and make them practise their signature. He refused to fill out anything that was signed with an 'X' because, he said, 'An "X" can mean anything. No one pays attention to an "X".'

Sometimes da would get up and leave the neighbour for a minute, coming over to the car, where the others would stand back from the engine to make a space for him. Then they would all look down on the riddle inside. 'Did you try that? What about that?' he would ask, pointing to the black lumps inside, but never quite touching them because he didn't like to dirty his hands. When he leaned forward you could see the baby bottle peeping out of his pocket. And it looked like a little pet mouse.

But then the barn was empty. Just a few crates of spare parts or the carcass of a wheel here and there and a few old tyres set against the walls, for after the war. Uncle Sam always said, 'You wouldn't know what might come in handy. After the war.'

There were bits of of a bicycle too, from when Herbert used to cycle to school, but it was too bockity to put together again. There was a punchbag hanging from a rafter, from when George used to be a boxer. It was all worn and dented by George's old fist-prints. Once it would have hung quite low, but the taller George grew, the higher up it had been hoisted. And George had been tall for a very long time. The punchbag was way too high for Charlie. Although once he pulled a stool up to it and stretched his fists up, pretending to be George. He pushed his voice down through his nose and gave himself a commentary: 'He wastes no time sizing up his man. He knows only one way to proceed and that is to go forward. He wades in, pinning his man against the ropes and crashing home left and right and left again.'

He gave the bag a few good punches for itself, but then he took his eye off it for a second and it came back on him with a spiteful swing. He fell backwards off the stool and for a few dark minutes thought he had broken his back.

When Herbert was his age he had made himself a hideout in the barn. Ma said it would take you forever to shift him. Sometimes he wouldn't even come in for his tea. So Charlie decided to do the same thing. He built it himself, with wood and nails, and he went down to Murray's piggery to beg for a bale of straw. Mr Murray made him run four messages before he gave him the straw. But four messages was nothing to Charlie – ma made him run messages all day. Up and down Thomas Street, to Saint Catherine's bakery with a pillowcase on his back or to the dealers' on Saturday evening so he could catch them at their cheapest just before they packed up their prams. Or to the shop in James's Street to buy blue duck eggs for da or a hack out of the salt-wrinkled ling that hung down from the ceiling. Up to Uncle Sam's garage to deliver a message and back to different shops on both side of the river. To shops with the smell of old clothes and the ticks of old clocks, and the room at the side where the moneylender pressed his blue fingers down onto a long page in a long green ledger, filling out sums in a special space that belonged to ma. And then crushing her name down into the paper with a little wooden contraption that rocked like a boat.

The straw had a smell of pig's piss off it, but if you tied it into a bale with a long piece of twine you could keep it out of nose-shot and only use it like a trapdoor to disguise your hideout when you weren't there, or if you heard anyone coming, pull the twine and drag the bale over to cover you in. This was in case the Germans ever came, or in case he ever wanted to do what he saw Herbert do one time.

His was a lovely hideout: it kept him busy for a couple of days just getting everything right. There was a bench and a shelf to put your comics on, and your tin with your marbles and a piece of paper and a pencil for writing letters to George and to Bennie too after he went away to America. There was a seat to sit on that he had pulled out of the old Ford Prefect that da used to drive. And a very nice little sofa it made too – dark red all over, except where the horsehair stuffing poked out, and still smooth enough to the touch, even though the skin had millions of creases on it. When he finished the hideout he wrote out one letter, then he copied it, word for word, onto another page. He filled out the top of the first one, 'Dear George', and wrote 'Dear Bennie' on the other. When he had finished the letters, he put them into envelopes and marked them 'Private and Confidential' – because that's what it said on the envelopes of da's letters – then he put them up until he had the money to buy stamps for them.

They looked so great sticking out from the side of the shelf with their foreign addresses all important – Belfast and New York – that he didn't really mind how long they would have to wait there because he liked looking at them. And anyway, Bennie never wrote back. And George did only the odd time. He didn't care if Bennie never wrote back or not because he only wanted the stamps. But he cared a bit about George.

When he had finished writing the letters he opened the tin of marbles and looked down at the crowd of dead eyes looking back up. He gave them a shake and listened to the rattle and then there was nothing else to do in the hideout. So he lay back on the seat with his hands behind his head and thought of all the things that had happened in the barn.

He tried to imagine what it was like when he was a baby and the place had teemed with hens and mad little chicks, and ma feeding them, pulling sprays of seeds out of a basket like Farmer Browne's wife in his old school picture book. He tried to make himself see her, with a bun in her hair and two fat, rosy cheeks going, 'Here . . . chuck chuck chuck.' But she wouldn't come into the picture.

The only time ma's cheeks went rosy was when she was annoyed or when she was looking for something. Like that time she took him on a visit to mad Aunt Maude's. It was the day Herbert got his exam results. It was before Herbert stopped being part of the family and went his own way. Mad Aunt Maude kept talking about how different things were now that she had no money. She kept saying it as though she had won a prize for being poor. She said, 'It's amazing, Greta, what you can do without when you have to. When I think of all those unnecessary little treats that I used believe were so *vital*, I'm ashamed of myself, really I am. Do you know what I'm going to tell you? The Wall Street Crash was the best thing that ever happened to me, and now, with the possibility of war, we're very well prepared. The last time I nearly went out of my mind trying to deal with the shortages, but this time? Why, this time I probably won't even notice. We've even planted our own vegetables, haven't we, Lucia? Lucia laughs at me because I worry about them so much, especially the potatoes. Their top growth – you know, the green, curly bits – well they're looking a bit floppy at the moment and I worry about them as if they were babies. What are they called again?'

'Haulms,' Lucia said.

'Yes, haulms. Well, I don't think they should be floppy at all, but Lucia thinks there's nothing to worry about. Still, we shall just have to wait and see. So you see, Greta, we're ready for the worst and at least we won't starve. Yes, we're ready to make the most of the little we have.'

But when Charlie looked around, he could see: two sitting rooms; a gramophone player; a piano with a dog-pawed stool in this sitting room and the legs of another piano showing through the gap in the door in the sitting room across the hall. A long-necked lamp with a beady fringe round its shade that whispered when Lucia opened the window. A tea tray with all sorts of silver carry-on, including sandwiches and cakes. And she didn't seem very poor to him.

But everybody knew that da's sister was half-mad: always doing mad things and saying mad things. 'She's half-mad, that one,' ma always said whenever Aunt Maude's name was mentioned. Ma said she'd never been right since her first husband died and she just got worse over the years, and then one day she just upped and left her second husband for no reason at all and caused all sorts of problems that ma could never bring herself to mention. And she wore trousers like a man, and turbans like a factory girl, and drove a mad little car that was always breaking down. But Aunt Maude had paid for Herbert to go to the high school so ma didn't really care how mad she was. And ma was nodding away at everything she said, managing even to look a bit surprised, as if she didn't know what it was like to be poor. He supposed ma was just trying to humour her because she thought Aunt Maude was going to pay for the university now. The university for Herbert. But ma was wrong. Charlie knew from the moment they had walked in and, looking over at Lucia, he knew she knew too: ma was barking up the wrong tree there. Ma was making a show of herself for nothing and ma was making a show of *him* for nothing too.

It was giving him a headache, ma making a show of herself that way, so he made himself think about mad Aunt Maude instead and how somebody should write a book about her. They could call it *The Adventures of Mad Aunt Maude* and you could have pictures of her in her mad little car, wearing her trousers and smoking her long cigarettes and singing lullabies to her potatoes at night with her face all worried, stroking their haulms, saying, 'Shh, shh, my poor little haulms.' And that would be a much better story than stupid Farmer Browne's wife. With her fat, rosy cheeks like ma's were now. Ready to burst.

It was taking ma ages to open her bag and pass over the little piece of paper to prove how clever Herbert had been. Aunt Maude took it in her hand and hardly looked at it and then she passed it on to Lucia. Then Aunt Maude smiled and screwed a cigarette into a little holder, saying, 'Oh well, now you must be very proud of him, Greta.'

But she still didn't mention the university.

She just kept talking about some recipe she'd seen in an English magazine for lettin'-on banana sandwiches for when the war came.

'Parsnips, you see,' she explained. 'You mash the parsnips and add a drop of banana essence and cut the sandwiches as normal and nobody is the wiser, apparently. Isn't that only marvellous?'

And ma said, 'I can't wait to try it,' in the posh voice she always used whenever she was a visitor or the odd time too maybe when somebody might visit her.

Charlie didn't trust the cake once he'd heard about the parsnip sandwiches and had a sly sniff of it before taking a bite in case it was made out of cabbage. But it seemed all right so he ate a big piece of it and then Lucia passed him the plate, all nods and smiles, as if she really, *really* wanted him to take more. So he ate another piece again, but this time he took one with a squeeze of jam inside.

Ma kept bringing the talk back to Herbert until Aunt Maude had to say something. So she said, 'You should have brought him with you – I could have congratulated him myself,' and ma said, 'Oh, you know what they're like at that age – so odd.'

But that wasn't why he had stayed at home; it was because the one suit he had was in the pawn. And the only other decent clothes he had were his school clothes. You couldn't wear them as street clothes when you were already finished school.

When they got up to go, Aunt Maude came over and kissed ma and then her neck went red as well. The last thing mad Aunt Maude said was, 'Well, whatever career he choses, I'm sure he'll do very well indeed.'

Charlie thought he'd never get home. Home safely with the ten-bob note Aunt Maude had given him for Herbert to buy himself something nice, and the half-crown she had given him because he was eleven. He couldn't wait to see Herbert's face: a whole ten shillings, it was – a fortune. But ma spoilt it a bit because she bawled all the way home.

And that was the thing about ma; she was always, always expecting too much. She was never satisfied. Even da said it sometimes: 'You know what your trouble is, don't you? You're never bloody satisfied.'

Charlie looked down at his feet and pretended he couldn't see her. He looked down at his feet and thought about the bag of honey bees he was going to buy with his money, and how he was going to suck them then slowly till the tubes in his ears squirmed inside, and maybe read a sixty-four pager from cover to cover. Read the comic quickly, suck the sweets slow. See which was finished the first.

'Let her stick it up her arse.' That's what Herbert thought of the ten-bob note.

He must have changed his mind, because after a while he called Charlie in and put out his hand for the note. That was the first time he took him to the pictures. The picture with no horses. And there was no more mention of universities after that. After that, Herbert got a job in town.

'Are you not pleased?' Charlie asked him.

'No,' Herbert said.

'Why?' Charlie asked him. 'What will you be doing?'

'I'll be learning how to be a plucked chicken.'

And Charlie thought about that for a long while, but he still couldn't figure it out.

*

You see all sorts of queer things in the barn. Some things you're allowed to see – like George's poker schools. When he played with the old men, they played off a table: a slab of plywood on two drums of paint, and a crate in the corner with bottles of stout. It would be Charlie's job to open them up and give them to the players and sometimes someone might give him a penny. When he played with the young men, they played on the ground and you wouldn't get anything. But you could listen to the curses and practise them to yourself, in case you were ever in a gang. And then you'd be able to say them out loud, instead of just inside your head. You could say 'Fuck' and then 'Shite' and then maybe even, 'You stupid cunt, go and ask me bollix.'

Once he even saw a ghost – his brother Danny – that he couldn't remember, just like the photograph ma kept hidden behind the dresser as if she was ashamed of him and only taking it out to show when da was gone out.

'You could have hung around a bit longer,' Charlie said.

'I couldn't. God called me.'

'Why didn't you just pretend you didn't hear him?'

'You have two other brothers,' Danny said.

'They're not brothers. They're men.'

And that was good too. Seeing his brother, swinging his ankles, from the rafter at the top of the barn.

That gave him a chance to get to know him.

Some things weren't so good, though, like the day he got the cold squeeze in his stomach, that time da forgot to come home. That was the time George went to Belfast and da had left him to the train and they didn't see him then for three days after.

'Where is he?' he asked ma each night.

'Nowhere,' she said, but he didn't believe her. Everybody had to be somewhere.

On the fourth day, Charlie thought he might never come back, so he felt safe enough asking the boys from Sunday school if they wanted to come over. They sat together in the hideout, Archie Evans and Teddy Daw; all stooped together hunker to hunker, and it was nearly as good as having a gang. They laid their marbles out between them on the red sofa, running their fingers over them, picking them up, examining them like the pawnbroker examining jewels; preparing themselves to discuss the swaps. That's when he got the cold squeeze in his stomach. He kept looking at the door of the barn. He just couldn't stop looking. After a while he got up and stood in the doorway to look at the archway out in the yard. The yard was bursting with sunshine but the archway was empty and dark. Yet he couldn't stop looking. Teddy and Archie followed him out and started talking to him about the swaps again. But he couldn't hear what they were saying: he was too busy with the archway.

'What are you looking at?' Teddy asked.

'Shhh,' Charlie said.

And then he saw da. Appearing suddenly out from the darkness. For a minute Charlie thought da was floating, because his two feet were a few inches off the ground, moving through the air. But when he advanced into the sunlight, there were two Catholic priests, black from head to toe, holding him up between them by the elbows because his legs wouldn't work. One of the priests said, 'Go in and get your mother, son.'

When Charlie came out of the house, he saw a crust of old vomit on his father's coat and his father's eyes all funny, as if someone had coloured them in with a red pencil. And the cross face on one priest. And the sad face on the other one. And Teddy and Archie clattering across the yard. That was the end of Archie Evans and Teddy Daw. That was the end of Sunday school too, because he knew, when he saw them doing a runner, that they were probably running off to tell everyone else. But at least they had left their marbles behind. In a way he sort of hoped they'd come back looking for them again, because then he could say, 'You're not getting them, you stupid cunts. Go and ask me bollix.'

But the best was the time he saw Herbert with his trousers around his ankles and two girl shoes on either side of his legs and Herbert's bare arse was popping in, out, in, like a cuckoo in a clock. It looked so funny that Charlie burst out laughing. And the girl said, 'Oh Gonny . . . Oh mammy.' And Herbert said, 'Get out, ye little bastard. And if you ever open your mouth . . . '

He stopped laughing then, trying to think. What did he mean: 'If you ever open your mouth?'

Why would he open it, when he had no one to tell?

When the last 'Yaaa' had bounced out of Francis Street and the last pair of legs had skipped out of sight, Charlie said goodbye to the albino horse and walked home himself. He held the pillowcase of bread out in front of him, batting the loaves away with the cob of his knee and trying to keep the swings nice and even. That kept him going until he turned into New Street, where, a few yards short of the house, he swung the pillowcase over his shoulder and slowed up his step, bracing himself to expect the worst. This was always how he approached the house; expecting the worst. Mostly he didn't get it, but sometimes he did.

He opened the back door, and there was ma sitting on a chair with her hands on her stomach. Charlie didn't like the look of her, so he closed the back door again. He thought da must be in there as well. Probably they were in the middle of one of their mill-ups if she had that 'I've-an-awful-pain-in-me-stomach' look. One of their mill-ups that never had room for him. Like a big balloon going up. Silence for ages while the balloon got bigger, filling up the room, rubbing its dry, squeaky skin against the walls – up, up, up; expanding to the ceiling. Then when there was nowhere else for it to go, 'Bang!' And you'd want to get out of there quick before it burst in your face.

So he decided to go to his hideout, where he wouldn't have to hear ma's screechy voice in a minute, and the back door slamming in another minute, and then da's uneven step going hop, hop, hop, away.

But when he got to his hideout, he found da already there. Da, sitting with a bottle of whiskey between his legs. Da had found the hideout and was using it for crying and talking to himself. And getting drunk. Charlie wanted to give him a dig, to crack the whiskey bottle over his head and make blood pour all over his face. Then he wanted to mash his face into the bale of pig's-piss hay. Give him something to cry about. Because he had ruined the hideout. He had made it no good now. How could it be a hideout, if da could find it and sit on its sofa and spill whiskey on it and cry like a girl? He tried to make da look at him, so he could see how much he hated him. But da couldn't see him. Da was looking at a squad of stray pigeons that had waddled in from the yard. Looking at them: swivel-eyed, as if they were rats.

Charlie reversed himself back out to the yard. He dropped down onto his hunkers and stumped himself along under the window so ma wouldn't see him. When he got to the archway, he pulled himself up and his legs felt a bit fuzzy, so he stamped them once or twice, but they just exploded inside into hundreds of sharp little sparks. And that felt very sore, so he started to jump them up and then down. And up again. And down again. A fraction of a second between each footfall.

By the time he turned into New Street, his legs could move in a perfect canter. He heard ma behind him, calling his name, all the way up the street. But the faster he moved, the fainter her voice became. Then it was gone altogether. He tried to get lost but he kept coming to places he knew. But if he pushed the canter into a gallop and made the gallop fast enough, everything went dizzy and only colours and sounds went whizzing past, all blurred up and unrecognisable. That was nearly as good as being lost.

And that was when Charlie decided, if he couldn't be clever like Herbert, or smart like George, or even dead like Danny, he could be a runner instead. He could be a horse.

PART TWO

I

Spring 1941

Mrs Abingdon leaned out the window, a bunch of loose linen held to her chest. She struck her arms out and flapped the cloth open; strands of corned brisket and shreds of spring cabbage trampolined off. She brought the cloth back to her, ducking into the room. And that was the Sunday dinner over with now.

This could be her favourite part of the week: Theresa out playing, the house to herself, all to herself. Nothing to do but nurse a fat pot of tea and have a long, slow look at the papers. Yesterday's *Irish Field* to recall the bets that hours of indecision had left jumbled up in her head; today's paper then to see how she had done. A short contemplation on where she'd gone wrong, or even – God be good to her – how she may have gone right. Worn out after that, she always had to take to the chair, where, with the sound of hooves gaining ground in her head, she would gradually nod off to sleep. Until Theresa came in to give her a shake.

Another sup of tea then, before seeing to the delft that had been steeping inside in the sink all afternoon. This was their lazy little secret: the dishes left till nearly six o' clock. And always she would say to her youngest child, 'Whatever you do, don't tell the others . . . ' and always she would gasp back, 'Oh mammy, as if I would.'

A night by an extravagant fireside to follow: Theresa drying her hair, school uniform pressed and hanging on the door – starched blouse and sponged tie and those long black stockings that she hated so much draped expectantly over the back of the chair. Little reminders of the week to come, but for the moment they could hold on to the week not quite gone. Just the two of them together up in the parlour; fried bread and cocoa. A listen to the wireless until it was time for bed; a bit of a chat in between. That was her Sunday; but only every second Sunday. Because today was an Agnes Sunday; the week after next would be a Betty one. A fortnight after that again, a Sunday for Margaret.

And so on and on, until Agnes's turn came back round again.

Mrs Abingdon pulled down the window and put to herself a string of questions, as she always did about this time of a Sunday every other week. Why could they not all just leave her alone? Why had they decided on 'taking turns' – as they called it – to annoy her every second week for the rest of her days? Why were they so terrified that she be left on her own? Could they not realise that, after rearing that amount of children, being on her own was just what she wanted? Inconsiderate children were one thing, but children that were over-considerate – was that not nearly as bad?

She held the cloth up to the light, examining it for stains. 'Yes,' she said aloud, 'we'll get another turn out of you – so long as there's only ourselves.'

Agnes's rusty voice struggled out of the scullery, 'Did you say something, mother?'

'No. Just talking to myself.'

Then Agnes's neat little head popped out for a glare around the room. 'Where's that Theresa one gone? I thought she was supposed to be drying the dishes.'

'Mmm? Oh, she's probably in next door,' her mother replied, tucking her chin into the hem of the cloth, drawing the corners together once, twice, until she had attained a manageable square. Her eyes fell on the odd, raised scar of a silky, darned patch and then picked on one that looked a bit off.

'Who sewed that one, do you think, Agnes?'

'Ah mother, how would I know?'

'I don't recognise the hand. I wonder who . . . ?'

She took it over to the press in the wall and, making an insertion between towelling and flannel, carefully edged it in.

'Unless it was your Aunt Grace?' she suggested, before turning back around.

Agnes frowning in the doorway, an irritated hand rubbing the bowl of her pregnant belly. What was vexing her now? The remark about the cloth? Perhaps she shouldn't have mentioned it. Perhaps it was just that sort of remark that made them think it was necessary to 'take turns' in the first place.

'I was only wondering, that's all. It's the sort of thing I notice – and your Aunt Grace, you know, always had a clumsy hand.'

'Oh mother, will you stop going on about the tablecloth. I don't care about the tablecloth.'

'What's the matter, then?'

'Nothing.'

'What? Tell me.'

'It's just . . . '

'What?'

'You have that one ruined, that's all.'

'Who?'

'Who do you think? Sneaking off like that. She's a bit too smart, now. And did you ever hear the likes of her, wanting to steep the dishes until teatime? I don't know where she gets her slovenly notions.'

Then her head popped back into the scullery again.

Mrs Abingdon took the paper to the table and laid it out flat. With a soft hand she lifted each page, her eye staying on it all the way up and on the way back down again, searching. Anything but the war. But everything was the war, in one shape or another. Every inch of every column; even the advertisements had to remind you – in case you could forget – shortages and scarcities; coupons and queues. Was there nothing bright to read any more? Nothing bright except . . . She came to the racing results and stopped. How had she done? Of course she wouldn't be able to check properly with Agnes here, but she could chance a quick look – if only she could remember her bets. Had she decided on . . . ? Or had it been . . . ? Oh yes – oh no. That's right, she had changed her mind at the very last second. Or had she, in the end, changed it again? But no use getting herself worked up unneccessarily – best wait until she had a chance to check the *Irish Field* first; the bookie's dockets tonight before she got into bed . . . The *Irish Field?* The *Irish* . . . She swallowed a gasp and, placing her hand over her heart, could feel a flutter tip out on her palm. Oh merciful hour, where had she left it? Oh Sacred Heart of the Divine, where could it be?

Her eyes jerked over the room until they found it: there, over there. Would you just look at it? Poking out from behind the coal scuttle, where Agnes would have had no trouble spotting it, with the mark of her pen all over yesterday's English meetings. She glanced towards the scullery before snatching it up, then, folding it roughly, hurried it across to the corner of the room, where she stuffed it deftly into the back of Theresa's school bag. It wouldn't do to let Agnes set her eyes on that. It wouldn't do at all. She scolded herself: careless, you're getting; downright careless. You were lucky that time. But you mightn't be so lucky again.

Agnes came through, a tea tray jangling over her bump. 'What are all them hot-water bottles doing under the sink?'

'They're leaking.'

'Leaking? Sure Jack'll fix them for you.'

'Ah, not at all – I keep meaning to throw them out.'

'You can't throw them out. Jack will . . . Are you all right, mother? You're a bit flushed-looking.'

'Am I? I feel a bit warm, right enough.'

Agnes settled the tray on the table, then homed in on the teapot; popping the cosy off, easing the lid up, dropping the stem of a spoon down through the steam, stirring. Then she came back to the hot-water bottles.

'He fixes them for all the neighbours; doesn't be a minute.'

'I wouldn't like to bother him.'

'Have you a puncture-repair kit?'

'I wouldn't think so.'

'Well get yourself one; he'll fix them for you some evening. How many of them are there?'

'I don't know . . . a few.'

'Well you better get two kits, so.'

'I always use the bed jar; I prefer the bed jar.'

'But the bed jar might crack. You might kick it during the night and it might fall out onto the floor and crack. And where would you be then, mother? At least you can mend the rubber ones, and there's no point in wasting them now, is there? Not with the war on. We can't afford to waste anything, not any more.'

Mrs Abingdon leaned closer to the stream of brown tea. 'Now

that looks to me like tea, Agnes – real tea.'

'I saved some from my ration for you, mother.'

'You're very good, Aggie. Very considerate.'

Agnes beamed like a well-praised child. And her mother felt sorry for her then. She looked at her daughter and she seemed to be just that: a well-praised child again, playing with a tea tray, pretending to be sensible. And what happens to them at all? What happens when they get married? What makes them into old women so soon? Talking like old women, thinking like old women. Agnes, for example – the giddiest of them all – Agnes, who had tittered her way through school; could never control herself despite circumstance or consequence. Sitting there now fretting her heart out over bed jars and hot-water bottles and what might and mightn't happen to them. Once she was full of life; of joy. What in the name of God ever happened to her at all?

'My ration's always gone before the week's half-out,' Mrs Abingdon said, for something to say – something to make her stop feeling sorry for Agnes.

'You could make it stretch a bit further if you dried the tea leaves in the sun. That's what I do. And a spoon of sugar in the pot; gives it that extra bit of strength.'

'I know, I know. I always mean to, but . . . '

'You give in to yourself too much, mother.'

And Mrs Abingdon nodded, no longer sorry.

Agnes pulled a chair to the table. 'She seems to be spending all her time next door.'

'Now don't start, Agnes. Gwen is a grand little one. They're a lovely family.'

'Jack would disagree.'

'Why? Because they're Protestants, I suppose. Oh for God's sake, he doesn't even know them.'

'He knows the brother – the one who works in the fire brigade. He drinks, mother. He . . . '

'What? What does he do?'

'Well, he gambles.'

'I never trust a man who doesn't take a pint. Always poking their noses in.'

'Jack doesn't drink.'

'Oh, that's right. I forgot.'

Mrs Abingdon brought her hand to her nose and gave it a mischievous little rub.

'I'm not saying there's anything wrong with the Nortons, mother, it's just that . . . well, they're different, that's all.'

'Nothing wrong with being different, Agnes. No doubt they find us a bit different too.'

'Well of course, but . . . '

Mrs Abingdon closed her tired eyes. What made them turn? Four married daughters, she had: four old heads on young shoulders. Was it the men they had married? Would that be it? Agnes's Jack, with a bicycle clip fixed to one leg, announcing himself by the lapel of his jacket: Pioneer pin; Gaelic speaker's circle; White League star to show his disapproval of bad language. And Margaret's husband – another beauty. His head stuck down to within an inch of his dinner; wouldn't even raise it to bid you good day. What sort were they at all? Or maybe it was her own fault – the way she had reared them? Her careless ways, her extravagant ways – her gambling? Had that made them afraid ever to take risks? Even the risk of enjoying themselves. Cautious lives; such cautious lives.

'Are you tired, mother?'

'No, no, I'm grand.'

She opened her eyes and tried to swallow the tea but the heat pinched her throat. Tilting her cup, she poured a drop down into the saucer, then began to lift the saucer to her lips, but Agnes's eye shamed her into lowering it again, leaving the tea to cool of its own accord.

'She needs watching, mother. You're far too soft with her. And she's gone as cheeky. When we were her age . . . '

'You had a father, Agnes, and each other for company.'

'So had she.'

'She had a sick man, bedridden and dying. Sisters and brothers already grown – that's what she had.'

'I don't see . . . '

'What time is Jack collecting you?'

'He's gone to the match, I told you.'

'Oh that's right, so you did.'

Mrs Abingdon took on the hot tea, while Agnes carried on giving out about Theresa. And it could have been any of her grown-up daughters sitting there opposite her, giving out yards. Because really, when she thought of it, they all had the same gripe, even if their approach was different. Agnes, now, would always be direct, whereas Kay was more likely to hint. And Margaret would just ask sly questions that seemed so innocent yet exacted answers that were full of guilt. As for Betty? Now Betty would . . . Oh, what did it matter how they complained? They were jealous, that's all; jealous because Theresa still had a spark. And they wouldn't be happy until she was like them, with that defeated, dissatisfied look in her eye. Nothing to look forward to but endless babies, and for entertainment – what? A watery husband to watch of an evening, mending rubber bottles while his wife sat awestruck in the background, as if he was a sapper defusing a bomb. Well, she wouldn't allow Theresa to become like that. Over her dead body, she wouldn't allow it. And one more word out of Agnes and she would let her have it. One more word and she would show her the door.

'All I'm saying, mother, is that if I was you, I'd watch her a bit more, that's all.'

Mrs Abingdon opened her mouth to speak but the sound of the front door slamming and the clatter of feet coming down the kitchen stairs made her close it again. She sighed. At least now she wouldn't have to fall out with Agnes. Poor little Aggie, pretending to be grown up. Poor little rusty gullet pretending to give out. Poor little child, just looking for praise.

'You have your own concerns now, Agnes. Your own little family.' In the end, that was all she had time to say.

'Mammy, guess what? You'll never guess what.'

'Theresa, shhh. Will you keep your voice down, like a good girl, please?'

'Mona Norton's got engaged.'

'She has not?'

'She has so. To a fella with a big black car.'

'Who is he? Do we know him?'

'No. He works in Belfast.'

'A chap from Belfast? Imagine?'

'No, no. He's from Dublin but he works there. He comes down every couple of weekends. They went to a dress dance in the Gresham last night and he asked her. Gave her the ring and all. He did; Gwen told me. I bet she looked beautiful; I bet he just couldn't help himself.

153

She always looks beautiful; she has such lovely dresses.'

'And why wouldn't she? Doesn't she work in a dress-hire shop?'

'Don't be so catty, Agnes. Don't tell me Mona is going to move to Belfast, Theresa?'

'No, he's moving down here after the war. He's going to open his own business.'

'What kind of business?'

'A garage, Gwen says. And guess what? He lives over a chipper.'

Agnes laughed. 'Well, I can't see Mona Norton living over a chipper.'

'Not here, Aggie. In Belfast, he has digs over a chipper. Oh, I'd love to live over a chipper.'

Theresa turned back to her mother and flung her arms around her neck. 'Gwen is going to be a bridesmaid,' she said.

'Stop swinging out of mother like that,' Agnes began crossly, and then, squinting up at her little sister, clipped her cup back down onto the saucer and drew her by the arm over to her side.

'Why aren't you wearing the scapular I bought you?'

Theresa put a guilty hand up to the vacant spot on her neck. 'I . . . '

'I hope you haven't lost it.'

'No.'

'Where is it, then? In your school bag?'

And Mrs Abingdon thought her heart would shove itself out and fall on the floor when she saw Agnes lift herself and make for the bag. But then Theresa turned and said, 'I have it here in my pocket.'

And her heart nudged back into position again.

'What's it doing in your pocket?'

'I was going to wash it.'

'Go away, you little liar. You wouldn't wear it in front of her. You're ashamed. In front of her.'

'I am not. I am not.'

'Ah leave her be, Agnes, will you? She's only a child.'

'I am not. I'm thirteen.'

Mrs Abingdon closed her eyes again and took off her glasses, knuckling her forehead, kneading her thoughts. A bit of peace and quiet; peace and quiet. Wouldn't she just give anything for . .

What were they talking about again? Oh yes . . .

'And when are they getting married?' she asked. 'Have they the date set?'

'After the war. Oh, mammy, will you be going to the wedding?'

'Don't be ridiculous, Theresa, how can mother go to the wedding?'

'Why not?'

'I'll go if I'm asked.'

'You won't go into their church, mother, surely?'

'I might,' Mrs Abingdon replied, winking softly at her youngest child.

'He's in there now,' Theresa said, 'talking to Mrs Norton.'

'What's he like, Theresa?'

'I don't know – I've never seen him. I heard him, though.'

'Heard him?'

'Yes. Last night he sent us in chips. We were in the parlour, and he said, "There's a few chips for the kids."'

'What did his voice sound like?'

'Oh for God's sake, mother,' Agnes said. 'You're worse.'

'He's coming down for Easter: his brother is getting married on Easter Tuesday. He's bringing them all to the races on Easter Monday. Even Gwen. And Mona's going to his brother's wedding. Oh, it's well for Gwen. I wish . . . '

'To the races?'

'Yes, he goes to the races all the time. And the dogs.'

Agnes sniffed. 'He's probably a bookie or something; that's how he got the car.'

'He's not a bookie. He builds ships for the war. He's in charge of loads of people, Gwen says.'

'I'm afraid they won't be going to the races, love. They've been cancelled for a few weeks on account of . . . '

'Oh mammy, oh no.' Theresa's face fell.

'He'll probably bring them on a nice drive instead.'

And Theresa smiled again. 'Do you want to see his car? Come on, mammy, come on up and have a look.'

'I can't go up there to look at his car, Theresa. What would Mona think?'

'Ah come on,' Theresa pleaded, pulling at her mother's arm.

'We've seen a car before, thank you very much,' Agnes said.

'The idea . . . ' Mrs Abingdon laughed. 'I most certainly will not.'

'Well, can I? Can I ? Please, mammy?'

Mrs Abingdon smiled and nodded and the child clattered back up the kitchen stairs.

At the top of the house, in the front-bedroom window, Mrs Abingdon and Agnes found themselves two minutes later peeping down through the lace at the big black car.

'He must be well off all the same,' Mrs Abingdon said, 'to have a car like that. I wonder what he's like?'

'Mother, how did you know there'd be no racing?'

'What do you mean?'

'It just seems funny you knowing. Mother, I hope you're not . . . '

'You hope I'm not what?'

'You know.'

'Agnes, I haven't been near a race meeting or a dog meeting; not since your father died.'

'I just asked how you knew.'

'It's all over the papers, Agnes. The foot-and-mouth disease. I do still read the papers, you know.'

'I just thought you weren't yourself today – sort of distracted or something, like the way you used to be when . . . You wouldn't lie to me, mother?'

'Do you want me to swear? Is that it? Give me over my missal and I'll swear before God. Is that what you want?'

'Mother, no. Stop.'

'How dare you.'

'I'm sorry, mother. I just don't want you to get into trouble again. I'm sorry.'

'And so you should be.'

Mrs Abingdon moved away to the side of the window and pushed the curtain aside just a fraction. She could feel the lace tremble in her hand and her face burning with what she hoped Agnes would see as rage. But she wasn't enraged, not one little bit. She was relieved; a giddy sort of relief. In fact she almost felt like grinning, as if she had lost a pound and found a fiver. Agnes had certainly been bold enough to cross-examine her like that – Agnes had been downright brazen – but for all her audacity she had overlooked one thing. She may not have set foot on a course or a dog-track since the death of her husband – that much was true – but she had set both her feet into plenty of bookie shops instead. ('You wouldn't lie to me, mother?' Not half, I wouldn't.)

Oh, Agnes was a bold one all right. But then again, Agnes hadn't licked it up off the stones.

She thought of her missal lying on the bedside locker behind her: stern and black; above reproach. The missal she had had since she was a bride. The edges of her holy cards peering out between its pages, faded now, as her fingers were with age; with touching. St Joseph; Padre Pio; His Holiness the Pope. Dead relatives whose sick old faces were scarcely recognisable. And somewhere in between, the bookie's dockets that she had always kept there for luck, only to be consulted in that quiet moment between saying her prayers and getting into bed. Since she was a bride.

Her face settled down after a minute, and the lace in her hand steadied up. She smiled quietly to herself down on the two young girls circling the car, watching it wide-eyed as though they expected it to growl at them. She stopped smiling then. 'Oh my God, they're after climbing into the car. Into it. The little gets . . . '

'Now, mother, do you see what I mean? *Now* do you see? Now.'

*

In the back of the car, Theresa and Gwen bounced on the seat and grinned at each other. It was like another world in here. A secret smell of leather and tobacco. It was like a little house.

'God, I can't wait to get a jaunt in it,' Gwen said, climbing across the seat with her legs all over the place and her shoes tipping against the back window as she went over the top.

'Gwen, *mind,*' Theresa said, ducking her head, then coming back up with the cuff of her jumper to rub the smudge Gwen had left on the window.

Now in the front, Gwen was making more smudges, running her hand along the board of shiny wood and stopping at the little press that was set right into it. She pushed the button. The small door sprang open.

'Oh don't, Gwen, you better not,' Theresa said, peering over the front seat to take a look anyway.

There were scraps of paper, a couple of pens, a few notebooks, a cigarette carton, a bow tie and an everyday tie coiled up like a snake. Gwen cocked her nose. 'Nothing much in here to report.'

Then she pulled out a thick paperback book. 'What's this?' she asked, holding it up.

'It's a form book – a book about horses,' Theresa said, and then, finding she was ashamed for knowing such a thing, muttered, 'I mean, I don't know, I'm not sure . . . '

'Oh yes, that's right. Sure Jimmy has loads of them under his bed,' Gwen said, not a bit ashamed at all.

'Has he?'

'Bundles of them.'

Gwen threw the book back into the little press and snapped the door shut, then, slipping over to the driver's seat, wrapped her fingers around the rim of the steering wheel and gave a little wiggle.

'What do you think, Terry? Does it suit me? Would I make a good driver?'

Theresa nodded. 'Oh yes, you'd be the best.'

She leaned over the seat, resting her chin on her hands. 'What's he like, Gwen?' she asked.

'He's lovely.'

'Has he got a nice manner?'

'A nice what? What's that supposed to mean?' Gwen laughed.

'I don't know. It's what mammy always says – what she says about Kay's husband: He's very plain-looking, God bless him, but he has a lovely manner.'

'Well, Mona's fiancé is not a bit plain-looking.'

Gwen was making herself at home in the front: kneeling up on the seat, twisting the little mirror that was hanging down, examining her teeth, now curling her eyelashes with the side of her finger. Next turning the mirror over to the side and making her smile follow it around. Theresa thought she might as well make herself at home too, so she stretched her legs out along the back seat and laid her head against the curve by the window. The upholstery felt thick under her; thick and tough like an animal's back; like that pony she had had a ride on one time at the zoo when Kay's old boyfriend had insisted – the good-looking one that had let Kay down. The one you were never supposed to mention. The leather felt nice on her bare legs, though: not hot and scratchy like her school stockings, but cool and smooth. She pulled her skirt up another little bit and then another bit again. Now she could feel it against her thighs, and that was nice too, but in a different way; warmer up there and a little bit sticky, especially when you pressed the back of your thighs down hard and then pulled them up quickly again. Ouch.

'He's tall,' Gwen said.

'How tall? Taller than your Jimmy?'

'Nobody's taller than our Jimmy. Except his brother is – the one that's getting married.'

'How do you know? Did you meet him?'

'No, Mona told me. He's nearly six foot four. Imagine. Now, as for Mona's fiancé . . . '

Theresa pulled herself up a bit then to watch Gwen's eyes expand into the mirror as they began to explain.

'Well . . . his hair is black; very black. He has beautiful teeth and his nose is dead straight.'

'Is this his hat?' Theresa asked, pulling a hat up from a shelf tucked between the back seat and the rear window.

'I suppose . . . '

She turned the hat over and looked inside. 'Borsolino', it said. She pressed her finger against the padding and then drew it slowly over the slanted letters. 'Borsolino'. It sounded lovely when she whispered it to herself. The minute she got back into the house she was going to try to write it down in the same slanty way. 'B' 'O' 'R' . . . She stuck her nose in. A familiar smell inside – an oily smell. It reminded her of the smell of her father's head that time when they lifted her up to kiss him goodbye. She turned the hat over and put it back on the shelf.

'You should see Mona beaming on him. Moony Mona, Jim calls her.'

Gwen turned around to show Mona's moony face and the two girls went weak with laughter. But then a rap on the window smartened them up, and they jumped. Oh Mona. Oh Janey. And there was her real face, right up against the glass and not looking moony at all.

Her voice bounced off the window.

'What are you two up to? Get out of that car this minute. The nerve of you.'

Mona opened the front door and pulled her sister out. Then she opened the back door and her head dipped in big towards Theresa.

'Come on, out.'

Theresa pulled her skirt back down to her knees. 'Congratulations, Mona,' she whispered, without looking up.

'Thanks very much. Now *out.*'

Mona bent down and pinched her sister's arm. 'He'll be out in a minute. He'll murder you if he catches you in there. I hope you too weren't rooting. You better not have touched anything – I'm warning you. I've a good mind to tell mummy on you, Gwen Norton. She'd split you in half.'

Theresa stood out to the path, her legs all wobbly, her thighs still stinging from the cling of the leather, that had seemed a bit reluctant to let her go.

Mona's finger wagged into her face. 'And I'm surprised at you, Theresa Abingdon, if you don't mind me saying. I expected more from you than this sort of behaviour. What have you got to say for yourself? That's what I'd like to know.'

Theresa looked up, red to the roots. 'I . . . I . . . '

'Well?'

'Oh Mona,' she sighed, 'your ring's only gorgeous.'

II

George pushed open the unlocked door of Enzo's chip shop. He tugged the blackout curtains away from the windows and a blast of sunlight broke in on the shop; one look around, and he felt like putting them back up again.

'Well isn't this just lovely?' he said. 'Just fuckin' lovely.'

The shop was a mess. Last night's sawdust stained with last night's traces: cigarette butts and a chip here and there dropped from a lax mouth on the way to the door. There was a stink of unchanged cooking fat and fish that was on the turn. He could taste the grease-sweat off the walls – see it too, in a misty film on the glass of Enzo's picture parade: Caruso and Verdi; Madonna and Child. And a damp day on the Bay of Naples.

He switched off the electric light and sat down on the ledge, pressing his eyes into the heels of his hands – letting the lights inside his head run for a while. He was tired; too tired to think – never mind deal with all this – working double shifts, a couple of hours snatched in between. Except for last night, when he hadn't bothered with sleep at all. Getting sucked into a game when he could hardly see the cards in his hand. How much had he lost? More to the point, how much had he borrowed so he could keep on losing? He raised his head and thought for a moment. Then, shaking the calculation away, he pulled himself up and looked over the counter.

The batter bucket hadn't been cleaned out: a lump of dead fish glued to its remains, slops of batter spewed down over the sides, a pool of the stuff curdled on the floor. Under the shelf on a spread of bloodied newspaper, a bluebottle took a leisurely graze along the black and purple nibs of fish gut. Another couple sniffed at the chip basket – across the rind of grease that had set hard on the surface or hung down like haemorrhoids out of its mesh-holes.

He moved to the far side of the counter: the shape of Enzo – dark, adamant – behind the flimsy strings of coloured beads, lying there on his side, tufts of black hair growing out through his singlet or in sprouts from the top of his shoulders. Face all twisted; mouth looking as if it was ready to drop off on the floor. He wanted to kick him. Kick him while he was down.

He flicked the beads apart and stepped inside, aiming his foot at the broad of Enzo's back, then redirecting it at a large potato that had rolled away onto the floor. The potato spun and wavered, then settled into the side of Enzo's leg.

'You bastard,' he said. 'You useless fuckin' bastard.'

He came back out through the shop and opened the door, beckoning to Harry Webb outside in the car. Harry came to the doorway, his whistle skirting the shop. 'For fuck sake. What's happened here?' he said. Then he followed George into the back.

The two men struggled to keep a grip on Enzo's body. George held the side door open with his foot and between them they dragged Enzo into the hallway. Harry paused and straightened up, panting.

'Where to?' he asked.

He watched George edge Enzo towards the staircase. 'Ah Christ, tell me you're not serious,' he groaned.

They sat at the end of the bed until they could breathe easy again; Enzo in a sprawl behind them, an occasional dry note creaking out of his nose.

'Will you look at the cut of him,' Harry said. 'Christ, if the signora could see him now. How long would you say he'd been laying there?'

'I haven't seen him since I got back from Dublin, Sunday night.'

'But today's Wednesday. You mean to tell me he could be laying there all that time?'

'No, he never misses shop hours. Probably started when he closed up last night; came down this morning with the jigs and decided to start again. He'll sleep it off and be back in business by this evening. That's the way he operates. Doesn't take too much to get him drunk – but he gets over it quick enough.'

'Aye,' Harry said, 'I know what you mean. My old man was like that. He could get drunk ten times in the one day. A wee nap, or maybe a gawk-up, and away with him at another bottle. He was only forty-two when he died, but he could make two days out of the one. What about your da? What's he like?'

'My oul'fella . . . ?'

'Aye.'

'I don't know. I've seen him drunk, plenty of times. I just never saw how he got that way.'

George stood up. 'Look, I need a wash. Here, throw that cover over him. And you better shove him onto his side, in case the bastard vomits.'

In the bathroom, he pulled his arms out of his overalls, plucked at his chin with the pads of his fingers, thought about a shave, decided not to bother, then stuck his head under the tap, rubbing his hands over his neck and face, spreading the lather he had forced out of the miserable bit of soap. He screwed his fingers into his ears, turning his head from side to side, cooler now; calmer; that hot little knot on the nape of his neck beginning, at last, to loosen. He shook himself off and backed away from the sink, searching for a towel. No towel. So he pulled up the overalls and rubbed his face in, cursing Enzo again until he felt himself dried. He could hear Harry pissing next door in the toilet, shouting at him over the splash, 'Are you sure you'll not come with us to Bangor? I say, are you sure . . . ?'

George came out to the landing, the now-wet overalls hanging over his hips. 'I've been up all night, Harry – I'm knackered.'

'Sure come anyway. I'll drive; you can take a wee snooze. What you want to stay in this dive for? It stinks.'

Harry turned away from the toilet, crossing his fingers over each other until the buttons of his flies were done up again. 'Heinz has the wireless set up. He's runnin' a good book too. Cleaned up, so I did, last Saturday when you were away home. Anyway, what choice do we have with every meetin' in the country called off? The way I see it, the disease could spread over to the mainland soon enough, and where's that goin' to leave us – racin' fuckin' butterflies? Come on, Georgie, what do you say? Can't we have a few drinks, maybe chase a bit of skirt after? Sure what more could you want?'

'I have a bit of skirt. Anyway, I'm back in work tonight.'

'Again? You'll have yourself kilt.'

'I've a lot to sort before I go on holidays.'

'I'll have you back in time.'

'You won't have me back in time.'

'I will too. I swear it. Look, the minute you want to go, you give me the billy-o, and if I'm not ready, go on you without me and I'll get a lift later on – I can't say fairer nor that.'

George nudged himself out of the rest of his overalls. 'How many times do I have to say it? I'm not going near Bangor. I'm going for a kip, then I have to call over to Fink: he's holding a few quid for me.'

'Fink? Sure the Fink'll be in Bangor today.'

'Are you sure?'

'I'm downright certain. He told me so. You'll not find him any place else this day.'

George thought for a moment. 'Nah, I'll leave it.'

'So I can take the car?'

'It's no good to me.'

'Fair enough. You better get me the permit so, in case I'm stopped. Have you them bets writ out yet?'

'I'll do it now. Here, you wouldn't do us a favour while you're waiting? Hang these things out on the line, will you? They're wringing.'

He rolled the overalls into a ball and flung them at Harry.

'What did you do, piss in them?' Harry asked.

George went into his room and closed over the door.

He patted his hand under the bed until it landed on a leather suitcase, slid it to him, undid the straps and took a look inside. Worse than he thought. There were four pound notes, a ten-bob note and a streel of silver change. Things had better look up quick or he could forget about going on holiday. He'd wages coming to him, but no matter how much overtime he clocked up, it wouldn't be enough – not when he'd paid back last night's borrowings. He'd have to see Fink. But the Fink was in Bangor. He pulled up the notes and shoved the case back under the bed. Then, walking to the window, shouted down, 'All right, Harry, maybe I will go along for the spin.'

Harry's voice came up from the yard, 'Good man, you do rightly.'

He opened the wardrobe door to look for his clean suit but all he saw was a gap on the rail. He looked at the remaining suits. A blue and a grey. The grey was too grubby-looking, the blue had held onto its shape a bit better. He put on the trousers, stuffed his money into the pocket, pulled out his good shoes and fired a spit on each toe before bending down to give them a rub with the corner of the bedspread. He went back to look for a shirt. Picking the one with the cleanest-looking collar, he pushed himself into it.

Then he heard Harry speak out behind him. 'What's wrong with your gob?' he asked.

'This. I mean, look at it. I haven't even got a clean shirt to put on me. He didn't bother his arse collecting the laundry again. Useless bastard. I tell you, if he doesn't shape up soon, I'm out of here. I mean it, I'm after new lodgings. Jaysus, I hate this. It's like Chinese torture putting on dirty clothes.'

'It's dark blue – who's going to notice?'

'I am.'

Harry peered through the mirror at him. 'Ah, come on, you're fuckin' gorgeous. Hurry yourself on – we've still to pick up the other pair.'

George pulled an envelope out from under the mattress, slipped the driver's permit out and put it into his inside pocket.

Harry followed him down the stairs.

'Jaysus, that's some sorry sight,' he began.

'What is?'

'Enzo's air-raid shelter.'

'What's wrong with it?'

'It's near ready to collapse, so it is, and it's that full of junk. It'll not hold up against a good sneeze, never mind an air raid.'

'You better not let him know you were in there.'

'Why not?'

'I don't know, he has a thing about it.'

'Right so. Here, Georgie?'

'What?'

'You didn't manage the petrol by any chance?'

'In the boot.'

'I don't suppose you got me sister's hair grips – don't tell me you got hair grips for her.'

'In the cubbyhole, along with your oul'one's sugar.'

'Me ma's sugar? Christ, but you're a right twister, you. How do you manage it at all?'

'Wouldn't you love to know?'

'Aye, I would surely,' Harry agreed.

He drove down towards Peter's Hill to pick up Kelly and Boyce. Harry beside him, the paper open on his lap, rattled off runners and riders. But his mind wasn't on the job: the traffic, dawdling along, was making him sleepy, and Harry's sing-along voice was beginning to get on his wick. The shabby shops on the Shankill Road fell over each other down towards the city; hard-hatted proprietors loitered outside, waiting for any bit of custom. The first man busied himself by adjusting second-hand goods, stretching up to them with a cautious hand as if he was dressing a Christmas tree. Lamps; pisspots; the snouts of gas masks; a swallowtail coat that swayed to his touch. The man at the next shop hawed at bits of fruit, then gave them a rub across his chest before putting them back on the barrow. The last man didn't even bother to look busy: he just stood and peered wistfully up the road, raising his hat when a prospect came into sight, lowering it again when the prospect passed by. George studied each man as the car edged slowly by.

But it was the last man that held his interest. Through the

wing mirror, he kept his eye on him, recognising something in his face. He knew then he wouldn't win a tosser at Bangor today. What's more, he knew why. It was the same reason he hadn't won last night; the same reason he'd been losing steadily for the last couple of weeks – it was a simple matter of desperation. He had to win today; needed it too badly. And the obligation was sticking in his craw. Sticking there like a lump of unchewed meat.

He thought about pulling over; getting out of the car and walking back to his digs. Walking back with his money still in his pocket, keeping it there until he felt the familiar gush in his veins telling him he was ready to bet again. If he could manage not to have a bet for a week or two, there would be no need to see the Fink today. What the Fink was holding for him would be as good as money in the bank: plenty to see him through a fortnight in Dublin. In the meantime, he could use his wages to pay off his debts. Just a week or two – what could be easier than that?

The car stalled behind a bus and he switched the engine off, ready to tell Harry he'd changed his mind – that he wouldn't be going to Bangor. But as soon as he saw the bus shudder again, he found himself restarting the engine, preparing himself to move when it did, to follow along in its shadow. It was as if the bus and the car were connected by a tow rope. As if it would be useless to try to resist such a pull.

He turned his head towards the butcher's shop on the corner – the only busy shop on the row. The shadow of the butcher and his boys shifted smartly from meat hooks to counter. Across the window panes, large white words bragged about the cheapest cuts of meat:

Pig's Feet and Pig's Cheek. Corned Neck and Corned Knees. Choicest and Best – Our Meat Can't Be Beat.

Confidence, that's what he was lacking. He straightened himself up, shrugging his shoulders. Confidence, that's what he'd have to regain.

Through the windscreen, the city took shape and passed him by in rectangular slaps of brick and glass. He pushed his way out of Donegall Place into the square, through army trucks and city trams. And bicycles, bicycles, hundreds of bicycles. Policemen and old men, women with shopping bags swinging from handlebars, others well-heeled in suits and hats, leather handbags and gas-mask boxes bumping off knees as they came up on the rotation. Hump-backed and straight-backed, they lined each side of the car. Wheel rims and ankles, turning and rising, and arses falling over saddles slid nimbly by. Everything seemed too big to his eye. Everything seemed to be moving faster than the car. The sunlight spat in his face; his head was beginning to pinch. And Harry's voice sang on and on.

He turned to the right, where the traffic narrowed suddenly to make way for the squat, red block of an air-raid shelter, and he lost his bearings for a moment. Were they still on Donegall Square? He leaned forward, looking up over the shelter to identify the upper halves of buildings. The peak and pillars of the Methodist church; the large initials of the YWCA a bit further down. Ferguson's showrooms stuck in the middle: rows of waxed cars hidden from sight. They were on the east side of the square. And uniforms everywhere; every shade and size; women and men in all shapes of khaki. The city was a tangled ragbag of khaki.

He turned to Harry. 'We'll be all day trying to plough through this lot. Jaysus, will you look at them. Where do they think they're going?'

Harry muttered, 'Ach, they'll be out lookin' for that war they've been promised. All dressed up and nowhere to go.'

He leaned his head closer. 'What? What did you say?'
'I said they'll be . . . George!'

A paper boy jumped up onto the runner of the car and waved a newspaper in front of him, and from behind the shelter a cyclist made a sudden swerve. He pounced, his hand hitting a long snort out of the steering wheel, his foot slapping a jolt out of the brakes. An English accent swore through the window at him. Harry rolled down his window and swore back, sticking his head out and carrying on swearing long after the cyclist had been grabbed into the traffic.

He pushed his hat back into position. 'Leave it, Harry, it was my fault,' he said.

'So? Who the fuck does he think he is?'

'Leave it, I said.'

Shaftesbury Square passed by without him noticing. Botanic Avenue came next. Billboard signs stepped out to contradict each other: 'Matinée Dance. Dancing Can Help. Keep Smiling. Don't Be Dull.' Another one warned, 'Mind Who You Speak To – Careless Talk Costs Lives.'

The traffic thinning out, the car picked up speed and the streets took on a smoother aspect. Shop entrances blocked by endless queues, leaking into each other, shop after shop. Hands clutching ration cards; sulky faces straining for the top of the queue. Side streets slipped by; sandbags and sandstone; the stubs of railings that had been ripped out and sent away to make bullets. Grabbed up by that war they'd been promised, like it had grabbed everything else – out of the shops, out of flower beds – vegetables growing in gardens instead of grass. Even the lawns of Queen's had been taken, carved up into allotments; the first feeble growth sprigged over humps of turned earth.

'Listen, George, you know I was sayin' how I cleaned up last week?'

'Yeah.'

'Well, you know yourself – a week's a long time . . . '

George drew the steering wheel through his fingers and took the corner for Stranmillis Gardens. 'You'll have to wait till I see the Fink.'

'Oh?'

'Talk to me then – I won't see you stuck.'

'I know you'll not, Georgie. I know that.'

George leaned back in the seat and put his hand in his pocket. He hesitated for a moment, then, pulling out two notes, passed them across to Harry.

'In the meantime, see what you can do with that.'

Harry fingered the notes. 'Are you sure you'll not be leaving yourself short?'

'It won't make any difference, Harry. Not one little jot.'

'I'll give it to you later,' Harry muttered, two blobs of red occurring on his cheeks.

He pulled to the kerb and sounded the horn.

The back seat darkened with Boyce and Kelly.

'So you're joining us today, Georgie boy?' Boyce said, settling himself in.

'Just for a couple of hours.'

'Aye, well now, I've heard that one before. So tell us, what do you think?'

'What do you think yourself?'

'Ach, I don't know, I can't make up me mind between . . . '

Kelly came up from the back seat, his small face slotting in between Harry and George. 'Never mind all that,' he said. 'Would you mind tellin' me somethin' else?'

'What?'

'What the hell is this geegaw supposed to be?' he asked, dangling something in front of George.

George glanced at it. 'I don't know – it was on the floor in the back. Is it not yours, Harry?'

'Mine? What would I be doing with that papist badge?'

'I thought it might be someone you had in the back.'

'He'd have more respect for his prick, would Harry,' Kelly declared.

'Yeah, I'm sure he would.'

'I might,' Harry said. 'Here, give it here. Come on, give me the fuckin' thing.'

He snatched the cord from Kelly's hand and rolled down the window. The scapular rubbed against the glass for a second and then slowly dropped back on the wind.

Kelly continued, 'Are you sure, nay, it wouldn't have been some wee Southern girl you were havin' a go at last weekend, eh, Georgie Porgie? Some wee Taig? I'd say, now, they'd be spicy enough, once you got them in gear. I'd say they'd be as good as the English girls. Oh, them English ones is as fast as a train, but the Romans might present more of a challenge. What do you say, Georgie?'

He could smell Kelly's face drawing nearer, feel his finger prodding his shoulder. He shrugged it off. 'I'm warning you, Kelly.'

'Oh nay, don't be like that. Of course you'll not have need for them Romans no more, and you on a promise.'

'Were you not told to shut your bake, Kelly?' Harry said.

'Sure isn't that why he got engaged, Harry? Of course it is. Oh it's a great man for the legs, the engagement ring. Wasn't I engaged myself five or six times. Amn't I right, Georgie – doesn't it do the trick?'

George elbowed him out of the way. 'Get back in there, you little bollix, or I'll fuck you out of the car.'

'Christ, what's got into him? I was only greasin' him up. Christ.'

Boyce spoke quietly into his other ear. 'You know what's up with you, Georgie? You're out of sorts, so y'are, on account of there been no racing, like. Oh aye, I'm tellin' you, you haven't been yourself – not since the standstill – and that's a fact. And I tell you something else, the lack of racing's left a gap in your head – you're taking things too seriously, son. Now you and I both know Kelly here was only greasin' you up. So why don't we just all forget about it nay and not let it spoil our day?' He lifted his voice then. 'So is it true you'll be leaving us?'

George didn't answer.

'I say, is it true . . . '

'He'll only be gone a wee while,' Harry said.

'When will you be coming back?'

'He'll be back the week after Easter.'

'What are we supposed to do for transport?' Kelly whined.

'He's leaving the car with me.'

'He is like fuck,' Boyce said. 'Sure how's he goin' to manage without a car? That's fella's forgot how to use his legs this long time.'

'His uncle has a garage – he can borrow a car.'

Kelly leaned over the seat. 'Where are you away to? Where's he away to, Harry?'

'Dublin.'

'For the whole fortnight? What the fuck do you want to do that for? What the fuck does he want to do that for, Harry?'

'His brother's getting hitched.'

'Christ on a bicycle, it must be a contagion. If I was you, I wouldn't be so keen to sit in the front, Harry.'

Boyce and Kelly chuckled quietly for a moment, then each man returned to his own thoughts, in his own corner of the car. And the rest of the journey was passed in silence.

When he got back to the shop, the floor had been cleaned and spread with new sawdust. The familiar sounds of Enzo came out from the back kitchen: the hum of an aria, the scratch of a knife, the plop of water each time a potato dropped in. He ducked into the beads.

'Ah, Giorgio.'

'Ah, Enzio.'

Enzo turned to him after a moment, a shy little grin on his face. 'Where were you?'

'I went to Bangor.'

'Back so soon?'

'I left early.'

'You win lots a money?'

'No.'

Enzo turned away again. 'Listen, Giorgio, about this morning. I'm so sorry. I collect your suit – shirts too. Everything nice and fresh in your room. New sheets on the bed too; everything nice . . . I am sorry.'

'So you said.'

'Look, I make it up to you. You bring the boys over for a game, I close up early, cook something nice. Eh, Giorgio? Before you go to Dublin – next Friday, is it?'

'I might wait till Easter Monday. He's not getting married till the Tuesday, and as long as I'm there in time for the wedding . . . '

'No money, heh?'

George said nothing.

'Why you buy a ring last week, if you broke? I don't understand.'

'I wasn't broke last week.'

'Always the same with you: up, down, up, down. How you gonna get married with no money?'

'When it's time to get married I'll have the money. It's tonight I'm worried about.'

'You want money? I give you money. I give you ten, twelve . . . how many pounds?'

'Ten. I'll give it back tomorrow.'

'Tomorrow? You win it back tonight, I suppose?'

'Look, I'll have it back to you tonight, one way or the other.'

'You lose it tonight, that's what you do.'

George looked away back into the shop. 'You've cleaned the place up, I see?'

'Sure I cleaned up. I always clean up.'

'That whiskey's going to kill you one of these days.'

'Me? Whiskey kill me?' Enzo laughed, slapping his hand off his chest. 'Look at me. I'm strong. You say so yourself – you say I'm like a middleweight. A Golden . . . A Golden . . . What was it again?'

'A Golden Gloves fighter.'

'Yes, yes. Remember? Remember the day we take them on? You and me, Giorgio, outside the shop? Boom, boom, boom . . . those Tommy bastards. Last time they call me Mussolini. Last time they call me anything.' He put down his fists and looked up at George, smiling.

George looked back at him. 'Next time I find you in that state, Enzo, I'm going to leave you in it.'

'Ah, you fuck off,' Enzo said, dropping the smile.

George waited for a minute. 'Are you going to lend me the tenner or not?'

'Ah, you fuck off. I give you nothing.'

'Suit yourself.' George stepped out of the shop and up the stairs.

By the time he came back down, Enzo was half-cut again: a slight slur to his movements, his eyes frantic and hard, his lips busy as if he was revising or maybe rehearsing some sort of an internal row.

'You better lay off that stuff,' George said to him, 'it's nearly time to open the shop.'

'You think I care? This country. I hate this fucking country. They don't want my wife, they don't want my children. They want my chips OK. Fuck them.'

'This country's done you all right.'

'They throw stones at me.'

'They don't throw stones at you.'

'In 1932, stones.'

'Ah for Christ sake, that was nearly ten years ago.'

'So that make it all right? They throw stones. In Victoria Station. Why? Because I want to go to Dublin for the Eucharistic Congress. Is this such a crime? Stones they threw. At women, at children. They take the good away from the day. Now they take my wife. Aliens – my children. My children. You know what I hope? I hope Hitler come and bomb the fuckers all. I hope he . . . '

'If they hear you talking that way, they'll send you back next. It's posted up all over town: Careless talk, Enzo. Careless talk.'

'After the war they be dead.'

'They won't be dead.'

'You read the paper? No . . . only the racing page. I read the paper; I read all the pages. You know what I read tonight? In Italy they call up boys of fourteen for service. Boys of fouteen. You know how old my son is? He is fourteen years old last week. My boy, a soldier . . . '

'I didn't realise.'

'A soldier.'

Enzo pressed his hands on the side of the table and lowered his head. He sucked in a couple of breaths and then looked up.

'OK, Giorgio, no more careless talk. So, you want to tell me why you were in my shelter?'

'I wasn't.'

'Somebody was. I know my shelter; I know when somebody was in there. I go out there when you were sleeping and I know. I know.'

'Well it wasn't me.'

'You didn't go out there?'

'No, I told you.'

'How these get on the line?' he asked, pulling George's overalls up off the floor and waving them in the air. 'Huh? You want to tell me?'

'What? They were hung out there to dry because I had to use them for a towel, because there was no fuckin' towel in the jacks, all right?'

'Well, somebody was in my . . . '

'Ah, you're talking through your arse. Look, I'm going to phone Mona.'

'You're going to phone Mona. And what are you going to say? Sorry, my darling, can't come for the holiday, I lose all my wages, it fell out my pocket. Does she know? Does she know the man she will marry? No, I don't think so. Does she know he will spend his whole life working for money that he cannot wait for one minute to throw away?'

'You think I'd be better spending it on drink, then? Like you?'

'I pay for my own drink. I don't ask you to pay for it. No matter how much I spend on whiskey, I never work all my week to throw every penny off on one lousy card game.'

'And no matter how much I lose, I never lie on the floor like a fuckin' dog and expect other people to drag me up the stairs.'

Enzo pushed past George into the shop. The grease was beginning to shift in the fryer. He threw a crust in and then, lowering his head slightly, listened to it whisper around the bread before raising the heat. 'I don't ask you. And here's something else I don't ask you: I don't ask you to go into my shelter.'

'How many time do I have to tell you? I wasn't near your fuckin' shelter.'

'Why can you not just tell the truth, heh? You a liar now as well as a loser? A no-good . . . '

'You better watch it, Enzo. If you weren't such a drunken slob, I swear to Jaysus I'd . . . '

'What you do? What you do? Hit me? Oh, you won't hit me, George. You know why? Because you're afraid if you hit me, I don't give you the money.'

'I don't want your fuckin' money. You can stick it. And as for that shed you call a shelter . . . Harry was the one who went into it, not me.'

'Harry?'

Enzo reached out and grabbed him by the arm.

'Harry? In my shelter? You let that bastard into my shelter? That thief?'

'You're not too worried when he's getting your whiskey for you. I don't hear you asking any questions then.'

'He is a thief.'

'Did he take anything? Did he?'

'No. Not this time he didn't.'

'Let go of me.'

'You ever let that thief . . . '

'Let go, I said. Get out of my fuckin' way.'

Enzo's face was up against his now; whiskey and sweat. Enzo's big face was making him sick. All he wanted was to get rid of that face, to get his own breath back and get out of the shop; feel some clean air around him; some space. He spread out his hand, brought it up to the face and gave it a shove. The face fell away, taking Enzo with it. George reached out to bring him back. But it was too late. Enzo was beyond his reach. George closed his eyes then, but they had already snatched up the picture. Of Enzo falling against the fryer, his fist out in front to break the fall. Enzo's shocked eyes; his scream. His fist.

And the grease exploding around it, rushing and ranting as if piranha fish had been waiting below.

III

The queue was double-banked outside the shop when he got back from the hospital. He parked on the corner and lit a cigarette, throwing a nod over to Bertie Rice in the doorway of his pub. Bertie came over, hoisted his elbow on the roof of the car and, peering down through its triangular frame, waited for the window to roll down.

'I heard the news about Enzo,' he said. 'Is he bad?'

'It's his hand. He'll be all right, but they're keeping him in for a few days.'

'Dear sake. Here, if I was you, I'd go round the back way. That's a right-lookin' shower down there. Look at them: they could turn nasty, so they could. I wouldn't want to be facin' them, anyway. How did the accident happen?'

'He was drunk – slipped and fell, his hand ended up in the grease.'

'Drunk? Well, seeing as how it wasn't in my pub he got drunk, I'm afraid my sympathy can only be minimal. It's a bad idea, that drinking on your own – I'm tired tellin' him. No joy in it at all. And at least when you're in company, if anything happens can't you always blame the other fella?'

George rolled the window back up and got out of the car. 'I'd no idea he was doing so well.'

'Oh aye, that there is a wee gold mine – if only he knew it. I tell you now not one word of a lie, but there are times when I do envy Enzo, so I do.'

'You're a publican, Bertie.'

'Ach, sure, what does that mean any more? You'd want to be away in the head to be a publican these days.'

'You're still raking in the money.'

'Oh aye, it's all pints of Double and small ones since the war, but it's them that's controllin' me, Georgie, instead of the other way round.'

'How do you make that out?'

'On account of nobody needin' the slate any more – they can drink anywhere takes their fancy. And don't they let me know it. See Enzo, he only has to tolerate a customer for as long as it takes to shake up a few chips, and then he's away up the road with himself and his problems. But see me, I have to be nice to bastards I wouldn't have let over the door two years ago – I have to be all about them. Poverty doesn't just keep a customer loyal, you know, it keeps him well-behaved too. Aye, there's no man more civil than the man under a compliment. That lot in there's like a pack of wild animals; aye, and I'm the zookeeper. You know simple-minded Caffrey? Well the boys in here do bunch up together of an evening to send him down for a wee bit of sustenance to keep the session alive. Christ, they'll be steaming when he comes back empty-handed. And I've nawthin' to detain them but a few slices of raw, salted tripe. I mind the time when tripe served in the pub was a guarantee you could hold on to the customers for the rest of the evening. But sure now that everyone's working, it's fish suppers or go stick it up your jersey.'

'As a matter of interest, how many fish suppers was Caffrey sent for?'

'I suppose a dozen, maybe more. And that'll only be the first batch. As soon as the smell of them takes a turn about the house, they'll all have the goo and Caffrey'll be run down again on the promise of a couple of pints. Well, he'll not be doin' much drinkin' this night, and that's a fact.'

George stood out in the centre of the road doing a quick calculation of heads. 'There must be over thirty people in that queue.'

'At the least of it,' Bertie agreed. 'And sure half of them's gone away home or away up to Fusco's.'

'Fusco's?'

'Aye. Or maybe Forgione's either. It's not that far, you know. Enzo'd want to watch himself, so he would, or he'll be comin' back till an empty shop.'

'Do you think so?'

'I know so. Here, you're not going to chance it, surely?'

'Ah, what have I got to lose?'

'Your balls, for a start.'

George laughed and continued on towards the shop.

He took the key out of his pocket and made for the door, the squall of complaints squeezing against his head as he pushed his way through. He had to give the door a good shove behind him to get it to shut properly and could almost feel the glass pulsate into his back when he leaned against it, closing his eyes. Thirty or so people. Most of them would want more than one order: women on their way home from work; runner boys that had been sent down from the docks, the mills or the munition factories. Caffrey and his dozen fish suppers, not to mention all the other Caffreys from every pub in the area. All that cash going down the Swanee. A tragedy, that's what it was. He took a deep breath and opened the door again.

A rubbery-faced oul'one was the first to pounce. 'Are you openin', or what?' she barked up at him.

'Hold on there a minute, will you, missus?'

'Don't you missus me . . . I just want you to tell me nay, are you opening this night or are you not?'

'I've got a family needs feeding,' another one wailed from the rear of the crowd.

'Well that's hardly my fault, is it?'

'You cheeky bugger,' rubbery-face said, shoving herself forward.

'Look, Enzo isn't well.'

'You mean he's drunk again. He means he's drunk again.'

'No, I don't mean he's drunk again. He's had an accident, if you must know. He's in hospital.'

'What sort of accident?'

'He hurt his hand. They're keeping him in for a few days.'

'For a hurted hand? Go away out of that.'

'They have to operate.'

'Well that's not much good to me, is it? I've a husband at home waitin' till his tea. We'll take our business elsewhere, so we will. Youse are not the only chip shop in the city, in case youse didn't notice.'

'Just wait, will you? Wait one minute. I'll see what I can do.'

George looked over her head. There were two boys sitting on the kerb pitching pebbles. 'Here, you two,' he called.

'Who, mister, us?'

'Come in here a minute.'

'Here, where do you think you're goin' with my sons?' rubbery-face demanded.

'I'll have them back to you in a minute, missus,' he assured her, while the two boys ducked under his arm and into the shop.

They gaped up at George. 'You know this area well?' he asked.

'Aye, we live just round the corner.'

'Do you want to earn a few bob?'

They looked at each other.

George continued. 'Can you write?'

'Do you mean like compositions?'

'No. Addresses, names – that sort of thing.'

'I suppose . . . '

'Right, hold on a minute.'

He pulled a notebook out of his pocket and tore it in half, then produced two pencils. 'Here, you'll need these. Go on, take them – they won't bite. Now I want you to listen carefully. Go out there to the queue and go to the women first: take their order and their addresses. Tell them to go home and put the kettle on, butter the bread and put their feet up – you'll deliver the order in half an hour. All right?'

'Thon women?' the older boy asked, his eyes bulging out at the prospect.

'If they give you any trouble, just call me out – but be sure to tell your ma I'm paying you. Do you hear me now? And tell her before you do anything else.'

'Aye.'

'Then find the runner boys and take their list off them; tell them you'll deliver the order as soon as you can. But whatever you do, don't get them mixed up – make sure you write on top of each list exactly where the order is to go. If it's the dockyard – which part of the dockyard. Or if it's the mill, find out if it's the spinning room or wherever, right? Do either of you have such a thing as a bike?'

'No. Our da has one, though.'

'We better leave your da out of it. Do you know Rice's pub at the end of the road?'

'Aye?'

'Go in and ask for Bertie. Tell him George – that's me, by the way.'

'Aye, we know. You're Georgie. From the South. The man with the car. Sure anybody knows who you are.'

'Do they now? Right, I want you to ask Bertie if I can borrow back the bike I gave him a couple of years ago. Then tell him you'll drop back in an hour to see if he has any orders.'

'Which of us'll be riding the bike, mister?'

'You can take turns. Now be quick, but be careful – no mistakes, mind – and when you come back in, knock at the door like this . . . ' He put his knuckles to the counter: rat, tat, rat tat tat. 'Let me hear you now.'

The boys came to the counter: rat, tat, rat tat tat.

'Good. Now, the quicker you are, the more money you get. And I'll throw in a fish supper at the end of the night, all right?'

The smaller boy raised his hand. 'Mister? I have a question.'

'Go ahead.'

'Would it be all right if I had a pasty instead of a fish – fish turns me queer spotty.'

'You can have *two* if you do a good job, how about that?'

The older boy turned a shocked face up to George. 'It does not turn him queer spotty – he's lyin', so he is. He just doesn't like the taste of fish.'

'Well he can still have two pasties, and I tell you what – you can have two fish.'

The older boy raised his hand then.

'What?'

'I don't really like fish that much neither.'

'You'd prefer a pasty?'

'Aye. Can I have two, like him?'

'Yes, yes, yes. You can have half a dozen for all I care. Now go on, get moving before I change my mind.'

The boys looked at George, then at each other, then down at

the pads and pencils, then back up at George again.

'Stickin' out,' the younger one yelped, and they both made a run for the door.

He could hear the babble outside as the crowd got used to the idea. Going into the kitchen to study the layout, he tried to establish the sequence of events in his head, first following the progress of the spud from dirty brown lump to long, waxy chip. There was a sack – almost empty, he noted – then a basin with ones that were already peeled. Next bare, chipped ones, steeped in water, ready to be cooked. There was fish cleaned and cut in squares piled on a plate, and the bucket of batter with a few more inside already coated. Back outside there was a basket of pasties that just needed reheating, and all along the worktop, salt, vinegar and sheets of newspapers threaded through twine, standing by and ready for the off. He played around with the frier for a minute, familiarising himself with its ways (and dismissing the notion that those speckles floating on the grease were in any way related to the fried skin of Enzo's hand). Then he pushed the buttons down on the till, catching the drawer when it sprang out and checking the float before pencilling the amount on the wall above. Everything seemed to be in order. A bit short on spuds, though. So where did Enzo keep the spuds?

Through the cupboards and behind the door, out to the hallway and under the stairs – no spuds. Out to the yard; boxes and bags of rubbish climbing the walls; a clothes line holding a solitary dishcloth that had been there as long as he had; a clothes mangler, its disused rollers clamped together like a pair of tight lips; a drum of paraffin; a tub of lard. And over to the lee side, Enzo's home-made air-raid shelter.

He took the flash lamp out from under the sink and, coming back across the yard, followed the cone of light through, turning it over the insides, stalling it when something particular caught his eye. In one corner, a rusty tricycle up on its saddle; behind it a large crate of cloth-covered shapes: whiskey bottles, old gramophone records and picture frames of various sizes. He pulled the largest frame out and parted the cloth a little way, and the big, bald face of Benito Mussolini glared out at him. He thought of Enzo's outrage any time Il Duce was mentioned and the brawl that night with the Tommies as a result of what had really only been a few childish jokes. Then he laughed out loud. 'You're some chancer, Enzo,' he said, edging the picture back down and resuming his search for the spuds.

A two-planked bench was fixed to one wall; tinned foodstuffs, rusty at the ridges, stacked neatly below. Higher up on the wall, corner to corner, was a long shelf holding a box of damp candles, a couple of Italian books, a sewing basket that had belonged to the signora and a large, glass-eyed doll, with a limb at every corner, that had belonged to little Francesca. Hooked out of a lathe was a tilly lamp and five gas masks: two adult-size and three smaller. Back beside him on the ground was a box of old toys and a suitcase spilling over with the once-bright clothes of women and children; the clothes were dull as rags now after soaking up the dust of a year in the dark.

He sat down on the bench, taking the light around again, tipping it off all the little sundries he could recognise as having once belonged to the rooms of the house. Enzo must have transported all traces of his family to the shelter as soon as they had been deported. Couldn't bear to look at them, probably – or was it the thought of anyone else looking at them that had made him hide them away? He stayed for a minute thinking about Enzo, picturing him sitting here on the bench, the whiskey bottle by his side, his hands reaching out to touch some memento – the hem of his wife's dress or some old toy that had belonged to one of his kids. The feel of his face felt suddenly fresh against his hand. He rubbed his palm into his leg a few times; the sting increased and then suddenly diminished. He rose to his feet.

'Ah, fuck it,' he said to himself. 'It was an accident. The stupid bastard. It was an accident, that's all.'

He spotted the potatoes then – a half-bag full, flopped up against the back wall – and, lifting the tricycle out of the way, stretched his arm out and pulled it over. It dragged a dull sound out of the ground and then, as if the ground had switched texture, suddenly changed its tune. George lifted the sack and bent down to have a feel: something hard down there. He brushed a part of the clay away and held the flashlight down on it. It looked like a large tin box that had been sunk like a coffin into the ground. He swept the remains of the clay away and lifted the box. Weighing the lock in his hand for a moment, he considered Enzo's outburst earlier on. There were all sorts of possible explanations for it; all sorts of things he wouldn't have wanted Harry to see – the picture of Il Duce; his whiskey stash; the possessions of his absent family. Or was it this box? Something in this box? He decided the box was the most likely explanation. Then, letting it slip back down to its place, he swept the clay back over with the side of his foot, lugged the sack over his shoulder and stooped back out of the shelter.

With a bucket of batter in one hand and a bucket of cut chips in the other, he came into the shop. Grease first. He turned the heat on full, then, plunging his hands into the bucket of chips, strained the water through his fingers. He tried to remember which way Enzo worked. All the times he had stood and watched . . . but it had been Enzo's speed and his chatter that had kept him amused, not his method. What was his method? What did he do first? Yes, that's right – he dried them. With what, though? He looked down at the wet chips, pissing onto his shoes and dribbling dark splashes along the legs of his trousers. He stretched out his arms and took a little hop back. Then Enzo's apron hanging on the back of the door caught his eye. He tugged it down and laid it flat. Folding it over to make a nest, he patted and rubbed, turning his face away from the musty whack of raw chips blending into Enzo's stains.

When the rat, tat, rat tat tat hit the door, he opened it and the two boys came panting in.

'Right,' he said, 'here goes – now read them out to me.'

'Mrs McCloy wants four ones and a fish.'

A mountain of brown chips sat in the warmer. George pulled one out, blew on it and tasted it. 'What's wrong with this?' he said, offering it to one of the boys.

The boy opened his mouth like a chick and sucked the chip in. 'It's a wee bit hard,' he apologised, 'in the middle like. But it looks very nice.'

The other boy tugged at his sleeve. 'That don' matter. I'll give them to my Aunt May for me Uncle Sam's tea. He's always drunk, he won't know the differ.'

'Great. How many does Aunt May want?'

'Only a one and one.'

'Well that's not much use to us, is it?'

George looked back at the mountain. 'Jaysus, what's wrong with them?'

'Did you do them twice?' the smaller boy squeaked.

His older brother reddened. 'Don't talk stupid. Don't mind him, mister, he always talks stupid.'

'I don't. I seen him. He always does them twice.'

'What would he do that for, you daft wee lig?'

'Hold on,' George said, 'he's right. He does do them twice. He *blanches* them first and then cooks them later. Fuck it.'

'Aye, fuck it.'

'Can you not just throw them back in?'

'If I put them back in now, they'll burn.'

'Aye, they will. They'll burn if he throws them back in.'

He scooped the chips back into the cage and handed it to the small boy. 'Here, dump these out in the yard. Run for it. And you . . . what's your name?'

'Alec. The other one – me wee brother – he's called Hammie.'

'Pass me over that bucket, Alec. We're starting again.'

He rubbed the wet apron over another load of chips and lowered them down into the fryer. The grease spat and snarled out and the boys jumped aside, screeching like seagulls, their arms shooting up to cover their faces.

'Jaysus,' he said, 'you'd need welder's gear for this job.'

The two boys laughed behind him.

'Did you get the bike?'

'Aye, it's out the lane.'

'Good, we'll do the dockyard next. When you're passing Rice's again, you better ask Bertie would he have a couple of towels.'

'Towels? What do we want them for?'

'To dry the chips, Hammie, otherwise your face will be one big blister from ear to ear. This thing here couldn't dry sand.'

He threw Enzo's apron to the floor and kicked it under the beads out to the kitchen.

After he had each bundle made up, he wrote the amount to be

charged on the side of the newspaper and stuffed them up their jumpers to keep them warm. 'Now run for it,' he warned them. 'Out the back way. Will you remember that? You go out the back way but come in the front.'

'Right.'

'Here, come back a minute – there's one other thing.'

'Aye?'

'Cash only. Bring back the chips if they refuse to pay.'

'Even me ma?'

'Especially your ma.'

By the time he had sent the last of the deliveries off and was ready to open the door to the general public, it was nearly half past nine. An air-raid warden was the first to come in – but he only came to check on the blackout regulations. The warden gave him a lecture on his careless ways and then George gave him a free supper. After that the warden made the blackout himself, going upstairs to hunt down every chink of light and even filling up the bath in case of emergencies – as if Enzo had ever bothered his arse with the like of that. A runner boy came in from the yard next, and it was only when George spotted him that he remembered he was supposed to be in work. Another free supper and the boy agreed to carry a message up to Big Sam to tell him he'd be along as soon as he shut up shop. Other than these two complimentary backhanders, it was all money in the till.

When the boys had finished their rounds, he set them to peeling and chipping potatoes. The three of them worked well together, and an hour or so later George heard himself whistle. He felt he had the hang of it by now: as far as the customer's eye could see, anyway – down on the ground it was another matter. His feet stuck to the grease on the floor or slipped on the dollops of batter that had dropped off each piece of fish (that was, unless his shirt hadn't first broken their fall). But his method was there in any case. He was working with speed: sprinkling the vinegar and shooting the salt, taking the orders and answering the wisecracks all at the same time. He watched his hands gain confidence and move speedily about, only hesitating, now and then, to wipe the sweat from his forehead. And that was only because it was dripping down onto the chips and he was afraid it might put the punters off. Other than that, he never took his eyes off the job, unless it was to watch the pile of money in the till grow bigger.

Alec was getting anxious, his little face popping out now and then through the beads.

'Have you a problem, Alec?' he asked him eventually.

'Them spuds is all peeled, mister,' Alec whispered. 'There's not a one of them left. What are we supposed to do nay?'

George took a quick look around. Only two bits of fish left, enough chips to make up a couple of bags and enough pasties to keep his promise to the boys.

'Ah, we've done enough. We'll close up shortly when we've got rid of this batch. I've got to go to work, anyway.'

'Can I help you here?' Alec asked.

'Sure – here, shove a bit of salt onto these.'

Alec took the tin in both hands and shook them at the chips. He watched George wrap them and bang the change down on the counter. 'You're no mug when it comes to making them wrappings,' he said admiringly.

'Here, have a go.'

'Ah, can I? Thanks.'

But Alec's effort was a failure and the chips came spilling out of the side. 'Ah, fuck it,' he whinged. 'I can't make it work.'

'Don't worry,' George said, reshaping the bundle, 'it takes a while to get it.'

'Get what?'

'The knack.'

'Oh aye, the knack.'

The queue of drunkards was getting wittier. 'What type of fish you sell in there, Chico? You speaka the English? I said what class of a fish . . . ?'

Hammie darted out from the kitchen to jump to George's defence. 'He's not Eyetalian, he only looks Eyetalian, but he's from the South, so he is.'

'Oh is he nay? The South? What sort of fish you sell in here, Southern boy.'

'White fish, but it's all gone.'

'White fish? Are you sure, now, it wouldn't be yella like the rest of you boys down there?'

'No, the yellow fish is gone too.'

'Probably hiding under the bed with Dev.'

'Who's Dev?' Hammie asked.

'He's the wee girl that runs his country.'

'Do you want the chips or not?'

'Aye, go on.'

George shovelled the chips onto the newspaper. 'That'll be two bob,' he said.

'Two bob? Away with you. It was only a bob last night.'

'Well it's two bob now – take it or leave it.'

'I'll fuckin' well leave it – and you and all.'

George slid the sheet of paper down off the counter 'Sorry, folks, that's it, I'm afraid.'

A woman's voice came out from the back of the queue: 'If the gentleman isn't taking those, I will.'

He returned the chips to the counter. 'Alec?'

Alec stepped up.

'Look after these, will you? I better hide the rest of the grub or they'll be over the counter after it. And remember to tuck in the sides *before* you roll up the bundle.'

'Aye, I will. I'll remember.'

George turned around to the fryer and switched it off. Then he pulled the lid of the warmer down on the remaining pasties. He could hear the sound of the woman's heels clicking up the shop, and then he heard her voice again. 'Well hello, George,' it said. 'I see you've come up in the world.'

He turned back around, looked at the woman, nodded at her and then turned away again, switching the knob on the fryer back on, then off again, lifting the lid of the warmer back up, then down again. He came back to the counter and took the bundle out of Alec's hands, unwrapped it and wrapped it up again. But the bundle seemed unwilling to be shaped, as if it was a pup or a baby or some live thing in his hands.

'What's the matter with him?' Hammie whispered to his brother.

'Nawthin's the matter with him.'

'Look at that wrapper.'

'What about it?'

'It's even worse than the one you made. He musta lost the knack, so he must.'

'So what brings you around here?' George asked the woman, raising his voice to drown out the whispers behind him.

'I'm helping out in the canteen on the Newtownards Road.'

'Doin' what?'

'Same as you. Feeding hungry buggers.'

'This is not my line, actually – I'm only helping out.'

'Is that so?'

'My friend, he had an accident. He owns the shop. This your husband?' he asked, when a man in uniform stepped up beside her.

'No,' she smiled, 'he's somebody else's.'

The soldier grinned foolishly and pretended to clip the back of her head.

George held out his hand and she dropped two bob on it.

'See you around,' he said.

'Yeah, see you.'

Then he called her back. 'Here, miss, you forgot your change.'

She nursed the shilling in her hand for a moment and then closed her fingers over it. 'Thanks.'

'You're welcome.'

'Well, that bates all,' the drunk called out. 'That fuckin' bates all, I have to say. One bob for her, two bob for the rest of us. And no need neither to ask what *she's* got that we don't.'

George turned away and into the kitchen. The stubble of his chin sang out to him as he caught sight of it in Enzo's shaving mirror above the sink; his face as dirty and greasy as if he'd had it stuck up against an engine all day. He looked down at his clothes, flocked with batter and grease and all sorts of shite. Then he whipped Enzo's apron up off the floor and wiped the last of his sweat into it. Beatrix Bumbury. Beatrix fat-arsed Bumbury. He felt like sticking his head into the bucket of batter.

IV

Beatrix fat-arsed Bumbury. She left a thick silence behind her; a thick, awkward silence with him somewhere inside it, fuming away. The two boys, sensing it, kept their heads low. The only sound to come out of them was the chips churning around in their gobs: slowly, painfully almost – as if they were afraid to enjoy their supper, in case it might cause him offence. Over at the till he made his own sounds: the abrupt smack of his lips on the butt of his cigarette every few seconds; the impatient rattle of coins in his hands; the rustle of notes. The jot of pencil-lead against the wall when he made up the sums of the night's takings – a heftier amount than he had reckoned on, too, but it still couldn't manage to cheer him.

He hardly touched his own grub – it couldn't compete with the sour taste in his mouth. So he passed it to Alec to divide with his brother, and he did so in silence – no argument or fuss – chip after chip and by gouging apart an unfortunate pasty between a pair of dirty, wart-dotted fists.

They were quiet when he paid them, quiet when he told them to come back the following night. Only when he bolted the door behind them did they come back to life, their voices like twin engines, sparked into action and revved all the way up the street, tapering into a gradual silence.

He went upstairs to put on his overalls and get ready for work but found himself naked in the bathroom instead, climbing into the cold bath the air-raid warden had filled. He scrubbed the skin off himself, then had a shave, even though he knew it was pointless at this hour of the night with nowhere to go but the dockyard and no one to see him but other dirty, unshaven faces. His body was hopping from the cold, but he couldn't seem to feel it. All he could feel was the heat of rage at being caught that way, looking that way (the very fact that he was raging at all was making him worse). He told himself that it wasn't a question of his own personal pride – he'd always regarded pride as being a waste of time anyway – it was more to do with the pride of his family: that legacy passed down from the last generation, with her grandmother, Mrs Gunne, acting as its chief curator.

His father had once been her grandmother's lodger; his mother her grandmother's maid – which was where they had got together in the first place, under the roof of that big fat sow. That was a time when his father's family would have been considered socially superior to the likes of the Bumburys and Gunnes. But that was a long time ago now.

And if Mrs Gunne had holes in her memory, where chunks of the past slipped conveniently through, the one thing it had managed to hold on to was that his father was a lodger; his mother a maid. She made certain no one else would forget either, taking every opportunity to remind them of the facts. For a long, sweet while these opportunities had been few and far between – until his mother had agreed to act as their dressmaker. In doing so, she had handed her an open invitation to personally supervise the decline of his family. Every disaster and every downfall – Mrs Gunne had been there in the audience, clapping the hands off herself, with her little eye glinting. You could see it had rubbed off on her grandaughter too, who even as a child used to speak to his mother as if she was still a maid, calling her by her Christian name, standing in her kitchen openly gawking around. As if she was thinking to herself, 'So this is how such people live.' While in the background a lurking Herbert would add to the occasion by drooling over her every move, his tongue hanging out in perpetual adoration.

Beatrix fat-arsed Bumbury. Her name kept spitting out in his head. Except she wasn't that fat any more. She'd pared down considerably – not what you could call a slip of a thing, but certainly not the lump he'd known back in Dublin. He kept seeing the snide face on her behind the veil of her hat, delighted to catch him off guard; couldn't believe her luck, probably. Working in a canteen on the Newtownards Road with a fur coat on her back – he knew the type. Dolling themselves up to serve out slops and hand around hunks of grey bread. Working not because they had to but to give themselves something to do with their lives; something to talk about. Between hands of bridge or over gin slings before dinner, between appointments at the hairdressers, or dragging officers into bed while their husbands were overseas. He could just imagine the kind of shite they went on with; acute but witty observations on the working classes; rolled eyes of complaint while they discussed the shortages of sugar or, more importantly, of maids. Modest little smiles in exchange for mutual compliments. They were all the same: stupid bitches. It didn't surprise him at all that she'd turned out to be one of them. Hadn't she been bred to be one, right from the start? A stupid, big-headed bitch.

Always trying to make people ashamed, too, or at least ill at ease, even when she was a kid. Usually succeeded with Herbert. But never with him – not until now. Except maybe the day of his little brother's funeral. The day he had decided to lighten the atmosphere by taking her off in the barn. The duck-arse walk, the whingey voice, the way she clipped those sprung ringlets off her shoulder every time she decided she had something to say. He had a go at the grandmother and her parents too while he was at it; staged a little play about the lot of them; had everybody in fits. When the laughter suddenly cut, he knew he'd been caught red-handed. He turned around to see who it was, relieved that it wasn't one of the adults of course, but a bit embarrassed to see it was Beatrix herself standing there. But funny thing, it didn't seem to knock a feather out of her. Any other girl would have cried – or at least have had the decency to blush. She just smiled, gave the ringlets a clip and said, 'Oh, please do carry on . . . '

She made sure to rat all the same. Her voice all sugar and spice: 'Oh granny, George is such a good mimic. You should see him taking me off. He did it for all the boys: the way I walk, the way I talk. It was so funny . . . He made jokes about mama and papa in India too – even the tic on papa's face. It was a scream. He can do you too, down to a tee – it's the funniest thing I've ever seen.'

'Taking you off . . . ?' Mrs Gunne gasped. 'Taking me off . . . ?'

'*George?*' his mother's shocked voice lashed out like a slap in the face.

'Oh, that's all right,' Beatrix said, smiling, 'I don't mind. Don't be cross with him, Greta, he was only having a laugh.' Then she put her hand up to her mouth, as if she had suddenly realised something. 'But of course you're cross . . . I forgot – it's not right to laugh, is it? Not today, of all days. Oh, I shouldn't have said anything. Oh, I feel just awful now. Oh, poor, poor Danny . . . '

Poor, poor Danny – as if she ever gave a tuppenny shite.

He started to dry himself with a dirty shirt, then, remembering the towels Bertie Rice had lent him, tiptoed naked down to the shop. He found one of the towels still unused: a rough, dry joy that he hugged to his chest all the way back up the stairs. Then he dressed himself up in the clothes Enzo had collected for him: good suit, white shirt, collar and tie. He patted the knot into place, settled his watch over his wrist, pulled down his cuff, tucked a clean handkerchief into his pocket and eased his hat onto his head, shaping the brim. He stopped himself then and sat down on the bed. 'What the fuck am I doing? What the fuck am I at, dressing myself up at this hour of the night? For what? To impress *her*? A tramp like *her*?

Yet he felt a need to impress her just the same, even if it was in retrospect. Not the usual need a man might have to impress a woman; none of that mushy stuff. It was more a need to let her see how well he'd done for himself. Next time, he wanted her to find him getting out of a car, newly polished, in a suit, newly pressed. Maybe standing at the bar in one of the better hotels, throwing money around, in company that could easily include some of the more impressive punters: Doc Woodside, maybe (she'd be bound to know him), or that spiv professor from Queen's. He wanted her to see him not as the sap she had seen tonight but as the man he could sometimes be. It was an irrational need; a childish need. It was a need that would just have to pass.

He knocked the hat off his head and began to undress again.

Now in his work clothes, he locked up the shop and came out onto the street. Relying on instinct to guide him along, he moved through the darkness down towards the docks. The blacked-out streets always calmed him down. After a few turns, she began to fade and he slowed up his step.

A ball of flashlight wobbled around the far corner, leading a group home, like a mad little dog on a string; the sound of footsteps from invisible feet and laughter from invisible mouths. This was the sort of thing he liked about the blackout: obscurity, invisibility, the distorted view through the long lens. Shapes ducked in and out of an air-raid shelter: a courting couple first; a few seconds later a drunk staggered in, excused himself when he saw the shelter occupied and pissed against its outside wall instead, singing 'Mr Browne in London Town' at the top of a perfectly controlled voice. An old man stood at Hyland's bookmakers, squinting into the window at yesterday's results. George stepped up to join him. The light trembled in the old man's hand but his eye stayed steady on George as they fell into a discussion on racing in general and odds in particular. The old man knew his stuff all right, and by the time they had finished the conversation George felt himself at ease again. He took the man by the elbow and brought him to his door. Then he continued on towards the docks, still thinking about odds, long and short.

All the time he'd been in Belfast, he'd only come across her twice before – the first time she hadn't even been aware that he'd seen her. It was just before the dim-out when the lights were still on in Belfast city. He'd been waiting in a car for Big Sam, parked opposite Thornton's on High Street. The light from the shop filled out the window, and there she was, standing paying at the till. The light from the shop filled out the window and she filled out her skirt. He lowered himself down in the seat and observed her from under the brim of his hat. She couldn't seem to keep still, squirming away while she talked to the proprietor: raising one foot, then bringing it down, shifting about, her backside struggling against the skin of her skirt. He smoked a cigarette and said nothing to

Harry; then the door opened and she came out of the shop. She edged her collar upwards, looked at her watch and crossed over the road. Then Harry saw her and whistled low. 'Did you see that . . . ?' he had asked George.

'See what?'

'That doll just come out of Thornton's?'

George shook his head. 'I didn't notice anyone.'

'Well you must be fuckin' blind.'

The next time he saw her, she was coming out of the Ritz on the arm of a uniform. Not the one she was with tonight: this one had the red tabs of an officer. He couldn't pretend not to see her then – he nearly bumped into her. She looked at him, waiting for him to say something, but he just looked right through her as if she wasn't there. Then he stepped around her and went on his way.

That was only twice; three times, if you included tonight. The chances of running into her again in the foreseeable future were small enough not to concern him. Besides, even if he did come across her again – so what? He'd only got himself worked up over her in the first place because the lack of racing had left a gap in his head. (Wasn't that what Boyce had said? And he hadn't been too far off the mark, either – he was letting anything and anyone get to him these days.) And she had only managed to make him ashamed of himself because he was already ashamed. After the amount of money he'd been losing lately, why wouldn't he be? And maybe the incident with Enzo had something to do with it too. But his shame had nothing to do with her. Let her look down her nose at his family if it made her feel better. Fair enough: he'd always looked down on hers. That made them quits. What did quits equal? Nothing.

He stood at the mouth of Pollock Basin watching the water follow its course. Down through the channels, over the lough, and out to the Irish Sea, in deep, tired breaths it edged itself on – even in sleep, it knew which way to go. Behind him the black city had suppressed all light. But the water made its own light, took its own shadows – from jib cranes and warehouses and acres of long, flat-roofed sheds. This was the furniture of the dockside: if not exactly visible, then certainly identifiable, like a room at night with the curtains left open. Cleaver's theory on the 'blackout fiasco' came into his head. 'You can black out whatever you like,' Cleaver always said, 'but you can't black out water, any more than you can black out the whites of your eyes.'

He looked up at the sky, pushing his eye along its ribcage, until his eye began to water. And for a moment he thought he could see the silhouette of a fighter-plane prod through the pleat of the horizon and sail into view, a round-capped head pressed to the window, calmly looking down. On the shimmering mat of water, the dockside furniture, the lantern lights winking a pathway; the outline of himself, then, standing in the doorway, with one sharp red dot jerking at intervals up towards his mouth. He drew his hand behind his back and let the cigarette fall to the ground, then brought his eye back to the lighthouse.

Its lantern dropped squiggles onto the water: on, off, on again. He blinked with them. Each time he opened his eyes, he forced himself to see another marker of his future move a little further along the course out towards the open sea. On, off, on again.

He flicked through the certainties. The racing would come back to normal. His luck would pick up. Enzo would recover. The war would end. He would move back to Dublin; take over Sam's garage in Terenure. He would marry Mona. He would be safe.

He stopped blinking. Satisfied, now – all sorted out – he openly studied the sky and the sea. These points in his future were the only things remaining. Everything else had disappered. The fighter-pilot of his imagination; Crawford's forebodings; his own sense of vulnerability: all gone. They had taken their place along with the countless other irritations of the long day he had just put in. The feel of a clammy shirt on his back; the smell of Kelly when he had leaned over the seat to deliver a coarse remark; a spit of hot grease on his face. A snide, scarlet mouth behind the veil of a hat. Insignificant. Transient. Nothing.

V

It is very like Berlin in shape, viewed from up here, ten thousand metres above sea level. This is Nordirland. Isolated by the lights on the rest of the island, its very darkness makes it stand out: a white dog with a black ear cocked. And you just can't help noticing how like Berlin it is. But it is better to see it as England's last hiding place; Churchill's pantry in the back of his house. Tonight the moon is three-quarters-way lit, as is the island. So far it has been a fine night; a light, south-westerly wind. The cloud, which was a little worrying earlier on, has broken up most obligingly. And now the visibility is exceptionally good.

Down there is the city of Belfast. Compared to other English cities, this is – as the English phrase goes – the runt of the litter. There are jokes made about it all the time. There are cartoons drawn. The runt that works so hard for its master; a master that leaves it so shamefully exposed. It is one week since we first came here. One week, and what has been done? A few extra guns; a searchlight or two; a smokescreen which will only serve to emphasise the areas worth taking – these are the titbits its master has thrown. As you approach other English cities, you are always afraid: you can feel the fear strangling your throat from the inside out. But here there is little to fear. This is almost too easy.

Silence and darkness. This is what the pathfinder sees. There is silence now. You can see this silence when you look down. But the first pinprick of the siren will change all that. By then, the rest of the convoy will have arrived. They are noisy devils, once they get going: Junkers and Heinkels. Sometimes they could drive you crazy. Such ugly sounds they make. The sights they bring, in contrast, will be beautiful; also elegant. Like some women can be until they open their mouths to speak.

When they fall, they will fall like slow snow falls, the small white parachutes which always go first. Gliding down at different levels, popping open at intervals; so wonderful to watch through the window. The ones that follow are larger and green; a little more clumsy. They land; their green silk drops. You wait. You listen. Twenty seconds later a crimson cloud; then, at last, a landmine that cracks open the ground.

Silence and darkness. There is darkness now. This is the path-finder's task – to introduce light. To make magnesium flares rope luminous against the darkness. Then it will be as bright as a summer's afternoon.

When the city turns white, you can see everything so clearly in the cockpit. You can read the print on the side of the cigarette packet. You can read the target file above the controls: '*Das Flugzeugwerk – Short und Harland. Die Schiffswerft – Harland und Wolff. Das Gaswerk. Das Wasserwerk.*'

You can look down at these places then, and the view is spectacularly clean.

After the white, there will be the red, in bursts soft and sudden. Showing for a moment something of a city – steeple; rooftop; dome; a crucifix that reminds you it is Easter. There will be the sturdier glow of fires that are thriving, reflected on the water and curling around the bowl of the city. This is the Luftwaffe's task. To fill up this bowl: red; yellow; all shades of blue. The colours of a city returning to the ground.

When the dawn comes, we will give them back their silence. When the dawn comes, we will go home. We will have cocoa and fried eggs for *Frühstück*. We will sleep then for a very long time. When we rise, there will be no more noise. Only the crackle of newspaper pages as we read about this moonlit night in the *Volkischer Beobachter*. This black land that looks like Berlin from up here.

Somebody will say, 'I hear it is a beautiful country.'

Somebody else will reply, *'Das sind sie alle, schöne Länder.'*

*

Slowly he came to terms with the room. Big bed; high ceiling; rose-printed wall at his face. Judging by the distribution of light on the wall, two long windows behind him. A large room, then; a large house. He shifted his eye cautiously along: the corner of a fireplace; the trim on a stool; the angle of a half-dropped drawer in a dressing table. An oval mirror above the dressing table reflecting the bottles and baubles of a woman's room. A woman's room.

Down to the floor. His clothes in a bundle; one shoe; a sock. A little way off, a woman's stocking; the sharp edge of a skirt; the softer drape of something satin. Things began to make sense. The strange heat behind him in the bed: a woman. The damp sensation against his bare thigh: the French letter she had shown him how to use with an expert hand.

This much he knew: he was half-drunk; he was buck naked; he was in some sort of danger. Everything about him felt weak and unreliable: his body; his will; his memory, especially. Only the urge to escape was strong. His instinct told him to wait. To remember.

A battered city was waiting outside; waiting to reclaim him. If he was to keep his head, he would have to prepare it to go back out there again. But first – how to get by this woman behind him? This woman he had been jigging away at a short while ago. He couldn't even remember if he had enjoyed it or not. Nor how he had ended up here in the first place – in this room, in this bed. The only thing he could recall for certain was that one sharp moment, just before he gave in, when it had seemed to him to be utterly necessary: the only thing he could possibly do. Now all he wanted was out.

He considered his options. A note. A note left with a suitable excuse – or any sort of half-arsed excuse. But he'd have to be sure she was sleeping. If he turned his eyes, hers might be waiting; then they would have to talk.

He could make a run for it. Grab his clothes off the floor, muttering something about going to the jacks. He could even go to the jacks, get dressed there and then slip quietly down the stairs. But he was unfamiliar with the ways of this large house and had no idea whether she lived alone or if the house was divided into flats. He might bump into anyone as he ran naked along the corridor. And anyway, what sort of a bastard would do something like that? This sort of a bastard, if he was to be honest with himself – or if he thought for one second he could get away with it.

He closed his eyes to cut out the room and give himself time to come up with a plan. It was dark in there: warm and dark. But no plan came to the surface. A few seconds' peace, then images of the battered city rolled into view. Buildings, streets churned inside out; all grey. And half-images too; fragments of red. A shovelful of bloodied matter; an open-mouthed wheelbarrow below; a shovelful again. He tried to get away; to pull himself back – but just found himself being sucked further in. And he knew then, if he wanted to get out, he would have to take the long way round.

*

The Queen's Yard. The Eastern Section. Only recognisable because of its location. A skeleton now: huge, prehistoric, steaming black from its big, bare bones. Hundreds of faces peer through the bones – silent; alert; each one intent on tracing some relic of his workmanship. He finds his own relic down at the far end – that corvette he has been working on for the past few weeks: stern-framing twisted, half-chewed. The carcass that he had last seen perfectly formed and almost ready to be fitted up, now on its side, buckled and crunched. Knuckles of engine parts; crippled girders; lumps of charred metal stuck all over the rest of its gut. Undigested remains of its last meal: this skeletal monster that used to be the Queen's Yard.

A man beside him starts to sob, breaking the silence. A blind hand, damp with tears, reaches out. He looks down at the hand about to touch his arm. He breaks away.

Following the water until he comes to the basin, he stops. The same basin – the same spot – where a night, two weeks ago, he stood looking out and thought he had seen his own future. Now he sees only a sky artificial with a sunrise that has nothing to do with the sun: red-shot; clawed pink; raw. Where clumps of black cloud stand out on their own and a broken-necked crane hankers for its reflection through the layers of dockside debris. A man takes shape a few yards away: a warden – a helmet under one arm, a handbell tucked under the other. He walks to the man and stands beside him. His uniform is powdered grey; face black; eyes crimson as if his head was bleeding inside. He studies the man for a moment. It turns out to be Cleaver.

After a while Cleaver acknowledges him. 'There ye are, Georgie. Aye, there y'are indeed. You're lookin' very neat, all considered. Were you away last night?'

'Up in Keadyville.'

'Ah. Who knows, maybe them cards did you a favour for once. Do you know what I've been meaning to ask you – did you ever sort out that wee problem with young Percy?'

'*What?*'

'You know – that bit of bother he got himself in.'

'For Christ's sake, is that all you have to think about?'

'Ah well, it's been on my mind like.'

'I had a word with his foreman.'

'Good man. So he'll not have to lift his cards?'

'Will it make any difference now?'

'Maybe not, Georgie, but it's knowing he's not sacked that counts. I'm thinking of his da, mind, not him. If it wasn't for his da, I'd tell you let the wee bastard go to the devil.'

He can't get over Cleaver, can't get over how normal he is, carrying on in his matter-of-fact way, as if it was any other day of the week.

'Aye, that's your blackout for you nay, that's your barrage balloon. That's your searchlights, and your smokescreen. And the biggest joke of all – your air-raid shelters. Oh aye, we saved them a lot of trouble with them air-raid shelters. "Don't you go botherin' your heads trying to peck us out one by one," says we, "sure can't we all go thon shelters and wait for ye there? Let ye catch the lot of us in one fell swoop."'

'The shelters?'

'Percy Street. Atlantic Avenue. God knows where else. Plucked asunder. Gone.'

'Oh Jesus.'

'They were only tickling us last week, Georgie – tickling us under the chin. But this time, they've shat on us. Oh aye, they've rightly shat on us this time. I tell you what . . . it's a bit early, I know, but do you think we might try somewhere for a drink? I feel now I might need a wee steadier before I face any more.'

'I can't. I have to get back to Dublin – my brother is getting married.'

'You'll not get out of Belfast this day, Georgie.'

'But I have to. I'm the best man.'

'You should have thought of that one before.'

'How was I to know? Anyway, I had to look after the shop and I thought if I caught the first train . . . '

'The first train? That's a laugh. Look, son, you may accept the facts as they stand. The roads is impassable, the stations either blown to pieces or them's not been hit are jammed to the ceiling. There's no way out unless you intend hoofin' it all the way.'

'I can try. I have the car – there must be some way.'

'Where's your car?'

'Outside the shop.'

'When did you come down from Keadyville?'

'When I heard the all-clear.'

'So you don't know?'

'What? Don't know what?'

'The shop's gone, George. The whole street. There's nawthin' left, son – nawthin' at all.'

'Oh Christ. What about Enzo?'

'Enzo's dead, son.'

'I don't believe it. Where is he?'

'Your first concern's your family and your wee girl. You best send a telegram home – that's all you can do for the moment. Look, here's a pencil – write it out there now you and we'll take it down to the post office. Put your mother's mind at ease, at least. Come on, son, steady yourself up.'

'But Enzo?'

'Come along you now with me.'

They walk in silence back towards the city. The heat on their faces from fires still burning, the cold at their feet where pipes have cracked open, spewing over pavements like rivers in spate. Uprooted tramlines; uprooted trees; the crustacea of burnt-out cars blown off the roads: sideways on footpaths, backways in buildings, or belly-up in a schoolyard, like a big black turtle kicked over. Shops with no windows; the frantic hammer of shopkeepers boarding them up. Shops with no fronts; sly-faced looters waiting to pounce. Royal Avenue: a crater punched into its belly and a queue of hundreds outside the post office. He sees Davy Wren and runs over. 'Is there any chance you'd do us a favour, Davy?'

'Aye.'

'Will you send a telegram for me?'

'Aye.'

'To let them know at home I'm all right. My brother, he's getting married this afternoon – do you think would a telegram get there on time?'

'Aye.'

'I just want to tell him to go ahead without me. Look, I've written it all down. Here's the money – this'll more than cover it.

You won't forget, will you? You won't let me down, Davy?'

'Aye.'

He looks into the dull eyes for a moment. Then he looks at the crowd for a more promising face but can't seem to catch any eye. He curls Davy's hand over the money. 'Thanks, Davy. You're a pal.'

Cleaver is over at the crater looking down. When he comes back, he's no longer normal – he's slightly insane. His two selves mixed up in an endless prayer. 'Our fuckin' father, our fuckin' merciful father in heaven. Help us now in our hour of need, for fuck sake will you not help us at all?'

George takes his arm and coaxes him along. 'Come on, Cecil, I heard someone say there's a pub open up the Antrim Road.'

Factories with the guts pulled out of them. Warehouses with their eyes sucked out. Ambulances and fire-tenders screaming their heads off. Military cars honking behind. A funeral parlour with the smell of burning horseflesh. Black, Belgian horseflesh he has often admired. A margarine factory weeps through its cavities. The stink of melting grease on the air. Rescue workers slipping and sliding. The high screech of a woman beside him: screeching, pointing, doubling up with laughter. A woman gone mad with grief. The Antrim Road is a foreign country. An exodus of refugees trudging along. There's a familiarity about it he can't seem to pin down. Spain. Maybe Poland. Some place he's seen on a Pathé newsreel. (What the fuck is he doing here, in a Pathé newsreel?) In another country, slow feet drag bundles and suitcases, long arms drag crying children behind or push prams with portable kitchens inside: coal scuttles; kettles; the spout of a teapot. The arm of a ukulele without any strings.

Side streets mauled down to rubble; mountain ranges of rubble where there used to be terraces. An occasional house sticks out like an insult. Half-rooms exposed in the sockets of half-houses. A perfect chimney breast on the top floor; the smooth, hard curve of a toilet bowl next door. A bit of a wall; the grimace of a melted clock, still holding on to its time. Down on the footpaths, rows of dead faces covered in white dust. Priests from different denominations whispering into dead, deaf ears. Cleaver still beside him. 'Our fuckin' father . . . ' The tonsil in his handbell waggling now and then.

They forget about the pub; drift in and out of these side streets instead, Cleaver's voice rising out of his prayer whenever he spots a familiar landmark – as if they're playing a game of 'Guess Which Street This Used to Be?' They stop to help, climbing like apes – hands over feet – clawing at concrete, pulling out rafters, passing handfuls along the conveyor line – man to man, hand to hand – dismantling the layers until the tightness gives way and holes began to appear.

A sock on a boy's leg. A strand of hair on a blonde head a little way above. Perfectly proportioned; anatomically correct. He gets all excited; thinks he's found someone alive; thinks he has even seen it breathe. He calls out, 'Look, look over here. A kid, still alive . . . '

Two soldiers hold a plank up between them, a sheet trailing over the sides. They lay it down, then climb to him and examine his find. They look at each other, then look away. They look at each other again. But they don't do a thing to help him. 'Go on, son,' one of them says after a minute, in a Lancashire voice softened down. 'We'll take care of this. Go get yourself 'ome, there's a lad.'

There's a lad? He grabs the soldier by the scruff of the neck.

'Don't you ever speak to me like that. If you ever speak to me like that again, I'll knock your fuckin' block off.'

The soldier screams back at him, 'Go on, you stupid bugger. Bugger off 'ome, I said.'

Then he cops – what the soldiers have obviously already copped. There can be no connection between the head and the leg. A girl's head; a boy's sock – how could there be? He looks over at the plank and it comes to him then. Body parts, that's what they are. Body parts that have been covered over, the way a butcher might cover his wares at the end of the day.

He stumbles back down the hill with the idea of running away. To find, like a dog, a quiet corner where he can puke up his ring in peace. But when he gets halfway down, his legs refuse him. They're well capable of staying balanced on a fallen door, which in turn has no problem resting across an uneven heap of masonry. Yet they can't seem to organise themselves to take a few easy steps back down to the ground.

And, balanced on that door, staring at that plank, looking like a complete and utter total fucking imbecile, she finds him.

The first thing he notices is her appearance: clean as a whistle, not a hair out of place. Hair, in fact, rolled up under one of those netted snood things. Lipstick, powder, all that kind of stuff – as if she's going out somewhere nice. He wonders to himself how she managed that, at seven o'clock in the morning with all this going on. Too fresh-looking to be last night's work: she would have to have done it today. Had she sat at a mirror, painting her face, lifting her arms up to curl up her hair? Grips between teeth, tutting at some little inconvenience like a stray bit of hair that wouldn't oblige, drawing the snood up, tucking it in, smiling then, pleased?

She looks so ridiculous beside all the other stained faces: ridiculous and beautiful. His legs start to work again and step down beside her.

'You look as if you could do with a drink,' she says. Then she stumbles and he catches hold of her arm.

Cleaver mistakes the stagger for shock; speaks to her kindly over and over. 'You'll be all right nay, girlie. You will be, aye surely. We'll take care of you, so we will. Would you like me to take you to the post for a wee cup of tea, girlie? A warm blanket? Or is your house still standing, do you know?'

She looks for a minute as if she might laugh in his face. But at least she has put a stop to his prayer.

As for himself, he already got the whiff of gin off her; saw the gin cloud in her eyes when he steadied her back up on her feet. She gives her address and stumbles again.

'Poor wee girl. You'd best take her home,' Cleaver says. 'So long as her house is still standing.'

And because Cleaver says so, he does what he's told. If Cleaver thinks it's all right, then it must be.

He tries to put her hand through his arm, but that arrangement doesn't suit her. She takes him by the hand instead and leads him along like a boy. Through the pulverised streets. The mutilated streets. The smoked-stenched, puked-out, shat-upon streets; her perfume twittering around the edges. Corner after corner, she pulls him on, until they part from the exodus and are alone on a road. Then up the granite steps of this house. There's a hole blown in the wall right beside the front door. A hole you could drive a truck through. But she doesn't seem to see it. She struggles with the latchkey, curses it, tries it the other way around, curses it again, pulls, then shoves, until eventually the door gives in. The hall is in tatters. She behaves as if it's supposed to be that way, throwing her handbag on a dust-covered table, unbuttoning her coat, palming the full snood to make sure it's still in place. He half-expects her to call out, 'Honey, I'm home.'

He follows her up stairs that curve close to the wall. There are daggers of glass sticking out of the wall. He leans away; she doesn't mind them. She's an inch off having the haircut of her life and she doesn't even notice. They walk through a door and she throws off her coat. A bottle appears, then two glasses. Yes, that's how he came to be in this room and that's how he came to be in this bed. Half-drunk and buck naked.

*

He opened his eyes and found himself longing for the uncertainty of the racetrack.

He stayed with his eyes on the wall for a while, watching the afternoon nose over its roses. Counting the roses: four small, one large, a long green stem leading into . . . four small, one large, all the way over to the door.

He came back to the idea of a note. The first line dithered in his head. 'Sorry I had to rush off but . . . ' 'I didn't want to disturb you, so . . . ' Then he felt a shift in the bed. The eiderdown flapped back; now the bed was suddenly lighter. A silk kimono slithered off the bedpost. Feet tapped across the floor, stopped, shuffled, then resumed, with the clack of slipper heels.

He looked at the door, willing it to open – willing the silk kimono to slither out of the room, taking her with it. But the footsteps stopped, the door stayed put and in a minute a voice came out from the side of the room, 'Are you awake?'

'Yes.'

He turned around as if to face her. But he didn't look at her face, he looked at the space beyond it.

'I suppose you're trying to think up an excuse?'

'What?' He managed a laugh. 'What are you on about?'

'You know, an excuse so you can go.'

'Don't be ridiculous. Although I suppose I better check on the shop. And a telephone – I don't suppose you have . . . '

'It's down.'

'Oh. Well, I'll have to find a . . . '

'Don't bother to explain,' she laughed. 'I really don't care.'

'Maybe we could meet for a drink later on?'

'Oh yes, that would be lovely. Did you have any particular bomb-site in mind?'

'I was only . . . '

'There's no need. I told you, I don't care.'

'Right, so you did. Will you stay here?' he asked the top of her hair when she tossed it back, the angle of her elbow when she shoved one hand down into her pocket.

'Why not?'

'What if they come back again?'

'Even the Gerries take the odd night off.'

She wasn't afraid. He looked at her face then. It looked like a mugshot: no expression. Nothing for him; neither hurt nor recrimination. Nothing for the Gerries either. Not even fear.

'My brother was mad about you,' he said then, because he too felt nothing and thought she should know somebody loved her.

'So I believe. He wrote to me once – told me all about it.'

She sounded bored.

'When? When did he write to you?'

'Oh I don't know, a couple of years ago.'

'Did you write back?'

'No I didn't.' She laughed at the absurdity of his question. Then she turned away and bent to the fire, poking into it, tipping, turning.

That annoyed him, dismissing Herbert that way. And Herbert annoyed him too: stupid bastard, what did he think he was at, writing to her, anyway? He was glad he was annoyed – it would make his departure that bit easier, better than any excuse. Getting angry, now that would even be better. He got out of bed and stepped into his trousers.

'You could at least have acknowledged the letter.'

'What for?'

'Unless you wanted to make a fool of him.'

'He'd already done that by himself, don't you think?'

'Well, he must have got over you anyway – he's getting married today. In fact he's probably . . . '

'What are you telling me for?'

'I just mentioned it.'

'What concern is it of mine? I don't care what he does.'

She stood up then and her face came through the mirror. Her mouth was still, yet she looked as if she was laughing at him.

'Speaking of letters,' she said, 'what have you done with yours?'

He pretended not to hear her, bending his head down to look under the bed for his sock.

She continued, 'You're not supposed to leave it on, you know. It can only be used once. You don't take it home with you, like a souvenir to pin to the wall: oh, what a good boy was I.'

'Why don't you shut your mouth?' he said, sitting back up on the bed and shaking the sock out.

She smiled.

He poked his foot in. 'Do you know something . . . '

She put her hand out to stop him. 'Now, if you're about to tell me what you think of me, don't bother, because it doesn't interest me. I don't care what you think of me.'

'Do you ever listen to yourself? "I don't care, I don't care." You're like a fuckin' child, with your "I don't care"s every other minute.'

It was meant to insult her but she burst out laughing. 'You're still a good mimic,' she said.

He stood up then, eyeing the floor for his other sock. 'I have to go.'

'Well, so long then.'

'Do you live here alone?'

'Yes.'

'Nobody else here? What about your husband?'

'He's not here.'

'Well, I hardly thought he was. Where is he?'

'I don't know. Plymouth, I think.'

She threw herself down in an armchair, crossing her legs, playing the castanets with her slipper against her heel.

'Look, I can't just leave you on your own.'

'Of course you can.'

'Are you sure you'll be all right?'

'Well, I'm certainly not going to cry, if that's what you think.'

'I didn't expect . . . '

'It's not something I do.'

'What isn't?'

'Cry. I never cry. At least I can't ever remember . . . '

'There you go again – more childish shite. "I never cry."'

He pulled on his shirt and lit a cigarette. 'You talk nothing but shite, do you know that?'

She stopped clacking the slipper then and pulled herself out of the chair. She walked to him, removed the cigarette from his mouth, took a couple of pulls on it, brought it to his lips again and slowly screwed it back into place.

'Let me tell you something,' she began. 'When I was ten years old, I lived with my parents in India. One day they put me on a boat and sent me five thousand miles, on my own, back to Ireland to live with my grandmother. My grandmother – you know, so I don't have to explain what that meant. The voyage took over a fortnight. I could count on this hand how many words I spoke to anyone else, and on this hand, how many words were spoken to me. I never saw my parents again.'

'What's that got to do with anything?'

'I don't care if you stay; I won't care if you go. You are under no obligation to ask me out, and to pretend to do so just insults both of us. I just don't care, that's all. Not because I'm childish. Not because I'm mad – and I can see by your face you're considering that possibility. Not even because I'm rude. The fact is, George, I don't care because I don't fucking well choose to.'

VI

She lied about crying. There was a time, towards the end of her childhood, when she seemed to do little else. It started on the return voyage from India, continued for a year or two, then, like any childish habit, she simply grew out of it. She also lied about being sent home from India alone. She wasn't completely alone – or at least it wasn't intended that she should be. Her mother had entrusted her to the recently widowed Mrs Carmichael, an officer's wife, with whom she had no more than a passing acquaintance. The widow was an elderly woman, nervy and frail. The only children she had known up to then were vague shapes in the background: houseboys or temple girls or the occasional colonial offspring that might have to be endured before dinner was served. You could see the strain on her bony face as she asked questions concerning her charge – in a manner which made Beatrix feel a bit like a dog. What should she eat, and how much? When should she sleep, and how often? Would she have to be played with? What about exercise and other matters of a more delicate nature – could she tend to these herself? And Beatrix's mother answered all these questions reassuringly – fondly, even – or as if, indeed, she was a dog.

At the Victoria Terminal in Bombay, her mother stooped low. 'You'll be a good girl for Mrs Carmichael?'

'Yes, mama.'

'And for your grandmother?'

'Yes, mama.'

'Do you promise me with all your heart?'

'I promise.'

'Good, in that case I promise you, with all my heart, we shall see each other soon – very, very soon.'

That was the last time they would ever look at each other, outside the frame of a photograph.

Mrs Carmichael rarely spoke to her, even at mealtimes when they sat alone. All around her the dining room hummed: orchestral music; laughter and chat; the low mumble of Indians at the far end of the room as they daily considered, then rejected, the strangeness of white, sliced bread. But nothing could drown out Mrs Carmichael's silence or the sound of her cutlery and plates, which seemed to grow louder as each meal progressed and always left Beatrix with a splitting headache.

Two years previously, she had made the same voyage but in the opposite direction. It had been quite different then: she had been with her mother. Her mother had already spent two months in India but, more importantly, had also spent a fortnight as the house guest of an Indian prince, a famous cricketer who owned a castle in Connemara. If there had been any doubts in her mother's mind about spending the rest of her years in India, those two regal weeks had booted them out. She wrote to Beatrix to tell her about it. Beatrix usually skipped over her mother's letters because they were invariably dull, but this time she found something out of the ordinary – in a paragraph down near the end:

The Prince – and I will give him his full title here: Colonel, His Highness Shri, Sir Ranjitsinhji Vibhaji Maharajah Jam Saheb of Nawanagar – is very gracious. He has been fishing with your father in the lakes. It is a pleasure (your father tells me) to watch his cricketer's wrist flick and flex over the fishing rod.

Beatrix underlined this paragraph and learnt it off by heart – she thought it some sort of a tongue-twister. Her grandmother made her recite it whenever they had visitors. It became her party piece; her way to get cake.

Her mother was in love with India. Or at least with the life she could lead there. On the outward journey she had used up all Beatrix's crayons to make Beatrix love it too.

'These are the trees in the compound,' she said. 'Palm trees and neem trees. The natives brush their teeth with sticks taken from the neem. A datun, the stick is called. It is better than tooth powder – that's why they have such beautiful white teeth.'

'May I use a datun to brush my teeth?'

'Certainly not.' Her mother laughed.

'Why not, if it works so well for the natives?'

'You must never do anything the natives do.'

Then she drew pictures of the Indian women – luscious with saris and amber skin, a star in the middle of their foreheads. They moved in groups; they fluttered. Like a flock of big, exotic birds.

'Are these women native?'

'Oh yes, they are better off than most – the higher caste, you know – some of them are even princesses, but they are natives, yes.'

'So I won't be wearing a sari?' Beatrix asked, sadly.

'No.' Her mother smiled, pleased that her daughter was already getting the hang of things.

She drew the verandah on the English club, where long, cool drinks were served all day and you could sit in the shade watching the tennis parties and the cricket matches and the stumpy polo ponies that ran close to the ground. She drew the verandah on the house too, where you sat in the evenings before dinner, watching a huge, soft sun slip down and run like honey into the river. By the time she had finished, Beatrix was in love with India too: she thought she would burst with love before the ship came to dock.

When she got to the house, there was a verandah, but it was an ugly house with no stairs. And it was just the same as all the other ugly houses dotted throughout the compound. They had the same layout of rooms, the same furniture, the same silent, brown-footed boy who pressed the palm of one hand on his forehead and bowed backways out of a room. And every verandah seemed to have the same red-faced Englishman, who said 'Indi-ar' instead of 'India', and who was drunk all the time.

There were a few other pictures her mother had forgotten to draw – or maybe she just hadn't noticed them. The skin-and-bone children begging for alms; the hordes of poor people sleeping at night on roofs of shack-houses. The big, fat flies and the long, thin rats and the thick, moist snakes that would get under the house and then at night crawl into your dreams. Nor did she draw the darker side of her honey-soft sun. The sun that had been waiting all its life for Beatrix to arrive. Hungry for the taste of roasted, white skin – the skin of a plump Irish girl.

She was looked after by an ayah – a sort of a governess – who called her 'Missie Sahib'. The ayah dressed her every morning down to her shoes, and gave her a bath as if she was a baby. While Beatrix crossed her arms over the two boils swelling on her chest, the ayah stared at her white skin and looked down quite frankly at the dashes of hair that had started to darken her private parts. Every morning the ayah would fling back the bedclothes with a suspicious eye, as if she was hoping to find she had wet the bed, and every night she would examine her underwear and say 'Ayayayay' through a tight, impatient jaw.

She brought Beatrix treats from the kitchen because she liked to giggle and point at her greed. Brown-shaped things that smelt of sweat, or honey-sweet cubes that shocked her teeth. The more she brought, the more Beatrix ate — at first because it gave her something to do, later because it brought her comfort and a vague sense of love. The ayah could bring all the treats in India — Beatrix would still hate her, almost as much as she hated the sun. But at least the ayah wasn't trying to kill her. In the end the sun almost did. She did everything she could to protect herself: covered her body with cloth and thick cream; stayed in the shade when it was at its keenest. But that only seemed to aggravate it. She stopped going out altogether. Yet it still managed to get her: its long, fiery fingers, prising through the slits in the wall, managed to cook her to a pink, blistered turn.

After the sunstroke, they sent her home. She knew she wouldn't see her father before she left because he was in the Punjab on business. But she didn't mind so much — she had never really known him anyway. To her, he had always been an oddity: a face that bounced with a souvenir tic from the Great War; a hand that signed cheques or patted her head; a voice that called her 'm'dear' whenever they happened to meet. You couldn't be lonely for a series of traits, and besides, she thought all the time that her mother was coming too.

It was only on the last night that she found out she was to go home alone. Through the verandah screen, she heard her mother say, 'I shall miss her, of course. But what can one do? Besides, my mama simply adores her,' in a voice that made her sound like an Englishwoman.

*

On the ship, the steward gave her a drink of lime and water to settle her stomach. She wasn't sick until she took the lime drink. She spent a whole day alone in her stuffy, one-eyed cabin, with her insides trying to crawl out, while Mrs Carmichel sat on a deckchair and waited for England to pop out of the sea. The next morning was the first time she found blood on her sheets. She screamed and screamed until people came running and there were raps on the door. The ship's doctor gave her an injection. Then he sent his nurse in to have a little chat. She told Beatrix there was no point in crying because she was a woman now. She was, of course, a little younger than most, but very well developed for her age. She said a lot of other things besides, but after a while Beatrix couldn't quite hear because the sentences started to melt away. After another while the nurse's face melted away too. The last clear thing Beatrix could remember seeing was the face of the ayah, standing in the doorway, holding the stained sheet up to the light and smiling around her big, white teeth.

When she woke up, she looked at her woman's face in the mirror, then put the pad the nurse had made between her legs and, to practise being a woman, took it for a little walk over the decks. It was sunset. The white people were below, changing for the farewell dinner; the Indians gathered above. They faced the same way, kneeling down, praying and chanting. Then they moved to the lower deck and huddled together for their evening meal. They pulled the lids of tins open and spicy breath hawed out at her as she passed by: pakora and *mittees* that made her mouth water. And big, jagged chapatti bread – bread they could understand, with contours and brown bits, like the map of a country – that they tore asunder in their dark, neat hands.

When the ship drew near Southampton, they practised being English. Giggling over English phrases and playing shop with pounds, shillings and pence. After a while, they fell silent. The ones with turbans bent their heads low. They began to unravel an endless strip of white cloth; long, black snakes came spilling out. They sliced a big silver knife through the snakes, rolled them back in the turbans and dropped them into the ocean. Then they took turns shaving each other. Unused to the task, they landed with blood blotches all over their faces. The blotches made them look as if they had a disease. So did the guilty look in their eyes.

Mrs Carmichael disembarked without her. Beatrix watched her sneak down the plank and stuck her tongue out after her. Then she saw her grandmother waiting below. It was the first time Beatrix had ever been glad to see her. It would probably be the last time too.

Her grandmother was the meanest woman she had ever known. Her grandmother's head was a ledger. Every outgoing had a calculated return: even the smallest square of chocolate would cost a kiss. Beatrix hated to kiss her grandmother, but she loved to eat chocolate. It was easy to see how her grandmother might believe she was loved.

Her grandmother was also a liar. She told lies about and to her friends. Lies about her past and, in particular, lies about her dead husband. Beatrix had never known her grandfather, but she had a firm picture of him in her head, because whenever her father was drunk, he liked to bring up the subject of Grandfather Gunne. Sometimes her mother passed it off as a joke, but mostly it made her cry.

Her grandfather had been a second-hand-clothes dealer. Out of a filthy back-street warehouse with a long, musty corridor of dead people's clothes leading to the office, where he would sit in his overcoat because he was too mean to put on a fire. A black bowler hat on his head; one finger on the cash book, the other stuck up his nose. But to hear her grandmother talk, you'd think he was a gentleman with gentleman's ways. You'd think he was the Duke of Windsor instead of old Grandfather Gunne. It had been easy enough to catch her out in the lies; it took a little longer to discover her sticky fingers.

Her father sent money to pay for her education – enough to cover one of the better schools. She was sent instead to a two-roomed hovel which was grandly advertised as Miss Nightingale's Academy for Young Ladies and consisted in the main of relatives of Miss Nightingale, all of whom were much younger than Beatrix. The rest of the money was pocketed.

She spent every day of those years alone with her grandmother: living with that meanness, listening to those lies, watching through the window the convent girls stream by. All dressed the same; all looking the same. Once she saw them in a religious procession, white dresses and wreaths in their hair, singing songs about a queen in heaven and sprinkling rose petals over the ground. She longed to be one of them.

'Why can't I go to that school?' she asked her grandmother,

'instead of that stupid academy where I have no one to play with?'

Her grandmother was shocked. 'Good heavens, child, you can't go there.'

'Why not?'

'They're Catholics.'

'So? You could ask them to make an exception.'

'They don't make exceptions. Besides, that's not the point.'

'What is then?'

'They're *common*.'

But she longed to be common. She longed to be the same. She had been different in India because she was white; she was different in Dublin because she was a Protestant. She had to come to Belfast before she could be the same. Before she finally got to feel like a native.

Sometimes they went to tea in other people's houses, where Beatrix knew they weren't really wanted. She knew they weren't wanted in George's house either, but she didn't mind about that, because she had an excuse to go. His mother, after all, was their dressmaker – she couldn't help it if she needed clothes any more than his mother could help needing the money.

In the end, she had more dresses then she could possibly wear, but she grew to love them in the way she had once grown to love the strange, sweaty smell of Indian food.

She loved George's house. The noise. The talk. The sound of the back door banging all the time, bringing new people in. People to watch; people to listen to. She loved his mother too – and the way she knew her own kitchen. The way she could handle several subjects in the one conversation; several tasks with the one pair of hands. But best of all she loved the way she could handle her grandmother: reduce her with one look, one cutting remark to the sly, lying thief Beatrix had always known her to be. It was the only time in her childhood that she could ever remember not being lonely, standing in his kitchen, surrounded by all that life.

She got married when she was nineteen years old, just to get out of her grandmother's house. She married her husband because he was the first man to ask her and also because he was kind. She hadn't realised that kindness and generosity weren't necessarily the same thing. They were still on honeymoon when it came to her like an icy hand on the back of her neck – she had married a man that was mean with his money. His kindness became irrelevant; his meanness became everything. He could only be somebody else not to care about.

When she got back from honeymoon, she wrote two letters: one to her father, the other to her grandmother. They were more like charge sheets than letters, really, listing her grievances over the years. There was nothing to read between the lines: neither bitterness nor reprimand. They were what she had meant them to be – simple statements of fact. Each one finished on the same note: a demand for compensation and a request that any further correspondence be conducted through her solicitor. She received a prompt response from both parties and continued to do so in the form of a monthly cheque. Hand-written letters, she disregarded. Letters from India were marked 'Return to Sender'. Letters from her grandmother were thrown in the fire.

Her husband paid for his version of 'the necessities': the roof over her head and the food on her table. In return, she took his arm at social functions. She kept the door of her bedroom closed. The war had been a blessing to both of them – he could get on with his kindness wherever he liked; she could get on with her life. As for her own money – that paid for her version of 'the necessities', insofar as the black market allowed: clothes, jewellery, cigarettes, gin. Such things as she now chose to care about.

On the afternoon following the Easter air raid in Belfast, she told all this to George. He listened to her silently, his shirt half-open, one foot bare. He listened to her carefully, his back to the fire, with the French letter she had shown him how to use crusting to his leg like a plaster. By the time she had finished speaking, it was almost dark and he was naked again. In her bed, in a big Victorian house, with a hole in the wall downstairs that she hadn't seemed to notice. And a hole for a window in the bedroom, where the glass had been blown out. And the wind sucked the blind in and then blew it back out again, like an asthmatic struggling for breath.

VII

Herbert's mot was up the pole – that's why he was getting married. He told Rafter one day, when Charlie was rummaging through the scullery box for his other runner. They didn't see him because they were standing at the kitchen door, smoking out to the yard.

'I'm getting married in three weeks' time,' Herbert said.

'Fuck off – you are not?'

'I am.'

'Are you fuckin' mad? What do you want to do that for?'

'The mot's up the pole . . . '

'That doesn't mean you have to . . . '

'Ah, what am I supposed to do?' Herbert barked.

'A bunk?' Rafter suggested.

Herbert said nothing.

'Well, that's what I'd do, anyway. Join the Raf or somethin'. Join the bleedin' circus if I had to. No woman'd ever snare me like that.'

Herbert still said nothing.

'Well, I think you're mad. Gettin' married. Gettin' fuckin' married. Mad.'

'Keep your voice down, will you? For Christ's sake, I haven't told them yet.'

Herbert's head tipped into the kitchen to show by 'them' he meant ma and da. That's when he saw Charlie.

'What are you moochin' around for?' Herbert asked him.

'I'm not moochin', I'm looking for me other runner.'

'Fuckin' earwiggin' again.'

'I'm not earwiggin', I'm lookin' for me other . . . Here it is, look.'

Charlie held up the runner and Rafter gave one of his grunty laughs.

'Bleedin' state of it,' Rafter said.

'What's wrong with it?'

'Bleedin' state of it. You wouldn't run snot in them yokes.'

'That doesn't make sense,' Charlie said.

'What did you say?'

'Nothin'.'

He went to the door. Herbert stepped out of his way; Rafter wouldn't.

Bridging his leg across the threshold, Rafter said, 'Where do you think you're goin'?'

'Out for a run.'

'Make us a cup of tea first.'

'Fuck off,' Charlie said. 'Make it yourself.'

'Yeh little bollix. Did you hear what he said? Did you hear him?'

Herbert laughed. 'Good for you, kid. You stick up for yourself.'

Charlie pushed by.

Out in the yard he put on his other runner. They couldn't even wait till he was finished before they started talking again. He didn't want to hear – and he did want to hear. But not enough to be called an earwigger again.

'I'll be out of your way in a minute,' he said, to let them know. But they just couldn't wait.

'I might as well tell you now – George is getting engaged,' Herbert said.

'George? Ah, for Jaysus sake. Don't tell me she's . . . ?'

'Who, Mona? No chance. They'll do everything the right way,

that pair – the respectable way. They'll have the house bought, the lot, you wait and see; there'll be no rush there.'

'And what about you? Where will you live?' Rafter asked.

'You know the other side of the house?'

'The part you rent out?'

'Uncle Sam's going to square it with ma.'

'But I thought you were supposed to be gettin' a new lodger?'

'Yeah, well, *I'm* the new lodger.'

Charlie went over to the archway and started doing his stretches. He was a good bit away from the house now; their voices were fainter, but he could still hear what they were saying.

'Here, where did you do it?' Rafter asked.

'Do what?'

'You know, stick her up the pole.'

'Fuck off, Rafter.'

'Ah, go on, tell us. Was it the barn?'

'Mind your own business.'

'Not the house, surely to Jaysus? Where then – the bank? It was, wasn't it? The bank? Did nobody . . . ?'

'When it was closed, you thick.'

'Oh, right. What about her granda?'

'The caretaker's flat is five floors up. He's half-deaf, anyway.'

'Gas, all the same.'

'What is?'

'You know – your mot and that. Amy wha'? Gamey Amy, after all.'

Charlie stood up. He wanted to let rip at Herbert. He wanted to scream at him for not throwing a dig at Rafter. He wanted to say, You're a chickeny bastard, Herbert, that's what you are, letting him speak about Amy that way. We have to tiptoe the words around you, but strangers can say whatever they like. You're a chickeny cunt, Herbert – George would've creamed him by now.

He shook his legs out, ready to run. 'Rafter?' he shouted.

'Wha'?'

'You're only jealous. You're only jealous because you couldn't get a girl to stick up the pole. You couldn't get a girl, you ugly, bandy-legged bastard.'

Rafter smashed his cigarette into the wall. A spurt of sparks; his hand hopped away and turned into a fist. 'You better start runnin'. I'm fuckin' warnin' you now. You better start runnin' before I catch a hold of you and break your scrawny . . . '

'You'd never catch me, Rafter, do you hear me? Never.'

*

That was three weeks ago. Three weeks and a day, and Herbert still wasn't married. The wedding was postponed on account of them all thinking George might have been killed in the Belfast blitz. The posh part of the house was all set for a wedding that wasn't going to happen, and ma had insisted on leaving it that way. 'It's only postponed,' she kept on saying. 'Any minute now, he could walk in that door.' Everyone was starving, but ma wouldn't let them touch a thing. Everyone was jacked too, but ma wouldn't let them go to bed, or change their clothes, or leave the house, until they knew about George. They'd only been allowed down to the kitchen once, and that was for bowls of sloppy porridge, and they'd all had to stand around the kichen table because all the chairs were up in the good room. But how could you eat sloppy porridge when George might be dead and when you knew that upstairs the table was stuffed with sandwiches and chickens, cream cakes and jam? Nobody ate the porridge except Amy's granda.

Now they were back upstairs again. Da kept looking at the bottles of stout; ma kept looking at the clock. Everyone else kept looking at each other. Charlie just looked at the floor.

After a while, ma wore the hope out of herself and sat down. 'He's dead,' she said, her face in her hands. 'He's dead.'

'He might not be,' Amy said, big eyes dripping brown. 'He might just be injured.'

Ma peeped out through her fingers. 'But surely . . . ? Oh, surely we'd have heard something by now?'

All morning, neighbours had been coming in and out – all the day before too – in nosy dribs and drabs. What had started out as a day for Herbert had ended up as a day for George. Except George was getting two days, because this was the second day that he was supposed to be dead. Neighbours. Coming in for a gawk at what sort of a wedding it would have been that they hadn't been invited to. Or maybe just to see what it was like in the posh part of the house. Or maybe just for a squint at Amy's belly. This time it was Mrs Fahy and Ma Grumley and a fat oul'one called Vera who had only one diddy. A couple more were out in the hall; another one on the way up the stairs. But it didn't matter who they were – they were all the same. Or at least they all had the same stupid things to say.

'And I believe the guts is tore out of Belfast, missus. I believe there's only thousands dead in the streets. Poor George. Poor, poor George.'

'And what about that poor child? Poor Amy, missin' her weddin' day. What's goin' to happen at all?'

'And all that lovely food goin' to waste . . . '

He could feel Mrs Fahy's attention pull itself away from the table, cross over the room and land on top of him.

'Ah, would you look at Charlie. I wouldn't know him in his suit. How old is he now? About twelve?'

Charlie looked at the wallpaper. There were trees and a river, a path and some birds. Over and over, the same little scene in diagonal lines up the wall.

'I'm thirteen,' he said.

'*Thirteen?* Imagine. But I never knew you owneded this part of the house as well, missus. Is this where the young couple was goin' to live? God help them, all the same. Wouldn't your heart go out to them?'

'The wedding is only postponed,' Amy said. 'Only postponed, that's all. The Canon said we've to send down for him as soon as . . . as soon as we know.' Then her big eyes cracked open and long, sloppy tears fell out. Her granda put his hand on her shoulder. Herbert put his hand in his pocket and leaned against the wall, glaring at the neighbours, until one by one they started to leave. Except for Ma Grumley, who seemed to think she was entitled to stay on, seeing how Mickey was Herbert's pal.

Charlie's suit was making him itchy, and the floor at his feet was starting to shrink. The walls were getting thinner. Thinner and thinner: you could nearly see right through the paper by now. He stuck his eye on a section in the middle, and the section in the middle got bigger and bigger until there was only one big scene. The trees on the wallpaper started to rustle, and the path running through them grew longer and longer. He could hear the birds twitter, see the water bristle – could taste the fresh air on his tongue. He had to get out.

'Ma?'

Mrs Grumley had the bottom lip bitten off herself with sympathy. She'd a hold of ma's hand now, smacking it softly, nodding away while ma talked through her arse.

'Ma?'

'I've been up and down to the police station more times . . . The sergeant, said it could be days before . . . And Samuel and Maude are gone to make a few telephone calls. They have contacts up there, you know. And . . . '

'Ma?'

'Poor Mona – his fiancée, you know. I wouldn't mind, but they only got engaged a fortnight ago. I'm expecting her any minute. She went down to the fire station to look for her brother: he was sent up to Belfast with the brigade, maybe he might know something. I'd offer you something, Mrs Grumley, but until we know where we are, I want to keep things as they are. You do understand; it's not out of meanness. He could walk in that door any minute now and . . . Oh God, I just wish we knew. I just wish . . . '

'Ma?'

'Ah, what do you want, Charlie?'

'Can I go out for a run?'

'I'll run you all right. Go down and make a cup of tea for Mrs Grumley.'

'Ah, maaaah.'

He went down to the scullery and looked at the kettle. The same poxy kettle he'd been sent down to look at every time another visitor arrived. He lifted the lid and stuck his face in, then sang slow and deep into its big, rusty belly. 'Ha, ha, ha. Hee, hee, hee. Ho, ho, ho. He isn't dead. He isn't even fuckin' dead.' He couldn't think of anything better to sing into the kettle's rusty belly so he started thinking about Amy and Herbert and where in the bank would be a good place to stick someone up the pole. He had seen the inside of the bank once when Herbert had sent him there on a message. But the man in the uniform didn't want to let him in; made him wait in the foyer for ages. Charlie tried to remember all the things he had seen that day through the big glass doors of the foyer. So where had they done it? On the long mahogany counter? But that looked a bit slippy, and you might fall off and break your back on the floor, especially if you had a big lump like Herbert lying on top of you. Or maybe it was on one of those desks in the middle? No, they were too short. Or what about the lift? But the lift had a grille gate and Herbert's feet might get caught in the grilles because he was so tall. That was all he'd had time to see of the bank because then the man in the uniform went over to the house telephone and then Amy came down.

When Amy came down, she gave out stink to the doorman. 'Why didn't you just send him up?' she demanded. 'Why? Why? Is he not good enough? Is that it?' Then she invited Charlie upstairs to the caretaker's flat for a cup of tea. But he said no. If she hadn't asked the doorman that question, he might have said yes, because he would have loved a look at the caretaker's flat and he would have loved a look at Dame Street, to see what it was like from all that way up, upside down. But the fact that she had asked it made him realise it was true. He wasn't good enough; the doorman knew his job. Then Charlie felt sorry for the doorman. He didn't feel it was right, an old man being given out stink to by a young one like Amy, and everyone who passed in and out of the bank able to hear. And he'd wanted to say, 'Ah, Amy, it doesn't matter, he was only doing his job.' But there was no talking to Amy when she got into one of her moods. She'd the hottest head of anyone he knew. Worse than George; worse even than Herbert. She was always fighting with Herbert too, especially when she got jealous, and she was always getting jealous. Once he even saw her spit in Herbert's face in the street and not give a shite who might be looking. Mona was different. Mona was all, 'Oh yes, George. Oh no, George. Oh God, you're only great, George.' She was much different, but Charlie sort of thought Amy was better.

He pulled his face away from the kettle and shoved it up under the tap. Unless you could do it standing up? Then you wouldn't need so much space. But how would you balance? Stretching one hand out to the bread bin, he pulled a good lump out of a loaf and pressed it into his lips. It filled his mouth up wall to wall, and he was dying for it to be soft enough to drop down into his belly. Standing up? But . . .

Then he heard a car coming into the yard. Oh fuck.

He thought it might be Uncle Sam coming back with news about George or maybe mad Aunt Maude coming to look for news about him. He opened his hand and spat the mush into it, then, pulling a nibble small enough to finish back between his teeth, dumped the rest into the bin.

He went to the window. It wasn't Uncle Sam and it wasn't Aunt Maude: it was a stranger's car with Mona's white face stuck in the window. A tall man got out the driver's side, walked all the way round the car, opened the door and then took her out by the elbow. A fireman. His uniform manky, as if he'd only just stepped out of a fire. The fireman brother. She was always going on about her fireman brother.

'I must get my brother to take you down to the station one day. You can have a slide down the pole,' she'd say.

'Really, Mona?'

'Yes, of course. He'll give you a day out very soon.'

Charlie knew there was no point in hoping that this would be the day. He wiped his mouth and opened the door.

'Where's your mother?' the fireman asked.

'She's upstairs. Oh, hello Mona.'

Mona forgot to say hello back.

She didn't look sad; she didn't look worried; she looked as if she had a right bee up her arse. As if it was George's fault that he might be dead. He brought them through the kitchen, calling out, 'Ma, Mona's here. Mona's here.' He said it a few times just to fill up the empty space on the way up the stairs.

Ma jumped up. 'Oh, Mona love, we still haven't heard. We still haven't heard a word.'

She opened her arms to Mona, but Mona didn't step inside. Da got up to offer her his seat, but Mona didn't take it.

'I won't be staying,' she said, and then everyone who had been avoiding her face suddenly turned to look at it.

'This is my brother. He's just come back from Belfast. He's got something to tell you. Jimmy?'

The fireman stepped forward. 'I've just come back from Belfast,' he said again, as if they were all deaf. 'I'm afraid I haven't had time to change. Mona wanted to come straight . . . '

Ma interrupted. 'Is it awful up there? Is it as bad as they say?'

'Yes.'

'Oh God. I've lost one son already, Jimmy, you know. I don't think I could bear . . . '

'He isn't dead.'

'Are you sure?'

'Not even scratched.'

'Oh, thank God,' Amy said. 'Thank God. Oh Mona, isn't that great news? Isn't that just . . . '

'Is it?' Mona said through her teeth. 'Is it indeed?'

Charlie was wondering how come Mona was acting so funny. He thought it might have something to do with whatever the fireman was getting ready to tell them. He could tell ma sensed it too, by the way she suddenly thought she'd never get rid of Ma Grumley.

'I wonder if I could ask you a favour, Mrs Grumley?'

'Certainly, missus.'

'I wonder if you wouldn't mind letting the neighbours know that George is safe. You're very good, thank you. Charlie, show Mrs Grumley out.'

Charlie whipped her down the back stairs, flew her through the kitchen and had to stop himself from shoving her face out the door into the yard. Bang went the door; skid went his feet across the floor; bump, bump, bump went the stairs, when he milled up them three at a time.

'To tell you the truth, this is a bit awkward for me, ma'am,' the fireman was saying.

'But I don't understand,' ma was saying back. 'If you're sure he's all right. I mean, *are* you sure? How do you know?'

The fireman said nothing for a minute.

Then Mona said, 'Go on, Jimmy, tell them. Go on.'

'Maybe I should talk to your husband, in private.'

'Just *tell* them, will you, for God's sake. *Tell* them.'

'I saw him.'

'You saw him?'

'Yes. He was . . . He was with someone.'

'With someone?'

'A girl.'

'A girl?'

'Well, a woman. He was with her, you know. With her.'

'Jimmy,' ma said, 'I don't know what you're talking about. Please will you just tell us what in the name of God you're talking about?'

Charlie looked over at da to see what he was thinking. Da had stopped looking at the bottles of stout; now he was looking at the whiskey. He took a glass, nudged the corner of the tablecloth in, rubbed it round, then inspected it against the light. He took another glass and did the same thing. He opened the whiskey bottle and the two glasses filled with dark, yellow light. He brought one over to the fireman, then handed him a cigarette, and the firman nodded thanks, and da said, 'Sit down, Jimmy. Take your time.'

The fireman took a gulp, a gasp, a dry smack on the butt of his fag and finally began. 'We were working for hours trying to get the fires out, and when we'd done all we could, I got Shay – that's our driver – to take me to George's digs. The digs were gone – razed to the ground – chip shop, the lot. Gone. The whole street in tatters. They were still taking bodies out, and I'd already been to where he worked – that was in bits too, so naturally I thought the worst. Almost gave up, then I saw a young lad and asked him if he knew George. He gave me the address of a place up the Shankill Road where he used to have digs.'

'The Cleavers'?' da said.

'That's right, the Cleavers'. So that's where I went.'

'And?' ma said.

'Give the man a chance,' da said, coming over and filling up his glass again.

'Mister Cleaver was there. He told me George was all right: he'd been with him earlier, and the last he'd seen of him, he was helping a young lady home. He remembered her address, so . . . '

'You went there?'

'I thought I might as well. I was thinking it was nearly impossible to get out of Belfast – maybe we could sneak him back with us, you know? Anyway, I found the house, and the young lady Mister Cleaver had told me about answered the door.'

'Young lady?' Mona snarled. 'Is that what you call her?'

'Mona, please,' Jimmy said, then he took another wallop of whiskey before continuing. 'The house was just about standing – damaged, but standing, just the same. She answered the door. She was in her dressing gown. I said, "I'm looking for a man I believe helped you home this morning. I was wondering if you knew where he went." She seemed to know all about his situation; told me he'd got someone to send a telegram to Herbert to tell him to go ahead with the wedding and that.'

'A telegram? We didn't get any telegram.'

'Well that's what she said, anyway. I got the impression she knew the family.'

'And did she tell you where he'd gone?'

'She told me . . . '

Jimmy stared down into his glass, his face boiling with blushes.

'What did she tell you?'

'She told me he was up in bed. Then I heard him call down to her and . . . '

'Up in bed?'

Ma stood up.

'Charlie?'

'What?'

'You can go out for your run now.'

'But I don't want to. I'm too tired.'

'Now, I said. *Now.*'

Charlie did in his arse go for any run. The only run he took was a quick sprint down the stairs as far as the door, to open it and then slam it shut again. And a swift crawl back up to listen through the door ma had so firmly shut behind him. He had to pin his ear right up against it to hear Jimmy say, 'The next thing, George appeared at the top of the stairs, and I knew.'

But then ma started shouting and he was able to take a safer stance halfway down the stairs.

'Ah, what did you know, Jimmy?' she was saying. 'What did you know? I mean to say, there could have been any reason for it. He might have hurt himself and had to lie down, or something. After all, you said it yourself: his digs were gone. He could have been a friend of her brother's or anything. I won't have you speaking like that about my son, not in front of me or my family, or Amy and her granda – what must he think? And look at poor Mona – the state she's in. Now I know you've had a rough time of it, but you've no right to come here and speak like that. You're mistaken, that's all.'

'Look, I wish I was. But I'm not. He was only getting dressed when he came to the top of the stairs, and I knew by looking at him, anyway – his face; everything about him. I knew what had been going on.'

'Ah, no. No, not at all. You're upset, I know, but I'm going to have to ask you to leave. We've enough trouble in this house without your . . .'

'I'm telling you, I confronted him, and he wasn't denying anything. He even said he was sorry and hadn't meant it to happen at all. Then he threatened me.'

'Threatened you?'

'He said if I opened my mouth to Mona or anyone else, he'd effin' well kill me. He said he was going to break it off with Mona his own way – whatever the hell that's supposed to mean.'

Now ma was crying. 'Oh my God, I can't believe it. I just can't believe it.'

'Oh, you can believe it all right,' da said.

Mona's voice came last and loudest. 'There's your lovely son for you now,' she roared. 'There's your son.'

She nearly knocked Charlie flying when she came thundering out of the room. He had to press himself against the wall to let her pass by; he had to close his eyes so he wouldn't have to see her face. The fireman brother came out after her. 'Mona, Mona wait.' Charlie thought he'd better stay as he was. Then he heard Herbert.

'Jimmy, a word?'

'What?'

'Who was she?'

'I don't know.'

'Was she from Belfast?'

'No. No, I'd say she was a Dublin woman – very well spoken.'

'What did she look like?'

'Blondey hair. Why?'

'Would it have been sandy?'

'Yeah, sort of sandy. Look, I better go.'

'Did you get her name?'

'Betty, I think.'

'Would it have been Beatrix?'

'Yeah, I think that's what he called her – Beatty.'

'Fuckin' bastard,' Herbert said. 'Fuckin' bastard. I'll kill him.'

Charlie opened his eyes. Amy had come out to the hall and was standing behind Herbert, staring at him, a funny look on her face.

'What's it to you,' she asked him, 'who she is or isn't?'

Herbert said nothing.

'What's it to you, I asked? It's because it's her, isn't it?'

'Ah, fuck off,' Herbert said. 'And don't start.'

She unscrewed the ring from her finger and threw it at his face. It hopped off his face and fell on the floor. It rattled and winked on the polished lino. Herbert put his foot over it and then it settled down. He lifted his heel and brought it down on the ring. Crunch. 'Don't fuckin' start, I said.'

When he lifted his heel the ring had stopped winking.

Charlie went out for his run.

*

He counts his laps, growing into them. He can hear his own sounds: the engine of his body, his blood turning it on, pushing it over. After a while he can hear the earth breathe under his feet, and it feels like he's running across the chest of a giant. Hair presses into the soles – the shape of each individual tuft, then each individual blade. Another lap. The pointlessness of going over the same ground again and again is making him tired. Passing the same scrawny tree, the same section of the wall; coming back again to the same starting point. Like George and Herbert. All that fuss for nothing. All that fuss, and now they were back to where they were before Mona and Amy. Pointless.

He'd like to break out of this lap; to leave the starting point behind, let his legs take him wherever: cross country. But his runners are frail, and cross-country land is harsh. He has two pair of shoes: runners for training; spikes for the real events. But each time he wears the runners he feels they have grown thinner, and the spikes, which were new at Christmas, now pinch his feet. His feet won't stop growing and he can't ask ma again, not so soon. Not yet. Not while all this trouble still hangs over the house. He had planned on asking his brothers – on waiting for the right moment to put it to them. The day of the wedding, it was supposed to have been. Somewhere between the sing-song and the first goodwill glow of the drink. He had planned on just asking – telling them out straight. 'If I'm to get on the cross-country team,' he was going to say, 'I could do with a decent pair of spikes.'

They give him things all the time: Meccano sets that stay in the box, books he never reads, ties like strips of wallpaper and jokes to pass on that he always forgets. But they never give him runners and they never give him spikes. They give him money too – a few bob at a time – but it's never enough. And he never thinks to hold on to it until the next few bob, and the next after that. Never thinks to, until he's standing outside Elvery's sports shop wondering what it might be like to go in and pick out the best pair of spikes. Then he says to himself, Next time I'll save it. But he never does.

Another lap. And he remembers last winter: the trials in Roscommon, when his Christmas spikes were new, following behind a sprinkle of blood a barefooted bogman had left in his wake. He'd watched the speckles pop out like a rash on the frost-whitened bumps of the land. The land the horse had softened the day before, and then in the night, when the ice had gripped over, the hoofprints had tightened into knife-edged craters that tore the soles of the bogman's feet.

He sits down on the grass, pulls off one runner, then pulls off the other. He puts his hands into them and studies them for a while. He lifts one runner over his shoulder and fires it away. He lifts the other one then and fires that away too. Rafter was right. You wouldn't run snot in them.

PART THREE

I

Incessant downpour: all day downpour, rolling down ridges on corrugated rooftops, sidling along in galvanised gutters, dangling in a string of silver pips off the downturned canopy of the Main Enclosure Stand. Nearer to the ground, it dripped off hat brims, slid off noses and lisped on the skin of bookies' umbrellas, and bookies, buttoned up to the neck, stood along a pier of stout, black boxes popping raw hands in and out, while a stub of damp chalk wriggled and slipped between the wet fingers of an attendant clerk.

Fred Slevin looked out from the concrete cave under the stand and remembered a time when he wouldn't have noticed a drop – when the weather was just something that determined the state of the ground, and he would be out there in the middle of it skittering around. That was when he had been a bookie's runner and always in demand. Then one day in Punchestown, his heart had suddenly refused – hit him a thump and pulled him down – and that had put an end to his skittering around. He had gone over to the other side for a short while after that, running for the punters. Fat cats who would plank their arses on a bar seat for the day, shove pokes of money at him and roar in his face if anything went wrong. All that abuse had played on his nerves: he'd got a bit sloppy, made a few mistakes, and it hadn't been long before he had begun to notice that whenever he walked into the bar looking for prospects, eyes averted. Up to the ceiling, down to the card: everywhere and anywhere except near him. And Fred knew, then, that the worst thing that could happen to a runner had happened to him: he'd been marked as unlucky. Nowadays, he had to content himself with laying the odd bet for whoever would have him: American soldiers, until they had the system copped, or tinhorn gamblers who liked to pretend they knew more than they did. Some days he wasn't needed at all. Those were the dud days. The days when he would wait until the last race was over to comb the bars for the most promising group, and if he hung on the periphery long enough, nursing his bottle of stout, someone would always buy him a drink. And you could say what you liked about the racing crowd, once your face was known, even the biggest bastard among them wouldn't see you stuck for a lift back to town.

Now all he had in his pocket was a two-bob bit. In the old days, two bob was something to flip at the tinkers in passing or press into the palm of a stranger's child. Today it was the most important thing in his life: wrapped in a scrap of newspaper to give it bulk and keep it safe until he found the right moment – the exact moment – to use it to its full advantage. A lousy two-bob bit. He put his hand down into his pocket, pushed the coin aside and pulled out a packet of fags. His numb fingers lifted the flap and eased one out, then, changing his mind, pressed it back in: better keep a few in case he fell into company later. Only one would he allow himself, after this race. Another one, the race after next. 'Ah, Jaysus,' he said, 'there has to be, just *has* to be, a better way than this.'

Realising, then, that he had spoken aloud, he slid over to the far wall, leaving the remark behind him – disowning it, like a fart.

A cackle of ruddy-faced dealers shuffled by, waterproof triangles stuck to their heads. In for hot toddies, no doubt, and hot little sausages that would roll in the mouth and hopefully might choke them. He stepped aside to let them pass. A man with his coat pulled over his head almost bull-butted him; he stepped aside again, and now he was back at his original spot. An umbrella twirled, then spat in his face; an old woman's voice came out shaky behind it. 'A typical Baldoyle day,' she sighed, and Fred nodded, as if he agreed.

It was a familiar remark – 'A typical Baldoyle day' – meaning rain and cold and a wind that would slice the balls off you. And no doubt about it, but the weather had the upper hand today: the gale riding in from the estuary and the Two Shilling Park a slush heap of guffawing tents and squealing caravans so that the hardiest of hawkers had abandoned their pitches; even the three-card-tricksters had long since folded their tables and gone to ground in the bar. But he had always liked Baldoyle; had only recently come to notice the harshness of its ways. Once he used even make a holiday out of the busier meetings – the August Bank Holiday or Paddy's Day, maybe, when the rest of the city was dry and it seemed as though every gargler in the county had developed a sudden interest in racing. He would take lodgings the night before in a house down the village, scoffing off rashers and eggs the jockeys were obliged to refuse, while their big heads and narrow shoulders stooped good-humouredly over sheets of dry toast. Then off with him for his morning stroll, the sun on the grass before him and the sun on the sea out in the lagoon behind. And coming to the course, where he would spend that sacred hour watching it shape up with the props and smells of a Baldoyle race day, until the first marching sounds came up from the early train, giving him the signal: the time to relax was almost over. One last cigarette then, smoked to the brown finger, because from then on, there would only be time for a couple of quick plucks between races. That, to him, had been a typical Baldoyle day – days that were kind. When everyone knew his face, his name, his place at the bar. And cigarettes half-smoked were thrown to the ground.

He glanced up at the tick-tack men transmitting odds he had no use for now and thinking to himself that today would be another of those days. A dud. He'd go home this very minute – walk all the way, if he had to – if it wasn't so wet and he wasn't so tired. And even though he had his dry patch here, he felt as if he was dripping wet all over, right through his clothes, into his chest, and down to the very heart that had refused him that day in Punchestown. 'Ah, fuck the lot of you,' he said to himself, then, glancing down at his hand, found the tail-end of a cigarette smouldering away – a cigarette he couldn't remember lighting, never mind smoking. 'And fuck you and all,' he said, for depriving him of the pleasure.

He felt the day draw tighter to him, darker; and a mad little voice nudged into his head. 'Punch the wall,' it said. 'Go on, punch it.' He lifted his fist and curled it tight but then, looking up, uncurled it. He tried not to smile but just couldn't help it. The day had suddenly, magnificently, opened out again.

Some men were good on faces; others on names. Fred's speciality had always been the gait of a man. He could identify any man by his way of walking: whether he was bustler or a straggler; if he led from the shoulders or more from the hips. Or if he was one of those slopers who introduced himself from the front: mickey first. George was a shoulders man. And Fred turned to watch them now, edging their way through the crowd towards the bar. He waited for a minute and then carefully followed behind.

II

Maude wriggled her hand out of the bite-tight loop of parcel string. She pulled off her damp gloves, rubbed the senses back into her wrist, then arranged her purchases on the seat beside her. A box of sorted fancies – most of which would go uneaten; a new pair of evening gloves – which she probably wouldn't wear; a book – the title of which she had already forgotten; and a selection of newpapers and periodicals for poor old Henry to fiddle around with. Futile purchases, perhaps, but those little packages seemed to allow her some sort of purpose: a busy woman who had more to occupy her week than afternoon tea at the Shelbourne Hotel with a friend she had known all her life. A friend to whom she had already said everything she was likely to say and from whom she had heard everything she was likely to hear.

All about her was the smug hum of small groups. Older women withdrawing pins from afternoon hats. Young women with softer hats kept on, rising to exchange Continental kisses. An un-accompanied man sat here and there behind a newspaper or else looked unashamedly about. Like the man beside the window to her left, a listless hand brushing a dandruff of pastry flakes from his knee, one leg stretched out in front of him, one arm lying across the back of a sofa. A self-contained man: no company necessary to seem complete. Different for them, of course. Can go anywhere they like; lift themselves backside first up onto a bar stool; a few pleasantries with the counter-hand. If they stay long enough, somebody is bound to come along and occupy the perch next to them; strike up a conversation. That's how they make new friends; yes, that's how they do it.

She looked down at herself sitting on the edge of the sofa, handbag cocked up on her lap, as if she was in the outer office of some domestic agency, waiting to be interviewed for a job. How ridiculous she must look. She heard herself sigh, then – an old woman's sigh. And, 'No thank you, dear, I'm waiting for a friend,' she explained as usual, to the usual waitress – who you'd think would know by now. Lottie was invariably late. And *she* invariably waited.

A flicker of activity came in grey from the foyer: the removal of raincoats, the separation of fingers from umbrella crooks. Rain-blearied eyes in rain-smacked faces looked past her down through the room for a friend or a vacant table. Out of the dowdy shadows, trolleys and tea trays came in a silver burst, clashing under the chandelier lights, up early to accommodate the premature darkness of a rainy afternoon. Almost half past and still no sign of Lottie. Supposing she didn't come at all? Supposing that? But no, Lottie would never, never . . . Still, you'd think she'd make the effort to be on time. Once in her whole life wouldn't kill her. She began to feel a rise of anger towards her friend but twisted it deftly back into herself, pulling her hat away from her head, laying it crossly beside her, unclasping her handbag and taking out her cigarette case, then sending her fingers guessing over the shapes inside. Where was it? Where was the lighter? Had she forgotten it? She pulled the lips of the bag apart and shifted it a little here and there until at last she saw it – the neat, silver tip. She hauled it up. A shaking hand. She felt like slapping it. (Stop it! Stop it this instant!) Too confined, that's what I am. A few years ago, this wouldn't have bothered me at all. A rut, isn't that what they call it? 'She's in a rut.' How many times have I used those words myself about somebody else? And now somebody else is probably using them about me. And when? When did I start to address waitresses as 'Dear'? With my old woman's sigh. Really.

Lighting the cigarette, she forced herself away from the edge of the sofa and back into its cushion, crossed her legs and settled her hair. There now, she reassured herself, isn't that so much better? Then she heard her name.

Coming out of the mouth of a small man in Shelbourne livery, winding its way through tables and sofas and bandy-legged chairs. 'Paging Mrs Cleary, Mrs Maude Cleary . . . ' It could only be Lottie. Who else would still call her by the name of her first husband? Who else refused to accept the fact that for twenty-odd years her name had been Masterson, after Henry Masterson, her second husband – or 'that man', as Lottie preferred to call him. Her name zoomed in closer, belting out over the tambourine tinkle of china and silver, encircling layers of sandwiches and cakes, skimming across bowls of fluffed cream and pots of wet jam, rising ceilingwards and then soaring down, wall to wall. Heads moment-arily lifted from cups to watch it pass by; the rumble of conversation stepped out of its way; the man by the window straightened himself up. What's that? What's that?

It's my name. *My* name. Like a budgie that has been let out of the cage for a turn around the room. Maude raised the cigarette towards the maroon uniform, now resting on his heels in the centre of the room. 'If you'd like to come this way, madam,' he said, flourishing his gloved hand and leaving it in midair until she fumbled to her feet to obey it.

Lottie on the telephone. All set for a nice long chat, and her standing at the reception desk while the clerk's tongue lapped at envelope flaps and his ear wigged blatantly in her direction.

'I tried to get you at home but there was no answer. I said . . . '

'I . . . I had some shopping.'

'What? What's that?'

'Shopping.'

'Oh, what did you buy?'

'I'll tell you another time.'

'A bit of a cold,' Lottie explained. 'Hope you don't . . . '

'Not at all.'

'And with the weather the way it is, I thought . . . '

'Yes, yes.'

'Have you heard from . . . ?'

'Lucia? I got a postcard.'

'But you told me that last week. Nothing since?'

'No, nothing.'

'Oh. Are you going up to see that man this week?'

'Yes – tomorrow and Wednesday, as usual.'

'But really, dear, why upset yourself? Why bother at all? I mean, if he doesn't even know you half the time . . . And it's not as if you have been living together – you've been separated for years. Good God, you owe him nothing. I'm sure you have more to be doing with your time. Are you listening to me?'

'Yes.'

'And if you must go, once a week is quite sufficient. You used to go only once a week, after all; it didn't seem to do him any harm. When did you start to go twice? And *why*, for goodness sake?'

'I must go now, Lottie. Take care of yourself. Goodbye, dear. Goodbye.'

'My friend,' she explained to the hotel clerk. 'Not well, you know.'

Worried about the hotel clerk; worried about her parcels all alone on the sofa; the cigarette she had left burning in the ashtray (supposing it had slipped off the edge and onto the table). Worried about all these little things, she had forgotten to suggest dropping in on Lottie on the way back from the nursing home tomorrow. Just a little visit to see a sick friend – an ideal excuse. Not like inviting yourself at all. Perhaps she could just turn up. Bring the box of cakes. Lottie was partial to iced fondants. Why not?

Yes. Something to look forward to while she sat with Henry. While she watched him choose newspaper snippets to stick in his scrapbook or supervised the mismanagement of the scissors in his hand. While she tried to be patient; tried to be kind. Yes, something to *do*, for a change.

III

He found George down at the back of the bar, seated on an upturned beer crate, racecard bridged between his knees. Fred had always enjoyed running for George. George was good to him after. Not just with the few bob: he sometimes even included him in, as if he was part of the company instead of a hanger-on with a bottle of stout growing warm in his hand. He had never been able to make up his mind if he liked George or not: sometimes he did, sometimes he didn't. He could be terrible sharp at times, but in the end generosity had always tipped the scales in his favour. Looking at him now, Fred knew he should probably leave him alone. He had that look about him: the look of a man who was already defeated and was now just putting in time. He wouldn't be needing a runner. Fred was looking at another pointless day – and he'd had his bellyfull of them of late. He didn't care if there was no use for him – if all he could hope for was a couple of pints – at this stage he would be happy enough just to have someone to row in with.

'You don't mind if I row in with you, George?' he asked, as soon as he saw George's attention shift from the card to the bottle of stout on the floor.

George said nothing – which, as far as Fred was concerned, was as good as an invitation. If he hadn't wanted him, he'd have said something – something like 'Fuck off.' He waited at a respectful distance until he saw the last drop of porter had been sucked away and a loose, brown web was all that remained on the inside of the glass. Then he followed through the corridor George had cut in the crowd and considered the young man before him.

He knew George this long time, going back to when he had been a bookie's runner and George a kid at his father's side. Yet he knew nothing about his off-course life. He knew he lived in Belfast, all right, because any time he ran into him, he was either coming from, or on his way back there. But apart from that, he knew little else: if he was married; what he worked at; where he was from, even. Someone once said he was a Prod; someone else said that was nonsense. There had been a touch of the Prod about the father, all right: a small man with a limp; a bit of a dandy; always polite. But George wasn't anything like him. Fred wondered if the father was still alive. He could ask – but he wouldn't. He had made that mistake once before, when he had enquired about the younger brother – the nipper that used to go racing with them.

'Whatever happened to the nipper used go racing with you – the younger brother?'

'He died, that's what,' George had snapped, and Fred felt himself buckle inside.

He hadn't felt right for the rest of that day, and even now, thinking about it, he didn't feel right again. But fair enough, he should have known better. He had broken a very important rule between punter and runner: never ask a man his business, unless you're more than certain that he wants you to. He had deserved to feel bad; in fact, he had probably deserved a good hiding.

Fred could never remember learning these rules; he just seemed to have been born with them in his head. The thing to do was to know your place. When to go with him, when to leave him alone; discuss when he wanted to discuss, otherwise keep your mouth shut. You could take your cue from him on occasion, but you had to be sure to water it down. Laugh when he laughed, but not so loudly. Back up his opinion, but not so strongly. If you ran into company, remember that it was his company, and your own private views didn't matter a shite. After that, your job was simple enough: run bets, check prices, and go up to the bar on his behalf. Keep your nose clean and your eye sharp; everything else would take care of itself.

*

The two men stood at the mouth of the cave, looking out at the ring. Fred accepted the cigarette from George's box and settled it neatly behind his ear. Then he lifted his eyes to the tick-tack men.

Fluttering hands – white, fluttering hands; head to shoulder; left to right. Now elbow. Now shoulder again. He was aware of George standing beside him watching, waiting. But the rain had stretched the distance, blotting the edge of the white hands so that he could get no sense. He might as well be looking at washing flapping on the line: no sense. He squinted again but that just made it worse. It wasn't his fault: his eyes were impeccable – always impeccable – dividing and cutting right down to the bone of any matter, no matter how distant. No matter how rigmaroled. It was the fault of the bloody weather, but how could he explain that to George without sounding as if he was making an excuse? How could he say . . .

'Would you believe? I'm after forgettin' me binoculars, and the rain, don't you know, tends to . . . '

George unharnessed himself from the straps of his glasses and passed them over.

Now Fred was all business. 'Four to one against,' he said.

'And . . . ?'

'Zigzag stays at fours. Silver Challenge gone out to twenty. The rest of the field . . . '

'That'll do.'

Fred lowered the glasses and passed them back.

Now it was his turn to wait for George. He could nearly hear his brain tick over, dragging the decision backwards and forwards through the inner dispute. He turned away to allow some privacy but his eye still managed to catch the hand jerk into the pocket and come back out again with a couple of notes, then pull them apart: one for Fred, the other for his pocket.

'Zigzag. Got to McFarland. Ask for 9 to 2.'

'Zigzag it is.'

A few minutes later he was back watching George slice the docket in two and flip it over his left shoulder, and he felt it as hard as if the loss had been his own. Only one note left; maybe he had the main wad in his other pocket. Ah, surely he must have. The procedure was repeated: glasses passed; tick-tack read; crucial moment. Decision pulled forwards, backwards. Decision made. Hand in pocket, and the last note came up. Fred reached out to take it but George shook his head. 'I'll do this myself,' he said. Fred nodded and stepped aside.

IV

Outside, the rain had been waiting for her, revolving doors slapping her parcels firmly out. Not a taxi in sight. She decided to walk home, just to fill the afternoon up a bit. An interminable evening ahead: a chop, a tin of peas. An hour or so of insipid Saturday-night wireless. If Lucia were here, there would at least be a decent supper; the pictures, maybe, afterwards. And they could drive there; she didn't mind driving so much when she had company. She was hopeless without Lucia, really – hopeless (tinned peas; tinned, pimply peas). Even though everybody, including Lucia herself, assumed it to be the other way around. But Lucia saw to every little thing. Besides, she was a pleasant companion. A little dull, perhaps, but after years of grinning at people you never really liked, engaging in conversations that bored you to tears – and were often subsequently held against you – being dull was sometimes a relief. They could go places together – the opera, the theatre – places where you'd look odd on your own. But Lucia wouldn't be home from Italy for another fortnight. Another two weeks on her own, and in the meantime, what? One afternoon tea, four visits to Henry, one visit to Lottie tomorrow – which of course would be a bonus but would also invite the inevitable lecture on Henry. ('When did you start to visit him twice a week?' she had asked. 'And *why?*')

He meant nothing to her now, of course: Lottie was right. Just some old man in a nursing home she went to see twice weekly. Some old man who didn't even know her name. And they were strangers now, this man and she. This man she had left years ago because of his constant infidelity. This man who had broken her heart and then snubbed her in the street a few months later, and who was still, come to think of it, snubbing her now. Ten years Henry had been in that nursing home. Sixteen years since they had separated. And yet his very existence still had a hold over her – still manipulated her thoughts, the way he had done when they were married. Here he was right in her head, all the way down Merrion Row, up along the tall squad of houses swaying into the curve of Pembroke Street, across to the kiosk in the centre of the road where she would stop to buy his sugary treats, on then up the Adelaide Road, all the way home: here's Henry.

Henry. Sometimes she passed the time chatting to other visitors. That nice police superintendent who sat with his sister, patiently answering her endless question. The same question – the one question – over and over. 'What time is it now? What time is it now?' Or that Bart Tully fellow, the one her sister Kate had left money to in her will. He was often there, visiting a man who used to work in his pub. A nice enough chap. Nice enough, in any case, to help her put in an hour that often seemed like several. Yet once that hour had passed pleasantly enough – for the first year or so, anyway, when Henry had been manageable enough, and of course the visits had only been once a week at that stage. She could take him walking through the roads and squares of Monkstown and Seapoint, their London names causing him some confusion – he always expecting some familiar landmark from his London days to suddenly emerge. Then down to the seafront to look over the railings at the small band of flabby grey beach. Poor children bathing in their underwear; parents sitting along the stone ledge behind. Henry rarely spoke, but sometimes he could be unexpectedly affectionate, kissing or stroking her face. But it could have been any face, really – the only thing about her that really interested him was the sweetie bag she kept in her pocket, and the intervals when she would reach up to him, so that he could feed like a horse from her hand. When he did speak, it was usually to indulge some dreadful outburst. Like the time they saw that man hopping out of the sea to kilt himself in a towel that was a bit too small for his particular bulk, then struggling with his trunks and frotting his bare backside, while he cast a modest eye about.

'You've missed a bit,' Henry had cried down joyfully to him. 'I say, my man, you've missed a bit.' And then, by way of explanation, Henry had pulled his coat-tail aside, stuck his own bottom in the air and prodded at it furiously. The poor man had nearly died. She thought she would die of embarrassment herself, although later, with Lucia, she thought she might die from laughing.

Sometimes you just couldn't laugh. Times when he might suddenly decide he had recognised somebody and wave; call out to a name, a face, that had climbed up out of the undergrowth of his memory; and then proceed to terrify some stranger on the street. Such episodes had grown more frequent in the past few years, while he had become more difficult; always at himself, pulling at his flies, trying to take his clothes off. But it was that day when he'd nearly got himself killed on the Monkstown Road that she had had to accept that she could no longer manage him at all.

It was the church that did it – the church that fills up the junction leading out of the village. Henry had gazed up at it, as if for the first time, and, before she knew it, had run out after it, like a child dancing after a balloon. She couldn't catch him; his long legs, hopping away from her, suddenly stopped. A bus screeched to a halt only inches behind him. A busload of drunken men, out on a Buck Excursion, pushing each other out of the way to get a better look. A better laugh. To laugh at him. At a man who had once been so proud; a man who could, just by his presence, command respect. Who, years before, at the outset of their courtship, had shown her this very church and explained gently the chess pieces on its crown and had had the grace, then, to be embarrassed when she had explained that she knew all about chess – was a ladies' champion, actually. Laughing at him. Not one beer-ruddied face pressed against one window had shown the smallest bit of compassion. She couldn't budge him; he wouldn't move. People on the pavement stopped to stare; somebody shouted out of a window. A nurse tutted from behind a high, polished pram, then turned it hurriedly to scurry down the road. As if Henry was going to hurt the baby. As if . . .

After that, she never took him out again. After that, she just sat in the window beside him while he played with his bits of newspapers. There had been that one exception, of course. That time when she did take him out, but . . . she would never think about that again. Never. Even now, it made her want to cry to think about it. ('When did you start going twice a week?' Lottie had asked. 'And *why?*') After that day it was – that terrible day. That terrible thing she had done. It was after that that she had decided the only way to make it up to Henry was to give him another day of her week. And she would continue to do so, week after week, month after month, year after year, until one or the other of them had run out of days.

V

George looked up at the blanket of faces. Now and then a ripple occured where a newcomer had managed to upset the balance, but other than that, the grandstand was solid. He could see the shape of Fred Slevin still cowering where he had left him and decided to chance the stand anyway, shifting his binoculars around to his chest, squeezing in, dipping, rising through the cram of bodies until the bench at the top came into view. He ran his eyes along it: every inch scalloped with the toes of shoes, boots and galoshes. There was even a man at the far end balanced like a cormorant up on one leg. He took two steps back down.

He'd never seen the stands so packed, the rest of the course so empty. He scratched his face, then rolled his shoulders. Itchy; he felt itchy. Crowds made him itchy at the best of times; since the air raids, he could hardly tolerate them. Endless nights stuck in a shelter, or that one night when he had traipsed with the ditchers to the safety of the fields outside the city. More than four years had passed since then, yet standing like this, shoulder to shoulder, breathing the used air of strangers, inhaling their smoke, smelling their smells, swallowing their coughs, he felt as though he was right back in the thick of it. All shovelled in like cattle looking out, waiting for something to happen. He almost expected the purr of the Our Father to break out around him, or the less optimistic chant of 'Nearer My God to Thee' to come drifting across from the neighbouring stands.

A man nudged in beside him, pulled off his cap, whacked the drops away and declared, 'A monsoon. A veritable monsoon.'

Further down the line somebody whined, 'Summer, me arse. Is it never going to stop?'

A drunk on the far side of him sighed out a whiskey breath and delivered a general statement. 'And the rain fell exceedingly for forty nights and forty days. On all the faces of the earth. On all the faces . . . '

Then the white flag was raised and there was silence again.

He lifted his glasses, but as soon as he had the eyepieces positioned, the back of a large head spilled into view. He adjusted the thumbscrew but the big head wavered – shrinking, then enlarging. George put down the glasses and looked at the thick neck with the barber's nick still fresh on its uppermost roll, and on top of the head an old-fashioned derby raised high at the crown. He wouldn't be able to see a thing through that lot. If he took off the hat, maybe . . .

And he was about to suggest it to the man himself when the drunk got in before him. 'Here, you – any chance you might like to take off your hat?'

The big man turned his head slightly. 'Any chance you might like to fuck off?' he growled back.

A young woman beside the big man gasped, 'Daddy!' and fluttered an apology behind her.

'Mutton-head,' the drunk muttered. 'Who does he think he is? Big fuckin' muttoner.' Then he rolled up his eyes and gave George a nudge.

George turned away. He looked down through the thick crop of heads. Down they went, step after step, giving way to a spread of black brollies where the roof cut off its shelter. He considered pushing his way through and over to the railings, which at least were deserted. But he had tried that earlier and had got no satisfaction – just blotches of rain on the lenses and a brown, indistinguishable stream taking the bend. A miserable day; he'd be glad to see the back of it. A day of mistakes and rain. He had the train ticket for Belfast in his pocket and enough for a bite in the buffet car. Once he got back he had a case full of money under his bed. Another bagful to collect come Monday. So why was he still here? Why couldn't he have left it alone?

On the way in, he had made a deal with himself: stay as long as the money in your pocket lasts, then as soon as it runs out, run out yourself. And it seemed to him somehow that he had been backing against himself all day, so he could do just that. He should never have come in the first place: he had too much on his mind; too much to do; too much to decide. And he was tired after a fortnight in Dublin. Tired and sluggish. And itchy, itchy, itchy. And, ah fuck this, he thought, what's the point? Then he indicated with a nod to the man beside him his wish to pass by.

'You're dead right, squire,' the drunk said. 'I don't blame you one bit. But you might as well stay where you are. Here, you wouldn't happen to have such a thing as a smoke?'

George ignored him and pushed on past. But the drunk couldn't seem to leave him alone. His voice followed him down the steps. 'Sure, be the time you get down, I say be the time you . . . And here, what about me smoke? I said, what about . . . ? Ah, hold on a second and I'll be down with you.'

George turned around to look for the face he was about to insult. But the big man in the grey derby hat blocked out the view. He looked hard at George. George held the look for a moment, then, just to annoy him, threw a wink at the daughter.

Back on the ground, instant relief – a feeling of freedom. He watched the diehards take on the rain: men with newspapers over their heads and storm collars tugged up to their ears. Women, blue with the cold, straw hats stuck to their heads, cloth flowers stuck to their legs. A man cocked up his umbrella and bailed out ahead of him. He got in behind him, head down, feet splashing, arriving back beside Fred just as the race stretched into the final furlong. He lifted his head, sifting through the din, until one name unravelled itself.

'Whelan has it,' he said.

'Did you not . . . ?' Fred asked.

'No.' He glanced at his watch. 'Sorry, Fred, I'm not carrying, I'm afraid. I'll have to catch you some other time . . . '

'Ah, don't trouble yourself, George . . . Don't trouble. So what are you doin' now?'

'Now? I'm going for a piss. Then I'm collecting my bag from behind that bar in there. And then? Then I'm getting the fuck out of this place.'

He stood in the lavatory doorway, swiping the rain off his face and hair; shrugging it off his jacket; flicking it away from his shoes. Then he spotted Old Bill standing at the latrine: dapper as ever and dry as a bone. He stayed back until the old man had finished and was ready to turn around. Then he stepped forward and made himself known.

'Ah, George, me old son . . . '

'Bill. You must be the first friendly face I've seen today.'

'I've just been this minute lookin' in the mirror and thinkin' the same thing meself. Hold on there you now, till I shake your hand.'

Old Bill turned away to the sink and washed his hands. He lifted the towel with the tip of his little finger and then dropped it again. 'You're a dirty shower of bastards down here, do you know that? Half of youse don't bother washing your hands at all and now some bugger's gone and blown his snout in thon towel.' He pulled a clean handkerchief from his pocket and snatched it over the top of his fingers. When his hands were dry, he offered one to George.

'You're gettin' better lookin' every time I see you.'

'You don't look so bad yourself.'

'At my age, George, what does it matter? Tell me, is it true you're moving back down?'

'I've to tie up the loose ends first, but yes, from Wednesday on, I'll be a Dublin man again.'

'A Dublin man that's the proprietor of a garage, if I hear rightly.'

'Half-right. I'm buying into a partnership. Starting next Saturday.'

'Saturday? You'll be working Saturdays? Dear sake, how you goin' to swing that?'

'There's a bookie's across the road. It'll have to do for the moment.'

'I'm pleased for you, Georgie – wish you all the best. Did you say you were going up to Belfast?'

'That's where I'm headed now.'

'Will you not stay for the Summer Plate?' He lifted his eyes to the ceiling. 'Summer plate? Christ, don't make me laugh. I know, why don't you stay down until tomorrow and come back up with me? I've a load of cigarettes to collect on the way. I'm tellin' you, Georgie, the cigarette famine up above's keepin' me goin'. Long may it last.'

'I can't, Bill, I'm cleaned out.'

'No luck at all?'

'I should be taken out and shot.'

'Ach, we can't have that, so we can't.'

Old Bill reached for his pocket but George caught him at the elbow. 'No, Bill, I don't need it. I've bucketfuls up in Belfast and I'm just as happy to leave now.'

'Don't be daft. There'll not be a sinner in Belfast this night. Everyone's away jollificating in Bangor for the holidays, and what difference can one night make? Here, do you remember the first time we met in Bangor? You fair cleaned me out, so you did.'

'Which time was that?'

'Ach, do you hear him now. The time I'd nothin' left to give you, so I give you me gran'far's bowler. Christ on a bicycle, but such a job as I'd explaining that to me poor old mother. Do you still have it?'

'I do.'

'Do you want to sell it back?'

'Not for a hundred quid, Bill.'

Old Bill laughed and grabbed him by the arm. 'You're a sound man, Georgie – you always were. You'll be sorely missed, so you will. The rest of us aside, the Millys will be throwing themselves into the Lagan.'

George smiled. 'I grew out of Millys a long time ago.'

'Oh now, nothing wrong with a good mill girl. Here, talkin' of mill girls, you never guess who I run into in Dublin last week? Ach, what's his name – you know him. Used to work in the yard with you. Do you remember? The boy you saved from getting the sack.'

'Percy?'

'Aye, that's right. Percy Paget.'

'I haven't seen him for a long time.'

'He hasn't changed not one little bit. Still talk the ears down offa your head. He's working in Dublin, you know.'

'Is that right?'

'Aye. He's managin' a dance hall.'

'That'd be just up his alley.'

'And it is, too – it's in an alley. Where was it now . . . ? He told me. Off Grafton Street, it is.'

'I know it.'

'Oh, he was full of you, so he was. And what a great fella you were – said he taught you how to dance.'

'He did in his arse. Did you ever see Percy dance?'

'You should drop in and see him.'

'It took me long enough to shake him off the first time around.'

'Oh aye, I can well imagine,' Old Bill said, and then stopped smiling. 'Here, I suppose you'll be wanting to have a piss?'

'That's the general idea.'

'Ah, not in front of me, George. I can't bear the sound of a young man's slash. Sometimes I do think it's not a doctor I do need, it's a plumber.'

George laughed.

'I'm not jokin'. I've been stood there for the past five minutes – all I got was a tinkle. I've spent most me afternoon in here. It's all the fuckin' rain, keeps making me want to go – and then when I get there, there's nothin'. *Me,* that used be able piss like a dog.'

Old Bill moved away and then stopped. 'Show us your card.'

George handed him the card. 'I'm not taking any money off you, Bill.'

Old Bill pencilled something onto the card, then eased a note away from his wad.

'Here, shove this on,' he said.

George looked down at the mark on his card and laughed, 'On Sh . . . ?'

'Ah, ah, ah. Don't say it. Don't mention the name. You know my wee superstitious ways. Go on, take it. Regard it as a good-luck gesture for your new venture. It'd be bad form to refuse.'

'Look, Bill, it hasn't a hope.'

'Oh, I don't know. Tell you what, if it does you any good, buy me a drink after, and catch you the later train.'

'Tell you what, if it does me any good, I'll go back into town with you this evening and take you up on that offer of a lift tomorrow. How about that?'

'That sounds like a fair deal to me.'

'But . . . '

'Trust me, George. Do it each way, mind. And on the tote.'

'On the tote?'

'Aye.'

'Each way?'

'Look, Georgie, when you get to my age, you realise one thing . . . '

'How's that, Bill?'

'You don't always have to come first to win.'

VI

Maude, in the doorway, drew her fingertips down along the spine of the umbrella until its skirt gave into a fold. She opened it again into a full pop, dispatching the excess drops down onto the flagstones outside her front door. She was inside.

The first thing to do was to walk through the house, reaching out to each light switch that she passed, until all the shadows were gone. Then she came back to the box of cakes. Had they survived? The box was a little damp but – she pulled the string aside and lifted the flap – the cakes were unspoilt. She would leave the box to dry out by the fire and return the cakes then, all set for Lottie's tomorrow. She got out of her coat and went into the sitting room, where she took a match to the fire. The doorbell rang, startling the match out of her hand. She listened for the second ring before getting up to answer it. It was Samuel.

'Samuel. How lovely,' she said. 'Come in, come in. What a nice surprise. Would you like tea? I have some cakes. Or perhaps you'd prefer a drink?'

A drink he had – the sherry glass like a bauble in his hand. She arranged the cakes on a plate and put them on the table beside him. His face all shy, he put the glass down and began to construct one of his home-made cigarettes.

'And how's the car going?' he asked, as he always did.

'Oh, fine. I only take it out on Sundays, really,' she replied, as she always did, 'or Wednesday afternoons, when the shops are closed and there isn't too much traffic. When I visit Henry, you know.'

'Still as nervy as ever?'

'Oh, Samuel, I'm hopeless. I must say, I'm looking forward to the day when Lucia can drive. No more worrying about traffic and signals and right-hand turns – and as for reversing . . . How are Lucia's lessons coming along, by the way?'

'She's doing well.'

'Oh good. She'll be a damn sight better than me, and at least the car will be put to some use for a change. I suppose I really am that "Only one lady owner" that I am told you salesmen use to your advantage.'

'Except nobody ever believes us.'

'I should write you a testimonial.'

Samuel smiled and the room filled up, fragrant with his tobacco.

She wished she had two chops, so she could ask him to stay for supper. She wished she had braved the rain and pulled a few potatoes up from the garden. She wished that, even if she had managed to master the rudiments of domesticity and had had all the necessaries for a good supper in her larder, she would only have the nerve.

'And how's young Maudie – or should I say "Mo"?'

'Ready to pop any day now.'

'Then you'll be a grandfather. Imagine. And I a grand-aunt.'

'I know.'

'What about Bennie? Is he still home? I had half-expected him . . . '

'Ah, you know Bennie – I've hardly seen him myself. But he'll be here for another while: he may honour you yet. He's been spending most of the time with Herbert and George – George has been home on holiday – running wild, I suppose; you know what they're like when they get together.'

'They're not the worst, Samuel. Did you know they went to see Henry?'

'No?'

'Oh yes, last week – matron told me. I could hardly believe it myself, but it seems they were out for a drive and dropped in. I thought that was very good of them. Poor old Henry, of course, wouldn't know them from Adam, but it was good of them, just the same. Apparently they had the place in an uproar – Bennie playing the piano, George and Herbert getting all the old ladies up to dance. They're so full of life.'

'You heard myself and George are going into business together?'

'Yes, I heard something . . . '

'That place I bought in Terenure before the war, it's been lying idle ever since and I haven't got the heart to start up another place from scratch, so George is going to take it on. We've been talking about it for years, but with the war and that, we've had to keep putting it off. Anyway, I wouldn't mind taking things a bit easier, now I'm getting on, and as I see it, there's no use in building something if you've to stand there holding it up for the rest of your life. And he's a good lad, George – not afraid of hard work. Bit too fond of the gallopers, but I'm told I have no cause for concern – which, I suppose, is his way of telling me to mind my own business. Still, he has the money to buy into Terenure, so he can't be doing too badly out of them. He's gone back to Belfast today to sort himself out; he'll be back on Wednesday and, all going well, the garage is to open next Saturday.'

'That's wonderful news, Samuel. I'm sure you'll both make a great success of it.'

He went quiet then for a minute, narrowing his eyes into the fire, sucking the last bit of life out of his cigarette. Then he spoke again.

'I was thinking maybe I'll go with you next week.'

'Where?'

'To see Henry. Tomorrow doesn't suit, nor Wednesday, but I could go with you next Sunday.'

'Oh, don't worry, Samuel, he's . . . Well, he's gone beyond noticing.'

'Still, I should. I'd like to.'

'That would be lovely, if you're certain.'

'I'll call for you – say, around two?'

'Yes, Samuel, thank you.'

'We can go for stroll, if you like, after – maybe have tea in the Royal?'

'I'd like that.'

'I usually use Sunday to catch up on paperwork, but now that I have a partner I feel I can skive off.'

She raised her glass. 'Well, here's to skiving off, then – and here's to George.'

'To George.'

He lowered his glass. 'I had hoped it would be Bennie, but . . . '

'He's not interested?'

'No, Bennie has no interest. All he wants is his oul' jazz music and galavanting all over the States with that band of his. He'll go back to America as soon as he can. I doubt he'll ever live in Ireland again.'

'Oh well, you never know – he might change his mind.'

'No, he's a Yank and that's the way he'll stay.'

He looked so sad; she longed to touch him. But of course she couldn't. She could change the subject, though – quickly. 'And tell me, is there no sign at all of any of those big lumps of nephews of mine settling down at all?'

'Not as far as I'm aware.'

'Strange to think, isn't it, Samuel – not one of the younger generation have married yet, apart from Mo, of course. I often wonder, did we put them off?'

He laughed. 'You may be right.'

'Of course, Herbert and George did manage to go as far as actually getting engaged, so they can't be completely against it.'

'No.'

'Shame they didn't go through with it, all the same. I liked George's girl very much, I must say. I knew her family, you know. Her mother told me she never really got over it. Four years – it's a long time for a young girl to pine.'

He put down his glass and looked at her. 'If it's a wedding you're after, I might be able to help you out. It's why I called to see you, in fact.'

'Oh?'

'I don't know how to say this, really.'

'Samuel?'

'Lucia . . . ' He pulled in a breath, paused for a moment and then released it on a string of words. 'That is, I've asked Lucia and she's agreed and we're to be married and that's what I've come to tell you. Lucia and I are engaged to be married. There, I've said it.' He laughed. She laughed. Out loud. Too loud.

'You and Lucia? I don't believe it. How? I mean, when?'

'I wrote to her in Italy, and I got her answer yesterday afternoon.' He placed his hand lightly on his breast pocket. The letter, *her* letter; precious in his inside pocket. Precious to his breast.

'We haven't told anyone else yet. Lucia was a little worried about telling you, so I thought I would come on her behalf, seeing as how I'm responsible, so to speak.'

'Me? Worried about me? Not at all. I'm just surprised. I mean, I had no idea . . . Well, you and Lucia. I had no idea – no idea at all. This calls for another drink.'

'You think it's ridiculous, and me about to be a grandfather?'

'We all deserve happiness, Samuel, no matter our age.'

'To tell you the truth, Maude, you'd get fed up being on your own.'

'Yes. Yes, you would.'

'There is an age difference, of course. But she doesn't seem to mind.' He smiled bashfully.

'No. No, she wouldn't.'

Too brightly, she crossed the hearthrug, raising the sherry decanter to his glass. A drop fell on the bridge between his thumb and hand. An amber drop, shining. 'I'm delighted for you both. Really I am.'

It was only then she realised; only then. Looking down on that tiny amber drop resting on his work-worn hand; only then. That she had always been a little in love with him herself. Even when he had been her first husband's chauffeur all those years ago, there had been something odd in the way he had made her feel. When he ran off with her sister, that feeling went, but it came back again when he did, after Kate had died. It was only when she saw him, spoke to him – his soft voice, slow eyes. Yes, she had always . . . If he had asked her, what would she have said? If he had asked *her*.

'We go back a long way, you and I,' he said. 'I used to call you ma'am. I have to stop myself from doing it still, at times.'

'Oh, Sam.'

'Do you remember that motor Pat bought? The hupmobile. He wanted you to learn to drive.'

'I wouldn't.'

'They don't make cars like that any more.'

'No . . .'

'I remember helping you into it and driving you both to the races. A long time ago, it was. Nineteen eighteen, just before the First War ended.'

'The First War? My God, 1918. And now the second one has come and gone.'

'You were having a tiff of some sort – you pretending to be cross with him. I envied you both, you were so close. I thought I would always be alone. Then Kate and I . . . I thought I would never love anyone again. But . . .'

'You do now?'

'Yes. It's a different sort of love, I suppose. But yes.'

He leaned forward suddenly and looked at her more closely. 'Maude? Have I upset you? I'm sorry – talking about Pat like that – I wasn't thinking.'

'No, no . . . It's quite all right. It's nothing.'

'Are you sure? I didn't mean to make you sad.'

'I'm not sad, really I'm not.'

She returned to her seat and filled up her own glass. Then, lighting a cigarette, looked back at him.

'What am I to do with you, Samuel? First you take my sister, now you take my companion. You won't be happy until I'm all alone, like an old goat on the side of a mountain.'

And she smiled her best smile for him, just to show it was a little joke.

After Samuel left, she sat for a long time watching the fire fade to grey. When she had finished the decanter of sherry, she took the plate of cakes onto her lap and dropped them one by one into the firegrate, waiting for the last fondant skin to shrug off in the heat and then cringe into the heavy smell of burnt sugar.

At seven o'clock she put the snib on the front door and pulled herself up the stairs, touching the light switches as she passed, leaving darkness behind her, as she had earlier left light. On her bed, she lay listening to the rain whispering on the pavement outside her window. She wondered how the puddle was getting on. For days she had been keeping an eye on it, watching it fill the dip outside the kitchen door, the rings expanding or tightening across its skin. And remembering how, as a child, she used to watch with a similar weariness the puddles outside her father's house. She had looked at it before she went out into town and was about to check on it again when Samuel had rung the bell. That was how she supervised the passing of the day: the puddle, the garden – grey in the morning, grey before dark. The light only changing for a short time in the early evening, when the sky buckled into darker bulges and an unseen sun pushed against it, causing a sudden light to relieve itself over the grass and the vegetable patch that Lucia had planted just before the war. This was how she had marked the passing of a rainy day when she was a child. This was how she passed it now. Now that she was old.

VII

Fred Slevin felt like singing, with the glow of whiskey rosy on his skin and the two ten-bob notes George had given him pressed between the pages of last year's pocket diary – still there, still square and . . . Oh, oh, Anton-io. Both still intact-io.

He would have loved an oul' sing-song: to spread his arms out to a tune, dip his knees down to it, then feel the words ooze up from his balls. A one, a two, and . . . Oh, oh, Anton- . . .

He studied the two men a few strides ahead of him: George (definitely a shoulders man) and Bill. Bill, now, would be more of a bustler: the sort of fella who pinned the jacket to his belly button before he ran for a bus. (Not that he'd ever have to run for a bus, mark you.) But whatever way they managed their gait, one thing was certain – they weren't the sing-along types. And so he swallowed the tune back down into himself and, for the third time in the last hour, climbed into the back seat of Bill Cassell's car.

'God, it's like a feckin' shop in here,' he said, throwing his head back and laughing. 'Do you not think?' Then, noticing he was alone, he cut himself short. The other two had remained outside and were now circling the car, tipping and nodding their way around its finer points, in the manner of a couple of cattle dealers.

Fred settled himself in between the cartons and bags laid out on the floor and block-bricked up against the far door, over which a yellow tartan rug was draped, by way of disguise. He fingered the fringe of the rug and, after resisting the urge to slip his hand under it, reached up instead to the leather hand-strap and slipped his wrist through it. And now, nice and steady, the time had come to have a stern word with himself: Think – think before you speak. And keep yourself to yourself, there's a good man. All that talk is just bursting to get out of you, isn't it? And we all know which exit it's going to take, don't we, now? That's right – the one straight out through your arse. So unless you want this pair to know you can't hold your drink, I'm warning you now – keep it buttoned.

Outside, the inspection was drawing to an end. A Georgeful of admiration stroking the bonnet; a Billful of pride patting the roof. They'd be back in the car in another few minutes, giving him just enough time to pull himself together and maybe indulge in his own little moment. And do you ever really know what's around the corner? he asked himself then. Did you ever even dream things could turn out so good?

He closed his eyes, remembering how he had been just a short time ago at Baldoyle. Slow steps dragging – and the only ones dragging. Everyone else seemed to be in such a hurry, running against time, while he just played with it, petering it out between races; between smokes. Up and down the grey world under the stands, looking for colour; looking in windows. Big windows with drinkers pressed to the glass; little, grid-covered ones where the toteman's shadowy hand slid in and out, the red of his spiked rubber thimble like an open wound against all that grey. Step by step and back again past the gusts of wind blowing in from the entrances. Blowing in thoughts of the evening to come. His room in Cuffe Street flats; sitting on the side of his bed; nothing to do; no wireless to listen to, even. Nothing at all – just the sound of his own breath or the bleats and bawls coming out of the tenements as the ritual of the weekly wash got under way: the wet slap of a mother's hand on bare legs; the child's screech that would follow. And then a long interval until the pubs would close. Women hair-bating each other down on the street; men singing sideways, careless with words. Correcting those words in his own head, as if they would hear or heed him.

That would have have been his Saturday-night entertainment. Only for that long, low whistle that had come soaring up behind him, spinning like a fizzgig through the crowd. He had stopped and turned, darting his eyes about until he had found the source of the whistle. And there he was – he suddenly was.

'George! I thought you were supposed to be . . . '

'Changed me mind,' says he, twisting the notes out of his pocket and passing them down low-hand. 'Will that keep you going?' (Will it *what?*)

'Oh, thanks very much, George. Much appreciated.'

Then Bill had come up on the inside with his hand out-stretched. 'Bill Cassell,' says he.

'Oh . . . eh, Fred Slevin.'

'Do you mind if I ask you a personal question, Fred?'

'No, I don't think so.'

'Do you take a drink yourself?'

'I do.'

'Well what the fuck are we hanging around here for?'

There he was then. And here he was now. Not a thing to worry about except his timing. When to offer his cigarettes (only the once so far). When to put his hand in his pocket (quick enough for them to notice, but not too quick so that, somehow, someone would always get in before him). But most importantly of all, when to go to the jacks. He had been afraid to go on his own in case they had spoken about him.

'Who's your friend, George?'

'I wouldn't call him a friend, exactly. He's just some hanger-on I took pity on. A washed-out tout – you know the type.'

As long as he stayed in their company, Bill would never have to hear those words. So he could go with George, but not with Bill, because Bill took too long and you had to wait for him, in case George might decide that he wanted to go as soon you got back out to the bar. It was like the fox, the goose and the bag of corn: it wasn't impossible, you just had to pick the right combination, that's all.

How many whiskeys was that he had had now? One at the races, when he had started to feel the weight of the ale, and one in each of the pubs they'd stopped off at so far. And no trouble getting the whiskey, either: none of this, 'We only sell whiskey between the hours of . . . ' or 'Sorry, sir, we've just sold the last of our quota.' It was ordered and it was served and it had been sat up to and discreetly relished. No batting of eyelids had occurred, on either side of the counter. Now that's what Fred called *class*.

He blinked out the window. The sun had decided to show itself at last; the sky scalded from it, the sea squeaky with light all the way back out to Howth. 'It turned out lovely after . . . ' he began. Then he saw the two men stoop into the car and, remembering he had said that the last time, the last pub – tapered the comment into a dum-de-dum dum.

Oh, they were the best fellas in all the world, all the same – you couldn't meet better. He would have liked to have told them, too. To have said it to them, out straight. 'Oh, you're the best oul' skins . . . ' But a little bell inside his head told him that it might be better left unsaid. Dum-de-dum dum.

Wasn't it enough to be seen with them up at the bar, just the three of them together. Ha ha ha . . . laughing their heads off; the best of pals. A man of importance with men of importance. Everyone looking at them, too; everyone must have thought it – the best of pals. And the way Bill kept grabbing his arm when it was time to laugh at a joke (which was just as well, because half the time he didn't know when the fuck he was supposed to laugh). And the way the George fella just left his money on the counter, Yank-style, so that Fred never seemed to have the time to get his own hand into his pocket. 'What are you havin', Fred?'

'Ah no, here, let me. Let me.'

'What are you havin', I said?'

'I'll have a small one so, thanks George. But I'm getting the next one, mind . . . '

'Ah, small one, me arse,' Bill says. 'Give the man a double.'

He could have had anything he wanted – anything at all. Although what he really would have loved was one of them ham sandwiches that had been grinning out from under the glass dome on the counter of the last pub: pink of ham and yellow of mustard; just the job to soak up the drink. But of course he couldn't have said that. Still, they might go for a bite yet; bound to ask him along if they did. And it wouldn't be for a ham sandwich, either, you could be sure of that. A lump of golden-vein steak; a spoonful of sloppy brown onions. Or what about a few mushroom buttons, sliding around in a puddle of steak blood. Next time he'd better make sure to buy. Slap his money on the counter the second the barman stepped up. Or at least put up a bit more of a fight. Next time.

He rolled the window down a fraction and a blurt of sea air

fell fresh on his face; just what he needed to keep him awake. If he was with anyone else he might chance forty winks, but not now. Not in front of this pair, with their hollow legs and constitutions of iron, as if they'd been drinking buttermilk all day. A cat's nap, that's all – just until they got back into town or to the next pit stop. Which would be where? He tried to think. How many more pubs before town? Fairview in a few minutes, then the North Strand. Plenty of pubs. Grainger's. Cusack's. The one at the Five Lamps. What was it called again? Or even better – restaurants. Hotels with grill-rooms, then? Someplace where they might stop for a feed. But the strain of thinking pushed down on his eyelids and . . . careful now, he warned himself – you're beginning to didder. Light a cigarette: that should concentrate the mind for a bit. He put his hand into his pocket and crept his fingers into the box: only the one left. Better forget it so.

Then Bill's hand came over the back seat, a white stem pert on the lip of a silver case.

'Smoke?' he offered.

'Oh, thanks Bill, I don't mind if I do. I meant to get some . . . ' he said, with a tutty-tut-tut at his own forgetfulness.

He leaned forward, steadying the tip of the cigarette into the blister of light. 'That's a nice lighter you have there, Bill.'

'This? Oh, I have this years. Got it in Monte Carlo, actually.'

'Is that a fact . . . '

'Here, have a look.'

'Oh, thanks.'

Not sure what he was supposed to do with it then, he played with it for a bit, turning it in his hand, flipping the lid open, then closed, giving the cog a bit of a thumb-flick: once; twice; once again. Then, when he had done all he could do – bar licking it –

to show his appreciation, finally weighed it a couple of times on his palm before handing it back.

'Very swank indeed.'

Then he noticed that something was different; something had changed. He thought for a minute, squeezing his brain . . . Ah yes, that was it – Bill had given the driver's seat to George and had taken the passenger seat himself.

'Don't be afraid to let her go there, Georgie – give her her head. Have a wee listen to her now and tell me what you think.'

Fred cocked his ear in case a comment would be appropriate. But how could he hear anything with Bill going like a machine-gun – yakking away. Although it pleased Fred no end to note that Bill had turned sideways, with his right forearm over the back of the seat so he could address them both at the same time; equal importance. And couldn't you just listen to him all day and all night, Fred thought to himself, and then, before he knew it, heard himself come right out and say it.

'Do you know what I'm going to tell you, Bill? Do you know what it is? I could just listen to you all day, all night, so I could.'

'You might bloody have to,' George said.

But that wasn't what he meant. 'Ah no,' he began, 'you misunderstand. I didn't mean . . . '

But the two in the front were laughing so much that his explanation never got over the fence.

He'd only been telling the truth, though. He did think Bill was a wonder: the things he came out with; the things he'd seen and done. A man of the world, that's how he'd describe him. If anyone were to ask him, 'Who's that fella I seen you with last week at Baldoyle?' he'd say, 'Oh, that's a friend of mine – Bill Cassell. From Belfast. A most sophisticated fellow. A man of the world, I'd have to say. A Protestant, too. Some of the nicest . . . '

A man of the world; literally, that's what he was. A man that had been to racecourses anywhere you'd care to mention. He'd been to Charleville Downs and the Kentucky Derby. Where blackies sang and danced before every race, oh yes. And every man you met was either a colonel or a brothel-keeper, and everybody went around sipping mint juleps (whatever the fuck they were). He knew the racecourses in Paris like the back of his hand. Royal Ascot, too: kept his own top and tails in a wardrobe in London just for that very event. And what about Monte Carlo? He'd thrown dice in Monte Carlo and a place in Germany that had a name you said twice.

Fred had noted that Bill never said 'dices': he said 'die', when he was talking about one; 'dice' for the plural. Now there was a thing to know. Die; dice. He must remember that. He leaned forward tilt-headed, regarding Bill, so that even if he lost the trail sometimes, he at least wouldn't let it be known. Bill's hands were up to all sorts, moving with the story right through the paces. First his fist was wriggling as though he was playing the bongos; now his arm was pushing in and out in a thrust-and-withdraw movement; now his fist gave another shake from the end of a loose fist. And Fred had to pull himself up: Jaysus almighty, what was he talking about? What could he mean? There was an air of obscenity about the whole demonstration. It looked as if he was talking about pulling his . . . pulling his wire. Ah, surely not? But then after a minute Fred picked up a few key words and got back on track. He sighed inside: thank Christ, he was only talking about the casino again – the croupier's rake, the throw of the dice (or 'die', rather, if it was only the one).

And Fred wanted him to continue about the casino. But George kept steering the conversation back to today's racing and how easy it would have been to cop the hotpot with all the favourites coming home first. And here's what Fred thought about that: if it was so fuckin' easy, it was a wonder George hadn't copped it himself. He felt like saying, 'Ah, listen here, George, we've heard it all before. Let's hear about something new. Let's hear about . . . '

The flight of marble steps to the oblong hall, and then you were in the atrium.

'What's this an atrium is again, Bill?'

'Ach, you know, a sort of a . . . a glass-roofed hall, class of a . . . you know?'

'Oh, of course, that's right.'

And sorry then he'd let himself down by asking at all, because now Bill was explaining every little thing to him.

'The Salle Blanche – that's the white room – ' he began; and Fred knew that – of course he knew that. How many horses had 'Blanche' in their name? Then George interfered again, bringing the conversation back to the racing and how the strain of all that travelling had been too much since the ban on Irish horses running in England had been lifted; all that toing and froing across the channel had worn them out, impaired their performance. And here's what Fred thought about that: Fuck them anyway, it wasn't as if they were expected to swim over to the English meetings and back again. And there was George going on and on about it, taking Bill away from him again. But this time Fred didn't mind so much because he needed a bit of time to think. To think about the Salle Verte – that's the green room, the smoking room – and if he had heard Bill right when he talked about its ceiling. Painted, he had said, edge to edge with pictures of women. Women with not a stitch on them. Nudey women, smoking cigars.

'Ah, surely now, Bill, you don't mean to tell me . . . You don't mean to say they would allow that?' He had to ask him, even if it did mean interrupting George again.

'Allow what?'

'The ceiling, in the casino, like. The women. Do you mean you can see everything?'

'Oh aye. Not a dolly on them. Naked as the day they were born – with a few improvements, of course. You've never seen such a display of nellies in all your life.'

'Nellies?'

'You know . . . ' Bill said, cupping his hands to his chest.

'Oh, right. And did you say they were actually smoking these cigars?'

'Aye.'

'Smokin' them?'

'That's right. They're holding them up in their fingertips like this.'

'Cigars?'

'Well, I'm near certain they were cigars, anyway.'

And the two up front laughing like madmen then. Although Fred couldn't see what was so funny and had to lean back and press to the window-pane his hot, bewildered face.

VIII

She woke with thoughts of Venice in her head. There had been no particular reason: no dream; nothing so definite as a dream. It was more a sense of Venice; light and water. A sense of shame, too, which she would always associate with that city. Why Venice? Why now, after all this time? Was it the rain that had put it into her head? Or had it something to do with the fact that it was the last place, the last time, a man had shown an interest in her?

Before the war, it was – the late thirties. She would have been, what, forty-nine? Good God, almost fifty. They had stopped off for a few days before paying a visit to Lucia's mother in Trieste. Almost finished the visit, too, when they had met him. That man, in the Café Florian. Now she could have allowed herself to stray with him. Although it was quite clear by the way he looked at her that all that gushing attentiveness would be gone in the morning. If Lucia hadn't been sitting beside her, she would have left with him. Oh yes. Allowed him to place his arm around her waist, lead her through the dark arcades along the side of Piazza San Marco, over the narrow bridge, up the marble stairs to her room. She would have let him do anything to her, say anything, with his clumsy English. Look at her, all over her, with his brown eyes, that were so beautifully, so softly insincere. It had been her last chance; she had lost it. Or rather, Lucia had lost it on her behalf.

Outside, on the terrace, upturned chairs were slotted onto tabletops. Inside, waiters fidgeted about, sweeping crumbs off velvet banquettes or crumbs very close to their feet. The small orchestra smoked and muttered, folding instruments into faded cases. The fat Arabian women looked down from the murals. And it had seemed to her that they all knew what he wanted. What she wanted. Everyone knew. Except for . . . ? No, not except for – *especially* Lucia.

They had watched each other across the table; had watched the opportunity slip away. Finally they had had to stand up and accept that the night had come to an irretrievable end. He had offered to see them to their *pensione*. Lucia, who'd scarcely uttered a word all evening, had suddenly taken charge and said, 'No need – it's only two minutes away.' And then she had stepped between them.

He had bowed them out; insisted on paying their coffee bill. But as he had done so, she could sense his interest had already waned. He wasn't the type to court: it was only one night he was interested in – one night with a foreign lady he would never have to see again. But he had already come to live in her head.

The next morning she had slipped out before Lucia was up, and had walked through the city, keeping herself in easy view. Should he happen to be out and about or looking down from a lunette, he would see her move through a *campo* or appear out into the sunlight from a narrow walkway. She had dressed herself as carefully as if she really had an arrangement with him. As if he had implored her, 'Please, won't you meet me, alone, tomorrow?' That was how pitiable she'd been.

She'd walked for hours, one *sestiere* looking much like the other: water, bridges, colour-rubbed walls; colours of turning leaves. Clusters of café tables, where people dipped early-morning *cornetti* into bowls of milky coffee. Later, as the morning wore on, the coffee cups would grow smaller, the coffee would turn black, letting her know it was mid-morning, getting on for lunch. Still she continued – in case, just in case. After a while, she came across a flock of red-cloaked schoolchildren. Noisy schoolchildren that were sure to attract attention. She moved amongst them, following their route all the way to the Accademia. Find me here, she had urged him in her head; find me. I am the silent one among them; I am the tallest, I should stand out. Wherever you are, look at them and you will find me towering above them. You will find *me*.

And when, from a corner by the Accademia, a brace of black-gowned priests fluttered towards her, a large-brimmed hat shading the face of one that had no business being so handsome, his beautiful hand coming down to pat the head of a child, she felt something weaken inside her: that unbearable yearning that a woman feels the morning after, as if . . . As if he really had been her lover.

She'd had to sit down, by a quiet *fondamenta* where the water was dark, the light pale on its back. Deep, dark water carrying the light in soft pats; pulling it along, gently along; out to the walls and up through a tunnel. Regurgitant, lazy; water and light. And all the time imagining what that would have been like. To have been his lover. To have stood at the shutter in her room looking down on the city, her eye following the rise and fall of scaly-backed rooftops, black and reptilian. Her ear, the sound of water slurping against the ancient stone below and his step behind her. Her hand leaning on the balustrade, his hand coming down to cover it, shyly at first, testing her out. More confident then, moving to her hair, fingers first, then palm, her scalp lifting at its touch. His hand lifting her hair aside, mouth coming to her neck. Leaving the mouth there and coming down to her breast, making it grow full, grow into it. Then taking her to the bed.

What would it have been like? To have lain on that bed with him then, his dark arm under her head. His dark leg lying over her white one (her legs would please him: long, longer than his; white). He would remark on them, she would kiss (no, lick) the remark away. She would not be interested in his predictable remarks; the absurdities of his pleasure. Only his dark hand, his flexible tongue. The taste of his tongue, foreign black. The feel of his hand, soft and then harder. They would know what to do, his hand, his tongue; regurgitant, lazy. Well-trained, they would make no mistakes.

No love between them, but because there was no love there would be no shyness. She would watch him, watch herself. Like a voyeur, she would watch the two of them, moving over each other, moving against each other. Pale and dark, light and shade, and not care if he saw her, watching brazen-eyed, relishing each second. Because he would be unimportant: a tongue, a hand, a body-part she would take whenever she was ready and whichever way she pleased. She would be the important one for the first time in her life; for this, her very last chance. It would be her body that counted, not his. Her pleasure only that mattered. What would it have been like? To lie naked with a man you knew cared nothing for you? Not to love, and to be unloved. But for a while at least to know the meaning of desire.

That afternoon the September rains came. They were not like any rains she had ever seen before: no wind, no slant, no variance in movement. Just a vertical onslaught, crashing violently to the ground so that the whole city appeared to be on a slow, constant boil. It filled the centre of the piazza, turning it into a lake: legs waded through; a gondola skimmed across; pigeons plopped down and floated bewilderedly about. The tourists were charmed; the Venetians were not (although they behaved in an efficient, if slightly put-upon, way). A series of wooden tables were erected around the periphery. Hands were employed to assist ladies up and coax them across. She had refused to be coaxed; climbed up unaided, crossing duckboards that sagged and rattled under her feet. Ladies squealed and laughed behind her. But, unafraid of falling, she made no sound. When she got to the end of the duckboard, applause broke out for her. She hardly acknowledged it. All she could think of was how best to tell Lucia that she would have to go on alone to Trieste. That she was going home. How best to say it without betraying the real reasons; that she couldn't bear the sight of the city now. This old city where nothing new could grow. She couldn't bear the sight of Lucia either: for taking her chance away; for knowing there had been a chance to take and for knowing how much she had wanted it. This had been her preoccupation. While Lucia crossed the duckboards, tippy-toed and laughing at the end of a kind, Italian hand.

Maude reached to the lamp and pressed light cautiously into the room, then turned away from it to avoid the eye of the clock. She knew by the undrawn curtains the evening was coming to a close. But she didn't want to know the exact time; didn't want to start counting the hours. The evening was coming to a close but the night had still to come. And already she had used up her sleep.

IX

The window-pane nipped the side of his head, wakening him, and he felt himself swing from the hand-strap, bounce off the driver's seat, then sway back into position. They were on the quays. They were back in town. He adjusted his eyes to a steel-stark river that sliced through his head like a fishmonger's knife gutting a mackerel. He tried to smarten himself up a bit, lifting his mouth up to his hand, wiping it dry, unnoosing his hand then from the strap and letting it fall down while the blood shimmied and pricked through his veins. He cleared his throat and addressed himself to the front of the car.

'I must have dropped off there for a minute . . . ' he began.

'A minute? You've been snoring away for over an hour,' George said.

'Aye,' Bill confirmed, 'and out of both ends too.'

Fred gave a little laugh and sat back again, trying to figure it out. Over an hour? Over an *hour*? Sure how could that be right? Fairview was only ten minutes away. The last time he'd looked out the window they had been approaching the maw of Fairview Bridge and he had seen the railings of Fairview Park stretch out in the distance. Over an hour? That couldn't be right. Then he noticed that Bill was back in the driver's seat and George was once more the passenger.

'Did you go in for a drink, be any chance?' he asked.

'We did.'

'Ah sure, you might as well, wha'?' He laughed, edging himself forward to show his good humour. But the lack of response edged him back again.

In for a drink. Left him outside with his face squashed against the window-pane, snoring his head off. In for a drink.

'My brother's up in Tully's, if you fancy it,' George said. 'He's with Bennie the Yank – my cousin.'

'The piano man?'

'That's right. He's home on holiday, I thought I might drop in and surprise them.'

Fred lifted a willing chin but then, realising it was an invitation meant exclusively for the front of the car, redirected it out the side window.

'No, Georgie, thanks, I won't,' he heard Bill say then. 'Do you know what, I can never seem to get going again after a feed.'

After a feed? After a *feed*? A drink bad enough, but they'd sneaked in and had a feed as well. Leaving him outside. Leaving him outside like an oul' dog in the car.

They looped off Butt Bridge and the pain in his head took on a life of its own, stretching out with the car, swerving, twisting, coming back into his head. Twisting again. And as if that wasn't bad enough, he was dying for a piss. He crossed his legs, pinching them in at the thighs, squeezing the load back up into his bladder. Oh, mother of Jaysus, oh Christ on the cross.

Now they were on Burgh Quay and Fred felt a panic as each pub passed by: the shadow of Kennedy's under the railway bridge; now the White Horse; the Scotch House any minute. The Scotch House might be nice. With its panelled walls and ballroom floor. Just the classy sort of a joint for a man like Bill: a real gentleman's place where the barmen called you sir and had the cigarette lit the second it sat up on your lip. And he wouldn't mind buying, either (in case that's what they were thinking). Oh no, never let it be said. The Scotch House; ideal. Quick now, before it slips by.

'I'm dying for a piss,' he piped up, as they came up to Corn Exchange and the Scotch House announced its entrance.

'Why don't you come into the Scotch House and let me buy you one, Bill, before you go away? To say thank you for the lift and all that. It's a lovely spot, you know . . . '

'I'm barred from the Scotch House,' came Bill's flat reply.

'Barred?'

'That's right. Barred for life.'

'Oh. Well, it doesn't have to be there, of course. What about somewhere else. What about the . . . ?'

'I've enough.'

'Are you sure, now? One for the road? You'd be more than welcome.'

'You might as well drop him here, Bill,' George said.

Then the car and his bladder jolted together.

'Right. Well, I suppose I'd better . . . ' Fred slowly uncrossed his legs and shifted himself towards the door. 'Are you not coming?' he asked George.

'No, I'll go on.'

'Oh right, fair enough. Well, goodbye. And thanks for the lift and . . . and all that, Bill. It was a pleasure.'

He waited for a minute to see would Bill want to shake his hand. But no hand came over the seat. And he knew then that whatever little booth or table they had sat at, and whatever little sneaky dinner they had ordered, his name had been in there somewhere. His importance had been chewed away with the steak. He was back to where he had started this morning: a washed-out tout. No, worse than that, he was a spectacle for passers-by to laugh at; a face squashed up against the window. An oul' dog, snoring out of both ends.

He pulled himself up out of the car and leaned in through the half-open door. 'God bless, now, and . . . '

Then he heard the door clip behind him.

'And fuck the pair of you,' he muttered, as he watched the car take off up the quay. 'A few years ago I wouldn't have spat on either of you. A few years ago, I'd a been up there in that Red Bank Restaurant eating rings around meself – no shortage of money, nor company either . . . Fuckin' Prods, you're all the same. Black-hearted, miserable bastards.'

The pit of his stomach pressed down again and he looked around for somewhere to go. The Scotch House, packed to the gills, with jackets and ties and some snotty little barman.

'Can I help you at all, sir?'

'Eh, I'm just going to the . . . '

And then pinning his eye to you on the way back to make sure you were going to buy. A glorified kip, that's all it was, and the price of the drink, pure robbery. Didn't even sell porter: a real man's drink. And apart from all that, a two-mile trek to get to the jacks. He'd never be able to make it.

He glanced around at Saturday-evening people going about their Saturday-evening business and he felt like a ghost. Across the river, couples, linked to each other, slipped into picture houses or upstairs to 'couples only' lounges. Back over here, commuters rattled in and out of Tara Street Station: normal people with places to go. Like a ghost, they made him feel, as if he just wasn't there.

He could barely move now with the pressure; would have to go and would have to go quick. He'd have to *now*. But where? He thought for a second, then . . . Right, if they were going to treat him like a dog, he'd fuckin' well act like a dog.

Around the corner, into Corn Market Exchange. He stepped into the doorway of a shop, hoisted himself gingerly out and waited for the message to get through to the pump. It's all right, you can go; go ahead; go on, my son. Ahhhh. It started off slow, relaxing into a lustier spurt. He guided the nozzle over the tiles, up and down in a neat zigzag movement, until the stream began to narrow down; then a nice little swirl to finish off. Ahhh.

They'd sneaked in for something to eat. And then they effed him out on the street. Lousy bastards. That's all they were. Dirty rotten lousy bastards. He tucked himself back in and came out to the street. Just who the fuck did they think they were?

Leaning his shoulder on the pole of a bus stop, hooking his fingers into the litter basket hanging on its hip, he steadied himself up. He still had his two ten-bob notes, all the same. He even had his original two-bob bit down in his pocket. And it was early enough, the night but a pup. He pulled out his last cigarette, strangled the empty packet between his hands and dropped it down into the basket. You could have a good night on a quid; with a bit of prudence, you might even have two. And there was no shortage of pubs between here and Cuffe Street. He struck a match and a little map of pubs lit up in his head, but he switched it off again.

He didn't need any map. He knew where he was going. He might make one or two stops on the way, but he knew where he would end the night. Treat *me* like a dog. I'll show them. I'll show them how a dog tracks.

He looked to the sky; raining again. But a slow, easy kind of evening rain. Long, large snot-drops, but random enough; no great hardship at all. He glanced back at the Scotch House and wondered about Bill. Barred? And for life? What sort would be . . . ? What sort was he, with his Monte fuckin' Carlo and his Kentucky fucky Derby? Who did he think he was coddin', anyhow? Fuckin' oul' chancer. Smuggler. Carpet-bagger, no less.

Sucking on the cigarette, he moved along up the street, increasing his step and swaying lightly as he went. Two ten-bob notes, one two-bob bit. Twenty-two shillings and a bellyful of drink. Fellas worked themselves half to death all week would have less to declare on a Saturday night. All considered, he wasn't too badly off. All considered, he was laughing up his sleeve. He dipped his knees as he came to the corner.

A one, a two. And . . . Oh, oh, Anton-io, left me on me own-io.

X

She was thirsty now; longing for a cup of tea to scald the film of stale sherry away, maybe calm her down too, help her to stop thinking about Lucia and Samuel. But she was reluctant, somehow, to descend the dark staircase with the skylight bleeding above her head; the mirror in the hall where she might catch herself sneak by; the cracks of half-opened doors; the narrow back stairs that led to the kitchen. Through the empty house. Imagining things. All sorts of things.

It was times like this she missed having a maid.

'I should be happy for them,' she said aloud. 'Why can't I be happy for them? Why do I have this terrible feeling they went behind my back?'

All those times he called, and I thought it was to see me. All those drives he took us on, to the mountains or the sea, I thought . . . Sitting up front, while Lucia sat in the back. Doing all the talking, while Lucia said nothing. Playing up to him, as if I was a girl. Stopping for tea or a drink; sitting myself down beside him again, as if it was my right . . . I thought – I always thought – it was me. Even today, when he sat on my chair, drinking my sherry, warming his hands at my fire, I saw it as a preview of how things could be. And when he said he'd come with me to Henry next week, a stroll afterwards, and tea . . . I thought . . .

Did he see it in my face? Did he know that look? That look of searing disappointment.

And she might have warned me; she must have known. I took her in; gave her a home. I talked to her. Told her things. Why? Why had she not returned the confidence? Why had she not prepared me? The driving lessons, of course, would have been what clinched it. Or my insistence that she go to a show – a picture with Sam on her own when I was up seeing Henry. When I think of all those opportunities I allowed; I never stood in her way. I never stole *her* chance, but then I didn't know she had a chance to steal.

Plain little Lucia. Plain little dull little Lucia. Now she has a man at last. A good man, too. While I have to keep myself in this old body, alone in this old body, while young thoughts continue to taunt and torment me. I want a man, like Lucia's man. Or any man at all. Not just for the bed thing, either; not just that. The other things: the differences, subtle but marked, that make up a life of a man and a woman together. I want to see those differences again. I want them to be mine to compare. The way he drinks from a glass; the awkward route he takes to look at his watch; the way he sits or reads a newspaper. The way he listens, or sometimes doesn't. The feel of his hand light on the small of my back as I precede him through the door or across a busy street. His arm about me in the back of the taxicab after a night out. Those things, I want. Instead of what I have. Loneliness.

Loneliness will be the latter part of my life. I call myself middle-aged, but I'm not. I'm old now. I am not middle-aged. If I was, I should live to be more than a hundred and fourteen. I will probably end my days just like Henry, in a chair by a window, telling my secrets to anyone who will listen, bombarding them with all those shameful things I have kept hidden inside. And who will come to hear them? Will it be Lottie? Will I know her if she does? Will I tell her then? (When did you start going twice a week? she asked, and *why?*) Why, after Venice, of course. After Venice. Will I tell her how it was?

How a week or so after I'd left Lucia, I went to see Henry. Uneasy, I'd been, all that week: restless, unable to sleep. I didn't know what was the matter with me; hadn't been myself since that man in Florian's – that stupid, stupid . . . When I went in to Henry and reached down to kiss him on the cheek, he put his two hands on my thighs and drew me over to him. But this time, instead of being embarrassed, I felt something gush warm inside me; something I couldn't ignore. I watched the glint in his eye as it followed a nurse across the room – the glint that used to cause me such heartache when we lived as man and wife – and I felt a greed take me over. A greed like his greed for sugar. I didn't devise a plan, I just did it. Without having to think about it at all. Leading him gently down the stairs, telling the porter I was taking him out for a little drive, reassuring the porter then, when he showed concern. 'Of course I can manage.' Putting him into the car, tucking the rug into his lap, driving off. Oh yes, I could manage all right.

I brought him home. Didn't even bother to show him around my new house. No offer of tea; no niceties at all (except for the sweeties, of course – the sweeties were the enticement). Straight up to my bedroom. 'Now, Henry,' I said, 'it's time for your little nap.' He did what he was told. Everything he was told. A man-child I so easily took advantage of. A man-child who would forget it all; would never think to tell. And even if he did, who would believe him? Lying him on the bed, touching him through his trousers, feeling it first small and soft, like the head of a little bird, then growing fuller, harder; hard enough. Removing his clothes, leading him through the motions, the way he used to lead me. Sitting on top of him then: it was very enjoyable too, I must say. Taking from him what I had believed was taken from me in Venice, I suppose that was the idea behind it. But the reality? It was madness. Wicked madness. Hoping since then that there is no heaven; no life hereafter. For how could I face them: mama, papa, Kate. Or Pat, my darling Pat? How could I face them after what I had done?

Afterwards, I consoled myself that Henry had enjoyed it too. That it had been good for him. That when he lay crying in my arms, it was relief, it was love. And then he called me mother. After what I had done to him, he called me *mother*. And I . . . ? I had the cheek to take offence.

I told myself it was loneliness that had made me do it, but it wasn't loneliness. It was lust and the evil will to carry it through. It was selfishness.

And I have always been selfish, taking what I want – however, whenever, with no heed for the consequences. It had nothing to do with loneliness. It was too big for that. Loneliness is made of small things. Things you can do nothing about. Loneliness is what I have now: a daughter who has no time for me – who cannot even bear to live in the same country as me. Relatives I scarcely know; relatives I have refused to help when they needed it – when I could have done. A first, beloved husband dead; a second husband who cannot recognise me. A car I haven't the nerve to drive. A kitchen I am afraid to go down to in the night. Yes, this is what loneliness is.

Maude sat up, coughing the lump out of her throat, sipping at the water she kept by her bed, and lighting a cigarette she didn't really want. She felt better now, knowing she had only herself to blame. Her mind eased up at last. At least if it was her fault, she could do something about it. Stop being selfish; that would be the start. Start helping others; that would be the way – unquestioningly, unselfishly. She could make her life change. She could be happy for Lucia and Samuel.

She leaned back into the pillow, the ashtray on her lap, and waited for the cigarette to yield a little. When Lucia came back, she would make a huge fuss; she would buy the most extravagant wedding present. She would help with all the arrangements: the trousseau, the reception. She would fill the house up with flowers.

On Monday morning she would advertise for a maid.

XI

It was a pub that explored the afternoon. Drawing daylight from high-set windows; smearing it gently over wood and glass; fondling it for a couple of hours before ushering it back out again. It was a place of slender sounds and comforting smells: Bovril, beeswax, a touch of yeast. Where the burr of conversation was never obligatory and there was small chance of finding yourself stuck in a round. It was a place where a sick head came to be cured. And where all sick heads were equal. That's how Fred Slevin had always known it, anyway. Now he was all confused. This was the first time – since before the war, anyhow – he could remember being here of an evening. It was like another shop altogether; it was like a madhouse, in fact. Nowhere to hide. And he needed to hide.

He took a quick scout round for a spot to squeeze into. The widow's snug already full, tops of widow-heads nodding away. Out here in the main bar, old men sat close together, backs to the wall; young men in rowdy groups took up the floor. Quieter types were pinned along the counter, heads going bob when pints were sent over or bottle after bottle of stout skimmed past. He checked a label just to be sure: 'Bottled by Tully's that sells no other brown stout in bottles.' It was Tully's shop all right. And if, during the day, all heads were equal, it was clear to him now that at night they were not. Labourers gathered down at this end; tradesmen kept to the centre. The back bar, hidden from sight by a frosted-glass swing door, was obviously reserved for the toffs: stout men and whiskey drinkers who took pleasure in paying over the odds.

He screwed one finger into an ear and gave it a rattle. His head was ringing inside; full of commotion, like a jam jar of bees. Glasses clattered; tills pinged; the snug bells belched long and low. The blare of conversation was no less than savage; every mouth in the house going at once. And the outside door admitting more by the second; each man instinctively making for his section of the pub. A couple of big nobs pressed through to the back bar: soft hats and long coats, black brollies and evening editions. Keen, respectable faces, all seeking the bossman out. All seeking to have their status confirmed. Fred Slevin, on the other hand, was not. He was waiting for the simple-faced barman down here to serve him. Because Simple-Face wouldn't notice if he'd had a few too many. Whereas the bossman would do more than notice: he might very well refuse him.

Fred could see him now, down at the far end of the bar, pretending to be otherwise engrossed. Tugging a cloth down from his shoulder; bringing it across the counter; stopping for a little rub-de-dub here and there. Examining a glass; lifting an ashtray; wiping it, then replacing it. A smile at this man, a nod at that one, a remark thrown in on a conversation; an instruction thrown out to one of the staff. An unobtrusive figure sinking into the background as if he was part of the bar furniture; a presence of little or no consequence. That's what he'd *like* you to think. But always the invigilator, his eye alert for short glasses tossed back into open mouths or tilted pint glasses with the tide going out. Each order was precipitated and passed accordingly down the line. And every time the door fell in, the lastest arrival was noted; demeanour duly recorded.

Fred was keeping *his* demeanour well out of the way. He ducked in behind the labourers, keeping one eye firm on his chance to be served, the other loose on the bossman, and ready to shift the second he looked down this way. A pint in his fist, that's all he needed. A pint in his fist and he'd be in for the night. A gap showed between the elbows: he tucked himself through, raised his hand, and opened his mouth to call. Then he felt a tip on his shoulder and the mouth of a whispering apprentice come close to his ear.

'What?'

'Mr Tully wants a word.'

'With me? Wants a word with me?'

The apprentice nodded, biting his lip.

He made his way down to the flap in the counter.

'Fred?'

'Ah, good evening, Mister Tully.'

'Well?'

'Well what? Oh, a pint a porter, please.'

The bossman leaned towards him, all confidential. 'Do you not think, Fred, you might have had enough?'

'Enough? Ah, God no.'

'I think you might be better off going home. Come back in tomorrow.'

'I tell you, Mister Tully, not a word of a lie – I'm grand. I'm as right . . . I'm as right as that rain out there.'

'Now I doubt that very much.'

'I wouldn't say it if it wasn't true. Anyway, I can't go home – I have an appointment.'

'An appointment?'

'Yeah, with George what's-his-name. You know – your pal lives in Belfast. I was with him in Baldoyle today, promised I'd meet him here.'

'George? You've an appointment with George?'

'Isn't that what I'm trying to tell you? He asked me to meet him here, and his brother and his cousin – the eh piano man. He was supposed to go up to Belfast this evening, but didn't he win a packet and wanted to surprise the others.'

'I didn't know you were in with that crowd.'

'Sure me and George, we're the best of pals. It was me gave him the tip, as a matter of fact. That's why he wanted me to come in, so he could show his appreciation, like.'

'The best of pals, and you don't know his surname?'

'Ah, of course I do, it just slipped me mind there for a . . . '

The bossman made him sweat it out for a minute, turning his back to him to go over to the till. Fred watched a bag of brown pennies tumble down into the till drawer and pulled his face up into what was hopefully a more sober arrangement. Then a man behind him belted out an order large and complicated enough to steer the bossman's attention away.

'Go on, then. They're in the back bar. But I'll be keeping an eye on you, mind.'

'Oh, of course, Mister Tully, of course. But there'll be no need.'

He stepped up to the swing door and gave it a shove. He was in. In for the night.

George wasn't exactly thrilled to see him.

'What are you doing here?' he asked.

'Here? Sure I always come in here.'

'I've never seen you before.'

'Ah, but you wouldn't, George – you'd be in Belfast.'

George lifted his glass to his lips, bit in, gulped down, smacked his lips together and then slid the pint back on the table. 'I'm in company, Fred.'

'Sure I was just coming over to . . . '

'I'm in company, I said.'

He sent them over a drink anyway. Partly out of spite and partly because, when he turned to the counter, the bossman's face was waiting.

'I thought you were supposed to be joining your friends?'

'I think I'll have a quiet pint on me own first. Send the boys over whatever they're having.'

'That's five drinks, Fred.'

'That's no problem to me, Mister Tully, and I'll have a pint meself while you're at it. Stout, that is, not porter.'

Five drinks: three pints, two small ones. Five fuckin' drinks at back-bar prices. It set the jam jar of bees off again in his head. But at least there was a bit of space in here; a stool, convenient up at the counter, where he could watch, through the backdrop mirror, the company that was too good for Fred Slevin. George in the corner spouting away; the big fella beside him – obviously the brother; the lad with the American accent next must be the cousin; and then, if you don't mind . . . Dinny Rafter the rat-catcher's son and Mickey Grumley out of Charlemont Street flats. Oh, lovely company indeed. Tenement toughs and jumped-up gutties. He was well off out of it, that's what he was; had had a lucky escape, that's what he'd had. A decent man would be ashamed to be seen with any one of them.

Passing his money over, accepting his change, managing not so much as to glance at it, gliding the pint towards him in short, small circles: he rehearsed his next movements. They'd be thanking him now in a minute. Well, they could stick their thanks where the monkey stuck his nuts. He'd raise his glass, but only slightly –

in a no-big-deal kind of a way. Wouldn't utter a word; wouldn't lower himself even to turn around. Then he'd finish his pint, nice and easy: not too fast so as they might think he was shook, but not so slow as they might think he was trying to tag on. Then he'd get down off the stool – 'Goodnight, Mister Tully. God bless, and thanks' – and head for the door, maintaining a dignified silence all the way. Maybe just give a sort of a half-salute as he passed them – more dismissive than friendly. Oh no, he wouldn't want anyone to think he was being friendly to that shower of dirty, low-bred bastards. That's the last thing he'd want anyone to think.

Through the mirrorscape, he watched the tray hover over the table and the glasses alight one by one. He waited to see the reaction, his pint ready to raise in its no-big-deal sort of a way. But he needn't have bothered his arse. George didn't even acknowledge the drink and, apart from a curious glance in his direction, the others showed neither gratitude nor surprise. As if they were entitled to have free drink sent over to them; as if that was why Fred Slevin had been put on this earth – to fill up the likes of them. Only the Yank was civil. Even thanked him when he came over a few minutes later to buy a packet of fags. Took a shine to him too, Fred could tell, by the interested way he leaned his elbow on the counter, his foot on the bar-rail, as he asked Fred a few friendly questions. Thought he was funny, as well; at least, he kept laughing all the time.

Then he said, 'Why don't you come over and join us, buddy?'

'Ah no, I couldn't do that.'

'Sure you could.'

'George mightn't . . . '

'He's not inviting you, *I* am.'

He'd a good mind to say no, with the sour face on that George fella, but as it was his only chance of recovering something of his investment (five drinks: three pints, two small ones; five fuckin' drinks at back-bar prices), he decided he might as well. He took care to choose the seat that was furthest away from George. He took care not to say too much either, but they all would insist on talking to him. They all would insist on making him the centre of attention. Everyone got on like a house on fire after. Fred had never known himself to be such a success; couldn't seem to put a foot wrong. Everyone wanted to hear what he had to say; everyone howling with laughter. Even Sourpuss cracked in the end – ha ha ha ha; the best of pals. And his brother got up and called for a drink. Fred was included.

'Oh, thanks very much. I'm sorry, I don't know your name.'

'Herbert.'

'Well thanks very much, Herbert.'

Then the bossman came out and laid down three big plates of sandwiches thick as doorsteps, which nobody seemed to feel obliged to pay for.

'Go on, Fred, help yourself,' the Yank said, shoving a plate under his nose. The smell hawed up at him, sweet of ham and sharp of mustard.

'Ah no, I couldn't.'

'Go on, get stuck in. You don't wanna offend Bart.'

'Bart? Oh, you mean Mister Tully. Are they on the house, then?'

'Sure they're on the house. Why wouldn't they be?'

It was shaping up to be the best of nights.

The next thing he knew, someone was shaking him. He looked up and there was the bossman's face.

'Ah, there you are, Mister Tully,' Bart Tully asks. 'What do you think you're playing at?'

'Me? What do you mean, like?'

'I mean, this is a pub, not a feckin' doss-house.'

'But sure I wasn't . . . '

'I'm not blind, Fred.'

'I might have closed me eyes for a second but . . . '

'Come on, home with you now.'

'I can't, I'm with me friends.'

'Fred, I'm warning you now: don't push me.'

'Ask them, they'll tell you: I'm in the company.'

He felt the bossman glance over his head. 'George?'

'Get him out to fuck,' was what George said.

His elbow was lifted, his knees unhinged, his arse sucked away from the seat. The table began to slip out of sight.

'I haven't finished me drink.'

'I'll put it down for you.'

'Ah, Mister Tully, will you be reasonable? I'm wide awake now, and we were only having a bit of gas.'

The bossman was gentler now, lowering his voice. 'Can you not see it, Fred?'

'What? See what?' Fred asked him.

'They're only makin' a laugh of you, Fred. They're laughin' at you,' he repeated, as the frosted-glass door swung behind him.

The backs of his knees started to hop as soon as he found himself out on the street again. He had difficulty putting a cigarette into his mouth; even more difficulty getting it to stay steady enough to light. Laughing at him – was that what Tully had said? No, Tully had it wrong; didn't understand, on account of having no sense of humour himself. Laughing, yes, but not *at* him. Not that.

Behind him, the door to the bar gaped open and a lizard-lick of noise slipped out for a moment. It came back to him then, the humiliation of being ushered out by Tully and the pattern of faces that had swerved out of their way: toffs, tradesman, labourers, a nosy bitch in the snug peering over the partition. A man on his way in, standing back to let them out. He looked at the clock above the pub: last call now in a minute; pub emptying shortly after that. He moved himself on.

The rain had cut out again, leaving its black glaze behind. Pools of light fell down on the surface from shop windows, street lamps, the goggle eyes of a car parked up the way. He watched his shadow trawl over the ground, then slither up a pane of glass on a shop at the corner. He faced his reflection, buckled and black. Laughing at him? But why? What was so funny? What was so *fuckin'* funny? His reflection slipped off the glass. He staggered after it and found himself at the bottom end of Grafton Street.

But Grafton Street refused to be gained, as if he was marching on the spot, while the pavement was gliding back under his feet. Over the shops, the top decks of buildings remained steady enough: he picked out a turret here, a deckle-edged gable there, the flicker of bunting over Switzer's shop. He tried to look up. But his head was heavy and kept bringing him back down again. It was driving him mad, this feeling that he would never pass the street out. He wanted to get off it. Now, right this minute. *Now.*

He took a step sideways.

The shudder of a harnessed horse; the jerk of braking wheels; the pinched voice of a jarvey shouting down – a sidecar in the middle of the street. He must have been very close to it because he could see the passengers' legs swinging at the side, the soles of their shoes wagging in a puddle the wheel-rims had pinned to the ground, and a woman's frantic hand flying down to cover her knee. Now there were several voices shouting. Somebody laughed.

'Who fuckin' laughed?'

He followed the force of his swaying arm round a ring of spectators. 'Who fuckin' laughed? Did *you* fuckin' laugh?'

'Get out of the way before you kill someone, you drunken, foul-mouthed cur.'

Somebody shoved him.

He got back on the pavement and started again.

The street was starting to fill up. Out of pubs with unfinished arguments or dress-dance hotels with unfinished steps, groups of pedestrians kept coming at him: down from the Green or up from the College; Harry Street; Duke Street; Anne Street South. Cyclists on the road veered around each other, a fluffy skirt on the crossbar of one, a khaki uniform, splay-legged, on the handlebars of another. A chain of scrubbers linked together passed a shared cigarette along the line and a group of lads behind him exploded: a roar from one, a wolf whistle from another, a catcall to follow, that made little sense. He sloped around them with a mutter of disapproval, then cut the corner into Anne Street South.

Groping his way into the first available doorway, he pressed his forehead to the window and passed an eye over the bleary interior: Vard's the Furrier's, that's where he was. Right, Vard's. He stepped back and let loose an exuberant gush from his mouth. It landed on the tessellated floor, unguinous and perfectly formed, like an omelette about to set to the pan, and 'Jaysuso Jaysuso Jaysus,' he whined as he noticed, through the window, the fur coats quit their stands to move around each other in a slow, cumbersome formation: a troupe of headless dancing bears. A second lurch in his stomach—

pit brought forward another heave-ho – a more liquidised consistency this time, landing in a flop that just about managed to miss his shoes.

He took a step to the side and, his back to the wall, slid down on his hunkers and buried his head in his knees.

Voices woke him; one of them laughing. 'Who fuckin' laughed?' He felt himself topple: head jerked back, knees snapped straight, hand slapped down into the pool of vomit. Voices. Voices out on Anne Street South. Some down this way; others across the road; more down towards Dawson's Corner. Stranger to stranger across the street, they called out to each other: an open-air discussion on where to go next.

'Did you not get in?'

'No. House full. We left it too late.'

'What about the Orpheus?'

'House full there too.'

'Ah, you're jokin' me?'

A familiar voice rose out for a moment and Fred felt his empty belly churn over.

'Is that place up the alley open?'

'Yeah, but you haven't a chance, pal, I'm telling you.'

'Oh yeah? Well, we'll soon see about that.'

The voice dipped down back to its own little group. 'Fella I used to work with in Belfast runs it. He'll let us in, no bother. Percy. Jaysus, wait'll you meet Percy.'

George. George and his crew, coming down this way. Would pass that doorway any second now. He struggled to his feet, wiped his hand on his dustcoat, then tucked himself into the far, dark corner, where the light from the street couldn't reach him.

When he was sure they had passed, he eased himself forward and peered around the edge of the doorway. Grumley, the Yank and Rafter the rat-catcher's son swaggering along the centre of the road. George and Herbert up on the path, leading the way. He watched the group come together at the corner. He waited until the alley closed around them. Then he came out of his hole.

The alley was long and jagged with shadow, blocked off at the far end by the high boundary wall of the Hibernian Hotel and the dance-hall entrance. Here was a concentration of light: one large blade from a solitary street lamp, one soft globe hanging down over the dance-hall door. Rear entrances to shops; boxes and crates; walls spiked at the top with fangs of broken glass; a tangle of bicycles sloped in an alcove. Rafter extracting one of the bikes and cocking his leg over, the wheels glinting in and out of the light. This was what Fred saw when he came into the alley.

The bicycle attendant broke away from his herd and danced around Rafter. Rafter taunted him for a while, then suddenly stopped, vaulted off backways and shoved the bike home. It rattled for a moment, then collapsed into the arms of the attendant.

Fred waited until the bike had been settled back in place, then, making his way around the edges, took up position at the side of the alcove. Checking this position for suitability – near enough to see the dance hall, far enough not to be seen himself – he nudged himself in behind the attendant and half-listened to his gripes on the youth of today and the city in general.

A fella had been thrown out for doin' the jitterbug, not five minutes ago – out on his ear. Every night it was the same effin' thing – more fellas thrown out for the jitterbug, when there were signs up all over the place saying it was barred, barred, *barred*. Could none of them read, would someone mind tellin' him?

And the women were worse, letting themselves to be fecked around like that: over shoulders, under legs, skirts up to the bejaysus. Had they no respect for themselves, that's what he'd like to know.

Fred obliged with the odd remark, a tut, a gasp or a simple nod of the head, while his eye carried on prowling the scene.

A few stragglers who had got browned off banging at the door wandered sullenly back out to Anne Street. A couple came out of the hall, his coat around her shoulders, his nose troughed into her hair. The music mumbled behind the walls, brassed out when the entrance door opened and shrunk back when it closed again, as if somebody was fiddling with the wireless knob. The Yank started to dance. Rafter joined in, copying his steps, one hand flat across his stomach, arse poked out behind. The two of them shouting down the big-band sound inside, 'Mist-er Sat-urday daa-ance.'

The Yank wasn't a bad dancer, all the same: loose-limbed, plenty of rhythm. The other fella moved as if he had a poker up his hole.

A man came out and whistled for his bike. Another one forgot his and had to be reminded. Next, a skinny young one in a huge plaid coat scrabbed the make-up off her face with the corner of a hanky and came tearing down the lane. The Yank danced after her a few jaunty steps, saying, 'Any time, baby. A-nee time at all.'

The young one increased her pace. Then she was gone.

Now all that remained in the lane was Fred, the attendant, George and his butties.

'Do you know what I'm goin' to tell you?' the attendant continued. 'This town's gone to the dogs since the war.'

'Is that right?'

'The shaggin' dogs. Didn't I catch a pair at it last Saturday night?'

'At what?'

'What do you think?'

'Go away?'

'Up there in that corner – you see, just beyond the dance hall. You wouldn't know it unless you were told, but between the hotel and the hall, there's this skimpy little cutaway. At it, the pair of them, up again' the wall.'

'Oh, that's a disgrace, right enough. What did you do?'

'Sure what could I do?'

George and Herbert up at the office door. Grumley skulking back on his own. The door opened; a chucker-out bent over the wicket gate, put the snip on the lock, then whispered something to George. The door closed again. George and Herbert stepped aside to the wall, heads close together: something to discuss.

'A bloody disgrace is right,' the attendant restated. 'It's all them foreigners, if you ask me.'

'Foreigners, would you say?'

'I'm tellin' you. Australians. Canadians. Then there's the Yanks. Of course, everyone thinks the world of them because they've the name of being big tippers. Well, here's one mug's never seen none of their tips. Messers, is all they are. There's a prime example of one of them up there: that fella dancin' – if you can call that dancin'.'

'Ah, he's not bad now. Moves well enough, of course, he bein' a musician.'

'How do you know?'

'Wasn't I drinking with them earlier.'

'With *that* lot?'

'Oh, I didn't hang around too long, let me tell you. They

wouldn't be my idea of company. I bought them a drink and got out as quick as I could.'

'Who are they, anyway?'

'Well, them two fellas – the tall ones over by the door – they're brothers. The Yank's a cousin. And as for that other pair of gutties . . . '

'What about them?'

'What?'

'You were saying, "That other pair of gutties . . ."'

But Fred's attention had wandered off, down to the hoarding at Newell's grocery shop and a bulky shadow behind the crates.

'Who's your man?' he asked.

'Who? Where?'

'There, over be Newell's. Look – behind them crates.'

The attendant stepped out and peered up the lane. 'I don't see . . . '

'There, look, he's lighting a fag now.'

'Oh Jaysus, you're right. You've very good eyesight, I must say.'

'In my line of business, you'd have to.'

The attendant came back into the alcove and lowered his voice to Fred. 'Oh, that'll be the gaffer – he owns the ballroom. He'll sort out that lot quick enough. He's like an anti-Christ, too – mustn't have done too well at Baldoyle today. He'll soften their cough for them, you wait and see.'

'Hard man, is he?'

'Hard man? Hard man? He's made out of effin' concrete, that's what he is.'

'He's a big man, right enough.'

The big man left his shadow and stepped under the street light, his large frame pouring into the bourn of light. He growled out a comment, and all heads down the far end perked up and took notice. A ricochet of verbal exchanges then from the big man to

Grumley; Grumley to the big man; back to Grumley again. Grumley was getting fidgety: shoulders and neck; a bit of hip movement too. The big man gave another growl and Grumley sidled over to him, his slight figure making a dent in the light. Rafter hesitated for a moment, then flipped his cigarette against the wall and calmly followed, his left shoulder leading him in. Next came the Yank, throwing himself at it blindly, like a kid jumping into the canal. Over by the wall, the two brothers turned to each other and started to laugh.

The big man, Grumley, Rafter, the Yank: a bit of shoving and pushing but all you could see for certain was the light flickering on and off the crown of the big man's derby hat, which was a head higher than any of the other three.

Fred stuck his head out of the alcove, craning his neck to see. Fast movement; difficult to make out. All plugged together, moving together, jostling away from the light.

He could hear the attendant's footsteps behind him, then the panting of words hot in his earhole, 'What's happening? I can't see a thing – what's goin' on? Jaysus, this is getting out of hand. I better get some help.' He fumbled with his coat and came out with a silver whistle.

Fred put his arm out and drew the whistle away from the attendant's mouth. 'Put that thing away,' he said.

'But I'm supposed to use it if there's any trouble. I'm supposed to let them know.'

'Ah, put it away.'

'It's not fair, three again one; it's not right, so it's not. And supposin' them other two big fellas get involved?'

'Not at all,' Fred insisted, softening his tone. 'Relax yourself.

I'm telling you, your gaffer has them taped.'

'Are you sure?'

'Of course I'm sure. Amn't I lookin' at it?'

The only sound was the scuffle of feet; the occasional grunt of exertion. They came back nearer to the light and bunted into it, still stuck together; still moving as one.

Half-laughing, George moved away from the wall and called out to his cousin. 'Ah, for Christ's sake, Bennie, stay out of it, will you? Come on now, it's nothin' to do with you.'

But the Yank wasn't listening. George took another step forward and tried again. *'Bennie!'* The Yank's head turned to answer George. The big man's paw stretched out and grabbed the Yank's head back. George was in now, with Herbert directly behind him, and the big man's hat was no longer visible.

There was a sudden lurch; the bunch came unstuck; one man fell to the ground. It was over.

One man down – leaving three distinct sounds for Fred to mull over. The smack of a fist against a jaw – clean, snappy: you couldn't mistake it. The thud of a body hitting the ground – heavy, deep: just what you'd expect from a cargo that size. The third sound was a sort of crack. It took Fred a minute to work out that crack. It was long; it was thin; it was delicate too: a crack no louder than a piece of china breaking. Yet there had been something hefty about it; something almost substantial.

Back in the alcove, sealed in its shadow, Fred waited for them to pass by. A scatter of legs; a scarper of feet. Two, four, six, eight – four pairs lashed back out to Anne Street. Only four pairs of feet?

One pair missing. Now where . . . ? He lifted his eyes to the far end of the lane until they landed on the high boundary wall of the Hibernian Hotel. A figure dangling by the arms; the missing feet scuttling against the wall; a final hoist, and the feet disappeared over the top.

The attendant's whistle snipped through the alley. The door of the dance hall smashed against the wall. The chucker-out hopped the gate. His heel tipped off the 'House Full' sign and it clattered to the ground. A young woman behind him struggled with the lock, then burst through, screaming 'Daddeeee . . . ' She flung herself down on her knees and began plucking at the big man's sleeve. The chucker-out picked up the grey derby hat, knocked it off his knee, brushed it, blew on it, then put it down again. Someone called out for an ambulance. Somebody else called out for the police.

He could feel the bicycle attendant shaking beside him. 'What was that noise?'

'His skull, I'd say.'

'Did they kill him, do you think?'

'I don't know . . . ' Fred said.

'Oh Jesus, oh Mary, oh Joseph. I thought you said he had them taped?'

'I thought you said he was made out of fuckin' concrete?'

'Oh God. It happened so fast. It happened so fast. I didn't see what happened because it happened so fast. Knocking a man down like that and then doin' a runner – thugs, that's what they are. Cowards. Did you see which one done it?'

'I'm not sure.'

'Well, at least we know one thing: they won't get away with it.'

331

'How do you mean?'

'Well, you know them. Didn't you say you knew them?'

'I said I had a drink with them, that's all.'

The bicycle attendant stared at him for a moment and then shuffled away towards the dance hall, his arm lifted, waving for attention. He started to call out.

'Here,' he said, 'this man, this man back here knows them. He seen who done it. He knows who they are.'

A cluster of faces looked up from the body. 'What man? Where?'

'There, back there in the alcove. Will I get him?'

'Well, you better, if he says he knows them.'

The attendant shuffled back down the lane.

But when he got to the alcove, there were only bicycles.

XIV

It frightened the life out of her, the sound of the door knocker crashing through the house at this hour of the night; she nearly jumped out of her skin. Past midnight, she knew, because a while ago she'd heard the chimes from Rathmines Town Hall tip out another day. She stretched over to the locker and turned the clock to her. A quarter to one? A quarter to *one?*

Bang, bang, bang. It came back again. Then again and again. Difficult to say which was more terrifying – the knocks, or the intervals between. Sometimes the button bell squirted drily behind, but it was the knocker that bore the brunt: big, brash, menacing; like something alive – something that was getting closer each time.

She took hasty stock of her room: stout walls; fastened window; telephone wire leading to telephone only a hand-stretch away. Under the bed, the granite rock the army man next door had plucked from his rockery and handed her one day. (What had he said she was to do with it again? Yes, that's right – lean out her window and drop it on the roof of his mad dog's kennel.) Telephone; mad dog; army man next door: whichever way she turned, help was near to hand. Yet she found herself feeling completely displaced. The room had pulled away from her; had become remote: that feeling you get from a hotel room on the last day of your stay. As if you're already gone. Or you've never even been there. This room would do nothing to protect her.

In the landscape of her folded body, she took refuge under the covers.

Bang, bang, bang. Louder this time. No indication that it would ever let up. Who would call at this hour? Bad news would come by telephone: a nurse's voice if it was a question of Henry, a London voice for her daughter Patrice, Lottie for a mutual friend or acquantance. Unless . . . ? Of course, of course – unless the bearer had no telephone, in which case . . . bad news. Perhaps even a policeman waiting to tell her something dreadful. Not danger at all. Danger is silent; danger sneaks in the back way. Danger doesn't wake up the dead.

She unfolded her body, threw off the eiderdown and hurried into Lucia's room at the front of the house.

From the upstairs windows of the house next door, stanchions of light crossed over her garden. The army man was obviously on standby – it gave her courage to know. She looked down. A few feet from her front door was the top of a head: a man's head, rather small. Yes, but what man? *Who?* He took a step back, lifting his face; she jumped back herself to avoid it. Then, remembering her vigilant neighbour-in-waiting, came forward again and examined her visitor.

There was an impudence about the way he was shifting his face from window to window, all over her house. But it wasn't an impudent face. In fact, it looked rather gormless. It slipped out of sight then, and she could hear the flap on the letter box lift, pause for a second, then snip back into place.

Looking in her hallway – that's what he was doing. Peering up her stairs – that's what he was at. Scrutinising whatever he could through the limited vision allowed by her letter box. He'd be stomping in the flower beds to look in the downstairs windows next (if he hadn't already done so). The nerve of some people . . . the utter, unspeakable cheek. She shoved the window out of its socket. And this time, it gave her satisfaction to note, it was the little man who nearly jumped out of his skin.

'Who are you?' she called down to him. 'What do you want? Who do you think you are, banging down the door at this hour of the night. Explain yourself, before I call the police. Explain yourself this instant.'

His face flinched up to her. 'Mrs Masterson?' he asked. 'Mrs Maude Masterson?'

'How do you know my name?'

'Your nephew . . . ' the man began, then suddenly lowered his voice.

'What did you say? I can't hear you. What are you whispering for?'

'If you could come down, ma'am. I have to speak to you.'

'I'll stay where I am.'

'I don't want to shout.'

'It's a bit late to be thinking about the neighbours. Did I hear you say something about my nephew?'

He didn't answer her, just urged her silence however he could: patting his palms on the air, casting his eye back over each shoulder, nodding and twitching – absurd yet intriguing. She decided she might as well go downstairs.

When she opened the front door, the sight of a smelly little man on her doorstep made her immediately regret having done so. A tie thick with stains; a dustcoat not much better; a tooth at every station, grinning at her now from a half-witted face.

'Well?' she said.

'I'm glad to see I didn't get you up out of bed, ma'am.'

'I *was* in bed.'

'Oh?'

He seemed surprised. She looked down at herself and could understand why. She was still fully clothed: skirt shifted around to the side; blouse tail halfway out; hair going God knows where; hole in the toe of one stocking. Then she looked back at the smelly little man; taking her in – judging her – just as she had been judging him.

'Naturally, I started to get dressed when I heard you knock. Now, if you wouldn't mind telling me what you want, exactly?'

'I'm very sorry to disturb you, ma'am, but I've a message from your nephew.'

'My nephew? Which nephew?'

'He's around the back lane, ma'am, waiting to be let in.'

'Waiting to be let in? Are you mad?'

'No, ma'am.'

'Then what makes you think that I'm going to go out there to open my back gate just because *you*, a complete stranger, tell me my nephew's out there.'

'It's the American lad.'

'My sister's boy?'

'Well, I wouldn't know whose boy he is, ma'am – I'm only taking the message.'

'Why didn't he just knock at the door?'

'He didn't want to be seen.'

'Oh, for God's sake, this is ridiculous. I'm telephoning the police at once.'

'Ah no, ma'am, I wouldn't do that.'

'And why shouldn't I?'

'Well, he's in a bit of bother already, and that's why he asked me to knock you up.'

'What sort of bother – not with the police, you don't mean, surely?'

The little man said nothing.

'Are you a friend of his?'

'I don't know him, and I don't know anything about him. As I said, is all is I'm doin' is delivering the message. He's hurt.'

'Oh God.'

'Not badly. It's just his hand. Cut it on a bit of glass, like. I only mentioned it at all, so you wouldn't be alarmed when you seen the blood, like. Is all he needs is a bit of a bandage.'

'Maybe I should telephone his father.'

'It might be better to speak to him first.'

'Yes, very well. All right, you'd better come in. I'll give you the key to the back gate.'

He nodded and stepped into the light.

She took a good look at him. 'Do I know you?' she asked. 'I mean, I have a feeling . . . '

He considered her question. 'To be honest, ma'am, I'm not certain.'

'What's your name?'

'Slevin, Fred Slevin.'

Half an hour later, she was back in bed, sipping that cup of tea she had been longing for all those hours ago. She wouldn't think about Bennie now. No, this was definitely *not* the time to start thinking about her strange American nephew. His shifty look; his rapid-fire speech; how much he'd changed since she'd seen him last; the terrible trouble he was in; or, worst of all, her willingness to help (which she was now beginning to regret).

And she had been willing: very willing. In fact, come to think of it – and if she was to be honest with herself – she had been more than a little thrilled by her involvement. He didn't even have to talk her into it.

She must have been mad. She must have been out of her mind.

She'd held his hand under the tap, the blood swirling into the flow of water. 'You're very pale. Are you sure I shouldn't take you to the hospital?' She had asked him that question three or four times. Each time, he'd said, 'Honest, it's OK,' and then sucked the pain back in through his teeth. She'd dabbed the iodine and wrapped the hand. She couldn't help but be pleased with the job she had done, and for a while she had felt like a nurse with a stranger. The cuts were all across the inside of his fingers, as if he'd grabbed onto something sharp. Glass, he told her when she asked. Glass and barbed wire.

'I don't understand, Bennie. Why would you?'

His answer made little sense.

She gave him whiskey and he became more coherent, but not coherent enough, so that she'd had to rely on that little Slevin man to fill in the gaps. There had been a fight, apparently – a fight outside a dance hall.

'What sort of a fight?'

'A serious one.'

'Is that how you cut your . . . ? Is that how he cut his . . . ?'

'No, that was when he hopped over the wall.'

'The wall?'

'He did a runner.'

'I had to, Aunt Maude, I had to. They'll blame me. They'll stick together. They always do – you know what they're like.'

'Who is he talking about?'

'Your other nephews.'

'They were with you? Bennie, they were with you?'

'George and Herbert. It was an accident.'

'But I thought George was in Belfast.'

'No, he was with me, and they'll stick together – they'll put it all on me.'

Then he started to cry like a baby.

'Oh, Bennie, come on now, pull yourself together. George and Herbert wouldn't do anything to harm you. You're family, for goodness sake. Whatever it is you've done, you must stay and face it.'

'I can't stay. I won't be let back in the States if this comes out. You don't understand, Aunt Maude. He's dead.'

'Who's dead? Who? Answer me, Bennie, answer me. Oh God. Mister Slevin, who does he mean? Not one . . . ?'

'No, no – he means the owner of the dance hall, ma'am.'

'Oh, this is terrible. This is just the most awful . . . Oh, your poor father. What will this do to him? Your poor . . . '

'You gotta help me, Aunt Maude – I don't have anyone else. They won't let me back into the States, and . . . '

'Yes, all right, all right. Keep quiet for minute, will you? I have to think. Do you have a cigarette?'

He put his face in his hands and started to sob again.

She gave him a moment to compose himself, then asked, 'Bennie, you must tell me the truth: did you do it?'

'I swear to God, you gotta believe me, I didn't do it, I didn't.'

'Did you see what happened, Mister Slevin?'

'I was there all right and, like the lad said, it was an accident – I don't think anyone meant to kill the man. It was just a scuffle that got out of hand. You know how these things happen.'

'I don't, as a matter of fact. Did he do it?'

'I couldn't be certain, but I don't think it was him.'

'I see. But surely that must mean that George or Herbert . . . ? And if I agree to help you, where does that leave them?'

Bennie lifted his hands away from his face. 'No. There were two other guys. They were the ones. It was their fault. George and Hebert – they'll be okay.'

'Is this true, Mister Slevin?'

'There was another pair involved, right enough.'

'Bennie, does anyone else know you came here?'

'No.'

She stood up, poured herself a whiskey and began pacing the kitchen, trying to think.

'Christ almighty, what in God's name am I to do? Will somebody please, please, give me a bloody cigarette?'

Bennie started to pat at his pocket. Mister Slevin started to fidget. 'If you don't mind, ma'am,' he said, 'I'd like to be getting on.'

'Yes, yes of course. But I need to ask you something first.'

'Ma'am?'

'I need to know, can we trust you? If I'm to help my nephew, I need to know.'

'You need have no worries as far as I'm concerned.'

'Thank you, Mister Slevin. Now you must allow me to give you something for all your trouble.'

'Ah no, ma'am, there's no need.'

'No, really, I want to. Dragging you into all this – all this dreadful business. Now, my purse is where . . . ?'

'Really, there's no need. The young lad's already taken care of me.'

'Oh?'

When they were alone, Bennie leaned across the table to her.

'Aunt Maude . . . ?' he began.

'I'll help you,' she said.

He gave her a cigarette, then held out the lighter. She couldn't help noticing how steady the lighter seemed in his hand.

She gave him two things; he didn't even have to ask. A loan of her car and all the money she had in the house. She even plotted the route he should take to get safely out of town and told him where the petrol was hidden in the garage; enough to take him to Cork, where he could arrange his passage back to America.

What else could she have done? He was her sister's boy; he was Samuel's son.

He'd get the car back to her in the next few days somehow, he promised. He'd come to see her again some time – maybe next year; maybe the year after. He'd come to see her again when all this had blown over.

'Yes, you do that, when your hand is better. And maybe you'll play the piano for me?'

'Sure I will.'

He stood at the back door, ready to leave. 'Aunt Maude?'

'Yes.'

'Will you tell the others I'm . . . '

'I can't tell anyone anything, Bennie. I can't let them know I've helped you this way. No one must know.'

'No, I guess not. I'm sorry, Aunt Maude. I'm real sorry about all this.'

And just for a moment he had looked like her sister's boy.

She must have been mad.

She finished her tea and listened to the sound of her car clearing its throat at the corner, edging out to the road, then spearing the empty night. Silence. She continued to listen. Silence? Had the rain stopped? Actually stopped?

And for days she had been keeping an eye on it: the puddle; the garden; the vegetable patch Lucia had planted before the war. Now it had stopped.

PART FOUR

BALLROOM TRAGEDY

I

The traffic was beginning to thicken, the afternoon getting on, by the time Greta and Samuel came out of the Rotunda Hospital onto the street. They stopped on the corner, where the northbound traffic lumped out of Parnell Street into the square. Greta accepted his arm to cross over the road to Conway's gilt-edged pub, where he invited her in for a drink. They'd have to have a little something, he said, to wet the new baby's head.

'Oh no, Sam, I couldn't.'

'Ah, come on, it'll be all right.'

He meant, of course, that it would be all right for a woman to come in, or at least that *he* would somehow make it all right. A nod to the barman to seek permission; a discreet nod back to grant it. A dark corner, then, where her presence would be least likely to offend: a snug or a funk-hole, or perhaps one of those cut-off corridors reserved for policemen and priests.

He asked her again. 'One little sherry? What harm could it do?'

He thought she was being respectable, but he was wrong. She was anxious, that's all – anxious to get down to Moore Street before the scavengers had picked it clean.

'Tomorrow,' she said. 'We'll celebrate then.'

Samuel nodded, gently unhooking their arms.

'And congratulations again, Sam. Congratulations on your beautiful, beautiful grandson.' She waved, moving guiltily off.

But wouldn't he be better off without her? Standing at the bar, he could brag about his grandson, put up drinks all round. (You could be sure a pub that close to the Rotunda would have plenty of resident backslappers to keep him company.) If she was with him, he would have to stay in that dark corner, never leaving her side. Yes, he would be much better off on his own.

Now making her way down towards Moore Street, she forgot about Sam and began to fret. What if there was nothing left? Or worse – only a few rotten ones? And she would still have to buy (if she were to inspect, she would be expected to buy). She stopped to adjust her hat, that was prone to slipping just a little to the right, then peered back down the street until the forehead of a bus shifted itself, revealing this side of Mooney's clock. It was past four – of course they'd be gone. As if the whole city wouldn't have been there before her, hoarding up. She should go back, have a little sherry for herself, get a lift home. It was simply too late; better to accept that now than to let herself turn that corner and have it slapped in her face. Wouldn't it do just as well to go home and say, 'I was going to go into Moore Street, but by the time I got out . . . ' Then they would know she had thought of them, at least. She took a step forward, then a step back, but still her mind wouldn't make itself up.

A batch of Girl Guides were waiting to cross the road, like little brown buns, watching her. The bus conductor, on the platform of a bus, swung his ticket machine over his shoulder and put his hand on the bar, watching her. And the Granby Lane girls, coming this way, strung together like the sausages they shaped, watching her. All watching her. She couldn't stand here forever: she would have to move, one way or the other.

She decided to hold firm with herself. Can't you have a quick look, and so what if they're all gone? It's hardly the worse thing that's ever happened to you, now, is it?

She took the corner with a decisive step and there she was at the bottom of Moore Street, still bustling as if it was the middle of the morning. The sun had lifted off the street, leaving everywhere nice and cool; the only traces of the hot summer's day were the hazy smells that had been left behind. There were two sorts of smells in Moore Street, she always found – male and female. The female was the fruit: slightly sickly after a day's turn in the late July heat; a prissy smell, trying to restrain itself, trying to be polite. The deeper smell was male: vegetables that couldn't care less if they stank to the heavens, even half-expected you to enjoy it. And funny the way they never really mingled. They might touch off each other now and then, but you could always smell them in seperate wafts. The rows of barrows grazed the corners of her eyes, in long lines up each side of the street, and she didn't even have to turn her head and look directly at them. She already knew.

Because the boastful cries of the dealers told her, and the wisps of fruit paper all at her feet and everything about the boisterous street. The barrow boys; the jostling housewives; the men in suits so comically out of place. Everything told her: they were here and they were plenty. And she wouldn't have to go home and say, 'I was going to . . . ', because she *was* going to, as soon as she had walked up and down once or twice (careful to avoid the eye of any particular dealer until she had picked the one she would favour), actually going to . . . And this – she said to herself – this will mark, for me, the end of the war. This is what I'll say to my grandchildren. Oranges. The day I saw oranges for sale again, I knew it was over. The war was *actually* over.

Blazes of them. There they were, past the slimy grey fish stalls and the dry, dun colours of second-hand shoes. And there they were further down on the other side, not afraid of the flowers – outdoing the flowers – blazes and blazes of them. And skins on the ground where people had been too excited to wait till they got home, ripping them apart there and then. Wouldn't she just love to do the same? For she couldn't remember when last she'd had a good suck of an orange.

And she couldn't remember feeling this happy, either – not for a long time. The whole day had been marked by happy moments; the whole fortnight, too. George home on holidays (the last time she would ever have to say that: by next weekend he would always be home). And Herbert's pay rise. And Charlie's news about being picked for the cross-country team. But best of all, Mo's new baby boy. She had held it in her arms; had forgotten how delicate they were – little baby boys. Herbert and George had once been like that, and Charlie too – hard to believe. And the size of them now – big men: George tipping six foot one, Herbert six four from stem to stern. Charlie catching up by the minute. (Had they really been that small?) No, she couldn't be happier. She thought so now, walking down Moore Street, and she had thought so earlier, sitting on the side of the hospital bed, a brand new life nested in her arms. Sam, proud grandfather, on the other side of the bed; Mo sitting up, unwrapping the gift she had bought for the baby. Slowly, so slowly: folding the paper first, putting it aside, winding the string into a put-by ball (and you could say what you liked about Clery's – dear hole that it was, they certainly knew how to wrap a gift). And all the time visualising the baby-bunting coatee, so that by the time Mo had pulled the last piece of tissue away and held it out, gasping, 'Oh, it's lovely, Aunt Greta. I hope you didn't waste all your coupons', she would be ready to discuss it without seeming too pleased. She had pulled herself back with a matter-of-fact tone: 'It's a bit on the big side, now, but he'll soon grow into it, and you must be very careful with washing it now, you must . . . ' But then she had caught sight of the oranges. Piled in a bowl on the top of the locker, behind the flowers and slightly to the left of a photograph of Mo's English husband. 'Oranges?' she couldn't help shouting out. 'Where did you get the oranges?'

Sam said, 'I got them in Moore Street, on the way in. If I'd known you'd be here, Greta, I'd have brought some for you.'

But she didn't want him to get them. She wanted to get them herself. That was half of the pleasure. And half the pleasure was too much to give up.

Mo offered the oranges around. She had refused. 'I'm only after me dinner.' She hadn't wanted to eat it – not in front of them. Not the first one, after all this time. Sam accepted his, rolling it between his palms to loosen the skin, taking his pocket knife to it, scoring out four sections, turn by hissing turn. He pulled the quadrants back on the blade and the orange was bare. He began popping segments into his mouth.

'Are you sure?' he said.

'I'm only after me dinner.'

While he ate it, they spoke about the baby: names and weight. About the father too, and what a shame he couldn't have got leave – what a pity. And all the time, she could smell the orange, acrid and sweet. A most contrary fruit, she thought it: you could never really tell what it was like till you got the skin off and had a taste. It could be plump and sweet, or maybe dried up and past it, with a whiff of halitosis that would knock you off your feet. This was a good one, she could tell, by the soft way Sam's lips moved over it; by the soft pouch it left in his cheek.

Then at last the whole business was over and he took a hanky from his pocket, dabbing his lips dry.

'Any sign of Bennie?' he asked.

'Bennie? No, I haven't seen him since Saturday. Why?'

'Oh, I just thought he might have been up to see his new nephew.'

'Ah, he'll probably be up tonight.'

Sam nodded. 'George got away all right?'

'Oh, he's not gone yet. At least, he was still here this morning.'

'But he was supposed to go back to Belfast on Saturday.'

'He must have changed his mind.'

'He's cutting it a bit fine,' Sam had said, gathering the bits of orange peel and getting up to find a bin and wash his hands.

When he came back, he was frowning.

'The new garage is to open this Saturday, you know. And if he's still to go to Belfast, then get back here on time . . . '

'Oh, I'm sure he'll manage,' Mo said, fingering the satin ties of her bedjacket. 'You're not worried, are you?'

'He's cutting it a bit fine, do you not think, Greta?'

'Ah well, that's George for you,' she had replied.

But now, taking her string bag out of her pocket – coaxing it open, holding it out while a dealer rolled oranges one by one off off a muck-dusted palm (praising each one as if she'd laid it herself) – Greta wondered why she had said, 'That's George for you.' Because it wasn't George at all. He was always so meticulous; so organised. He had explained it to her on Saturday morning while he got ready for the races, and she had only half-listened, knowing of course that it was really himself he was explaining things to. Going over it, again and again: 'I'll go straight from Baldoyle. I need at least a couple of days in Belfast, and I've still a load to see to down here: ads, spare parts, gas converters – all that. I want to give those two cars another look over, make sure everything is in order.' He had seemed so sure of his plan; had had all his details written down in one of his notebooks.

'In case I forget,' he had said then, moving away to the door, 'will you remind Charlie to come up on Friday – give the windows a rub?'

'He's hardly likely to forget – the amount of times you've told him.'

He had turned to her and grinned. He knew she knew him. Knew him well enough to know he was nervous about the new garage, just as she knew him well enough not to suggest that if he was that short of time, he could always skip the races and get an immediate start with his business. She handed him a packet of sandwiches.

'Thanks,' he said, squeezing the packet down into his pocket. 'I'm off, so. Expect me on Tuesday – Wednesday at the latest.'

But it was Tuesday now and he hadn't even gone yet.

But no matter, she thought then, eyeing her change as it came up and out from the dealer's greasy pinny pocket. Whatever way he organised it, he would be home by the end of the week, for good; forever. And he would change the course of things, she felt sure of that. Yes, George would be the man to sort them all out.

She continued up the centre of the street, scanning the barrows on each side. The pathways were packed, and you'd have to feel sorry for the pork butcher-hands, on strike in this weather, flies beating against the windows to get at the stench of unsold meat, heads ducking past the picket under the canopy and into the shop. Trying to maintain a picket line with this crowd; trying to maintain a bit of dignity. And having to make do with a scowl and a snarl, each time the picket was passed, with a policemen perched on the corner, watching their every move. And where are their winks and their nudges now? And their chirpy low innuendo about the length of a sausage and the width of a pudding. 'And do you want stuffin', Missus?'

Should she buy a bit of fish for supper?

Who'd be there for supper? She counted the heads on the tips of her fingers, pressing them into her bag. Charlie, Herbert, himself (who probably wouldn't eat a bit of it but would have to have the plate put in front of him anyway). Bennie, maybe, although not since Saturday. Where could he have got to? Drunk, probably, somewhere. With a woman, probably, somewhere. He was too fond by far of both – did Sam know? Now who else? George? No, no point in counting George in, because he'd *have* to be gone by now.

Had Sam seemed a bit displeased? Even Mo had sensed it (fingering the satin ties of her bedjacket). Which was the way with men that were as easygoing as Sam: the slightest frown on their face and they had everybody all upset. It was Sam's garage, she supposed: she hadn't asked the ins and outs. But George was putting money up too. And George would be the manager, in Terenure. Where they used to live. He could say it to the customers too. 'We used to live here, just down the road. You know Eaton Square? Well, we used to live there.'

Better than saying we live in New Street.

And was that a crate of potato-onions she could see between the calves of that dealer's legs? Such legs. Bulging down from under her skirt like two prize marrows; bruised all colours. Being on your feet all day does that, of course. She took a quick glance down at her own right leg, stepping it out. Not a mark on them: spick and span. Not bad for a woman her age. Potato-onions fat as you like, kept hidden for pet customers no doubt, and the little fecky bulblets she had on display. But how would she carry them? She'd never manage. Would Sam still be in Conway's? Potato-onions; a bit of fish; yes . . . She could see the dish in her mind for a second: jagged smoked cod, rusty and thick; a silky white sauce, bumped with onions all around. Herbert's favourite. Maybe put a bit of colour on his cheeks. Peaky, he'd been, for the last few days; not himself at all. If she went back to Sam, she could manage all right, and she'd get her lift. And her glass of sherry. They could talk about the baby. But then she remembered Samuel's frown. She'd make do with the onions she already had.

She settled the fish bundle into her bag and turned towards Henry Street, moving lightly along. It made her feel young to be out and about, with gloves and a hat, a few bob in her purse, feet tipping off fruit paper and her good high heels on. She didn't feel like herself at all. Even the voice in her head had acquired that tone you keep for people you meet at parties or a friend you might have. Someone you didn't know well enough to tell your troubles to, but an acquaintance you went on outings with: an afternoon matinée, for example, or the teatime fashion show in Arnott's café, discussing this or that over tea. But never the worries, and never *ever* the husbands. The children would be all right, she supposed, in a vague sort of way.

'And tell me about your sons, Greta. What do they do?'

'Well, my youngest now, he's waiting to be called for the civil service, you know.'

'Oh, how nice.'

'And my eldest, he's a law searcher, although we had hoped he'd be a solicitor. He went to the High School, you know.'

'Really? Well isn't that nice?'

'My middle son, George – the one I told you lives in Belfast – well, he's coming home, to start a new venture: his own garage in Terenure. Where we used to live.'

'Terenure? Well, indeed.'

'For the moment, he'll be selling reconditioned cars, but there's a very nice showroom, a flat upstairs he's going to do up, and pumps out front, for whenever there's petrol to pump again.'

'Oh, well now, they do say the motoring age is about to return.'

'And just as well, because my boys are motor-car mad. Except for my youngest – he'd rather run. Has the legs run off himself, that fellow. He's just been picked for the cross-country championship, in December, you know.'

'Well, isn't that only marvellous? And I believe, Greta, that your lads are all fine-looking fellows?'

'Oh well, I don't know about that . . . '

She came into Henry Street shaking her head; shaking the conversation and her friend away. Silly, really.

Now Arnott's window. She leaned towards the glass. Assistants nipping forward and backward, sliding box drawers into walls or peering down into glass-lidded counters. This one, madam? You mean this one here? A manager presenting a bentwood chair for that lady to sit on. She felt like going in, being presented with a chair herself – maybe buy something that didn't need coupons. But you couldn't go into Arnott's carrying your string bag with your oranges sticking out and your smoked cod plopped on top. Another day, she told herself: there would be other days to wear your high heels and Sunday hat. Yes, other days.

She moved to the next window and caught sight of herself in a side-view mirror, a strand of hair sticking arseways out from under her hat. She fidgeted for a moment and, there now – hair re-tucked, hat realigned, she was ready to move off again. Ten windows, in all, she believed Arnotts had, although she'd never actually counted them. You'd have your hands full cleaning and dressing them. Poor shop boys out in all weathers, whitening the masonry round each one; hawing on the window-panes till they were all out of air. How did their mothers allow it?

She turned the corner into O'Connell Street; broad and suddenly bright. And it always looked well at this hour of the day, this time of the year. This was the hour she knew it best, because it was about this time that she used to go to work when she was waitressing in the Gresham Hotel. And later then, in a banqueting room, putting the final touches to the table – a canister here, a decanter there; bowls of flowers all up the middle – it used to put her in mind of the centre island that cut O'Connell Street in half. With the evening sunlight raking over it; tubbed flowers and black monuments and the Pillar at the centre wreathed with colour; a pramful of fruit; a bench of old soldiers. Yes, that's what it used to remind her of then, when she was young and inclined to see something in everything: a banqueting table as the island in the middle of O'Connell Street. Silly, really. Always so silly.

She stopped at the corner as if she was waiting for someone; laying her bag down at her feet; giving her arms a little rest. The widest boulevard in Europe, some man she used to work with had told her. The widest. Imagine.

From behind the columns of the GPO, paper boys popped in and out, roaring like elephants, and the occasional uniformed man swaggered by – Australian officers; Canadian air force; Johnny Doughboys – hands in pockets (always in pockets). They had a certain way of walking, overseas men. You could never imagine them actually marching. Full of themselves, of course, with their easy limbs and big shoulders. Think every woman is looking at them, with their tanned faces and pale eyes. Think they're only the business, with the hair on their hands whenever they take them out of their pockets. And their fancy strap watches. Think they're . . .

A newsboy jumped up beside her waving the *Herald* under her nose. She frowned at his feet. You'd think, with the Herald Boot Fund, they'd look after their own that were always on view. What must they think, these overseas men? Boys in bare feet, roaring like elephants. He waved the paper again. Something to read on the bus? She paused for a moment, considering. Why bother, when Herbert always brought the paper home? She could look out the window on the way home instead. Somebody would give her a seat, surely, with this great bag of messages to hold like a child on her lap. She could look out and enjoy the antics of the rush-hour city. The herds of black bicycles swarming the bridge; the policeman's white glove guiding them. The well-to-do ladies and what they were wearing. The street photographers snapping at random – office girls posing sweetly arm in arm; accepting his card; giggling. Businessmen rushing past; brushing it away; scowling. So much to enjoy. Why spoil her glow with all that bad news they were shouting at her, vying with each other in their fishwives' tones. Pétain and Reynaud, Churchill and Attlee. All those names that meant nothing now. Now that the war was over, actually over.

The paper boy came back to her, holding up a dirty, defiant face. (What sort of mother . . . ?) But she didn't want the paper, could he not understand? And she hadn't got three ha'pence handy. She shook her head, lifted her bag and moved to the edge of the street.

She waited to cross over with the rest of the crowd. Men hot in shirtsleeves, hats pushed off their foreheads, jackets slung over one shoulder. Girls cool in cotton, tossing loose hair into breezes that leaked out from the gaps between streets. Summer, all summer – after weeks of rain and grey.

Behind her the paper boys continued to bray, the odd bit of sense breaking in. Pétain on trial. Honshu blasted. Churchill leaves Potsdam. Faraway names. What did they matter? Then closer to home. Calves slaughtered in Leitrim. Mailboat stranded. City man slain in a ballroom tragedy. What did any of it matter today?

She crossed over the road and stepped onto the island. Nelson's Pillar was behind her now, freeing up the view down through Earl Street and the bridge of Amiens Street Station right at the bottom. Incongruous-looking, it was, as if it belonged somewhere else: Spain, or somewhere like that. As if someone had found it and stuck it up in the wrong city; shoved it into that space that happened to be free at the bottom of Earl Street.

A train slid over, chewing up the light bit by bit, then spitting the light back out bit by bit. The Belfast train, maybe. With George on it, maybe.

II

The outing was over and supper was served; she was back in her slippers – back on her patch in the scullery lino that had faded over time into a map of her feet. She whipped a cloth round the base of a pot and cocked her head to the kitchen: her experienced ear could detect only one set of cutlery in use.

She came to the doorway to see for herself. Vacant chair and full plate where her husband was supposed to be. Charlie's plate next: good lad, almost finished. Herbert's plate, she couldn't see – his back was too broad.

'Have you enough there, Charlie?'

'Yeah, ma, I'm grand.'

'Are you sure you don't want another little bit?'

'I can't, ma, I told you, I'm training after.'

'Keep a bit of room for your orange, anyway.'

She came over to the table, peered into the milk jug, fiddled with the bread plate, swabbed at a sauce-blob with the corner of her cloth. Herbert hadn't even picked up his fork.

'Are you not going to eat your . . . ?'

'In a minute.'

'I've a bit of butter put by from your ration.'

'No, thanks.'

'Ah, Herbert, will you not even try? I got it specially.'

'I'll just finish this smoke.'

She turned to her husband, seated by the fireplace – a book held up to his face. 'Your dinner's on the table, in case you didn't notice.'

'What is it?' he asked, lowering his book.

'Smoked cod.'

'Smoked cod? Is that so?'

He closed the book back up to his face.

A skin had taken a grip over the two plates of untouched food. Like old snow, it looked, grimy and grey. She thought of the waste – money, food and sense, not to mention her time – and felt like picking up the plates and mashing them into their faces.

'I should have saved me legs and kept me money, that's what I should have done. After all the trouble I went to, and what thanks do I get? I wouldn't mind, but Sam invited . . . ' Then the back door pushed open and there was George – in rolled-up shirtsleeves, oily up to the elbows – heeling the door shut behind him.

'George? Don't tell me you're still here?'

'Well, that's a lovely greeting, I must say.'

'I was only talking to Sam up at the hospital . . . '

'I suppose you told him I hadn't gone?'

'Well, he asked me.'

'The water's still not turned on, would you believe,' he said, lifting his black forearms out in front of him and following them into the scullery.

He stepped back to make room for her at the sink. She hoisted the dishes out, then poured a measure of washing powder down into his cupped hands.

She stood aside and watched him for a while, rubbing his hands together, working the grains into the creases until a thin, black lather formed. Flashing them now and then under the running tap, sliding the lather up and down his arms. Saying nothing, of course, just rubbing, rinsing. Rinsing again.

'Well?' she asked at last.

'Look, I'll be gone in the morning and back by Friday.'

'I thought you were supposed to have a million and one . . . ?'

'I decided to take care of things this end first.'

'And how are you going to manage without any water?'

'I *said* I've taken care of it. So you can tell Sam he's no need to check up on me.'

'He wasn't checking up, he was just wondering, that's all. You should have told him you'd changed your plans around.'

'What difference does it make once everything's done?'

He flicked the drops off his fingers and reached for a towel.

'Ah no, not that one,' she scolded, pulling a rag out from under the sink.

They came back out to the kitchen. 'And he's looking for Bennie,' she said.

Herbert looked up. 'Bennie?'

'Yes. Why, do you know where he is?'

'How would he know where he is?' George said. 'He's probably gone back.'

'Now he'd hardly go back without saying goodbye to his father.'

'Ah, he'll turn up, all right. I wouldn't go worrying your head over Bennie.'

'Greta reached down for her husband's plate, swiping it away. 'No point in wasting this,' she said. 'Sit down there, George, and I'll heat it up for you. I wasn't expecting you, son. Go on, sit yourself down.'

Her voice trailed behind her, still speaking to George.

'That fella's eaten nothing again. I don't like the look of him at all.'

'What?'

'I said, that fella's eaten nothin' again. Not a bite.'

'Who?'

'Herbert. He's not one bit well. Look at the colour of him.'

'He looks all right to me,' George said.

'I said it to him, I said: It's not right, a man your size losing his appetite. He should go to the infirmary.'

'Too many late nights, that's all.'

'What are you talking about? Apart from work, he hasn't crossed the door since Saturday night.'

'Maybe that's what's wrong with him.'

'You know that chap he works with was carted off to the sanatorium last week? And I passed the Enrights' house yesterday – the windows were all open.'

'So?'

'Well, there's only one reason that lot would have the windows open in the lashings of rain. George, are you listening to me?'

'What?'

'The Enrights had the windows opened.'

'Maybe they couldn't stand the stink of themselves.'

She stuck her head out and looked at him. 'George, I'm serious. It could be TB.'

'For Christ's sake, the things you say. Herbert hasn't got TB.'

'Did I say he had? Did I? I was talking about the Enrights.'

'Did anyone get a paper?' the Dancer asked.

George sat down and gave Charlie a nudge. 'What's up with you?'

'Nothin'.'

'Are you not out training?'

'I'm goin' now, in a . . . '

'Did anyone get the paper?' the Dancer asked again.

'Where are you training – the Park? I'll run you up, if you like.'

'No, I'll go on the bike.'

'Did anyone get the bloody . . . ?'

'How many times do I have to tell you,' Herbert snapped, 'I forgot it.'

'What about you, George – did you?'

'What? Oh, I must have left it in the car.'

The Dancer put his hand up to the mantlepiece and pulled himself up, then slid his cigarettes and matches to him and went out to the yard.

George looked across the table at Herbert. 'You better eat it,' he said.

'I can't.'

'Eat the fuckin' thing, will you?'

'I said, I can't.'

George leaned over, plucked the cigarette out of Herbert's mouth and threw it in the fireplace. He picked Herbert's fork up, then began feeding himself from Herbert's plate: a spike of fish, a lump of spud, a scoop of onions. Then he put the fork into Herbert's hand and got the food down his own gullet and the chair back under his arse just as his mother came back in, the reheated supper held high in a cloth between her hands.

She looked at Herbert. 'Well, that's a bit better,' she said, and smiled, laying the plate down in front of George.

'That's a right mystery . . . ' she began.

'What is?'

'Bennie.'

'Bennie's a big boy,' George said, lowering his head close to his plate. 'Any chance of a cup of tea?'

When she left the room, he took Herbert's supper and divided the remainder between his own plate and Charlie's.

'Hey . . . I have to train tonight.'

'Ah, shut up and eat it – it'll do you good.'

Charlie stared at the mess on his plate, then beyond its rim to the little red checks on the oilcloth. And then the blue stripes on the salt cellar, and just in front of that, the blistered ring on the oilcloth where somebody drunk had been careless with the teapot. He didn't want to look up from the table. With Herbert's pale face opposite him, hanging like a moon on its own. With George's crabby face beside him, looking up between gobfuls over at the scullery to check on ma or across at Herbert to give him a glare. He didn't want to see the glimmer of George's knife brushing off the wall when he held it up and said, 'You better get a grip on yourself, Herbert – I'm warnin' you.'

He could hear the scullery noises inside: the drill of water hitting the kettle, the click of the flint, the fart of the gas ring. Chattering dishes; chattering ma, shouting out to George. George shouting back. One face for ma, the other for the table. One voice for ma, the other for . . . He lowered his head to a forkful of mash and felt a cold squeeze in his stomach.

Her voice came out from the scullery again. 'Ah, you should see the baby, George – he's only gorgeous.'

'What's she calling him?'

'She doesn't know yet.'

'Well, I hope it's something better than "Mo".'

'Ah, that's because she just hates the name Maude.'

'You mean she hates Aunt Maude.'

'No she doesn't.'

'Maybe we'll go up to see her after.'

She showed her face for a minute then, and it was all lit up and thrilled with itself. 'Would you? The three of you? Oh, she'd love that, she would.' Then it slipped back into the scullery.

Herbert reached for his cigarettes. 'I don't want to go,' he whispered to George.

'We can talk on the way.'

'I don't want to go out.'

'But ma . . . ?' Charlie called in to her.

'Ah, can't you miss training for one night? Go up and see your cousin's new baby? Anyway, you can't run yet – not till your food is settled. It wouldn't kill you to stick your nose in for a minute.'

'Ah, for God's sake, ma.'

'Well, can't you go straight from the hospital, then? I'll give you a note for Mister Shanks.'

'I can't give him a note, ma. It's the Leinster team, not school.'

'Ah, let him go,' George said, patting Charlie on the back. 'A champ's got to train – isn't that right, kid?'

Charlie pulled his chair from the table and picked up his kitbag. When he got to the door, he turned back around. 'Will you be stopping the night?' he asked.

George's eyes came over his shoulder. 'Why?'

'I just wanted to know what to do about the mattress.'

'Leave it where it is. I haven't had a chance to get a bed for the flat yet.'

'So you'll be staying?'

'Yeah. If you've no objection . . . '

Charlie shook his head and pulled the door to him.

'Charlie?'

'What?'

'We haven't been disturbing you, have we?'

'No, I didn't hear a word.'

'I didn't ask you if you heard what we said, I asked if we've been disturbing you.'

'Well, you haven't.'

'Good. Are you all right for a few bob?'

'Yeah.'

'You're sure, now?'

'Yeah.'

'Here, kid?'

'What?'

'You forgot something.'

Charlie dropped his bag to the floor. He lifted his hands in the air and watched them snap down on the orange.

He put his hand on the saddle of the bike and pushed it in front of him: over the yard, under the archway, down through the tunnel, where da was standing looking out at the street.

'What's the puss for?' da asked, when he came up beside him.

'Nothin'.'

'What?'

'I have to sleep on that bloody mattress again.'

Da pulled the cigarette in and out of his mouth and nodded. After a while he spoke. 'I don't know what he's talking about – there's no paper in his car.'

'I hate sleeping in the kitchen – I'm awake half the night.'

'It's not like him, not to have an evening paper. It's not like either of them, come to think of it.'

'And anyway, if he has no bed in the flat, why can't *he* take the mattress and leave me to my own bed? Me training's all off – Mister Shanks even says it. I can feel it in me breathing – and me legs. Me legs weigh a ton. And another thing – she keeps making me eat, and I'm not supposed to eat for two hours before training.'

'Did you not tell her?'

'I did. She won't listen. She says, "Ah, there's only enough there to keep up your strength. Eat it quick and you won't even notice." She just won't listen.'

He saw da's lips move around the butt of the cigarette, and it might have been a smile, so he decided to continue. 'Between that and the lack of sleep, I'll be thrown off the team.'

'Indeed you won't.'

'They stay up drinking till all hours. They bring Bennie back and all sorts, and . . . '

'Bennie hasn't been the last few nights, has he?'

'No.'

'What are you worried about then?'

'Well, he could turn up tonight.'

'Not at all.'

'How do you know?'

'Bennie's gone.'

'Do you know where he is?'

'No. But they do.'

'Oh?'

He waited for a minute to see would da say anything else about Bennie or about ma or about the mattress even, but he knew by his eyes that the conversation was over. Charlie wheeled the bike out onto the road and cocked his leg over.

'Mind you don't fall, now,' he heard da say.

III

You think of the kitchen. Lying behind the curtain on the mattress in the corner, tasting the dust on the floor, the greasy stench of the mattress. Afraid to let go, always listening – for the sound of footsteps coming back from town, or a car coming back from a bona fide pub in the mountains. The rattle of the latch, the clink of large bottles; voices outside struggling to whisper. Coming inside then, they forget about whispering; start acting as if they own the place, until the purr and snap of shuffling cards finally quietens them down. Your brothers, your cousin, Grumley, Rafter, or a stranger they might have picked up on the way. And you know there's no point in complaining: one tut and you're bollixed. One tut and they'll drag you out just to keep themselves amused. But if you keep yourself quiet – if you eat your own breath – they might forget you're there. But that doesn't mean you'll get any sleep.

You think of the kitchen, last Saturday night. Hearing the first noises out in the yard, waiting for the sequence to continue. But this time only two voices come in. Two voices hushed. Hushed and at the same time heavy. The scrape and grunt of kitchen chairs, and you can see from under the curtain two pairs of feet settle under the table.

George doing most of the talking, repeating things to Herbert, as if he was trying to make him learn something off by heart. Herbert saying nothing at first, but you can hear him breathe. You can hear the fear in his breath. He's afraid of something. They're both afraid.

'As long as we keep our heads. Are you listening, Herbert? Are you listening to me? As long as we keep our heads. I'll have to go to Belfast tomorrow.'

'You can't leave me. You can't just . . .'

'Look, I'll only be gone a couple of days.'

'Can you not just stay?'

'I can't. I told you, I have to get the money.'

'I'm not staying here on my own. I'm fuckin' telling you – if you go, I go.'

'Shut up, will you? Keep your fuckin' voice down.'

'Let's get one thing straight, George, one fuckin' thing straight – I'm not staying here to face this on my own.'

'Oh, for Christ's sake. All right, all right. I'll stay a few days, but I'll have to be gone by Tuesday.'

'Tuesday?'

'Wednesday, then. If anything's going to happen, it'll happen by then.'

'George, what are we going to do?'

'Nothing, that's what. We're going to do nothin' and say nothin'.'

'What about the others?'

'We'll just have to . . .'

'Have to what? Trust them? Oh, that's fuckin' great, that is.'

'They'll be all right. Leave them to me.'

'They'll squeal like pigs.'

'Herbert, listen to me. Listen. If we keep our heads, it'll be all right.'

'If we keep our heads?'

'That's right.'

You're not used to seeing your brothers afraid. You're only used to seeing other people afraid of them. By the time they're finished talking, you're afraid as well.

*

He decides to skip training. Doesn't want to have to feel himself struggle behind the rest of the team; or to hear Shanks roar out his name more than the others; or to see the look on his face later on, when he draws him aside to give him a bollocking. He doesn't want to risk losing the rag, either – end up telling Shanks to stick his team up his hole. Because he's sick of Shanks now – sick of being told what to do and which way to do it. He gets off his bike and starts to walk.

He ends up down on the quays and tries to remember how he got there. But there's no route in his head – no streets – only people: a Jewman locking up his shop; the Vincent man knocking at a tenement door, a charity parcel under his arm. A man stepping out between greyhounds who said goodnight to him. When you're running, you never notice these things. When you're running, you only notice the shape of the streets.

He gets to Kingsbridge, pulls the orange out of his pocket, takes a bite out of it, gnaws a hole into its face, then throws it into the Liffey. The taste of the fish is still there in his mouth: the tang of the orange. Leaning over the wall, he sucks on the air, but there's only the sulpherised rot of the river. He spits into it. A long, greasy gob: an insect on top of the water. He croaks his throat and spits again.

He comes back into New Street and sees the man with the dogs again. The dogs are tied to the railings outside the public jacks. The man is stooping down to one of the dogs, rubbing his hands all over it. The muscles on the dog stand up to his touch. The other hounds, jealous, pant into their muzzles, frantic for their turn to come around.

The man calls him over. 'You're the Dancer's son, aren't you?'

'That's right.'

'I think you might have a bit of trouble.'

He follows the man's nod down the road to a big black car parked at the archway.

'You better warn your da,' the man says.

'Me da? Why?'

'Your da, or whoever. Can you get in the back way?'

'Who are they?'

'Cops.'

'Cops?'

'Plainclothes. The worst sort,' the man says, then goes back to rubbing his dog.

He slows up his step as he comes to his house. Big, black car; four men inside. The window rolls down.

'What's your name.'

'Charlie.'

'Do you live in there?'

'No.'

'Do you know who does?'

'No.'

'Where do you live?'

'Somewhere else.'

'Go on then, scram.'

He nearly runs through the wall at the back of his house; has to pull himself back before he can throw himself at it. His feet reach into the familiar footholds. He can hear the slap of car doors out on the street; the march of feet coming in through the archway. A fist pounds on the door three times.

He knows he's too late, but he pulls himself up anyway.

IV

Henry lives in a house by the sea. A tall house with box hedges all round and a pebble path that stops at the gate. He sits in a picture window and looks down at the gate. It has an iron strip at the top half and iron bars at the bottom, where outside legs stroll past: flat-footed children; lean-calved women; men's legs, with brisk sticks swinging in time and sniffy dogs lagging behind. Not all legs pass by: some of them stop. Then the bell downstairs hums into the hall, and soon the porter's baldy head comes out the front door and down the front steps. He flaps his arms when he puts on his jacket; his feet scuff over the path; then the tired old gate gives a laryngitic groan and the legs bring a whole body in, hat and all.

He sits in his window and looks at the top of the bus, when it stops and juts over the hedges. And a row of quarter-profiles look down into the garden, then take a greedy glance all over the house before the bus swims lazily by.

He looks at the sea: sharp elbows of swimmers saw through the cracks; white quiffs of sails claw over its muscular back; gulls pull and pluck at its skin.

It's a very loud house, this house Henry lives in – full of old theatre people who talk of old things. Old acts and ariette, burlesque and buffa from long-ago days and long-ago theatres that Henry can't always remember. The theatre people call him Mister Masterson. The nurses call him Henry. They comb his hair and shave his face and read from the paper to him, then help him cut out the interesting bits to stick in the book he is making.

A woman comes to sit with him sometimes: a woman with anxious eyes and hair that may once have been chestnut. She brought him sweeties, so he called her 'mother', but that just made her cry. So now he doesn't call her anything at all. In case it pops out by mistake: 'mother'. Sometimes he thinks the woman must mistake him for someone else. She tells him about the interesting life he has led; all the things he has seen and done. She tells him, for example, that in his lifetime he has seen people progress from carriages to motor cars, and now when they want to go to another country, they fly through the sky to cross over the water.

But he has been watching the sky all day; all days. And he has seen the birds fly like a burst of soot flakes across it. And he has seen it plump with clouds and transparent grey and curdled with light and all shades of blue. He has seen it all ways, always. But he has never, ever seen the likes of that. She is talking rot, of course. But he doesn't mind that. Lots of people talk rot in this tall, loud house.

He is always dressed for an outing: a buttonhole, a shiny shoe, a pressed trouser end. These are the things he sees when he looks down at himself. But he never goes out. Not now. Once, he escaped. When the baldy porter was new. Henry came down in his street clothes and simply asked, 'Has my taxicab arrived yet?'

'No, sir.'

'Ahh . . . ' Henry had said. 'Damned taxicabs. I'll just go and meet it at the corner, so. Good day.' The baldy porter had fallen for it and opened the gate. Then Henry was outside, his shining shoes following each other all the way up the road.

They had found him in the evening time, without his coat. On the tip of Dun Laoghaire Pier, watching the mailboat's dinky little lights. His trousers were wet: stuck to his thighs; sore when he walked. Little, nervous sores all huddled together that stayed itchy for weeks. The roundy nurse patted gentle cream on them with her pink-padded fingertips and then they went away.

Now her hand is holding a scissors; her other hand a piece of newspaper. She turns the scissors around the corner and the piece falls away from the page. 'Where?' she asks.

'Here,' he says, 'this is the page. "B" for ballroom.'

'Why "ballroom"?'

'Because that's where it happened and that was the very first word in the very first caption. "Ballroom tragedy" – see?'

'Yes, I see.'

'And today is . . . ?'

'Sunday.'

'Yes, Sunday. So it goes here in the space beside Saturday.'

The nurse dabs the cutting with stiff, sticky paste, lays it down, presses it in and smooths it out with her nice roundy fingers. Then she tells him he'll have to put away his book because it's nearly time for his visitors.

'What visitors?'

'Mrs Masterson and some man called Samuel.'

'Mrs Masterson? Some man called Samuel? I don't know them.'

'Mrs Masterson, who brings you the sweets.'

'Oh, her.'

The bell goes off in the hall and she gets up to leave him.

'Where are you going?'

'To let them in.'

'Why not the porter?'

'He isn't back from his dinner.'

He looks at the section she has stuck in his book and sees something new. Something that wasn't there yesterday. He puts his face close in and begins to read.

The bells from the church bounce around the house. The door opens behind him. The nurse says, 'Henry, your visitors are here.'

He reads the section again, this time using his finger. He whispers the names that his finger points out. Then he reads them again, this time out loud.

PART FIVE

Winter 1947

They released him in the dead of winter: the Black Winter of '47. The wardsman stood in the doorway of his cell, a bundle on the crook of one arm: carrier bag, clothes, a pair of brown shoes. He let the bundle drop down on the bed. 'You're getting out,' he said. 'I'll be back in half an hour.'

It took five minutes to dress. He folded his prison clothes, then sat on the bed and waited.

When the wardsman came back, he glanced round the cell and nodded at the empty bag. 'What about your stuff?'

'What about it?'

'Are you not even taking your books?'

'I've read them.'

The wardsman shrugged and stepped aside. 'You're expected down in the governor's office. Good luck to you, now.'

He walked alone down the wired-in gallery, past the rows of cell doors on the A1 Block. The first time he'd walked this way without being part of a shuffling troupe: grey ghosts in the light of a thirty-watt bulb – just enough to see by when you emptied your slops. The first time he'd walked this way without the rattle of keys in his head, the snide, low sneer of a warden herding him on. The first time he'd walked anywhere on his own for nearly two years.

His shoes felt all wrong – too big and too slippy – and the way they clanged on the metal floor was making him feel guilty, like he was rubbing it in. He could sense the raw eyes of long-term lags watching him through the hatches in cell doors. He looked straight ahead and kept on walking. When he got to the end of the gallery, there was a sudden eruption: whistles and cheers; hand-slaps on walls; feet-thumps on steel doors. He didn't look back, just raised one hand in acknowledgement, and, using the other hand to steady himself up, grabbed a hold of the rail, then clanged downstairs to the gallery below.

He stopped at the triple cell that passed for the prison hospital and thought of the things that had happened in there over the past eighteen months. The IRA man on hunger and thirst strike, tongue-shrunk and withered, trying to say his prayers. The tinker who'd been dunked into the big main bath filled with freezing water, then dragged out to die a day later. An old man who'd fried himself after he'd been given an inspection lamp with the gutta-percha hanging off it and ordered to hose down the boilers.

He stood in the open doorway and thought about the things he used to try to make sense of when he'd first come in: *mens rea*, *actus reus*, murder and manslaughter. He looked at the empty beds and thought about death.

The governor explained the terms of his release: the ramifications of a Convict's Remission Licence. 'What it all boils down to is this: any messing and you'll be straight back in.' Then he lifted the prison stamp and thumped it down on the paper. 'It's bloody cold out there. Have you no winter coat?'

'It wasn't winter when I came in.'

'Oh, that's right,' the governor said, checking his file. 'Not to worry, your mother probably brought one with her.'

'My mother?'

'She's outside,' he said, with a gesture towards the window.

Outside the prison walls, it looked like Siberia: a wilderness of snow and sky. For miles and miles, snow and sky, nothing else – except a Morris Oxford carved like black stone against the candescent light, and his mother and brother standing beside it, waiting for the prison gate to open. His brother lit one cigarette off the other and stamped his feet on the driveway, which was thick-ribbed with ice. His mother wore mittens and fur on her collar. There was no winter coat in her arms.

Faces started to come into his head: faces he hadn't thought of in months. The screaming white face of his mother when they pulled her two sons out to the yard and clapped the handcuffs on. The breathless white face of Charlie watching the squad car shriek up the street, then watching his brothers being folded into it. The silent white face of the Dancer limping towards the phone box on the corner. Other faces too: faces in the witness box, fingers pointing him out – some bollix from Belfast he'd only met for a second; some other oul'fella he could barely remember who'd sent him over a drink in Tully's back bar. And Grumley and Rafter, squealing like pigs, squirming their way out of it, under the expert guidance of their senior counsel. As if he'd be stupid enough not to guess a deal had been made behind the scenes.

Weeks of waiting and newspaper headlines, from 'Four Men Arrested' down to 'One Man Found Guilty.' The way he used to imagine people who knew him all over the city opening their morning papers. Across kitchen tables and office desks, shop counters and bar corners, reading the details out to each other; some of them shocked, more of them smug. Saying the sort of things you say when someone is dead, like, 'God love his poor mother' or 'I wouldn't mind, but I was only talking to him the other day.'

And the way he kept recalling something his old schoolmaster once said about knowing he'd hear of his former pupil one day and be proud.

Behind him, the governor was making a speech about second chances and rehabilitation. 'People would surprise you,' he said. 'Their ability to forgive, forget.' And he could see himself the day he was sentenced, being escorted down the narrow stairwell from the courtroom to the cells below, then being escorted out of the Bridewell into the prison van. Local kids hissed at the prison guards, an oul'one made the sign of the cross. A barrister cut his swagger short, put his hand on his wig and turned to look back at him. He stooped his head to get into the van: hissing kids, praying oul'ones and Wally Caper's eyes burning into the back of his neck.

He looked down at his mother again: the mittens on her hands, the fur strip on her collar, and the turn of her head looking over each shoulder, as if she was afraid someone might see her. It came back to him then, the feeling of shame, and he remembered the relief of being able to let go of it once he'd settled inside, where it had seemed a bit pointless, like a black man in Africa worrying about the colour of his skin.

He glanced back at the governor's desk and the big brown envelope marked with his name: his personal effects. A notebook full of redundant phone numbers; the watch Amy had given him their first Christmas together; a few other bits that he had happened to have on him. Everything waiting to be reclaimed.

The governor told him the world might seem a bit big at first: to ask God for help if he felt a bit lost. 'Talk to your priest,' he said, 'go to Mass, receive. Never underestimate the power of prayer.'

'I'm not a Catholic,' he said.

'Oh that's right, so you're not,' the governor said, checking his file again.

He came back to the desk and signed the release papers. The governor gave him the envelope and held out his hand. He looked at the hand, swallowed a spit and turned away.

His mother broke down the minute she saw him. She cried like it was his suit that was making her cry and not him. She took off her mitten, put her hand on his jacket and plucked at the sags of loose cloth that used to fit into his body. 'Look at your suit. Your lovely good suit. Hanging off you. Will you just look at it. How could you have lost all that weight?'

'Ah, think of the fun you'll have fattening him up,' his brother said, half-laughing, half-crying; shaking his hand; pulling away then to take off his overcoat. 'Here,' he said, 'shove this on you before you turn blue. And there's something in the inside pocket to welcome you home.'

He got into the car and they drove through the midlands: the snow-swollen midlands. Everywhere paralysed; everything dead, or near-enough dead. Crows scattered like black rags on top of the snow. Solid sides of frozen cattle sunk down into it. A scrum of sheep, barely alive in the corner of a field. No sound existed except for the engine and the turn of the tyres retracing their tracks to keep a grip on the road.

The dense silence outside pressed against the car. They were afraid of the silence; kept chipping away at it. Taking turns to talk, or talking sometimes together.

His mother told him about the new house in Crumlin, the geyser that heated water, the bus that stopped right outside the door. Then she broke off and started crying again. 'I just can't get over it, son. You're so thin. Not a pick on you. I just can't.'

He wanted to tell her why. To tell her about the screw from Roscommon, sucking the gravy off the lumps of meat, dropping them back on the aluminium tray, wiping his fingers in the arse of his trousers, before opening the cell door and sliding the plate across the floor. He could see the picture of the screw in his head but he couldn't seem to shape the picture into words.

'Ah, the grub wouldn't be up to much – not after what I was used to,' he said to her, and smiled.

She seemed happy with the smile: stopped crying, anyway, smiled back at him and said, 'Your teeth are lovely and white.'

'Plenty of time to brush them, anyway,' he said.

Then they both told him about the Black Winter. People dying of the cold. Farmers going out into blizzards to look for lost stock and never making it back. Chestnut trees on residential roads being hacked down for firewood. Milk shortage; fuel shortage. People burning their good furniture: the best of stuff. Men shovelling snow off the quays and throwing it into the Liffey. Gangs of kids skating on the ice in the quarry. Three boys died when the ice gave in.

His brother told him what it had been like living in Tullamore after the garage in Terenure fell through because of all that business in the newspapers. Tullamore, the arsehole of nowhere – a whole year stuck in that kip. He'd recovered, though – had his own place now: a place off Baggot Street, the cars driving themselves off the forecourt, things were going so well. He said he'd hoped they could work there together. 'I've the sign painted and all. Both our names on it. You only have to say the word and I'll nail it up over the door. Partners. What do you say, Herbert?'

The sound of his Christian name startled then saddened him. 'I'm finding it a bit hard to say anything at all at the minute. Only used to my own company. Solitary and that. Twenty hours a day.'

'You take your time,' his brother said. 'A few pints, a decent dinner, you won't know yourself, Herbert.'

He pulled the coat closer to him. The snow was making him tired, stinging his eye, and he wished his brother would stop using his name.

'Twenty hours on your own?' his mother said, after a minute.
    'Twenty-two on Sunday.'
    'It must have been terrible lonely. Why did you stop taking visits?'
    'Why did I stop taking visits?'
    'Yes. Surely it would have helped to have a few visitors?'
    'It breaks the continuity.'
    'What do you mean?'
    'It makes the time go slower.'

They left him alone after that: just the odd word here and there, mainly between themselves. They got to the Curragh and he looked out the window: out at the empty space; the plush, warped land; the unreachable distance. He wanted to get out and walk. To feel the snow suck on his feet. To walk through the dense silence and hear nothing but the sound of his shoes breaking into the crust on the snow.

He woke at six because he thought he heard the chime of the triangle outside his cell door. But it was only the echo of last night's welcome-home party still raging inside his head. Countless voices going at once, like an opera without any music. He looked up the wall for the window of his cell. But it was a bigger window, and it was lower down, with his mother's hand-sewn curtains instead of bars. Across the room there were two other beds. Two other heads waiting to wake up and start talking. He lay still until the morning started to stir outside, then listened for a while to the sounds of the street. Buses, cars, slamming front doors. Voices. He listened until the thick, salty smell of frying rashers came into his stomach and turned it over, then, finding his way out of the room to the jacks, puked into the toilet. He came back into the room and got dressed. He lifted the packet his brother had given him, opened it up and rubbed his thumb against a thick wad of notes. He folded his pyjamas, then went downstairs to tell his mother he wouldn't be able to stay.

EPILOGUE

EPILOGUE

1953

He rarely thinks about prison now, though he still scrubs out the space he lives in each morning and he still wakes on prison time: the first shift towards day. He lies on his back and waits for the darkness to fall away, the furniture to solidify into angles and curves: big belly-stove, table and chair, bench by the wall covered in miniature plaster-cast figures – Venus de Milos and Pietàs, bought from the deaf mute who lives down the lane.

The bedpost presses into the soles of his feet and there's a taxi-lady sleeping beside him: one of the new girls, not used to his ways – otherwise she'd be gone by now. He gets up; sets a match to the oil burner; holds the flame low so there's just enough light for her to see on the way out. He places a small ball of money by her handbag, includes the cut for the taxi-man who acts as her pimp, then picks up his clothes, goes through to the workshop and dresses.

Standing at the iron door, he feels the silence around him, then grabs it by the throat. A yank at the chain: it clanks and rattles against the door; slides down off it to the floor. A shove with his shoulder; the door crashes open. He winces. Then reaches out, grabs the door by the sharp edge and gives it another couple of jolts, just for good measure.

Behind him, there's a jangle of bedsprings; a startled female gasp. He comes back and takes a look round a corner formed by a stack of crates. She's up on one elbow, gluey-eyed and heavy-faced, gawking around: at the corrugated iron, the concrete floor, the timber rafters. Taking it all in and wondering how the fuck she ended up in a shed.

He slips out the door before she's a chance to see him and moves round to the side of the shed. He can hear her gather herself together, stumbling around. There's a break in her movement and he guesses she's plucking up the money, transferring it into her bag, and maybe she's even remembering her careless words of the night before, when whiskey and the heat of the bed blurred the surroundings as well as her judgement: 'A good-lookin' fella like you shouldn't have to pay for it.'

He follows the clip of her heels till they reach the workshop, the iron door slightly ajar. He sees her then, coming outside. She stops short and blinks at the canal.

Trotting up the incline towards the bridge, her head turns from side to side: main road, bus stop – she locates herself. He comes back inside.

He comes back inside and walks the length of tin wall, almost a hundred feet, from the workshop out front to the living quarters he's rigged up at the back. He likes the wall: the feel of tin on his hand and the monotony of rain beating off it at night. In winter he stuffs sacking into the gaps; in summer he pulls the sacking out again.

As soon as it's light, he pins back the doors, puts out his sign and waits for the customers. Surly-faced farmers drive up from the country first thing in the morning to look at his gates. They stand stiff in the doorway, hands in pockets; won't loosen up till they're ready to deal.

'Are you the gatemaker?' they always ask at the start.

At night he takes the sign back in, locks up shop and strolls down to the pub on the corner. He sits in the snug and listens to the talk of old men. Sometimes he plays chess with the deaf mute. Sometimes he just gets drunk. When he feels the urge coming on, he goes out to the bar and makes a call to the taxi-man.

His family have stopped visiting now; stopped calling to ask him what he's doing for Christmas, or Sunday dinner, or if he fancies going for a pint or a spin somewhere or the other. Charlie might drop in from time to time, on his way home from training. He comes in half-drunk and boyish on adrenalin, all full of chat, usually about George. Still living in the Ormond Hotel, he'll say, or over in England at the races. Getting married soon to a young one they haven't yet met. Years younger. Catholic, too. Funny name – can't remember it now.

'Where do you think he got all that money?' Charlie asks.

'What money?'

'You know, the money to set himself up and that.'

'Maybe he won it.'

'I doubt that. He never makes use of money he wins – gets rid of it straight away, like he never really wanted it in the first place. Do you know what ma says?'

'What?'

'Ma says that man he had digs with in Belfast left it to him. You know, the Italian. I can't believe that, can you? Leaving all that money to him in his will.'

'Maybe he didn't leave it in his will. Maybe he just left it.'

Charlie thinks about that for a while, sitting in his running gear, a blanket around him to sop up the sweat, a double sheet of newspaper stuck up his jersey to stop a chill setting in. They drink tea together and then Charlie grows quieter – begins to lose his boyishness – pulls the newspaper out from his jersey and rolls it up into a ball. He puts on his work clothes, gets up on his bike and goes.

He hasn't seen George for months, then suddenly there he is, standing in his doorway at half six in the morning, just as he's getting into his stride with a farmer who's stopped by on his way to the market.

'Why these gates?' the farmer is saying.

'These gates? Well for a start, they prevent gate-climbing, so you've no need to worry about trespassers.'

'Aye, and . . . ?'

'And no bull will get his head stuck in there.'

'Are you sure about that?'

'Look at the bars – they're diagonal. How could they?'

The farmer, tilting his head, puts himself momentarily into the mind of a bull – a sure sign a deal is about to be struck – then George steps in and makes his announcement.

'He's dead.'

'What?'

'He's dead. He's dead.'

There's no need to ask who he means.

He's holding a clothes hanger up at shoulder level: long black coat, black suit, shirt and tie. He says it again, 'He's dead.' They look like a pair: his brother, the clothes – they look like a ventriloquist and his dummy.

'I brought these for you,' he says.

'For what?'

'The funeral. You'll come to the funeral?'

'I don't think so.'

'Ah, for fuck sake, he was your father.'

'Not according to himself.'

'That was only drink talk. He reared you, didn't he?'

The farmer starts to shuffle towards the door. 'Listen,' he says, 'I'll come by another time.'

'You do that.'

'Maybe next week, or the one after that. Aye, that's what I'll do, and I'm sorry, now, for your troubles.'

'Thanks.'

The farmer's banger struggles away. They stand listening to it for a while, then he turns on the blowtorch and lifts the kettle. 'Do you want tea?'

'No.'

He watches the spears of blue flame spike the base of the kettle.

'It was a heart attack,' George says. 'Ma found him when she came in last night, sitting in the chair with his coat on. Thought he was asleep. Jesus, it's fuckin' freezing in here. How do you stick it?'

'It doesn't bother me.'

He lets a few moments pass. 'So I hear you're getting married to a young one,' he says then.

'What? Oh, right. Do you remember Mona Norton?'

'She's hardly a young one.'

'It's a girl who lives next door to her, used to be pally with Mona's younger sister. Theresa Abingdon's her name. Terry. And she's not *that* young, either.'

The water is beginning to shift; the handle is hot in his hand. He sees George studying the layout of the workshop, following its order with his orderly mind. He clips the hanger of clothes up onto one of the rafters. The clothes sway for a few seconds, then stop. Hands now free, he touches and shifts; the empty frames leaning on one wall; the boxes of diagonal bars cut to various sizes; the jig on the ground with a half-made gate waiting to be fitted up. The completed gates then, stacked in a corner. He touches and shifts, prods and pulls until he has it all worked out in his head.

He turns off the blowtorch, takes the teapot outside and lashes a slur of tea leaves at the side of the wall. When he comes back in, George is on his hunkers, testing the weight of a gate.

'Are they selling?' he asks.

'Can't complain.'

'Good idea that, the diagonal bars. What made you think of it?'

'Oh, I don't know, a story somebody once told me. I suppose it just stuck in me head.'

They come outside and stand at the car.

'Nice motor.'

'She doesn't like it – Terry. Thinks it's too showy. Have to park round the corner when I collect her from work. So will you come?'

'Where?'

'To the funeral.'

'I don't think so.'

George opens the door and puts his foot on the runner. 'Well, it's the day after tomorrow, ten o'clock service in Crumlin. In case you change your mind.'

'I won't.'

'Well in that case, you know what you can do.'

He climbs into the car and starts the engine, drives past him, turns into the lane, then reverses back out and passes him again. He stretches over and rolls down the window.

'Herbert?'

'What?'

'You weren't the only one to suffer, you know.'

'I don't hold any grudges.'

'Yeah? Well, I'll tell that to ma.'

He watches the car slope towards the bridge, hesitate, nose out and turn. Then he watches the top of the roof slither across the bridge and slip into the main road. He looks back through the door of the shed, the hanger with the funeral clothes still dangling from the rafter. He decides to forget about the tea, pulls up his hat, puts on his overcoat, closes over the door and starts to walk.

He goes as far as the seventh lock, not thinking about much: George, for a minute, living in his hotel, meeting people at every turn – in the corridor, in the foyer, every time he sticks his nose into the dining room, having to have a word. Then he thinks about him driving through the countryside on his way to the races, in the car his fiancée's ashamed of, seeing the gates now everywhere he goes. Pointing them out to whoever happens to be beside him. 'See those gates . . . ' he'll say.

He thinks about Charlie for a minute: winter evenings training in the dark; cycling up to the track on the hill; dismounting his bike; then carrying it like a bride up the steps. Climbing up past it over the wall; sliding down the far side until he can feel the ground reach up to take his feet. Running the resentment out of himself because relatives of convicts don't get called for the Civil Service.

Running his guts out, lap after lap after lap in the dark. Like a blind man, running.

He gets fed up thinking, sits on a bench, smokes a cigarette and watches the pipistrelle bats comb the water for insects. After a while, he gets up and starts walking again, crossing the waterway at Ballyfermot Bridge, then returning on the opposite bank, eastwards to Harold's Cross.

The shapes of the morning are starting to form around the canal. He can see the curbing stones of the locks and the outline of the church's dome against the scratches of first light. A barge comes into view at Portobello and clears the lock, its Bollinger engine blowing vertical smoke rings – perfectly black, perfectly formed. It comes to Emmet Bridge and the helmsman throttles back the engine. The smoke collapses and spreads, then squeezes with the barge under the bridge.

He's back at the shed now; back where he started. He decides to carry on; slopes down the bank to stay close to the water. He keeps to the towpaths and the narrow ledges that run under the bridges. It's difficult to see down here, away from the street; away from the street lamps. But he knows the canal, the changing face of the water: the grimy heads of long-haired canal weed below, the lily pads that rise like scabs on the surface. He passes under the trees and under the bridges, and he knows the long shadows he walks through.